FALLING FOR THE JERK

VAUGHN BROTHERS

AMY ALVES

Editor: Lilypad Lit

Proofreaders: Tiffany Hernandez & Virginia Tesi Carey

Cover Design: KiWi Cover Design Co.

❀ Created with Vellum

VAUGHN FAMILY & FRIENDS TREE

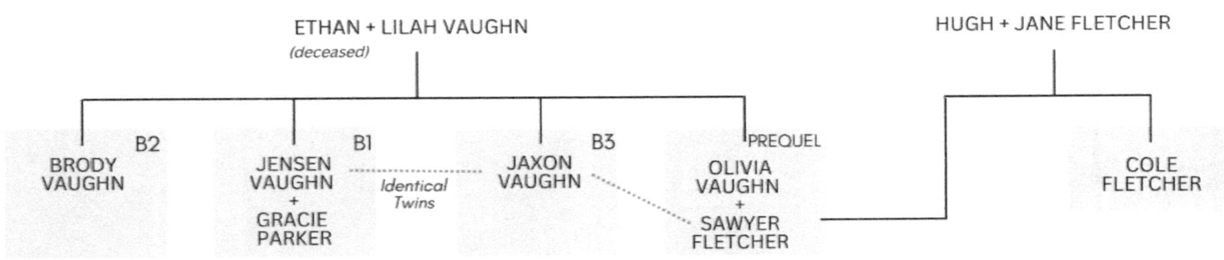

Other Series Characters

MIRANDA — MAYOR
MR. GILLESPIE — RETIRED GROUCH
MRS. LANGERHAM — "THE VINE"

LEGEND

——— = Family Relation
·········· = Best Friends
NAME + NAME B# = Series Couple & Book #

"Don't touch that," I bark.

Jaxon sets the apple back down onto my desk and raises his hands innocently. I bet if I turned the piece of fruit around, there'd be a missing bite.

He knows better than to fuck around with my snacks. Which means he wants something.

Pissing me off has always been my brother's way of getting my attention. At a glance, he may be a mirror image of me, but we couldn't be more different. Jaxon is the life of the party, everyone's friend. He's charming and fun. Growing up, my disinterest in parties and having a social life were the easiest way to differentiate us. And the fact I don't walk around with douchebag sunglasses all the time.

So the way he's hovering, fidgeting, pretending to be interested in the administrative work I'm doing means he's about to ask me to do something I won't like.

Determined to avoid whatever it is for as long as I can, I open another email inquiring about the Vaughn Volunteer Firefighter Training Program. I've been working toward this for two years, wanting to improve and staff our county departments. It's something Dad would have loved, and something he'd mentioned after I got my full-time position here. There are a lot of accomplishments he's missed, but also moments I'd hate for him to have seen.

I attach the program details document and press send, collapsing against the back of my chair.

"Gracie just joined the Hospital team for the Fire & Ice Game."

"Absolutely not," I tell him, snagging the apple and taking a bite, ignoring the missing bite he was probably banking on distracting me.

"Already a done deal." Jaxon's easy grin taunts me.

"We'll see about that." She works at the outpatient clinic attached to the hospital. Does that even count?

"This is your fault, you know," he tells me.

"How do you figure?"

"You poked the bear. Practically dared her by telling her she wouldn't be able to keep up on the ice."

Someone had to say it. The charity hockey game is my responsibility and every year, it runs smooth as butter. Because I make sure it does.

Each year, public service departments in Vaughn team up for an annual charity hockey game. Last year we had teachers face off against the police department. This year, it's the hospital versus the fire department.

Allowing Grace to play would be a huge mistake. She'll end up hurting herself or someone else.

My jaw clenches. "Who gave her the idea?"

"I don't see how that's relevant," my brother states, lifting his feet to rest them atop my desk.

"I'll talk to Leo," I tell him, opening up my email again. "I'll get him to tell her they're all full up."

Leo might not be the coach, but he's the hospital liaison

tasked with the administrative side of organizing their involvement in these fundraisers.

"Some of their best athletic candidates are away at a medical conference that weekend. They're scrounging for a few more players."

I shut my laptop. There's no way to ask him to turn her away without coming across as a complete asshole.

"She works at the outpatient clinic," I argue. "Can she even be considered hospital staff?"

He shrugs. "It's part of the hospital, and she insists she can skate." Un-fucking-likely. "That's all Leo will care about."

I grunt in disbelief, shaking my head.

A shit-eating grin spreads across his face. "Why don't you ask Sullivan to talk her out of it? He's the coach."

The charity this year supports the pediatric unit of the hospital, which means Dr. Tanner Sullivan is running the team. And Dr. Sully, as he prefers to be called by his pediatric patients—and to everyone he introduces himself to because he's that kind of self-important prick—has a thing for Grace. Apparently, he's willing to subject himself to that kind of trouble for a pretty face and a tight ass. Can't blame him, I guess, but it's become a spectacle. The town has been talking all about his attempts to woo her.

But because of his little infatuation, I know there's not a chance he'll risk kicking her off the team.

"If you frown any harder, that forehead vein is going to pop."

Some days, I'm astounded he's a paramedic.

"Listen, worst case scenario, she gets a little ice time just to prove you wrong and then sits the rest of the game."

"No." Does he even know her? There's no chance she'll sit out most of the game.

He tsks. "Not your call, bro."

An alert tone sounds from the speakers overhead.

"EMS," I say. "That's you."

Jaxon jumps up and jogs over to the doors connecting the admin office to the bay area. Before disappearing, he shouts, "Don't piss off Gracie! As much as it would please me to watch her tear another strip off you, she hates you enough as it is."

And sometimes that bothers me. But not when it's a safety concern.

Now that Jaxon's gone, I finish scheduling the two new probies for extra training days so we can get them in rotation.

We have enough full-time career firefighters to run a three-shift schedule, but during the high tourist season and holidays, things get tight, and we often need additional support from volunteers in the county.

I spend the last hour of my shift scheduling community engagement events, but my mind's not in it. It's on a blond-haired, amber-eyed, petite pain in my ass.

It's been nearly a year of heated arguments, pointed glares, and avoidance. All because she barged into my life at the worst possible time.

Dragging out my phone, a part of me questions my sanity.

> If I needed someone pulled over and detained a couple of weekends from now…could you make that happen?

BRODY:

> I already told you no.

> No, you didn't.

> Shit. Sorry. Jax asked me something similar a few months ago.

Fuck. If he's mixing me up with Jaxon, I'm going to need to dial it back.

> What's this about?

Forget it. I'll find another way.

You brought me into this, now spit it out.

Just trying to prevent a tiny hellion from bringing her special brand of chaos to the Fire & Ice game.

I'm not arresting Gracie Parker.

Technically, I didn't ask you to.

That's a headache I don't need. Everyone loves her. I'd have half the town calling me or barging into the station.

Yeah, everyone who hasn't seen her vindictive side loves her. All the people who don't have to save her from herself. Repeatedly.

And maybe she is fun and sweet or whatever they think. But she's not that way with me. Never with me.

And I prefer it that way.

Boots echo down the hallway right before the fire chief walks through the doors with a small pink and teal box in hand.

Declan stops in front of my desk. "Dani made these for you. She said they have extra filling."

The box lands on my desk with a thud. I flip it open to reveal two cream-filled mini eclairs, drizzled in chocolate, and sprinkled with nuts and toffee bits. If Dani wasn't my best friend's girl, I'd be tempted to date her—strictly for her top-notch baking skills.

My cheek twitches as I wonder what Declan would do if I voiced that thought.

Deck me. And then never bring me all the special treats she's been having him drop off for me.

Wait.

I point to the box. "As soon as I finish these, you're going to tell me why your girlfriend's been sending me pastries all week."

Declan chuffs before striding over to his office. "Keep the last weekend of the month free. I'm moving Dani in with me and told her you'd help."

With a mouth full of eclair, I mumble, "Don't tell her I agreed yet. I want a few more days of treats."

"You'll have earned it."

I narrow my gaze at him. "She's not a hoarder or something, is she?"

"No. But—"

A bell rings, loud and persistent, through the station. A cheer goes up. Everyone celebrating the free drink they'll be getting at the end of this shift, likely courtesy of Bradford.

The chief sighs. "You think Bradford left shit in one of the trucks again?"

Before I can answer, Bradford's voice rises over the commotion. "Fuck off. That wrapper fell out of my pocket. I'm not buying you bastards a damn thing."

Declan strides away with a grin, turning his head as he reaches his office door. "I'll buy you as many beers as you want if you keep him from coming in here to bitch."

"Done. But we're not going to The Hole. It's Spin to Win night."

Declan shoots me a look of disgust over his shoulder.

Our dive bar does all kinds of crazy shit to keep customers drinking and entertained. Tonight they'll bring out a giant spin wheel, and for a few bucks you can take a spin. There are some great prizes: bottles of top-shelf liquor, cash, tablets, a night of unlimited free drinks. Occasionally, they'll even have a couple of tickets to NFL or NHL games.

But there's also shitty "prizes" that feel a hell of a lot more like punishments. Things like getting serenaded throughout the night, drinking a beer out of someone's shoe before claiming your unlimited free drinks, or choosing a prize from the bin of crap people have left behind.

Regardless, I'm no longer permitted to participate in special event nights at The Hole. I'd like to blame my brother for how that went down, but my actions were my own. Jax and his best friend, Sawyer—who is now our little sister's fiancé—convinced me to go out the weekend after my girl left me and moved away from Vaughn. I drank myself into a stupor, accidentally got into a fight, and then threatened the manager about looking closer at potential fire code violations. I was a complete dick. So I went back the next day and apologized, but we agreed it would be best if I refrained from partaking in their events for the next year. Which worked out perfectly for me, but had people talking about the scene I caused for weeks. At least it gave them something other than my brutal breakup to gossip about for a while.

"Fuck that. We'll meet at Rocky's after I get some sleep," he tells me.

This is why we're friends.

The day they added Dec to our crew, we got on the same page. Being his second in command has been pretty damn easy. It's a lot like how I imagine being a zookeeper feels. I'm in charge of training, ensuring everyone follows protocols, and prevent the monkeys from throwing shit at each other or anyone else. Some days are harder than others. But in a small town, sometimes that's more on the residents than the crew. Which is why I'm also in charge of media relations.

Declan got promoted after only a year here because we needed someone to clean up the mess former Fire Chief Nanton and his assistant chief left behind. Mistakes made on scene that weren't handled properly, neglected ongoing training for senior crew members, extramarital affairs. Our community information bulletin, *The Vine*, had a field day with all this. They run our town's main social media account, and while I won't say they aren't an important part of the community, they can be a colossal pain in the ass. Especially since their posts and articles are an even mix of community events, news, and straight-up gossip.

"Oh, hey." Declan leans out of his office door, just as I shovel a handful of almonds into my mouth. "Congrats on the Mayor's Award nomination. We've needed that Volunteer Training Program for years, and the Town Council recognizes that." He taps the doorframe. "Hell, I'm just glad someone else is heading it up. I don't have the time or patience for that shit." He gives me a nod and then ducks back into his office.

I shake my head, shouting back, "That was heartfelt. Thanks, buddy."

"What? You want a hug or something?"

"Sure don't."

"Then get back to work. And don't forget to block out that last weekend of the month." I pull up my phone and start entering the details. "Oh, and Gracie's going to be there, so I need you to tone down the hostility."

Fuck.

"Dec!" I shout, much less amused than it was a moment ago. Unease churning in my gut, I toss the bag of almonds onto my desk.

She's fucking everywhere, entangled in too many aspects of my life. My town, my hockey game, my friends' lives. It might not be intentional, but it's a problem all the same.

He appears at the door again. "You rappel into dangerous situations, walk into burning buildings, and extricate people from nasty MVAs. But you can't handle one tiny woman?"

"She hates me and if allowed within reach, probably bites."

"Whose fault is that?"

I scoff. "Her wrath has a hair-trigger."

My friend and chief leans a shoulder against the doorjamb, his disappointment clear. "You could apologize."

That's a no.

"Too late for that," I mutter.

She wouldn't believe it, and even if she did, it would mess with our dynamic. The one where she does her best to ignore me, sasses me when she can't, crosses the street to avoid me, and begrudgingly lets me help her when she needs it. And I try to keep her from doing ridiculous shit that could get her hurt. Because despite what she might think, I don't hate her, but she infuriates me. A little too much, and a little too often.

She ignites every protective instinct I have—and other kinds of instincts I've suppressed. Some days I'm hanging on by a thread.

Even after our numerous spats, hostile interactions, and harsh lectures, she still gets in my face, charges ahead with little regard for her own safety, and challenges me at every opportunity.

And all that fire and sass has been thawing my icy resolve.

But I'll never stop calling her out on the stupid shit she gets herself into, and she'll never stop hating me for it—or our past.

We met under shitty circumstances—I was a miserable jackass with newfound trust issues whose fiancée had just left him.

Then there was the incident with her car accident...

The fire tone blares over whatever he was about to say. I push away from my desk and head to the bay to gear up.

After my shift, I'm heading straight to Dani's bakery to milk a few more treats out of her. Then I'm heading home to watch the Kings play the Sharks.

Then I'm coming up with a way to keep Grace out of my charity game.

CHAPTER
TWO

GRACIE

With only five laps left to go, my calf muscles start cramping. I know better than to push hard during a workout without making sure I'm well hydrated first. Hell, I haven't even eaten anything yet today.

I've let my hate-fire fuel me as determination has my heart beating in a furious rhythm.

Jensen Vaughn is trying to push me out of the Fire & Ice charity hockey game. And the thing is…I wasn't even going to play. I'd have happily sat in the arena and cheered for my coworkers, helped raise money, even coached if needed.

But then that arrogant bastard said I'd be a hindrance. That I probably couldn't skate worth a damn and was too big a risk to let on his ice. *His* ice!

So now I'm skating laps, getting my stamina up, trying to build balance again. It's been at least a year since I've skated, and I'm more than rusty. I'm a wreck. Which has been made obvious by the blooming bruises on my hips, butt, and knees. I'm sore, frustrated, and starving.

Skating and swimming were activities I took up when I was younger to help with my developmental delays. I loved sports, especially team sports, but my motor skills were abysmal, and my sense of balance was nearly non-existent.

I'm fortunate to have a mild case of Developmental Coordination Disorder—though I prefer the term Dyspraxia.

Several young students I've treated at Vaughn's elementary school and other schools have more severe symptoms—poor visual-spatial awareness, working memory, thought organization, and speech impairments.

While my condition impacts many of my daily tasks, I don't let it define me.

Some days are better than others, and I don't conquer every challenge I face—but I always try. I've come a long way since my early years of physical struggles, but since falling down on this ice is my constant state of being, I'm questioning that assessment.

Upon finishing my final lap, I decide to stick to dry-land training for the next couple of days. I need a chance to heal, and I can hone my balance with a few targeted exercises I recommend to the athletes I treat.

But tonight, I'm going to grab some food—I would do despicable things for a burger from Stuffed right now—and then call my bestie so she can talk me down from my spiral of fury and disappointment.

BECAUSE NO WAY am I letting Jensen Vaughn tell me I can't do something. It might not feel like it right now, but by next week, I'll be able to say with confidence, "Oh yeah? Watch me," and mean it.

I SHOULDER OPEN the door of the bakery, inhaling the mouthwatering scents of sweet treats and coffee. Hands down, gaining a baker for a best friend is the best choice I made since moving here last summer. I've already gorged myself on a burger with extra pickles, but couldn't help stopping by Baked Delights to get a pick-me-up.

I slip to the back of the short line, scanning the shop for Dani, but don't see her. At the back, there are some seniors setting up for their weekly bridge tournament, and Dottie's grandkids with their schoolbooks out while she works behind the counter. My eyes roam over to the display window that runs the length of the bakery. A grin pulls at my mouth when I spot the fire chief's command vehicle parked across the street.

Guess I'll have to ask Dottie if she knows when the boss will be back. We've both been victim to barging in on Declan and Dani, and I'd rather not have those two appear uninvited in my dreams again—or worse, collapse in a fit of sexually deprived envy.

Returning my attention to the line in front of me, I'm met with a set of wide shoulders and bulging trap muscles that weren't there a moment ago.

It takes my stupid hormones a few seconds longer than my brain to clue in on who stands in front of me.

"Back of the line, hotshot," I tell the man responsible for my sour mood and aching body.

He turns around, a rare grin on his full mouth. "Didn't realize you were in line. You going to come at me, Smalls?"

Relief and amusement twist my lips into a half-smile.

I've made a point to tell the Vaughn twins apart. For my first few weeks here, I thought they were the same man—a man with perplexing mood swings. But after my contemptuous introduction to Jensen, I realized my mistake.

Because the man had the gall to flirt with me—or so I thought.

And after what he said to me at Rocky's Tavern? I was livid.

When I was done giving him a piece of my mind, I spun

around and faceplanted into the sculpted chest of the asshole I thought I was reaming out seconds before.

Dragging my eyes up to his face, my jaw dropped. And to my utter humiliation, I mumbled, "Holy shit. There's two of you."

Jaxon had laughed, hooked an arm over my shoulders, and apologized for whatever his brother had done. Jensen stormed off with renewed determination to be a pain in my ass, but Jaxon has been surprisingly friendly.

Since then, I've made sure to pay closer attention.

Because I wasn't going to make that mistake again.

I scrutinized how they walk, their quirks and habits, their facial expressions. Beyond their distinct personalities, there's Jaxon's glasses and tattoos, and the tiny freckle below Jensen's eye that somehow draws a little more attention to his dark gaze. I can only spot their indiscernible differences in hair color if they're standing next to each other. Jensen's is a deeper, warmer brown whereas Jaxon's is ashier.

But you weren't looking at his hair, Gracie. What does that say about you, hmm?

From behind, their differences are nearly impossible to notice.

"Hey, Jax," I greet, softening my tone. "Sorry, I'm in a mood. Just don't take the last caramel apple muffin, and we're square."

"You mean this caramel apple muffin?" Jensen's deep, mocking tone drawls.

I lean to peek around Jaxon and lock eyes with his brother. He dangles a white bag with the muffin—my muffin—in it.

"Not today, Jesus," I pray, despite not being religious. But I will accept any help available to keep from committing a crime today.

I point at him. "I refuse to choose violence."

Jensen's mouth curves into that perplexing upside down grin of his. "Didn't think you ever *chose* the mayhem you cause, Grace. You seem to come by it quite naturally."

"I have many talents," I answer. "And it's *Gracie*." I've corrected him many times over the last eight months.

"So you've said. I like 'Grace' better." He dips his head and whispers, "Gives you something to strive toward."

This. Asshole.

I lunge at him and snatch the bag out of his hand. I slap a five-dollar bill into his now empty palm and bolt.

Jaxon's deep laugh follows me out of the bakery. As I push through the door, I sneak a glance at the two men. One is bent over covering a laugh, his hand clasped onto his brother's shoulder, the other one hasn't moved. He's still holding onto the money I thrust into his hand. And glaring daggers at me.

With a wide smile, I blow him a kiss, which seems to break whatever trance he was in. And the moment he takes a step forward, I run, racing around the side of the building. My muscles scream in protest, and I suck in a pained breath before I slip into the alley between Dani's shop and the next.

I glance at the alley's entrance as I bang on Baked Delights' back door. Hopefully, Dani is in the kitchen and picks up on my urgent knocking.

The door swings open, and I rush inside.

"Lock it!" I whisper-shout.

I look up into a stern face that does not belong to my bestie.

"Gracie..."

"Chief." I nod, giving him a tight smile. "Seriously, lock it." I tip my head at the door.

He sighs and does as I ask.

Through the door, Jensen bellows my name.

Declan's gaze narrows at me, and I widen my eyes innocently back at him.

"Gracie!" Dani greets me. "Why'd you come through the back?" She darts a glance over to the connecting door that leads to the front counter.

"Stole this," I tell her, holding up the pastry bag. "Had to make a quick getaway. Who'd guess I'd circle right back around to the scene of the crime?" I wink at her as she rolls her eyes.

"Fine, don't tell me." Her gaze locks on me, eyes widening. "I'd rather hear about your lunch with Tanner yesterday anyway." Declan blows out a breath, muttering something as he grabs a broom from the storage closet. "How many dates does that make now?" she asks.

I barely stifle a groan.

That's yet another thing that went wrong this week.

"It was fine. But I wouldn't call them dates. We occasionally eat lunch together in the hospital cafeteria or in one of the staff break rooms."

Her excited smile falls. "Uh oh. Didn't go well, huh?"

With a sigh, I collapse against her prep counter. Truth is, it disappointed me. I was hoping it was just an off day, but then he kissed me.

"You know when a man kisses you and it makes your head spin? The world around you fades to black, and all rational thought flees your sex-muddled mind, making dry-humping him on a picnic table at a public park during a family barbecue seem like a reasonable idea?"

She hums, "Mm-hmm, yep," and shoots Declan—who's been doing his best to ignore our conversation—a *you fuck me in public places and I love it* look that makes my vagina perk up in interest only to remember we don't have our own firefighter beast to fuck.

If a vagina could throw a tantrum, mine would need to be dragged out of this bakery kicking, screaming, and holding her damn breath until some brawny, big-dicked hero gave her what she needs.

"Yeah, I haven't felt like that since I was a teenager," I admit. "And that was because of hormones and a persistent case of impulse control issues."

"The kiss was bad?" she surmises with a grimace.

"So bad," I whisper.

"Well, first, I feel I need to point out that if there was a kiss at the end of lunch, it was a date. Second, I'm so sorry, babe. But at least you know now instead of wasting your time."

I lift a shoulder in a defeated shrug.

"Can a vagina spontaneously dry up? Go on strike? Withhold solo orgasms until she finds a suitable mate?"

An indelicate snort leaves her as she moves closer, settling in next to me. "You're the medical professional, so your guess would be better than mine. But I'm going to go with probably not."

I let out a pathetic whine. "He just had so much potential. He's nice, smart, loves kids, and is ready for a committed relationship. On paper, he's perfect. And he seems to like me. So why can't I summon even a few crumbs of desire? Just a pinch of anything beyond friendship and respect?"

"Just because he seems like a great choice, doesn't make him good for you, Gracie." She places her hand on my arm, giving it a gentle squeeze.

"I know. I wasn't interested in dating anyone right now anyway, but then I got my hopes up. Why can't I like nice men in admirable professions who treat me well?"

"Maybe you don't like the sweet, golden retriever type? Have you tried letting your heart choose?"

"Oh, sweet, sweet Dani." I turn and lift a hand to cup her cheek. "My heart is a moron and would have me panting after the first sexy, scowling face who grunted a terse greeting in my direction." I drop my hand and blow out a breath. "Or I'd end up trying to tame a man-whore into falling in love with me. I'd thrive off the challenge at first, but then wind up brokenhearted and alone again." I shake my head at her like she doesn't know my history of chasing after assholes. "You've grown soft and forgetful in your state of near-cohabitating bliss."

Her hands fly up with a squeal. "That reminds me! I gave

notice to give up my apartment. I move in with Declan in less than a month."

A soft smile pulls at my mouth. "I heard."

She tilts her head. "How?"

I scrunch my brows at her, surprised she even has to ask.

"Right. It's probably all over town already." She rolls her eyes and laughs. "Anyway, I still believe you need to be daring when it comes to your love life. I mean, take Declan, for example. He was a total grump, and look at him now." She nods over to where Declan is sweeping, but no longer pretending he can't hear us.

"I'm not doing this because I'm sweet, cupcake. I'm trying to get us out of here faster so I can take you home and get you naked."

Biting my lips together, I glance at Dani. Her cheeks turn pink as she presses a hand to her chest, a glimmer of mischief in her eyes. I follow her lead and press a hand to my own chest.

"Aw!" we say together.

"So romantic," I add.

"The cutest, right?" she responds.

"He's like a living version of those teddy bears holding a heart-shaped box of chocolates." His jaw tics as he exhales a grumbly, irritated breath. "But like all muscled and protective." I glance at the broom. "And domestic. Are all firefighters as sweet and cuddly as you, Dec?" I flutter my eyelashes at him.

Dani giggles, and the chief's eyes soften.

But then that gaze comes back to me with one brow raised. "Not sure. How about we open the back door, and you can ask that again, but a little louder? There was another firefighter out there just a minute ago. I'm sure he'd love to make friends and answer all your questions."

Well played, sir.

"No need. But quick question..." I school my expression before asking, "Do you usually befriend random firemen who hang out in alleys? If so, pretty sure we found the theme for next year's Vaughn Fire Department Calendar fundraiser. We can rent a smoke machine, get some of your department's equipment to use as props, rub you all down with some oil, and have you all wrap those powerful, life-saving arms around each other."

He blinks once and resumes staring.

Back straight, with poorly hidden amusement plastered on my face, I attempt to maintain eye contact. And fail. Fire Chief Declan Walker is intimidating as all hell.

"I have no idea what you guys are talking about or why a fire-fighter is hanging out in my alley, but I'm on board with the calendar idea, Dec."

In under three strides, he's scooped Dani off her feet.

"Go home, Gracie," Chief Walker bellows.

My best friend sends me an amused but apologetic smile as she waves at me from Declan's arms.

"And try not to cause any shit with my crew on your way," he adds, carrying Dani into her tiny office.

I salute him in response.

Dani shouts, "Tomorrow, drinks at Rocky's!" just as the door slams.

Hightailing it out of the kitchen, I take a quick peek out of the swinging door that connects to the front of the bakery.

Jaxon and the Jerk are nowhere in sight.

Dottie gives me a knowing smile as I emerge from the back. With a wink and a finger wave, I leave Baked Delights, pastry bag clutched tight in my hand.

On my walk home, I savor every morsel of my muffin. And knowing that I deprived Jensen of his sweet treat tonight makes it taste even more delicious.

THREE

JENSEN

"Alright...spill. What's got you brooding on my couch, honey?"

My mouth dips down. "I'm not brooding."

Mom's eyes widen as she nods. "Mm-hmm. Well, you've got a few beautiful acres of peace and quiet at your place, and a fridge full of beer you like. Instead, you're here, knocking back a blueberry ale and watching *Sister Wives*. Sorry for thinking you might have something on your mind."

I swivel the bottle in my hand, studying the label. Huh. Blueberry. That's why it tasted weird.

"It was already on the TV," I mumble.

She turns it off and faces me.

"What's going on?"

I swipe a hand over my face. I didn't come here to spill my shit. I came here to check on her. And maybe for food. But she can always tell.

"Is this about your dad?" This time of year is always the hardest, and I try to make it a little easier on her if I can. It wasn't in the plan to get all mopey and lounge like a miserable oaf on her couch. "The anniversary of his death is coming up, and I know it's been a long time, but sometimes old wounds don't heal all the way the first time and rip right back open. I know you and Brody don't like to talk much about it, but it can help, and I'm always here to listen. You don't have to be worried about bringing him up."

"I know, Mom. But I'll always worry, so there's no sense in warning me off."

She drops her chin, eyeing me from above her glasses, waiting for me to tell her what's going on.

I blow out a resigned breath. "Part of it's Dad. I'm missing him...wishing he were here to see me get nominated for the Mayor's Award—two years before he got his first one." Right before he died, I bet Dad that I could win this award before I turned thirty-five, which was when he won his first one. Now if I do win, it'll mean more but be bittersweet.

Mom shakes her head in amusement. "He would have doubled down and challenged you to win *two* by then."

I give her a half-smile, and nod. "Yeah, he would have."

She tilts her head. "What's the other part?"

"I got a call from Liv about her wedding." Mom's mouth tightens into a sympathetic half-smile. "And I handled it like an asshole. So now I'm feeling like shit."

"Ah," she says. "Is it the wedding or the fact your baby sister is getting married again that's bothering you?"

Sawyer Fletcher's a good guy, so that's not an issue. When I found out Livvie was a contestant in our town's ridiculous reality dating show, I might have barged into Rocky's to shut it down. But I realized Liv loved the hell out of the dork, and I got on board. But not before messing with him a little.

"I'm not 'bothered.' I knew this was coming."

"The fact you're still drinking my fruity beer says otherwise."

Shit.

I set the bottle down and lean my forearms onto my thighs.

"I'm happy for her. They are kind of perfect together. And I don't want my bullshit to darken any part of her wedding day."

Mom hums. I lift my gaze to hers, finding her deep in thought.

After a few moments, she says, "And you think you will?"

"I sure as shit hope not." I shrug. "But I don't know. And I hate that."

Snagging the half-empty bottle off the coffee table, I take it into the kitchen.

Mom walks in right when I pull out the cleaning supplies she keeps beneath the sink so I can get under there. She sighs in a knowing way.

"You need a garbage disposal. I'll pick one up. Should only take me a couple of hours to install. Sunday work?" Easing out from under the sink, I return her cleaning supplies before standing. The look she gives me is one I've seen many times before, but not for a while.

"I'm fine, promise. The shitty memories took me by surprise, that's all." She doesn't seem convinced, so I move over to her and wrap her in a hug.

"You're still avoiding your feelings about the wedding," she says. "Did you and Jaxon ever talk about what happened? Or did he just make a joke about the whole thing while you clammed up waiting for the moment you could sneak off to brood alone?"

She clearly knows the answer to that question.

I mean, we talked but it was short and consisted of him coming up with ideas of how to stick it to my ex. And then me fielding all his Vegas and Spain trip ideas to get me out of my "funk." It was his way of trying to make it up to me somehow. But he did nothing wrong, and there's no way I'd let Erika come between us. We're solid, always will be.

"We're good, Mom." I smack a kiss to the top of her head before I walk away to grab my jacket from the barstool on the other side of the kitchen island.

She grumbles while following me to the front door and out onto the front step.

Turning back to her, I admit, "Projects give me something easy to fix when I don't know how to fix the other shit going on." I shrug.

She smiles at me. "I guess that's better than shutting yourself into your cottage in the woods and only coming out for food and work." Yeah, I handled the breakup really poorly. "Or getting hooked on dope. Is that what people still call it? Either way, your brother says the opioid crisis is an ongoing problem."

Squeezing the back of my neck, I make a mental note to ask Brody to stop telling mom crazy shit.

"Yep," I say, trying to keep a straight face. "Installing garbage disposals is better than doing drugs."

She scrunches her nose at me with a chuckle. "You are too easy to mess with, honey."

I shoot her a half-hearted glare before heading to my truck.

"Call your sister," Mom shouts from the door. "She's already talking about searching for locations outside of town to have the ceremony. I think her exact words were, 'I will not let the memory of Fuckface Erika ruin another wedding.'"

Shit. I won't be letting Liv change a damn thing about her wedding just because I was caught off guard and reacted poorly.

Out of the corner of my eye, I spot Mrs. Dodson easing closer to us as she pretends to prune her hedges.

"Will do."

I'll have to call Olivia as soon as I get home. I've got an early shift tomorrow, and it's Friday the 13th. I'm not superstitious, but it can't be a coincidence that these days always bring a new level of insanity. Or maybe people use it as an excuse to act like morons. Either way, we stay busy.

And this time, I might welcome the challenge. Tackling the crazy is exactly what I need right now.

I take it back. Welcoming a challenging Friday the 13th was stupid.

We've been on scene for half an hour getting the details from the middle-aged couple who spiced things up in the bedroom and tried bondage. And now need technical rescue support.

I'd like to say this is the first time we've had a sex-gone-wrong emergency in Vaughn. But it's not even the first one this year, and it's only February.

Fucking Fifty Shades of Grey.

Ever since the first movie came out, we get at least two calls a year where someone has tried bondage without knowing what the hell they're doing. Our population is about one-twentieth the size of the closest city, yet I'm confident if we kept statistics on bedroom accident calls, we'd have Santa Rosa beat.

And somehow, I'm always the one scheduled on these special days.

"Mrs. Mancuso, we'll have you out soon, but I'm going to need you to be still until I'm finished."

The middle-aged woman in a shiny, black polyurethane teddy bites her lip, giggling. "That's what my husband always says too."

Absolutely not. Nope. Wiping from my brain.

At this point I should just be grateful she thought to drape a sheet across her bottom half. Mr. Mancuso didn't have the same sense of propriety.

She shifts again and hiccups. An odd noise gurgles in the back of her throat, and her playful expression morphs into one of stark concern. "I think I might have to throw up."

Great.

"Did you have any alcohol last night or early this morning, ma'am?" I tip my chin up at Ross, my newest volunteer fire-fighter. He nods, weaving through the rest of the team and around the anxious husband to grab something for our patient to throw up in.

"A bit last night," Mr. Mancuso huffs behind me. "Fine. Maybe we had a bit more than usual. We were nervous! Got too drunk to attempt the cuffs last night, so we gave it another go this morning."

The cuffs they've used are the real deal. Which makes them a hell of a lot harder to get off, and the metal also causes injury. Especially for clueless beginners.

The kicker is that the handcuff keyholes are both facing the wall, and the huge headboard they added to their frame—and attached to the fucking wall!—leaves me with no space to maneuver them.

"Universal key isn't going to work," I tell Ross as he returns with a puke bag from our EMS guys. "Let Kelly know we need the bolt cutters from the truck."

"Sir, are you experiencing any stomach pain or breathing problems?" Jax asks the husband.

"No, not at all. It was a clean swallow," he answers. "Wait. Will it hurt coming out?"

"The key is small and those kinds of things pass without incident, but if you have any abdominal pain, fever, vomiting, or difficulty eating or drinking, you'll need to head to the hospital."

"I didn't mean to swallow it. It was between my teeth, and then I got excited."

When Ross returns, I show him why we can't just unlock the cuffs.

I let him cut Mrs. Mancuso loose while getting the rest of the guys to pack up. Then I prepare myself to run through some bondage safety protocol with these two sex fiends.

At first, researching this kind of information to prepare us better for the increasing number of calls we were receiving was a running joke amongst the crew. But I can tell you for a fact that my shift knows a lot of shit they didn't before, and I haven't heard a single complaint.

Until we get on a call and people are being dumbasses.

I stride up to the couple, arms crossed, speech prepared.

"First, you don't mess around with erotic play unless you've done your research. Second, you need a safe word." They frown at me, waving me off in disagreement. "Yes. You do," I bark at them. "Third, start slow, maybe with a blindfold or something. Then, when you eventually work your way to bondage, don't start with metal cuffs. Look at your wife's wrists, man." His eyes dart to her red, chafed wrists. "Try something a little less risky. Velcro straps work well and wouldn't require all this." I jerk a thumb at the men packing up around me. "And lastly"—I stare at Mr. Mancuso —"unless the emergency is time-sensitive, let's remember to put on pants before opening the door for the first responders. Got me?"

Hell, I'd have settled for just removing the cock ring.

But pants would have been really fucking appreciated.

He nods, tightening the robe one of my guys asked him to put on earlier.

"Alright. Play safe, you two."

I'm the last one out of the house, making sure we're all wrapped up before we head back to the station. I radio in to let dispatch know we're clear and returning.

We don't even make it all the way into the bay before the tones go off again. I check my phone to see where we're headed next.

The construction site on Lougheed Avenue. Shit. You never know what you'll find when you get to a construction site accident, but it can be ugly. Equipment accidents, motor vehicle collisions, electrocution, crush injuries, vehicle versus pedestrian.

As we roll up to the scene, there are people everywhere. Some waving at us, others gawking. We get the truck positioned to divert traffic and then assess the scene.

Jax and Anders wait for my go-ahead before jumping in to provide any medical support.

One of the construction workers beelines for us.

"You call it in?" I ask him, as the crew moves on to secure the scene, stabilize vehicles, and assess injuries.

"Yeah. A vehicle sped through here, careened into a parked car, and I think they hit a cyclist too."

While I walk over to the involved vehicles, I check in with dispatch. "Dispatch, Engine 2 and Ambulance 1 are on scene at Lougheed Avenue. Assistant Chief 1202 reporting an MVA and possible vehicle versus cyclist." One of my guys calls out that the scene is stabilized, two injuries. "Area is secure, two injuries reported, paramedics have made patient contact."

That's when I see the bike.

A bright purple hybrid commuter bike lays mangled on the sidewalk.

"Fuck," I say, my strides lengthening.

That flashy bike with the obnoxiously loud horn belongs to Grace.

CHAPTER
FOUR

GRACIE

THE VINE COMMUNITY UPDATE

Cunning vandals evade law enforcement once more, leaving their mark on several road signs throughout Vaughn. Witnesses have reported three large, hoodie-wearing young miscreants wandering the streets sometime between midnight and 4:00 a.m. Areas that were subject to sign vandalism early this morning include the road construction site on Lougheed Avenue, and the residential subdivision of Spring Hills.

So far, all speed signs with the blacked out "S" and "D", as well as the "Men Twerking" construction signs, have been identified in these areas. Please contact the Vaughn Police Department's non-emergency line if you spot any other graffiti or altered town signs.

G rinning, I veer off my usual biking path, taking the long way to work just to ensure I pass through both "vandalized" areas of the town.

A snicker works its way loose as I pass the "PEE 25" sign.

I hope they leave the sign for a little while. I imagine the kids in the area are loving them.

The ride becomes a little bumpy as I roll over loose gravel on the uneven terrain of Lougheed. Maybe coming through here wasn't the best idea. I better get a twerking show for my efforts when I pedal by the workers.

I keep to the bike lane, and a car passes me, honking at the construction workers ahead. The teenagers in the rusted sedan crank a Cardi B song and holler at the men.

The kids slow down, laughing and chatting with some flaggers who are diverting traffic. I pull over onto the walking path next to the road and take a few pictures of the sign. One worker who I see at the gym spots me and grins. The moment he realizes I'm taking photos, he struts over to the sign and starts gyrating, lifting his shirt and flexing.

And...send! My mom will love that one.

She thought I was crazy for moving to a small town instead of staying in Sacramento after college. After growing up in a big city, I wasn't sure if small-town life would be a good fit for me either. But the friendly community atmosphere, being nestled in the Sonoma Mountain range, and the convenience of never having to drive over ten miles to get to a winery, has made me forget about life in a large city.

And while her initial concern for the lack of opportunities here—both professionally and romantically—is logical, I see it as a plus. The fact Vaughn doesn't have as many resources as bigger cities means I can do the most good here.

MOM:

> Fine. I'll put that in the pro column. But I doubt this strategy will work as well on your dad. He refuses to move anywhere new that doesn't at least have an NHL team. Or places in town that stay open past 8:00 p.m.

I roll my eyes. We have two bars and a couple of restaurants that always stay open later than that. Well, usually.

My parents and I have been going back and forth about whether I should move back home or they should move here. We're at a stalemate. Both sides have made good points, crossed lines, used dirty tactics. But I love Vaughn, so I'm hoping one day they'll cave. Because I miss them.

> Do NOT show dad. He'll drive over here and interrogate the poor guy.

> I was kidding, honey. I'd be showing your dad this picture for other reasons. I love what his jealous side brings out in him. *wink*

My nose scrunches as I type my response. Dad is protective and intense when it comes to his ladies, but I did not need to know how much mom likes it. Or the implication why.

> Gross.

> I'm off to work. Do what you will with that picture, but do not implicate me in your devious, kinky plans.

> You're not still biking to work, are you? Dad's been looking into another car for you. The safest on the market, with all the bells and whistles.

> I'm fine walking and biking, Mom.

Mom's a worrier. But she's also the nurturing type who has been my pillar of support since we first found out I have Dyspraxia. My developmental delays became more pronounced around kindergarten, and even more so once I started playing sports. But I wasn't going to let that stop me.

I did, though, throughout all of elementary school. And that's when my dad stepped in, making sure I knew that he'd back me every time someone tried to keep me from anything. Because there was no way he was going to let anyone or anything keep his baby girl from a single damn thing she wanted.

And now I don't. Those bullies at school, the ones who teased, laughed, and excluded me? I punched one in the face in fourth grade. Well, maybe I missed and hit his neck, but it hurt him all the same, and while he was whining, I took his place on the soccer field at recess. And I scored a goal. Accidentally, but it was a win either way.

When they called my dad into the school to talk about my "violent outburst," my giant, construction worker father let out a raucous, "Hell yeah! That's my baby girl!"

So fuck the people who tell me I can't. I do what I want, and you can bet your ass I'm willing to work ten times harder. Not only to prove I can, but to show them I can do it better than they ever could.

My one exception lately has been driving.

All because of that one accident I can't shake.

> It's very unlikely you'll have another accident like that, honey. And you said all the chatter about it died down after a few months.

> My nips were plastered all over our community news website and social media accounts, Mom! And I was new in town. It was humiliating.

The Vine has eyes and ears everywhere and doesn't pull any punches. They are a force to be reckoned with.

> That was a gorgeous lace bralette. Sheer, yes, but lovely. How many people can say they look hot even after their car rolls into a ravine?

> It wasn't a ravine.

It was steep enough that they had to use
harnesses, Gracelyn.

In my defense, there was a mountain lion in the middle of the road.

Or a wolf.

Maybe a fox.

Either way, my reaction time sucked when I swerved. I panicked, over-corrected, and couldn't get back on the road in time.

Now I bike, walk, or catch rides wherever I need to go.

Tell Dad I'm fine. My legs are killer. I could
probably do that watermelon crush challenge
easy peasy. Especially with how much I've been
training for our charity hockey game.

You two are still coming, right?

You bet. Prepare yourself though. Your father
hasn't gotten to play the part of hockey dad in a
while.

I only played hockey for a couple years before I
moved on to cross-country running and swim
team.

My phone rings, showing a video call from my mom.

I answer and she starts with, "Swim meets have a totally different energy, Gracie." Her blond hair appears freshly cut, falling to her shoulders, and her reading glasses are perched on her nose. "And waiting for you at the finish line of your runs wasn't quite the sporting experience your father was prepared for."

Yeah, a six-foot-five, two-hundred-thirty-pound man cheering, giving out unexpected high-fives, and busting through other waiting spectators to run the last twenty feet with me might not have been well received those first few meets.

He's straight-up crazy, and I love it.

"As much as I know I'm going to regret saying this, you can give him the green light on letting all his overzealous hockey dadness out."

She chuckles. "Alright, but I'll be moving sections if he tries to start a chant. Know that I still love you though."

Sometimes it's astounding how my parents even ended up dating. They are so different. My mom is a homebody introvert who keeps a tight circle of friends and loved ones. Dad is the wild extrovert who makes friends everywhere he goes. He showers her with affection, makes her laugh, and coaxes her out of her shell, while she grounds him with her calming presence and devotion. It's the fucking cutest.

So when my mom noses in on my romantic life, my go-to "mind your business" retort is to point out that she and Dad have clearly set the bar too high and none of the men in my life have come close to passing the Erin and Cam Parker love test.

"Completely understand." I check the time with a frown. "Shit, I'm going to be late," I mutter.

"Get going. We'll do a video call this weekend. Love you." She sends me an air kiss.

I return it. "Love you more."

I shove my phone in my backpack and hop on my bike.

Hopefully, Phyllis isn't out in her golf cart leaving "My son's an optometrist and would love to help you with the vision impairment that has made parking a challenge for you" notes in the hospital parking lot today.

She attaches a business card, and it amuses me to no end. It's the sole reason I chose her son as my eye doctor. But her golf cart escapades tie up traffic.

When I slip back into the bike lane, I wave at the construction crew and pick up the pace while my leg muscles scream in protest. Skate training is killing me.

Tires squeal behind me, making me flinch.

My body locks up at the unmistakable, deafening sound of a car crash. Metal screeches. Glass breaks. The sounds seem to come from all around me.

Don't look back. You'll lose your balance.

Is the vehicle weaving, striking multiple other vehicles? Is it right behind—

Seconds pass in a perplexing blur of agonizing dread. The parked car next to me lurches as if it has a life of its own, clipping my bike.

Turns out it wasn't skating I should have been worried about.

My inability to back down from a challenge might be the end for me.

And I'd been trying so hard to stay out of *The Vine's* local news bulletin.

The headline *"Gracelyn Parker Meets Tragic End In Unfortunate Men Twerking Accident"* flashes across my mind the moment my body becomes airborne.

CHAPTER
FIVE

I found Grace wandering away from the scene of the accident, like nothing happened. That was over fifteen minutes ago, and she's been vocal about needing to head back to work for each one of those minutes.

My older brother convinced her to stick around to give her statement, but when I told her she also had to get checked by Jax before we could let her go, she ignored me.

Thankfully, no one was seriously injured, and my crew is wrapping up. She's standing off to the side, not far from my brother's squad car, waiting on Jax to finish checking on the guy whose airbags deployed after he hit the parked car.

But the obstinate woman is getting antsy, and I know she's going to make a run for it. I can feel it.

I plant myself in front of her. "Show me," I demand.

"Show you what?" she asks. "I've already explained to you that my bike got clipped, but I'm fine. Believe it or not, I'm a bystander in this situation. In fact, it's offensive and presumptuous of you to think that I had anything to do with this accident."

The frustrated breath I release rattles in my chest.

"Don't growl at me," she says through clenched teeth. "Oh look, the tow truck driver is here. Brody seems busy with the whole policeman thing, and while your other brother over there may look a lot like you, his bossy pants aren't shoved as far up his ass as yours, so I'm not sure he'll be able to handle all that. Look!" she shouts, tipping her head toward the tow truck. "The people need you!"

"Did you hit your head?" I ask, crouching down to examine her pupils. Those amber orbs stare back at me, brows dipping in irritation. Her creamy skin is paler than usual, making her plump, rosy lips more pronounced.

"You'd like that, wouldn't you?"

I force my eyes from her face, and continue my assessment. Her helmet looks intact as it dangles from the straps hooked over her delicate wrist as she grips her forearm as if she's holding herself back from throttling me.

Frowning, I reach toward her to check for a head wound, but she jerks away, grimacing. Pulling back, I place my hands on my hips instead. She doesn't want me to touch her, fine.

And that's when I notice the droplets of red sprinkling the ground by her feet and soaking into her floral-patterned Keds.

Still clutching her arm, she shifts, attempting to hide the blood-splattered shoe behind her calf.

I pinch the bridge of my nose. "Parker, stop wasting my time and show me your damn arm."

"It's fine. Just a scratch. Move along, hotshot."

"Yeah? Then you should have no problem releasing the iron grip you have on that forearm."

Her warm honey eyes turn to steel, her jaw clenching.

After several moments of enduring her stony stare, her fingers loosen. Then, after a few more seconds, she drops the arm.

She cocks her head at me in challenge, her stare unwavering in intensity.

I break the connection first, my gaze darting straight to her arm. Intermittent drips fall from her fingertips.

Shit.

"Jax!" I shout over my shoulder.

Grace startles and follows my gaze to her arm. Confusion sweeps over her face, and when she glances back up at me, she's pale. Too pale.

I reach for her a split second before she sways.

"Stretcher!" I call to my brother as I sweep Grace into my arms. Her head lolls into my chest.

Fuck.

My heart pounds in an unsteady rhythm against my chest as Jax and Anders roll up with the stretcher. We position her on it while they take her vitals and check her for wounds.

"Vitals are good. Pulse is slow, but that's expected after fainting," Jax says. "She's got a nasty laceration on her arm though. We'll need to take her in."

Ross jogs over. "Chief, you should see this dashcam video of the accident." He tilts his head at Grace before adding, "She said her bike took the brunt of it and she was fine. Walked away, whatever. But she got rocked pretty good."

He holds up the dashcam, and I watch Grace get tossed across the hood of a car, and tumble to a jarring halt onto the pavement.

"Goddammit, Grace," I mutter, radioing into dispatch to give them an update.

We wheel her into the ambulance, and I hold pressure against the sterile dressing Jax applied to her wound.

Jax raises his brows at me when I hop into the ambulance with him.

Grace's eyelashes flutter as she comes back around. She blinks up at the two of us.

"I see him freaking everywhere," she whispers, using her uninjured arm to point at me.

The corner of my mouth tips up as my brother chuckles.

"Hey, Smalls. You woke up just in time. We're about to take you on a ride."

"Both of you?" she asks, confused. She lets out a breathy sigh. "My sex dreams have gotten *way* out of control." She frowns, eyes closing once more. "So weird. I don't even like threesomes. My brain must be punishing my vagina for being so damn thirsty."

Well, I don't think I'll ever be able to get that visual out of my head. Or the fact that she has reoccurring sex dreams.

And why the hell does her dislike of threesomes leave me with a smug kind of satisfaction?

Jaxon snorts, "Sorry, sweetheart, not a dream."

Knowing I shouldn't say a damn thing, but unable to help myself, I add, "Though I'd be interested in hearing the details of those dreams, Grace."

Her body stiffens.

"What?" she gasps, eyes flying open.

"There she is," Jaxon announces.

"Why am I in an ambulance?" she asks, eyes darting between the two of us.

Barely holding back the lecture that's on the tip of my tongue, I press my lips closed, letting my brother field her questions until I can get my anger in check.

"You were biking to work and got into an accident. Then you fainted. Jensen caught you before you hit the asphalt. Scooped you right up, all heroic-like. You'd have hated it, so it's a good thing you were unconscious."

"Oh god," she mutters, turning her head away.

"We're taking you to the hospital to get checked out, and that cut on your arm is going to need stitches," he adds, as Anders gets us moving.

No one says a word on the drive.

When we pull up to the ambulance-access doors of the ER, Jax and I get her out of the back and wheel her in.

She tries to sit up, but I place a hand on her shoulder, cutting a glare her way.

As soon as we maneuver her into the curtained waiting area, a nurse comes over and we start the paperwork.

"Ah, shit," Grace hisses.

I gaze down at her. "What? What happened?"

She blows out a breath. Her face is tighter, pain making her eyes water. "Nothing. I just realized that we're stuck with each other until they admit me."

Her attempt at a cheeky smile is off.

"Want me to make him go sit in the chairs over there?" Jax asks, pointing at the row of seats across from the tiny ambulance-access stalls. "After many hours spent waiting with the patients, I can confirm that they are super uncomfortable."

Grace gives him an amused but tired smile before her gaze moves back to me. "Hurts," she finally admits.

"Pain meds should kick in soon, Gracie," my brother assures her.

"What hurts? Your arm? What else?" I ask.

She shakes her head, flinching. "Everything. Everything hurts."

Grinding my teeth, I respond. "Yeah, well, getting hit by a car makes everything hurt. Even if you pretend it didn't happen."

My brother reaches over Grace to punch me in the arm.

"What the fuck, Jax?"

"Gracie's in pain, so she couldn't do it. And you deserved it."

"I'm just pointing out the obvious. If it wasn't for me, she would have cracked that big, stubborn head of hers on the pavement and been a hell of a lot worse off."

"Jensen?" she whispers, her fingers brushing across my hand that's still holding pressure on her wound.

Hmph. She's going to thank me, and it's been a long fucking time coming. Because with the amount of shit she gives me, I still saved her ass several times this year.

Even though she came after my job.

Even though she infuriates me.

"Yeah, Grace?"

She hooks a finger, beckoning me closer.

I dip my head down to hers.

In a raspy voice, she whispers, "Not even getting hit by a car will stop me from showing up to play in your hockey game. So you sure as hell won't stop me either, hotshot."

My cheek twitches, a surge of something warm swelling in my chest.

"Bring it, Damsel."

Her eyes shoot flames. "I'm *not* a damsel in distress, if that's what you're implying. This one wasn't even my fault."

The tightness in her face is relaxing, only to be replaced with her usual death glare. Either the pain relievers are working, or I've got her so worked up she's not feeling it at the moment.

"Oh, so you're finally admitting that the other scenes we've been called out to *were* your fault?" I prod.

She points a finger at me. "Not what I said. And I didn't get directly hit by the car. So it shouldn't count. Make sure they include that in any reports." She's shit out of luck if she thinks people aren't already talking about what happened. Her gaze reaches me again, looking less lethal than before. "Or maybe leave my name off the reports altogether."

Her blinks are getting longer, eyelashes fluttering with the exertion of remaining awake after the pain meds.

"Sleep, Grace. Tomorrow, when you're feeling better, you can read *The Vine's* Community News Update about how Assistant Chief Vaughn saved you from certain death after you tried to triple jump parked cars to impress the 'men twerking.'"

Her forehead wrinkles. "Triple jump? Like track and field?" she asks in a tone that's soft and breathy. "You should know...I'm more of a jogger."

Yes, I've seen her. Hard not to with the intense way she hits the trails. She doesn't see anyone, hear anything. Her focus is on running. I've found myself jogging behind her a time or two, and she's been completely oblivious—which is dangerous as fuck. So when I do see her out on the trails, I follow, making sure she doesn't get into any trouble.

And the view doesn't hurt either. Her thick, toned thighs are on full display in those cute little running shorts. They're nearly as distracting as the athletic leggings she usually wears.

Fuck. What were we talking about?

Right, triple jumps…

"I meant motocross jumps." She squints an eye, even more perplexed, and my brother smothers a laugh. "It's dirt bike jumping. I dirt-biked a lot in my later teens. Kept me busy, and mostly out of trouble."

"He still does it, annoys the hell out of some of the kids at the track. I've been meaning to tell you…" Jaxon stares at me from his spot in the chair opposite the hospital bed. "It's embarrassing. Stick to off-roading on your own property."

Grace snorts, her eyes drifting closed. "I can't imagine you being a motocross kid. Or getting in trouble. Or doing anything dangerous. Answer me one question…"

I narrow my gaze at her. "What's the question?"

She eases one eyelid open. "In elementary school—before the motocross bad boy stuff you tried out—were you voted hall monitor, or did you volunteer?" Her eyes close again, but there's a lazy, teasing smirk on her lips.

"Hall monitors got free chocolate milk at lunch, a key to the staffroom full of snacks, and could leave homeroom early every day."

She doesn't respond, but her smile grows a little bigger.

"Definitely volunteered," Jaxon confirms, not bothering to look up from the paperwork he's filling out.

Before I can defend myself or explain that I had a harder time making friends than my brother did growing up, a nurse arrives to talk to Jaxon. On the other side of the curtain, she tells him they'll be taking Grace to acute care soon.

I glance down, expecting Grace to be ready with another taunt. Instead, I get the serene sweetness of her sleeping face surrounded by blonde tresses. I brush a stray piece that's slipped over her face, my fingers slipping through the silky strands.

Not sure what compels me to lean in until I can smell the subtle scent of her hair. "Hmm, peaches," I murmur. "That might need to be your new nickname."

"Apricot," she mumbles. She can't even keep her eyes open, but she can summon the energy to correct me.

"That's not as cute as 'Peaches.'"

"Tough shit," she mutters, pulling a wide smile from me.

I catch Jaxon watching us with a curious glint in his eyes.

"Your stubborn ass is set on ruining me, isn't it?" I ask her.

Her cheek twitches.

Inching closer, my mouth grazing her light, golden hair, I whisper, "If you can stay accident-free until the game, I might let you on the ice."

"Screw you, Jerksen. I'm playing." Her voice is weary and her eyes still closed, but there's a comforting heat in her words. She's going to be okay.

As the nurse wheels her off to acute care, she reaches out and waves at me with her uninjured hand. But she seems to only have the strength to use one finger.

Yeah, she'll be just fine.

Dammit. I look down at the taco strewn all over the floor. The first bite of taco is always the best, and that pleasure was stolen from me.

And since it's the *only* pleasure I'm getting that isn't self-given this Valentine's Day, it's especially tragic.

I scramble for napkins to pick up the mess, but there's none at the table. Harper is working behind the bar, pouring a drink, and I wave to get her attention. When she glances my way, I mime using a napkin.

She blows a piece of glossy black hair out of her face and lifts her chin up at me, mouthing, "What?"

I point at the floor and then lift my hands in an apologetic shrug.

We should come up with some kind of signal for when I drop shit. Especially since Harper is one of only two people who knows I have a neurological condition that causes my motor coordination issues. Not because I'm hiding it or ashamed. It's more about the annoyance of having to explain. It's the pity, the doubt, the change in their perception of me.

People can either accept me as I am or not. The details of my medical history are irrelevant. I've improved over the last decade, and fought hard to overcome the worst of my cognitive disabilities. So usually people just assume I'm an absent-minded klutz.

Harper holds up a finger and calls one of her servers over to the bar. As the manager of Rocky's Tavern, she often has to fill in, and on the days she's behind the bar, she rarely gets a break. But since my plan today was to get sweaty at the gym, go home alone, and then set up a romantic evening for one, complete with a luxurious bubble bath, candles, and a waterproof vibrator, I figured it might be good for both of us to get out. Even if it's at her place of work.

"Really?" Irritation and disbelief lace the tone of the man who's come to a halt beside me.

Without moving, I sneak a peek out of the corner of my eye. On the floor beside my seat lies the scattered remains of my taco. With one large boot in the center.

"Grace." Jensen's voice resembles a growl.

Ah, shit.

With a sluggish turn of my head, the enormous pain in my ass comes into view.

I release my lips from where they were trapped between my teeth. "Hotshot."

"This yours?" he asks.

The weight of his gaze is intense, magnetic.

"*Hm?*"

Harper appears, setting a platter of tacos on the table. She looks down at the mess and tsks. "Got distracted by Gracie's killer legs and dropped your food, huh? Five second rule?" she teases.

Jensen glares pointedly at me, but not before I catch his earthy-hued gaze dip down to the bare expanse of thigh my ruche, off-the-shoulder sweater dress has revealed. His glare remains in place as he shakes his boot off, muttering, "More like *Corgi* legs."

Another jab at my height and short legs.

"They're long enough to shove my foot up your ass if you ever compare me to a dog again."

I might only be five foot two and bestowed with puny legs, but what they lack in length, they make up for in shape. Running and weight training has left my thighs luscious, and my calves toned as fuck.

Curious if he'll look again, I cross my legs.

He doesn't, but that muscle at his temple jumps. Close enough.

Without another word, he strides away, and I wait until the heavy tread of whatever kind of hiker-slash-work boots he's wearing fades before turning back to Harper. She's sending a small, awkward wave to Brody. The hint of a nod is all she gets in return before the eldest Vaughn brother's gaze returns to his beer.

Brody may be more of a miserable grump than Jensen, but the difference is, Vaughn's prickly police chief has never once chastised, complained about, or humiliated me in public. Not that I know of anyway.

Harper drops into the chair across from me and reaches for a taco, bringing it to her mouth with an indecent moan.

I grin at her, knowing she rarely gets to sit down during a shift, especially when she's working the bar. While she munches, I duck down to clean up the taco with the napkins she tucked under the platter.

"I wouldn't judge if you decide to launch that taco at him."

"Thought about it, but Mrs. Langerham is having her neighborhood watch meeting right over there." I tip my head at their table on the other side of Rocky's dining area. "They are brainstorming a trap for the vandals, but if they saw me tossing tacos, I'm sure they'd carve out some time to interview my first to fifth grade teachers to find out if I had a history of instigating food fights. Do a big expose on my early years. Wouldn't be pretty."

Harper's gaze shifts to where the nosy Nellies are meeting, then immediately jerks away.

Never draw attention to yourself.

With a wink, she says, "I have a pretty good idea who the vandals are anyway." She picks the jalapeños off her taco and takes another bite.

I snatch the peppers off her plate, shoving one into my mouth. "Who?"

She leans in. "Think about it. The pranks and 'vandalism' are only ever in that one neighborhood—Mrs. Langerham's neighborhood—and the paint turned out to be *washable*." Huh. That *is* kind of odd. "And who went over and cleaned all those signs while offering car washes for department donations?"

"I don't know." After my most recent accident, I stayed off social media for a few days, not wanting to know what anyone might have said about my involvement.

"*The Vine* covered the story *with* pictures of all the guys wet and shirtless..." she hints.

No fewer than five people sent me photos, one of whom was my mom—who is *not* supposed to be following *The Vine's* socials anymore. It's a lot harder to understand the crazy that happens in Vaughn unless you live here. It's a vibe *and* a tribe.

I lower my voice. "You think the fire department is involved? That they're targeting specific neighborhoods for publicity?"

"And donations. They've been trying to raise funds for the new Volunteer Firefighter Training Program. Or that's what Anders told me a couple of weeks ago." Her taco spews lettuce all over the table as she waves it around while explaining. "And then a truck full of buff, heroic firefighters show up to clean up the neighborhood. Washing cars, chatting up residents, giving safety tips? And some of the most notorious busybodies in Vaughn happen to live there..."

"There's no way half of those guys would skulk around town, painting signs, and relocating lawn decorations and furniture to other yards, trees, and Town Center Park in an attempt to raise money for their department."

"Agreed," she says with a quick dip of her chin. *"Half* of them wouldn't."

One of her employees comes to clean up the residual taco mess, and I thank her profusely before returning to my food.

I pour some hot sauce onto my taco, taking my time with it so this one doesn't end up on the floor too. Handheld foods are usually significantly easier to eat than those requiring the use of cutlery, but apparently not today.

"You think Dec or Jerksen, or hell, even the new guys trying to toe the line, would draw *The Vine's* attention with a mysterious town drama and then change the optics into a heartwarming community endeavor?"

Harper snatches the bottle out of my hand, her eyes flickering between me and my taco. It's drowning in hot sauce. I shrug and take a bite anyway.

So good.

"There's no way Dec or Jensen would allow the guys to pull that kind of crap. Even if it's harmless." Her smile widens. "But whoever's doing it, in a weird way, it's helping the community. And Ava loves pranks, so I kind of hope it continues and they head to our neighborhood next."

I raise my brows at her. "Because of your daughter? That's the only reason you hope the pranksters hit your neighborhood next?"

She drops her elbow to the table, resting her chin on her fist. "And the hot firefighters and EMS guys cleaning my car would keep me going for months," she admits before sighing.

"You could start dating again, you know."

With an eye roll, she says, "I'm a single mom who works six days a week. I don't have the time or energy to nurture a plant, let alone a relationship. Add in getting to know each other, figuring out if we're compatible, and uncovering their baggage?" She slumps back in her chair. "No, thank you."

With a tight smile, I clutch her hand. If anyone deserves a nice guy with no baggage who's good with kids, it's Harper. For a moment, I wonder if she'd let me set her up with Tanner. But that might be super awkward since Tanner asked me out again just a few days ago. I dodged that like a pro by pretending he didn't mean a date and agreeing that we'd be better off as friends.

I slapped the guy on the back with a *"see ya later, buddy"* and speed-walked back to the outpatient clinic. Not my best moment. But it's still better than, *"I'm only interested in men who are bad for me."*

In the past, guys have been understanding about my clumsiness right up until they experience the daily, ongoing symptoms. After a while their sympathy wanes and they can't understand that it's not as simple as 'trying harder' or 'listening better'.

This is me. If I'm 'too much' for you, move the fuck along.

But there's just something about a man who is rude and growly, protective and surly, with a massive soft spot for his woman—almost embarrassingly so—that I desperately crave.

And this is why I'm alone on Valentine's Day.

Those men don't exist.

"I know. But I think you should still get out there. You're hot, kind, and smart. Some guy out there is waiting for you to give him a chance, already half-hard." She snorts, glancing around the bar to see if anyone heard me. "You make better choices than me, so you've got that going for you. And I would think, as a bartender, Valentine's Day would be the perfect day to pick someone up. Guys are bound to come sit at the bar to get away from the love-fest out there. You could score someone who just got out of a relationship and is looking for a sexy shoulder to cry on."

Harper's upper lip hitches in disgust.

Eh, not the most enticing example. I'll give her that.

"Okay, a man who isn't looking for a serious relationship and doesn't care for all the romantic, Valentine's Day crap, but just wants to have fun?"

She rolls her eyes. "Sounds charming."

"Oh! I know! The 'got stood up' guy!" She sighs. "Or what about the temporary buffer guy?" She tilts her head in question. "You know, when a group of people go out for the night, but one guy is clearly there because the other two are just looking for an excuse to go out together. Soon, the two who are hot for each other get closer, murmuring in each other's ears, sharing soft touches. An eager caress along his arm. A possessive hand on her thigh. Yearning gazes and flushed skin. He'd lean in and cup her—"

Harper clears her throat, eyes wide.

"Got a little carried away there. You can blame the stack of romance novels I stocked up on for my big V-Day plans."

She grins, twirling the straw in her soda before taking a sip. "Oh! You have plans?"

"The 'V' in 'V-Day' stands for 'Vibrator' this year."

Sputtering on her drink, she grabs for the napkins. "Dammit, Gracie. That went up my nose," she coughs out with a laugh.

I lift my margarita and clink the salted rim against her glass. "Happy Vibrator Day, Harp!"

A shout from across the bar has us both craning to see what the commotion is.

Harper groans. "Crap. Lars is crashing Connie's date again. Poor guy refuses to move on, and she seems hellbent on dating every young twenty-something-year-old she can just to piss him off after she found out he offered her up as a prize in some kind of bet."

"Oh, hit me up with those details later."

She flicks me a look that says, "not happening."

I should be grateful she doesn't enjoy adding to the rumor mill like most everyone else. And while I'd like to pretend I'm above being intrigued by *The Vine* and the many other town happenings, I'm really not. As long as I'm left out of any embarrassing public scenes or *Vine* posts, I soak it in. People in this town are crazy as all hell, and it's fascinating. I've almost convinced myself that my humiliating introduction to Vaughn was par for the course.

Harper rises and beelines over to the threesome. "I'll send over your complimentary Valentine's drink. Anyone who comes in solo tonight gets a free glass of wine," she calls out to me without turning around.

I'm choosing to be excited about the free wine, not depressed about being served pathetic loner wine meant to cheer up all the loveless patrons who had the balls to go out alone on today of all days.

"Awesome," I shout back at her, infusing extra enthusiasm into my tone.

I don't even bother looking around to see if there are any single guys I could spend some time with tonight. I'd end up choosing some intriguing but emotionally vacant bastard who would call me his pretty girl, flirt, and later get me down on my knees. Like a good girl. And it would be good. But he wouldn't want to keep me. Wouldn't want to put up with my clumsiness. Apparently, it's only "cute" in small doses.

A few minutes later, my white wine—now nicknamed Pity Pinot—is delivered, looking crisp and cool. I prefer red wine but never drink it when out because it stains, and more than likely I'll end up spilling some of it.

The person delivering my Pity Pinot is a tawny-haired, gray-blue eyed man wearing dark jeans and a button-down shirt.

"Harper said I should bring this to you and join you."

"Oh!" I jerk my head over to the bar where Harper is mouthing *nice guy*, while pointing at him.

He's cute and had clearly been talking to Harper, so I wonder what convinced her to send him over to me instead.

"Hi, thanks for the wine. Much appreciated." I hold out a hand. "I'm Gracie, Harper's friend."

He takes my hand in a firm, warm handshake. "I'm Zach." He gestures to the seat across from me, asking permission to sit, and I nod.

"Sorry if this is awkward. I'm fairly new in town. Joined the police squad a few months back."

Ah. *That's* why Harper wasn't interested.

"And I think your friend felt bad for shutting me down and sent me over here." His mouth pulls to the side as he grimaces. "I probably just made things more awkward by admitting that didn't I?" I bite back a smile, taking a sip of my wine. "You're super pretty. Like a sweet, sexy angel. And I didn't ask your friend out tonight, so it's not *that* weird. I was talking her up last week. Twice. But she doesn't date cops, and...I'm bad at this."

I bark out a laugh. "If it makes you feel any better, I'd want to date Harper too. But sadly, she is not my type."

"Oh, you're, uh, you like women?"

"I do, but not sexually. I experimented in college though," I add with a wink.

I didn't, not really. I kissed one girl, and she tasted like strawberry lip balm and the only interest I had was in asking her if it was an original Lip Smackers flavor.

"Really? Huh. That's um, nice. I think that's good. When girls —women—experiment. You know, I like to try new things myself. Maybe if—"

Oh god. No. Please no.

"Sorry to interrupt." I'm really not. "Would you mind asking Harper to make us something with tequila in it? I think we're going to need it tonight." I give him an encouraging wink, and he shoots me a grin before taking off for the bar. Shit. I hope he didn't take that as a come-on. I am literally going to need tequila to make it through this conversation.

Twisting around, I shoot Harper a death glare and she hits me back with a disappointed head tilt and a "give the poor guy a chance" expression.

I roll the delicate stem of the wineglass between my fingers, as I contemplate a way out of spending the evening with the cute, nice, but a bit too eager—

"When do your stitches come out?"

The husky voice beside me sends a jolt of surprise through my body, causing me to flail. The glass flies from my fingertips, smashing against the wooden floors of the pub, spraying Pity Pinot in every direction.

"Shit."

I jump up from the table to clean it up but rebound against a hard chest. I'm sent flying backwards, the chair behind me taking me out at the legs.

On my back, wind knocked out of me, legs and arms askew, all I can get out is, "Oof!"

"I'll send someone over to sweep that up, Gracie," Harper shouts from across the room. "Do *not* pick up the glass yourself. Remember what happened last time?"

I let myself rest on the floor, needing a minute before trying to get up. I'll only embarrass myself more.

And then the breeze on my ass alerts me to the pinnacle levels of embarrassment I was worried about a moment ago.

I'm flashing my panty-covered vag directly at my nemesis.

I grip the hem of my dress and tug, but it's caught underneath me. And I realize too late that lifting my hips only serves to provide him with a much better view of my panties.

Dying inside, I lift my gaze, hoping he's looked away. Instead I catch his eyes slowly drift up from where they were locked on the area beneath my dress that's currently on display.

If he makes even *one* lady taco joke…

He kneels in front of me and yanks at my dress. "Are you capable of acting normal?"

No, I'm fucking not.

Once I'm properly covered, Jensen stands, holding out his hand to help me up. But I bat it away and rise from the floor on my own.

Somehow, this man knows what to say and where to poke to inflict the most damage. And some day, I'm going to stop letting it get to me.

"Fuck off, asshat."

That day is not today.

He swipes a hand over his face. "Ah, hell. I shouldn't have said that. It's been a shit day. And I wanted to ask about your stitches and if you're still playing next weekend."

"Is this your attempt at making sure I'm unable to play?"

His tall body stiffens, the color rising on his high cheekbones. "*You* rammed into *me*."

I inhale long and slow, holding it for a few seconds before responding. "You startled me."

"By talking to you?"

"My jump-scare threshold is fairly low. In case you hadn't noticed." My brother called me Queen of the Jump Scare growing up. The joy he derived from pranking me resulted in years of sibling warfare.

"Hard not to." He looks over his shoulder at his brother, lifting his chin in some kind of bro-code thing that Brody must understand because he shifts over to the bar and takes a seat. "Look, I just came over to see how your arm was doing."

Be nice.

Nope. Can't.

Be polite?

"They come out tomorrow. Just in time for the game this weekend. Barring any more ogre-sized men thrusting their chests at me unexpectedly, I'll be in top form."

"Ogre-sized?" His expression appears aloof, but there's a tightness around his mouth that gives him away.

"What's your best lap time?" I ask.

His forehead crinkles. "Lap time?"

"If repeating all my questions is a new way you've devised to grate on my nerves, it's working."

His hand comes up to work his jaw. "I don't time my laps."

Disappointing. "Huh."

"That was a judgy 'huh,' Grace."

"Nope. Just surprised you're not taking this as seriously as I thought you would."

Oh, the temple tic is flaring up again.

He turns to give another silent signal to his brother. "See you at the game, Peaches. If you could try to be less...*this*,"—he gestures to the surrounding area, my table, and the floor where our server is once again cleaning up my mess—"that would ease my mind about having you on my ice."

I step toward him, ready to ream him out, when Zach appears behind him.

"So, should I sit back down or are you two a thing?" Zach asks, gesturing with the two drinks he brought back.

Jensen spins on his heel, moving toward where his brother waits.

Releasing a deep sigh, I tell him, "I'm going home."

The excited glimmer in his eyes has me clarifying. "Alone. I'm going home alone." And because my parents raised me with manners, even if they're forgotten some days, I add, "It was nice to meet you."

But before I leave the bar, I give Harper a hug, whispering, "Never again. You are wing-woman fired. Love you." I brush past Jensen on my way out, knocking into his arm slightly harder than intended, earning a muffled growl. And then I run away from attempting to "people" on Valentine's Day.

CHAPTER
SEVEN

JENSEN

THE VINE COMMUNITY UPDATE

Tonight marks the eighth year of the Fire & Ice Charity Hockey Game. If you haven't gotten your tickets, a few remain and can be purchased at the door. All proceeds will be going toward the Pediatric Care Unit and the Volunteer Firefighter Training Program.

Rivalry antics continued today as fire trucks traversed Main Street, handing out pucks and tossing out charity shirts—which were modeled by our local heroes. The truck's last stop was the hospital where players from the opposing team were waiting.

A highly anticipated addition to this year's game is the inclusion of Fire & Ice's first female player. Gracelyn Parker joins the Hospital Healers and is rumored to have it out for Fire Fliers captain and organizer of this event, Jensen Vaughn.

The two were spotted at Rocky's Tavern on Valentine's Day, celebrating separately, but an altercation still ensued. The interaction left many wondering if this was part of the *charity game's rivalry week or a continuation of their ill-disguised feud.*

"**H**ey, jackasses. This is *our* charity game—not a gamer tournament in your mom's basement with stale Cheetos and edibles. Get your shit together," I shout at my team.

While some guys are making side bets and showing off, I'm the only one taking it seriously. Declan *was*, but he gave up on us as a coach halfway through the first period.

We're still winning, but the guys aren't putting on the show for the spectators like they should be.

"I need three of you to go out there and help with the intermission show. Miranda and a couple of Town Council members are choosing volunteers from the crowd to come down for the sponsor games." I left our mayor in charge of that, and Miranda doesn't half-ass anything, so I imagine it'll be quite the show.

"Then two of you will need to work the crowd a bit. We have a fake fight going down at 17:30. Bradford, that's all you." I point at him and glare until the shit-eating grin leaves his face. "Under no circumstances are you to actually throw your weight around or land a punch. Greer's a cocky shit but he's needed in the ER tomorrow. Got me?"

There are certain traditions we uphold every year and having at least one fight is the most expected. A couple years back, it was police versus fire department, and the game was a lot scrappier than intended. But that's what happens when you put three brothers on the ice who have been playing hockey together since before their voices stopped cracking.

To the town, my older brother may seem all buttoned up and professional, but off the clock, the stoic police chief is a beast— quiet and fierce. There were four fights in that game, and Brody was involved in three of them. It's a reminder of his younger years, before he joined the military, when he was getting into shit all the time.

"How much contact do we need? I know one feisty, adorable blonde out there I'd happily tap, Chief," Erickson says, earning a grin from a few of the guys. The idiot nods at them like they're in on the joke together. Our newest volunteer firefighter doesn't realize that the guys are grinning because they know something he doesn't.

"Yeah, Erickson? I'd almost like to see you try. She'd knock your teeth into the back of your dumb as fuck head." I look at the guys on the bench. "Apparently, I need to say this again. No one touches Grace. She's already had a few close calls, and I don't need the extra headache of added casualties." She's only fallen once, but she had an unexpected collision with one of her teammates who is startlingly bad at skating, and the chances of something worse happening has me on edge. "And if Erickson gets within ten feet of her, you have my permission to take him out."

"What the fuck, Chief? I was just messing around. You'd turn on your own teammate?"

"Do stupid shit, win stupid prizes," Jaxon chimes in, his eyebrows jumping in amusement. "It's like you don't know how we work, probie." The whistle blows, and he jumps onto the ice.

I spend half my shifts on the ice sticking around Grace to make sure she doesn't cause any problems. Hell, if I didn't know how much she hates needing help, I'd *almost* think she does it on purpose.

"You playing zone defense, or do you just like the way my sweat smells?" Grace chirps, flipping around to face me, skating backward.

I keep my face neutral, ignoring her and tapping my stick to call for the puck. My brow scrunches as I pick up my pace, maneuvering around her without replying.

"Why are you following me around?" she demands, brushing up next to me.

"Someone has to babysit you, and I drew the short straw."

As I skate past her, I catch her cheeks turning bright pink.

Fuck. Why couldn't I have just said, *"I want to make sure none of these idiots forget you're out here and crush you."*

There's something inside me that enjoys poking at her. I could just keep my distance, stop opening my damn mouth and egging her on. But I don't. And too often, that leads to me saying stupid shit.

Wanting to keep her safe, being protective, is simply a reaction to having rescued her from several situations—both serious and absurd. That's all.

But *sometimes*…I actually enjoy her zeal. Even though most of the time it chafes.

If you truly wanted to push her away, you'd leave her alone. Or at minimum, approach her with the same level of stark indifference you've enacted over your personal life for the last ten months.

I hustle to the net, my anger simmering too close to the surface. I've got to knock this shit off. I'm the assistant chief. I have long-term professional goals to focus on, and an obligation to contribute to our community.

I'll rationally explain to her that I'm merely trying to keep things safe and friendly. The guys can get out of hand, and she just healed from the—

Something hits my ankle mid-stride, causing me to lose my edge.

My stick flies out as I go down hard on my side. A player crashes onto me and we slide across the ice, stopping just short of the boards. The crowd goes up in an uproar, and a whistle blows.

Blonde hair tickles at my chin. Christ. I took out Grace. I've done little else but attempt to keep her safe all fucking game, and *I'm* the one who took her out.

Her elbow goes straight for my spleen as she shifts on top of me. I lift her upper body, assessing her state. "You okay?"

She twists to face me, her eyes connecting with mine. There's humor dancing in those orbs, sending a rush of relief through me. Her face glows as she hovers above me, and the sudden urge to flip us over and take control makes me pause.

That thought cuts off as she straddles me.

"Two minutes, tripping, number twelve," the ref announces, pointing at the tiny player sitting astride me.

Grace grins down at me, offers an unapologetic shrug, and then rises to her skates.

The tiny menace *tripped* me?

I jump up, watching as she glides over to the penalty box. Grace glances at me over her shoulder with a satisfied smirk.

We're not even through the first period and she's already playing dirty.

Distracted, I play for a few more minutes before heading to the bench at shift change.

Declan lays a hand on my shoulder. "I assume you deserved that?"

My jaw clenches, yet I can't seem to keep the corner of my mouth from lifting. "Yeah. Maybe a little."

"Didn't think she'd come after you like that, did you?"

I shrug, rethinking letting him coach.

"Your face after she took you down was something I'll remember for a long fucking time, Jens. It was like a real-life David versus Goliath. Dani cheered so hard she's probably lost her voice."

"I'm sure your neighbors will thank me," I mumble.

After a few minutes, he adds, "She's good. Faster than I expected. Smart. Her shots are a bit off, but otherwise good. Better than half the guys on her team." I nod and glance back at him, his weighted glower packing the heat behind his hushed tone. "So tell me why you kicked up so much shit about her playing?"

I lift my gaze to where she sits in the penalty box, chatting up spectators behind the glass, making them laugh. Admitting to him that I expected her to be a wreck probably makes me a bigger asshole. Because from the minute I got out on the ice with her, I was impressed—and shocked as hell.

"Fuck if I know anymore," I mumble as she leaves the box.

SHE'S FUCKING BLEEDING.

And I don't know whether to feel vindicated, aggravated, or impressed that she made it through nearly two periods without bloodshed.

One of our guys got her in the mouth with their stick. Bumped her or something, I don't know. Everyone on the bench clammed up the minute I asked what happened.

"You good, bro?"

Not bothering to take my eyes off the game, I respond, "Fine. Why?"

"Oh, no reason." Jaxon's shoulder bumps mine. "You just seem tense. This is the event you most look forward to every year. And that includes Christmas, much to Mom's disappointment."

He's not wrong. I do look forward to it. The town loves this game, especially with all the other activities we include. When we amp up the rivalry in the weeks leading up to the game, and draw out the drama on the ice, it's a guaranteed hit.

This year, the proceeds are being split evenly and will help the pediatric care unit and our new volunteer firefighter training program.

"I've been working on raising money for the training program for the last two years. I can't be serious about that?"

He grins as the buzzer for the end of the period goes off. "Sure. Let's go with that."

A few of the guys go out onto the ice for the intermission

show. Miranda has giant bread slice costumes and all the plastic, life-size sandwich fixings ready on the center line for tonight's second Sponsor Showdown.

"This year's game might be my favorite yet," he says, a teasing lilt to his tone that I really don't like.

I follow his gaze and find Tanner Sullivan—the coach who's supposed to stay behind the bench—leaning over Grace. He's running his thumb over the cut on her lip.

That's really fucking unsanitary and being a doctor, he should know that. Maybe she doesn't care because they're dating, and his dirty hands are on her all the time.

Grace waves him off with a smile and goes to the center of the ice with the rest of the players, helmet dangling from her fingers. She helps choose two members from the audience to represent her team in the competition Miranda has set up. My players do the same as our mayor explains what they have to do to win the prize—getting to drive the fire truck, and a week's worth of free lunches at The Sandwich Ship.

Yes, it's actually called that. The owners originally named it The Sandwich Shop, but they printed all their menus and signage with the typo and went with it—nautical theme included.

The pairs of contestants get into their ridiculous bread slice costumes and head to opposite ends of the rink. A loud cheer goes up when the competition starts and two opposing slices of bread zip back and forth to bury their partner under gigantic sandwich fixings. The first bread slice to launch themselves atop the pile to complete the sandwich, wins.

Would I have done this for some free sandwiches and a ride-along? Hell no.

It's by far one of the stupidest things I've seen all week. And as a firefighter/EMT I have seen some idiotic shit. Last week, we got called out to a constipated twenty-something-year-old's home. He tried to dig the shit out of his rectum with a spoon, and it got stuck. But as I witness a grown-ass man grab a mattress-sized piece of cheese and throw himself bodily onto his partner, I have to admit that at least the spoon debacle made some kind of sense.

But no matter how inane this game is, I'm keeping a close eye. Because there's another prize being awarded during this intermission. And that one, I'm *very* interested in.

CHAPTER
EIGHT

GRACIE

I thought the hardest part of my day would be tying my skates —regular shoelaces are bad enough, but skates are the worst.

Nope. My biggest challenge today has been keeping my cool around the man determined to rattle me.

Though maintaining a straight face during this sandwich competition is a close second.

When the fire department's bread slice hurls himself into the air seconds before ours, their whole bench goes out onto the ice to congratulate the winners and claim their prize, which provides some kind of advantage in the third period.

It's my first year attending this event, and I'm thinking I should have asked more questions instead of blindly joining the team.

"Congratulations to Tim and Brent for winning our Sponsor Showdown." Miranda motions to the big screen above us, displaying sponsor information. "And thank you to our generous sponsor, The Sandwich Ship, for providing not only the showdown prize but also contributing to our raffle and the post-game snacks for all of our players and VIP ticket holders. We will keep the fire department's team captain away from the food until everyone else has had a chance." She winks at Jensen, who's standing a couple of players down from me, on the other side of Tanner.

"I won *one* eating contest six years ago," he grumbles.

I snort. The man's appetite is boundless. I'm not sure how many subs The Sandwich Ship provided but based on the number of tacos and wings I've seen him take down at Rocky's, I'd say he's earned that reputation.

Then again, I have no idea how much food a man several inches over six feet and weighing two-hundred-plus pounds eats to stay in the shape he's in. Given the article and photos *The Vine* posted last summer about the fire department's Summer Fitness Program, I'd say he's earned the right to eat whatever the hell he wants.

"Growing boys and their hollow legs, right, Mrs. Vaughn?" Miranda gestures to where Jensen and Jaxon's mom are sitting.

"If food was a love language, it would be Jensen's. Keep that in mind, ladies," she shouts from the stands.

"Great," Jensen mutters, swiping a hand over his jaw but still smiling at the crowd. "Now I'm going to have a parade of women armed with casseroles and pies showing up at the fire station." His glistening, golden face turns ruddy as the color rises on the tops of his cheeks.

I find more amusement than I should that Jensen Vaughn's mom just embarrassed him in front of hundreds of people. "Not from me," I comment.

"Good. Death by food poisoning would be a shitty way to go," he says under his breath.

A scoff leaves me as I look away. I'm a fantastic cook. Baking though? Not so much. Precision and kneading are not for me. I haven't given up on baking, but with a talented baker for a best friend, I've been much less motivated. She keeps me supplied with Danishes, pies, and more kinds of cookies than I even knew existed.

My stomach roils as Miranda calls the team captains forward. I get mildly nauseous if I eat before big workouts, but particularly ones that require a lot of movement. Because of my neurological condition, I'm also more prone to motion sickness. And the combination of hunger, nausea, and the euphoric high of a good workout are making me jittery.

"As is tradition, we like to change things up in the third period. The winning team from tonight's second Sponsor Showdown have also won a game advantage at the start of the last period."

There's chatter amongst the crowd, most people having already found their seats in anticipation of this next part.

Shit. I really should have asked more questions.

"Jensen Vaughn, team captain and our fire department's assistant chief, will choose one of the hospital's players for a special task. Personally, it is my favorite part of the game. This player will sit out the first five minutes of the period."

Well, fuck me.

Like a shy middle school student, I keep my head down and hope I'm not called upon.

"Anybody have suggestions for Jensen as he contemplates who to pick?" she asks the crowd.

The cocky captain skates to the end of our team line, then circles back holding a hand over the heads of each of the players, playing it up for everyone with a wide-eyed, questioning expression.

It's possible he won't choose me. Not if he's going with the audience.

He could be putting on a show. Lulling you into a false sense of security.

A roar goes up as he approaches one of our most skilled players—Darnel, an orthopedic nurse.

Darnel laughs, slashing a hand in front of himself and mouthing, *No!*

Jensen continues down the line, and I hold my breath when I feel him move behind me.

A loud, "Let her play!" comes from the crowd, and I look up to see Dani standing, hands cupped around her mouth, a *Fliers* glitter sign leaning against her legs. Beside her, Harper and her daughter are holding a sign for the Hospital *Healers*.

"Not my Gracie Girl!" my dad booms from his spot in the stands.

With a slight chuckle, I wave at them all and then motion for my dad to sit down.

A grumbled "Hmmm," reminiscent of Geralt of Rivia, comes from behind me, and I shiver.

What the fuck was that?

No more thinking about Henry Cavill as *The Witcher* while Jensen the Jerk is around. My ovaries are getting confused.

He moves on and I finally exhale.

"He's going to pick you," Tanner whispers.

"Nah, I'm not a big enough threat," I respond, infusing confidence in my tone.

Tanner's gaze darts from me to Jensen and back, unconvinced.

"For those of you new to the Fire & Ice Charity Hockey Game, the person chosen will also perform a special task while in the sin bin." Miranda glances over at us. "They will receive a microphone so they can provide running commentary on the game and players. However,"—she holds up a finger—"all commentary involving their opponents must be enthusiastically complimentary."

Jaxon skates out a few feet to face us. "I'm told my best features are my face and as—butt!" he modifies for the younger spectators. "If that helps." A wide grin pulls at his smug, roguishly handsome face.

"Your butt and face look pretty similar, so that checks out," Bradford calls from the end of their line. The team laughs, and someone pulls Jaxon back into the line.

"Let's keep your face and butt to yourself for now, Mr. Vaughn," Miranda says into the microphone.

"I'll take both!" a woman in the audience yells.

Jesus. I roll my eyes, unable to keep from smiling.

Miranda scans the stands, looking for the culprit. She shakes her head, biting down on a grin as a wicked gleam Jaxon should be wary of lights in her gaze.

"Mr. Vaughn—the younger Mr. Vaughn—come on up," she requests.

Huh. Jensen's the youngest Vaughn brother?

He skates over, coming to a stop beside her.

"Who is spending the first five minutes in the penalty box?" Miranda asks.

The crowd shouts their suggestions as Jensen takes the microphone.

I do my best to avert my gaze, but my curiosity wins. When I glance over at him, he's already looking at me.

Shit on a stick.

"The Healer's player chosen to spend some time in the sin bin singing our praises, is..."

He pauses dramatically, and I force my eyes back to the ice.

"Grace Parker."

I close my eyes, trying and failing to keep my agitation in check.

He skates by to rejoin his team, ignoring me entirely.

My stick flies out before I think better of it and pull it back in, but he's already gracefully hopped over it.

The crowd laughs, used to our antics by now.

"Careful or you'll get an extra two minutes in there."

"Well worth it," I mumble, but he hears me and the hint of a grin tips up the side of his mouth.

My brows dip down into a deeper frown. I've seen a version of that grin before, given to his crew or his brothers. It's almost a carbon copy of his twin brother's, yet somehow completely different.

While the event staff cleans up the ice, the teams head to the bench, and I skate over to the box that Jensen's using to exert his control over me. He didn't want me to play, thought I'd be a disaster. And when I held my own—for the most part, my ass is one enormous bruise and my puffy lip still stings—he put me in a timeout.

Big mistake.

WITH A MICROPHONE GRIPPED in my hand and a box of Oreos beside me to stave off the hunger—consequences be damned—I deliver an entertaining and dramatic running commentary on the game. All very positive. In the back-handed way a condescending, elderly aunt might compliment your outfit for hiding the extra weight you've gained.

And the crowd is eating it up.

Darnel has attended every Fire & Ice game and mentioned the commentary is usually full of cheap shots and roundabout ways of actually cheering for your own team. He said to have fun with it, so I am.

"Number fifteen, forward Wyatt Bradford somehow remains upright after a light check from number twenty-three, defenseman Ronnie Shore. Though Bradford had to cling to Shore like an overly attached girlfriend to do so. No shame in Bradford's game!"

After a few lighthearted chirps from Bradford as he skates by, the team gets a little more intense and I get a little too into commentating.

This might actually be better than playing. The idea of volunteering to be the commentator for next year's game becomes more appealing by the minute. Especially given how badly it would chap Jensen's ass.

But would it bother him more than me being on the ice with him? Hard to say.

I focus back on the game as the Fliers take possession of the puck.

"The better Vaughn twin skates up the ice, passing to his rude but not completely unskilled brother. Shot on net!" The goal horn goes off as the puck slams into the back of the net. Shit. "Goal scored by Jensen Vaughn, assisted by Jaxon Vaughn. That puts the Fliers in the lead, 7-5."

Jensen circles the back of the net, fist bumping his teammates before skating past me. His darkened gaze locks on mine, and there's a hint of hurt in those steely irises. A moment later, irritation sweeps over his face once more, making me wonder if I imagined it.

With another two minutes left in here, I make the most of it.

"Anders's shot on net goes wide. *Way* wide. Was that a pass? Yes, that would make the most sense. Excellent 'pass' to the open space by the boards, number thirty-one! If only someone had been there."

Things get sloppy as my team tires out. Less than half of the hospital staff players have the stamina needed to skate—even intermittently—for several hours.

"Coach Tanner has put one of their wingers in for defense. That's a bold choice. Perhaps the coach is trying to confuse the other team by making outlandish choices. Or the Healers are looking to hand the win over to the Fliers early."

Tanner ignores me, focusing on the shift change.

"The Fliers captain annihilates our winger, taking control of the puck. The Fliers wisely use that to their advantage. Must be frustrating for the Healers," I say, an obvious edge to my voice as Tanner looks my way. I lift a hand to bang on the glass at him.

Tanner finally makes some changes, and I'd like to think that's what led to our next goal. It could also be that a few players are completely incapable of filtering out my nonsense.

"Jaxon Vaughn gets distracted by his reflection in the plexiglass, letting Carter skate past. Carter passes to Stanson who winds up for a huge shot. Big block by Fliers goalie, Lyle Emerson. Rebound snagged by Carter. He shoots!" The goal horn sounds again, tying up the game. "And that ladies and gents ties this game up."

My release from the box counts down, with only thirty seconds remaining.

"Some testosterone-fueled shoving happening just behind the net. Oh, here we go! The Fliers captain grabs the Healers captain's jersey, getting in his face." I let out a loud, lascivious sigh. "I love when men grapple. All sweaty and fired up. Think they'll take their jerseys off, ladies?"

Some hoots echo through the stands.

"Rhodes takes Vaughn down easily. A few love taps and he's down for the count. It's unfortunate our assistant fire chief's muscles are mostly for show." I keep going and take it further. "Disappointing. Oh shoot! I'm supposed to be complimentary. One second. I'll come up with something to stroke his ego. Hmm, at least he's pretty to look at? You know, for those who like that sort of thing. And he skates well. Gives an impressive mean mug. Don't worry, ladies. If he appears weak right now and lacks the He-Man vibes you'd expect from a burly firefighter, I've got some strength-enhancing exercises to help him out—"

Jensen lets out a roar of frustration, causing Rhodes to rear back and crash into the net. The poor pathology assistant falls to the ice, knocking himself in the chin with his stick. He's yanked up off the ice and flung over Jensen's shoulder like he's nothing more than a hand towel.

Miranda comes on the speakers, explaining that the ice crew will need to clean up the blood and reset the net before the game can continue. The camera scans the crowd as raffle winners are announced and spectators pop up on the screen for the kiss cam.

My eyes widen as the firefighter skates over to me. He glares at me while Rhodes twists to look at us while hanging upside down. "I thought I was supposed to win," Rhodes says. "Man, what are we doing? Hey! Are you listening to me?"

Sorry, buddy, he really isn't.

With a swift motion, I turn off the switch at the bottom of the microphone, preventing anyone else from listening in on our stand-off. "Regretting your penalty box choice right about now, huh, hotshot?"

Neither of us blinks as we glare at each other, ignoring Rhodes's agitated sounds.

Eventually Jensen puts Rhodes down, allowing him to join me in the penalty box. I move down the bench to make room while he gets into the adjacent box for his team.

The two penalty boxes are separated by a short divider between the benches, making me wonder how many fights were broken up on the ice only to continue in here.

"Trying to save you from yourself always seems to fucking backfire," he says, sliding closer to the paltry partition separating us.

I grit my teeth and hiss, "I don't need saving." His choked exhale mocks me. "Not from you."

It bothers me. Every time he's helped me, sweeping in to un-clusterfuck whatever mess I'm in, leaving me flustered and with his stern voice on repeat in my head for hours afterward...bothers me.

Why is it almost always *him* on-call?

He rips off his helmet, muttering, "How I wish that were true, Grace."

I ignore him, directing my focus up to the screen as they show more kissing couples—including my parents. My dad lays it on thick as he tips Mom out of her seat with an obnoxiously long kiss.

Then the player's bench comes up, showing Bradford and Jaxon sitting next to each other. Bradford notices first and waves off the camera with a frown. It pans away to another couple for a few moments before returning to the firefighter's bench. I laugh along with the audience as Jaxon wraps his arms around Bradford and kisses his helmet.

Sneaking a peek beside me, I watch a grin pull at Jensen's face as he shakes his head.

Whistles mix with the laughter, as the energy in the arena changes.

"Fuck," Jensen mutters.

Curious, I glance up at the screen and immediately regret it.

It's Jensen and me in our penalty boxes.

"Nope," I say, reaching for my Oreos. I cram three in there and have another on standby. I might choke, but then I definitely won't be forced to kiss the loathsome man beside me.

Jensen shoves over, hoping to get out of the shot, causing the crowd to boo at us. The camera pans away, and relief sweeps through me.

"Fucking fine. Let's just get this over with," he grumbles.

What? No. Not fine.

He leans over the divider, grips my shoulder pad and hauls me into him. His face is inches from mine and all I can do is blink up at him. From this close I can see the stubble on his jaw, appreciate the thick lashes that frame the earthy hues of his copper-flecked eyes.

I draw a hand between us, listlessly placing a cookie between my lips as if that will stop him.

He chuffs out a breath as his bemused gaze moves from the cookie to my eyes.

"That for me?" he murmurs, his tone teasing. And then his warm, minty breath is teasing my lips, his mouth briefly brushing mine. Our gazes lock as his teeth clamp down on my cream-filled treat.

He pulls away, grinning around my cookie trapped between his teeth. I'm left gaping as he eases farther down the bench, his jaw working as he chews.

The sounds of excited spectators draws my attention away, unsure of how much time has passed since. When I glance up, the screen is showing one of my teammates with the puck.

The game started?

I turn my microphone back on and rattle off a few more minutes of commentary.

I'm still fuming as I emerge from the penalty box on a mission to win this game for us. I don't have the finesse to outmaneuver the firefighters, but I do have speed.

But I only have a few minutes of freedom before Jensen leaves the box. He sticks to me like glue, even blocking a few of his own players who come near. Is this his way of proving I need his help?

Instead of continuing my attempts at evading him, I slow down, pretend I'm going off the ice, and then rush the net, hoping like hell my team can get me the puck. Jensen catches up, but I throw a shoulder into him, shoving him into the boards just before the puck meets my stick.

I take my shot, putting as much power behind it as I can muster.

The horn goes off and my team swarms me. I've put us ahead by one, but we still have half the period left.

"That was a bit more than *light* contact, Parker," Jensen says, his expression unreadable.

Hands on his hips, he stands in front of me breathing heavy. My smile widens as I shrug.

An arm wraps around me. "Don't let him fool you, Gracie," Jaxon says. "He liked it."

Jensen's eyes never leave mine as he heads to the bench, knocking into his brother on the way.

"Jax, what did I say earlier?" he shouts from behind us.

Jaxon's arm slips away. "Right!" He lowers his voice. "He warned us not to touch you. Got all riled up about it."

His words make me recoil in surprise, and I frown at him.

"Shit, you're cute. Don't think too hard about it. Just keep an open mind." Skating away from me, he calls over his shoulder, "He's not the asshole you've pegged him as, Gracie. Well...not a *complete* asshole."

I'm more confused than ever. Jaxon occasionally tries to diffuse the tension between Jensen and me or sits back and enjoys the show. But he's never tried to mend the rift before.

For a few moments I'm distracted, stealing a glance at Jensen as Jaxon's words circulate. Why would Jensen tell the guys not to touch me? Because he doesn't think I can hold my own or because he was trying to protect me?

I'm so lost in thought as I skate to the bench that I don't see the enormous shoulder coming at me until it's already on a collision course with my face.

CHAPTER
NINE

JENSEN

I knew this day was coming for weeks. But knowing didn't help.

Declan tips his chin at me as he spots me coming out of the house. "I need Dani's help with something in the laundry room."

I shake my head as he tries to keep his smug smile in check. "Right. You want her to make sure the spin cycle is how she likes it?"

"Shut it. Remember how I chopped all the firewood you'd need for the rest of the winter?"

"I think I actually have Dani to thank for that," I say. "You're the one who fucked up and decided that tackling my wood pile was an easier task than getting your woman to forgive you."

He clears his throat like he does at the station when the guys are being idiots and he expects us to shut up.

"Fine," I tell him. "Dani's needed for a small problem in the laundry room—"

"It's a *big* problem, asshole," Declan barks at me.

Light steps sound behind me as Grace makes her way up the porch.

"Sure," I placate him. "But it'll probably only take a minute or two. I'll let her pain in the ass friend know so she can eavesdrop on you two christening the laundry room."

"Gross," she says, coming to stand beside Declan. "Did you just imply that I'm a voyeur who enjoys listening to my friends fucking?"

I shrug, trying not to let my amusement show at how she embellished my harmless teasing.

"How about you two bring in the last couple of boxes instead of going another round?" Declan asks.

I shift closer to stare down the blonde pixie who sprayed coffee everywhere at the sight of me pulling up to help this morning. Apparently Dani and Declan didn't tell her I was helping.

Her reaction was a welcome diversion from my thoughts at seeing her for the first time since the hockey game—the one her team lost. Normally I'd have used that to instigate an argument or as a way to poke at each other. But I didn't dare bring it up. I wasn't in the right headspace. Because the moment her eyes landed on me, I could taste that damn cookie, feel the light brush of her soft lips as I stole it from her.

"Or just grab a beer and chill out. You two are driving me nuts."

Ignoring Declan, my focus stays on Grace and that little butterfly bandage peeking out from under her hairline. One look at the wound that's dangerously close to her temple has my teeth grinding. She had plenty of medical professionals on hand to close the wound and check her over, but it was that unprofessional dickbag Sullivan who insisted on taking care of her. He's exactly the type of guy she probably likes. And it's none of my damn business. I'm comfortable with the tumultuous dynamic we forged from the moment she moved here. It keeps us in check. Keeps *me* in check.

Because she might be nice to look at, cute as fuck when angry, and has the mettle that rivals most of the guys on my crew, but she's the combustible kind of dangerous.

And I know all too well how that ends.

The deep breath she takes does nothing to quell the fire still burning in her gaze. Closing her eyes, she mutters, "This is fine. Pretend he doesn't exist. I can do this," like a chant.

A forced smile stretches across her face. "There are still the boxes, and that chaise left to bring in. What's your preference?"

My head rocks back at the cordial tone coming from her lips. She's always at least given it to me straight, no filter. The false niceties leave a bitter taste in my mouth.

"Dani's not here. You don't have to uphold whatever promises you made about being nice." Her jaw clenches. "Now…what the fuck is a *chaise?*"

She jerks a thumb at the truck behind her. "The last piece of furniture back there. It's French for—you know what, never mind." She waves off whatever she was about to say.

"The long-ass chair. Got it," I say with a wink.

That stupid wink turns into a wince as I wonder what the hell I'm doing. I don't wink at women. Especially *this* woman.

Jaxon does, though, all the fucking time.

I force myself to rein in my wayward thoughts and return my focus to the task at hand. "You take the boxes. I'll bring in the awkward French furniture since it'll be way too—" I cut myself off, knowing what will happen if I finish that thought.

With a tone sharp enough to eviscerate, she asks, "Too what?"

I shake my head, refusing to play this game. There's no way in hell she can take that chair-thing in by herself, and I won't say the words to seal the deal.

I press my mouth in a firm line, determined not to let her goad me.

"First, I wasn't asking if you wanted to take it in by yourself. I wanted to know which of those two jobs you wanted to tackle first." She takes a step closer, somehow glaring *down* at me despite the foot of height I have on her. "Second, I can carry that by myself with no problem. It's not that heavy. Just prop the door open for me."

An unintentional chuffing sound escapes my throat at her bold statement. Her eyes widen and her head tilts to one side, eyebrows raised.

Well, fuck me. I know without any doubt this strong but tiny woman is going to attempt to carry a piece of furniture twice her size.

I take on the full heat of her glare and remain silent, tucking one hand into the pocket of my jeans.

"Dec, tell your sexist friend I am capable—" Her eyes dart around. "Where did he go?"

At some point, Declan must have left. I tip my head toward the house while wondering if I could also slip away unnoticed while Grace continues fuming.

An irritated sniff comes from her. The intricate braid she wove through her golden hair flies off the slender curve of her shoulder as she whips around, storming over to the truck. *Parker* is written in baby blue letters on the back of the white Vaughn Bowling Babes beer league shirt she's wearing. The cuffed sleeves show off her little biceps, but it's long on her, covering her ass. Makes me wonder what a large men's shirt would look like on her.

Unbidden images of her in a dark gray Vaughn Fire Department shirt flash across my mind. The red and white logo sitting neatly on her left breast, *Vaughn* sprawled in large block letters across her upper back.

Christ. I need to get a grip.

If I've sunk so low as to fantasizing about Gracelyn Parker in my clothes, waiting for me in my bed, knees spread wide to take all of—

Fuck!

"You going to help or just stand there gloating?" Grace

shouts, bounding out of the moving truck with two large boxes in her arms.

Gloating?

She stops at the bottom of the stairs, shifting the boxes. "You're being weird." Concern softens her tone as she asks, "Did you work yesterday? Is this when you'd usually be sleeping?"

"Day before," I answer, swiping a hand over the scratchy growth along my jaw. "I'm fine."

I glance at the truck as she heaves up the steps, and that's when it clicks.

"Thought you were bringing in the chair?" I nod toward the "chaise" which is now a few feet closer to the ramp.

"These were in the way, so I'm taking them in first."

No way in hell am I giving her another chance to hurt herself. The little spitfire may be strong, but I'm not willing to chance it today. Or any day. If she'd let me, I'd swaddle her in bubble wrap and strap a helmet on her before she left the house each day.

As she storms up the stairs, I lean one shoulder against the porch column. "Mhm, sure." The heated embers in her eyes flare at my tone. "But now that you've cleared those mighty obstacles out of the way, I'll go grab the chair."

"What? No, I can—" She spins to face me, causing the back of her heel to slip off the edge of the step. She gasps.

In agonizing slow motion, I'm forced to watch as the most stubborn woman I've ever met falls backward off the porch steps.

I lunge for her, my feet pushing off the rough wood. Before my fingers wrap around her forearm, I realize I'll have to twist my body and pull sharply to get her back on the step.

In my rush to get to her, I pushed off a little too hard. Lunged a little too far.

I didn't consider the best way to save her while also keeping myself safe. There was no time.

Instead, I've traded places with Grace Parker, leaving me on a one-way flight down the Fire Chief's staircase. Something I'll probably never live down.

And that's when the edge of my foot connects with one of the steps.

Crack.

CHAPTER
TEN

GRACIE

My stomach drops as I lose my footing. I sway backward, cursing myself for losing the tight rein of control on my body that's required whenever Jensen's around.

What are the chances I back dive down a flight of stairs and come out unscathed?

None, Gracelyn!

My mouth opens on a gasp as the top box in my stack crashes to the stairs. Household items scatter everywhere as the cardboard bursts open.

That's your future!

Jensen's fingers curl around my arm and tug—hard.

I didn't even see him move.

The last box falls from my grasp, and I brace to meet the wooden surface in front of me. My knees hit as I fall forward, my palms slapping against the porch.

Several thuds sound from behind me.

I crane my neck, not moving until I can do so without falling again. Jensen's sprawled on the ground at the foot of the stairs.

"Fuck." He grimaces.

"Oh my god," I mutter, floundering to free myself from the boxes and their contents that exploded all over the stairs.

A pained grunt and a few more expletives come from the man I nearly killed.

"Are you okay?" I ask, picking my way through the real-life representation of the wreckage I cause. "Don't move! You could have neck or head injuries."

Oh god. I broke the most reputable, brawniest—something I would never admit to his face—firefighter in town.

Jensen Vaughn…

Over two hundred pounds of pure muscle and dominating authority.

Member of our town's founding family.

Youngest Assistant Fire Chief our county has ever seen.

This year's top-contender for the Mayor's Award.

Taken down by Graceless Parker.

Swatting aside the shitty nickname that followed me through high school, I finally make it to his side. I drop to my knees and assess him. His warm brown hair is mussed, he's holding his right arm in place, and his ankle is definitely swelling. His shirt is askew, showcasing several inches of tan skin, impressively tight abs, and a hint of redness. I lift the fabric of his long sleeve tee to assess the damage and discover bruising over his ribs.

But when I reach up to palpate his skull, he shifts away with a growl.

Crap. We need to get him to the hospital. He'll need a full exam, x-rays, concussion protocol…

I might have been a little overconfident about my ability to carry that damn chaise, but I know I won't be able to maneuver this hulk of a man anywhere by myself.

"Declan!" I shout as I search for my phone.

Spotting it on one of the steps, I stretch, reaching for it. I turn it over and the screen lights up—the cracked, useless screen.

Can't catch a fucking break.

Dani races out of the house, clothes askew, face flushed.

"Dani! Thank god." I toss my phone on the ground. "My phone's smashed, and I think Jensen broke his ankle. I'm going to stabilize it." A sharp grunt comes from the man beside me. "Can you call an ambulance?"

"Don't call an ambulance. I'm fine," Jensen says, his voice barely above a whisper, but the deep rumble cuts through the stunned silence. "Chief can take me in."

Declan runs out a moment later, stopping at the top of the stairs. "Take you where? And why the hell are you on the—Jesus fuck. What the hell happened to your ankle?"

We answer at the same time.

"I was on the stairs, bringing in the last—"

"She thought she could carry the damn chair on her—"

My head snaps over to him. "If you hadn't—"

"This isn't on me." His brown eyes fill with anger as he cuts me off. "So point that finger somewhere else."

I retract the finger I inadvertently pointed his way and sigh. "You're right," I mumble.

"What was that?" he asks, surprise widening his eyes. Before I can answer, his gaze darts over my shoulder and he tries to sit up while groaning.

Behind me, Declan jogs down the stairs with his medical kit. I help him stabilize Jensen's ankle and shoulder before all three of us carefully haul him into the Chief's command vehicle.

I slide into the backseat with Dani while Declan peppers the man I broke with questions, his voice a gentle murmur I can barely hear.

Dani leans over and whispers, "Gracie Parker, did you push him down those stairs? I've got your back, but I need to know what we're dealing with here."

Nearly choking, I answer with a raspy, "No. God no." I bring my hands up to cover my face, letting the reality of the situation settle in. "He's going to be off work for weeks, Dani. Maybe even months. He's going to hate me even more now." Seeing the questioning concern in my friend's eyes, I try to lighten the moment with a dramatic eye roll, but that only worsens the humiliating telltale stinging in my eyes. "If that's even possible."

"You care if he hates you? I thought *you* hated *him*?"

"No one likes being hated, Dani. And I just took out a town hero."

"So, you *did* push him?"

I narrow my gaze on her, grumbling in exasperation.

"I'm kidding. Sorry. I'll behave." She drops the playful facade, rubs my arm, and takes a calming breath. "He'll be fine and back to work soon."

After arriving at the hospital, we wait in tense silence until they take Jensen back to get examined and booked for x-rays.

He dislocated his shoulder. That's probably four to six weeks of physical therapy. Then his ankle depends on if it's broken and if it requires surgery. But it could be months.

The damn man just had to save me.

He'll probably be touted as the victim of another puzzling incident that reeks of Gracie Parker's usual mayhem.

And they wouldn't be wrong.

I should have been more careful around him. He always makes me so nervous, and I should have known to be more intentional with my movements, to slow down. He's already been privy to many of the embarrassing moments I've gotten myself into.

But this?

There are no positives, no ways to look at the good like I usually do—other than "Hey, he didn't die!" and that's not where I want to be drawing the line.

I can't flip my hair, say something haughty and walk away as if I don't have a care in the world. Not this time.

THE SWEET RELIEF I'd found in avoidance and distraction at work the last few days was fleeting. Especially as I make my way to Jensen's property on the outskirts of town.

His condition keeps circling as I mindlessly pedal—fractured ankle requiring surgery, dislocated shoulder, multiple contusions.

My nemesis is a wreck. And the guilt is gnawing at me. Followed by irrational anger. Then regret.

And with Jensen not giving any details about what happened, whispers abound. Multiple theories are running amok, even after I gave my statement to Brody, who questioned us after receiving several calls about a potential assault.

My favorite rumor so far is I finally snapped and pushed Jensen Vaughn's ruthless ass down a flight of stairs. That I intentionally maimed a town hero.

Is he a bossy, rude, loathsome dickhole? Yes. Most of the time. Except for a few baffling moments.

We're *low-key* enemies, not *homicidal* ones.

And it's been making me question my standing in this town. Do they believe I'm that unhinged, or do they simply think this has been a long time coming?

Hell, maybe they're just creating drama for the sake of drama. The last town meeting *was* disappointingly tame. I mean, Mr. Drever only interrupted to discuss his escape-artist Pomeranians once, and no one called anyone else an "old hag."

Regardless, they should know by now that I don't do this shit on purpose! And I give back more than I mess up. I'm at the elementary school once a week to help the students with developmental and motor skill struggles. Dani and I serve on a few town committee boards. And I buy local with glee, spending more of my paycheck than is reasonable on lattes, books, local wines, and eating out.

I pump my legs harder, putting this latest wave of outrage to good use. It's taken an exhausting amount of concentration to ride on these roads compared to the ones in town. I've never been a strong biker, but in the last few years, it's become easier.

I slow my pace, swipe the sweat from my temple, and grip the handlebar again. Wiping out isn't an option. I refuse to drop in unexpectedly on Jensen while sweaty, emotionally unstable, *and* bleeding. He always yells when I'm bleeding.

My bike slips on the gravel again, the seat punching up at my vagina like a dick who just discovered a legit excuse for "accidentally" fucking someone else. "It slipped" is about to take on a very unpleasant new meaning.

Guilt. Apprehension. Sweat. And now a sore coochie. Not a great start to this impromptu visit.

When I finally turn off the gravel road, I sigh in relief at the dirt road in front of me. This should lead to Jensen's acreage, which probably has a no-trespassing sign and an electric fence.

But as I roll up to his driveway, I stop pedaling.

Just like his personality, the road to get here is rough, with irksome gravel, potholes, sabotaging tree roots, and uneven dirt. But his house...is beautiful.

While I walk my bike to the garage on the far side of his house, my eyes admire every detail of the cute ranch-style home. A beautifully stained wood and wrought-iron railing encases the wrap-around porch. On one end of the wide, covered porch there's a cushioned swing swaying in the breeze, and on the opposite end, a pair of Adirondack chairs, perfect for watching the setting sun. The four structural posts along the front have string lights draped between, giving it a modern rustic appeal.

But my favorite part might be the front door. It looks hand-crafted and is painted a cerulean blue. Did he choose that color? Was it already like that when he bought the place?

Tearing my gaze away from the porch, I pull up my big girl panties—literally; the rough ride shifted some things—and climb the front steps. I can't help but frown at the thought of how he'll manage these stairs, or if he's even leaving the house.

Dani told me Jensen arrived home early yesterday morning. Declan claims he's being obstinate about needing help, even from his family.

It doesn't surprise me. I've known plenty of guys who don't like to accept help or who shut down when they're wounded. Doesn't deter me in the least. There are ways to work around that, to appeal to their rational sides.

Straightening my shoulders, I prepare myself for the likelihood of that situation.

Knock. Knock, knock, knock. Knock…Knock.

I grin, knowing he's going to hate that knock.

Shit.

I'm supposed to be checking in, being nice. Easing my conscience and cleaning up my mess.

The gorgeous door swings open to reveal a bleary-eyed, shirtless Jensen. His eye color is softer today, a mocha brown instead of his usual bright chestnut. They give me a tired once-over, before delayed surprise has them widening.

"No."

The door starts closing, but I stick my hand out. "Wait! I'm not knocking on your door to see if you've found Jesus or want to buy some Girl Scout cookies."

His chin drops to his chest with a groan. "Why are you here, Grace?"

"How are you feeling? Got everything you need? Book your physical therapy consultation yet?"

That earns me another annoyed groan. But the door hasn't closed yet, so I still have a chance.

"Can I come in?" I ask, gently.

With his uninjured hand, he reaches up to grip the top of the doorframe for support, his bulky bicep invading my senses. I drop my gaze only to catch another glimpse of that pronounced 'v' of muscles I'm sure makes most women drool. "No."

His voice draws my attention back to his face.

His eyes lock on mine, and there's so much swirling in their depths. Irritation, pain, but also devastation. An uneasy pinch in my chest causes my breath to falter. The urge to slip through the door and take care of him is overwhelming. And absurd.

He keeps his gaze locked on mine for several beats longer than is comfortable, longer than he's ever looked at me.

Even while injured, he could easily overpower me and close the door in my face, but he doesn't. Maybe he wants my help. Maybe he needs someone who will ignore his bullshit and get him out of his own broody head.

I keep my eyes from wandering and instead take in his injuries. His casted leg is bent back, hovering off the floor by a few inches, and his arm is tucked inside a navy-blue sling.

"You shouldn't be up walking around."

He glares at me, his mouth a grim line.

Alright then.

I rise up on my toes, neck craning to see past his large frame, and peek into his house. It's an open floor plan with the front entry leading into the living room, an expansive dining area off to one side. A large island with several stools separates it from the kitchen. Prescription bottles and a myriad of bags, papers, and random items litter the table, but the kitchen is tidy, counters devoid of clutter.

The living space looks as if he's been set up there for a while. Blankets cover a portion of the couch and a plump pillow rests against the arm. More pillows are piled high on the coffee table that sits in front of a gorgeous wood-burning fireplace. Tilting a little farther, my gaze lands on a set of stairs leading up from the living room.

He shifts and blocks my snooping with a bare, bruised shoulder. The sling isn't positioned properly, and I'm wondering if he had someone show him how to put it on. With all the Velcro and angles, it's hard to do on your own.

"I'll come in and help you get set up. Where's your bedroom? I hope it's on the main floor—"

"No."

I wave him off. "It'll only take me a few minutes." Well, that part anyway, but I don't tell him that or he'll never let me in. We still need to talk about arranging physical therapy, and then there's the occupational therapist who will need to—

"Whatever this is—misplaced guilt, a new torture—stop. I won't be inviting you in, and you definitely won't be seeing my bedroom. Ever."

Remember, you prepared for his dickishness.

"You're angry, I get that. But I literally do this for a living." I step closer, giving him a reassuring smile. "Let me help you."

"Is it so hard to imagine why I wouldn't want to put any part of my recovery in *your* hands?" His voice is harsh, gravelly.

"The chances of you 'helping' instead of making things worse are low. Real low. And that's not a risk I'm willing to take."

The strangle-grip I thought I had on my emotions before walking up to his enchanting door slips. "I see the fall made you *more* of a prick."

The regret is instant. I close my eyes briefly, chastising myself for responding to his lashing out.

I open my eyes to the pretty blue door slamming in my face.

Yep. I deserved that.

"Your sling is crooked," I shout at him through the thick wood. "That arm needs to be at a ninety-degree angle, Vaughn. Don't make me call your mom." I don't have his mom's number, but he doesn't know that.

Silence greets me.

Little does he know that his reaction only reinforces my resolve to help him.

ELEVEN

JENSEN

Pounding at my door rouses me from a drug-induced sleep.

I've only been home for a couple of days and all I want is to sleep off the grogginess from the pain pills. But no, I have to hobble my way over to let in another well-meaning but intrusive family member. Or I'm hoping it's them and not the persistent blonde tormentor who was here yesterday.

After snagging one crutch from beside my bed, I wince as I maneuver it to the left side of my body since my arm is still in a sling.

Shockwaves of pain ripple through every sore part of my body with each hop down the steps that lead up to my bedroom. Teeth clenched, I finally make my way to the door during the third round of obnoxiously loud knocking. The force of those knocks tells me who is standing on the other side of the solid wood door.

Using my uninjured side, I grab the handle and yank, stopping it with my open palm. Brody stares at me, fist suspended mid-knock.

"I'm fine, alright?" I grumble. "But it's annoying as shit to come to the door, given my disabled state." Something like pity flashes across his face. "So how about everyone leaves me alone until I no longer look like I got the shit kicked out of me?"

One of his eyes narrows in consideration. That hesitation tells me he's going to either leave me to stew in my shitty situation or he's about to lay into me.

"No," he says, pushing into my house uninvited.

His shoulder barely brushes my arm as he passes, but fuck, that still hurts like hell.

"You've got two options," he tells me. "One, continue being a whiny little bitch, holed up out here with no one but the squirrels to keep you company. Two, admit you need some help."

"If one of you nosy assholes will drop off snacks occasionally, then option one sounds great." I nod at the thermal bag he's holding that I know is full of food from Mom.

"Nope," he says, holding the food up like a hostage. "Whatever Mom put in here is contingent upon your acceptance of the second option."

The muscle in my jaw tics. "I'm on medical leave for weeks. Then light duty for *months*." He's quiet, listening as I bark at him, spewing my pissy mood all over the damn place. "I've had to delay the start-up for the volunteer firefighter training academy. And the Mayor's Award..."

Brody sighs. "You'll be off for a while. But they will not rescind your nomination because you have to push back the opening."

"The Town Council nominated me because of that program." When I read their email yesterday, I could hear the worry in their words as they asked how I was doing and if my injuries would put plans for the training program on hold. I realized this injury might cost me the nomination. Because I'm the only certified trainer, which means the program can't run without me. Emerson is working toward getting certified as well, but won't finish the process until the summer.

And I didn't realize until Grace showed up yesterday how

aggravated delaying the program, and possibly losing my award nomination, has made me. There was something about the bet I had with Dad coming to fruition that made me feel connected to him again.

Brody runs a hand through his already mussed hair. More than a handful of years in the military ingrained a few habits in him that stuck, and the outer appearance of control was one of them.

I'm about to ask what's eating at him when he says, "Does this have to do with Dad?" I lift a shoulder. "What do you think he'd do if he saw you sulking like this?" My brother doesn't wait for me to answer, and I knew he wouldn't. "He'd kick your ass straight out that door to whatever therapy you needed so you could get back to work."

"He'd let me have a couple of fucking days to get level, Brody."

"Which is why I gave you a pass at the hospital when you were snapping at everyone. Time's up now."

"Oh, fuck off. After this disaster of a year, I poured everything into work, the training program, the community. And now look at me! Is it too much to ask that *one fucking thing* go right?"

"Oof. Knew we shouldn't have sent Brody in first," a sweet, teasing voice calls from the doorway. "You're both broody assholes when you're hurt."

Brody turns toward our baby sister. "I'm not hurt, broody, or an asshole."

Liv scrunches up her face. "Um, even Ava calls you Police Chief Broody."

"She's five years old," he mumbles. "And I'd bet Harper gives the kid money every time she shouts that in public."

"Doesn't make her wrong." She shifts her focus to me. "And you. Like a wounded bear retreating to his cave to lick his wounds in solitude. We've gone through this once already with you, and I hated it."

Her tone is light, but a flicker of sadness sweeps across her face. I know I retreat into myself and shut everything else out when hurt, but that's my choice. It's how I deal with shit.

"Not sure he ever came out after last time," Jaxon says, strolling up behind Liv. "For fuck's sake, think about the location of your house. Close enough to town to come in for work and shit, yet hidden in the woods on the outskirts of town to better give off those loner recluse vibes." He holds his hands out at my cozy, almost completely renovated, *normal* home. This house, the land, the peace…it gave me what I needed when I needed it. Still does.

It's not the house Erika wanted, of course. It might actually have been the opposite. We went looking for houses after we got engaged, and she wanted sleek, modern designs with no character or warmth. She wanted shiny and flashy. Guess that should have been a clue.

The good thing about being left on your wedding day is getting to do whatever the fuck you want afterward, like letting her deal with the fallout. I bought this house a week later and immediately started on renovations. Projects give me purpose, and that was what I needed. Because I wasn't going to do anything other than what I wanted or be anything other than who I am. Not anymore.

I turn on my crutch, moving toward my room. "Eat a dick, Jax."

"Don't be such a stubborn ass." My twin brother's voice rises at my back. "Let her help you so you can get back to work sooner."

I ignore him and continue to my room.

No one asked who "her" was, which means they all know Grace visited and why. Grace found my house without issue yesterday, which means she got that information from someone in this room.

I knew texting Jaxon after she left was a mistake. But she

arrived on a cute new sky-blue cruiser bike, which only further aggravated me. That bike is no match for these roads. So I asked my brother to come pick her up before she got too far. Because if she found trouble, like she usually does, I wouldn't be able to save her.

Liv catches up to me before I've made it up even one stair.

"JJ," she whispers. Fuck. When we were younger, she called me that for years but now only pulls it out when she's trying to soften me up.

"Livvie," I respond on a sigh, waiting for whatever she's about to hit me with.

Her hand reaches out to rest on my good arm. "She didn't do it on purpose."

My gaze drops to the stairs as some of the anger dissipates.

I *know* it was an accident. But there's a part of me that still wants to press her up against a wall and blast her for being so damn careless. I'd watch the fire build in her honey eyes, and the minute she opened her mouth to argue, I'd shut her up in the way I've often been tempted to. And maybe she'd actually listen and stop doing the stupid shit that one day is bound to get her seriously hurt.

Grace can barely walk from one end of the room to the other without incident, yet she hikes, plays hockey, paddle boards, canoes, and rides that damn bike everywhere. Last year, she even joined the roller derby team. That one was shut down and banned after a huge tournament brawl that landed Grace in the back of Jaxon's EMS truck with bruised ribs and a mild concussion. She grinned at him and rasped out, "Worth it."

With every month that has passed since she moved here last summer, I've come a little too close to the sweet-faced disaster of a woman being the death of me.

"I know you, Jensen. And while Brody is right about you being extra dickish, I understand why. But we will not let you disappear on us again. This is a minor bump in the road."

"I'm not going to disappear, Liv." She gets a half-smile from me. "I've got way too much shit to do."

It's been nearly a year and I haven't handled it well. But I thought I was getting back to the guy I was before Erika. Just a little rougher around the edges and unwilling to put up with bullshit.

Fine, I was still acting like an asshole, but I was never a ray of sunshine. So, people can accept that I'm not a sweet-talker or they can fuck off.

"I've seen the way you look at Gracie, the way you *almost* smile when she's storming away from your ornery ass. And since you don't hate her like you want her to believe, take her up on her offer." I frown at what she's implying. "That way you can get back to the station a hell of a lot sooner. But if you want to work with a different therapist, fine. We can help you find someone else."

Lowering my voice, I tell my sister, "I'll look into it, okay?"

She nods, hope brightening the hazel eyes that change with her mood.

"Tomorrow," she demands, with a wide, confident smile. "Gracie told Jaxon that you should be starting therapy for your shoulder next week, but your ankle will need more time to heal first."

It's a good thing I love my family because they are overstepping shits sometimes.

You'd do the same if the situation were reversed.

"Tomorrow," I agree. "I'll make some calls. Now get those assholes out of my house." I glance back at my brothers. Brody's hands are on his hips, looking irritated as usual. Jaxon is grinning, the bribery bag clutched in his hand as he swings it at me. "Leave the food or lose the hand."

His other hand rises in surrender, and he slowly side steps to the coffee table. As he drops it, he looks at Liv. She nods at him in silent communication of a task accomplished, and then he walks to the front door.

"Love you, bro. Don't slam the door in Gracie's face again or I'll be back." I tip my head to the side, flattening my mouth in indifference. "And I'll also intercept as many of your food deliveries as possible." He jerks a thumb toward my living room. "Including mom's sympathy meals. I took the carrot cake out of there this time as a warning."

Fucker.

I throw my crutch at him.

He laughs and runs out the door.

Liv gives my uninjured side a quick hug before she follows him, yelling, "We're splitting that piece of cake, Jaxon, or I'm telling Mom!"

I shift my focus to my older brother. He gives me a slight shake of his head, as if to say he had no part in jacking my dessert or anything else to do with those two crazies.

"I'll come by this weekend to mow. I'll let myself in. Leave the keys for the ride-on mower on the hook."

I might hate that I'll be a hindrance to everyone I know for a while, but the reality is, I won't be able to do shit for weeks. Even showering is a pain in the ass.

I dip my head. "Thanks, man. I appreciate it."

His brows raise. "Even if I mow in circles?"

My lip curls in disgust. "Don't you fucking dare."

He grins at me and then motions to the stairs. "Want help to move your shit so you can sleep down here? At least until you get your walking boot?"

I shake my head. I can at least climb a few damn stairs a couple of times a day.

"Alright, I'll let Mom know you settled on option two with little coercion." He pulls his phone from the holder on his work belt, clicking away. "She's coming over tomorrow to make sure you're all stocked up on whatever you might need. Heard she recruited some people to lend a hand."

The fuck?

"Nope."

With a quick jerk of his chin, he says, "Already done. I've got to get back to the station." He moves toward the door. "Eat your meatloaf and get some rest. Call if you need anything."

With that, he's out the door, locking it with the key he had but decided not to use earlier.

I hobble over to the couch and gingerly lower myself onto it. Then I set aside all other thoughts and focus on the bag of deliciousness in front of me.

Once the meatloaf and mashed potatoes are sitting heavy and happy in my belly, I lie down. Thinking about climbing those stairs again is causing my muscles to lock up in protest, so with my casted foot propped on the back of the couch, I close my eyes. The stairs can wait until after a quick nap.

Then I'll look into my physical therapy options.

Grace Parker can't be my only option in Vaughn.

TWELVE

GRACIE

S weet, seductive bliss meets my lips.

I put the decadent fudge brownie down and check my phone while Dottie fills a bakery box for me. Nervous tension fills me when I see a reply from Jensen's mom.

LILAH:

Thank you so much for all the information about ankle and shoulder injuries, Gracie. I've forwarded it to Jensen, along with a reminder to book his therapy.

Phew. I wasn't sure if she would be upset with me after what happened to Jensen. And there's no way she hasn't heard the speculative stories that are going around town.

No problem. Anything I can do to help. Seriously. I feel awful.

It was an accident. We all know that, honey.

Do we? I feel like a select few do not. And her son is one of them.

> Jensen is just stubborn, but he'll come around.
> His father was the same way. When they're sick
> or hurt, they turn into big, grumpy babies.

Pretty sure that's her son's usual state.

Dottie slides the loaded box across the counter toward me. I tuck my phone away and peek inside.

"You're sure these are his favorite?" I ask the spunky sixty-something-year-old woman now refilling the scones in the display case.

She tsks, throwing me some side-eye.

"Don't pretend you wouldn't love the drama that would ensue if I brought him food he hates when trying to make amends. He might not want my help professionally, but I'm going to keep apologizing until he accepts."

And means it, because the grunted, "It's fine," he responded with at the hospital somehow didn't feel genuine. The door slamming in my face did though.

Dottie wipes her hands on her apron and moves over to the sink. "I won't deny that I get more than a little thrill out of watching you two have a go at each other. But it's for reasons you don't want to hear."

This should be good.

I raise my eyebrows in question.

She mouths, *It's hot!* and winks before picking up a bus bin and moving out from behind the counter.

"It's not hot," I whisper, storming after her as she goes around to each table, collecting stray plates and cups.

"Have you seen the man?" She looks over at me, widening her eyes dramatically. "The times he's towered over you with that muscle in his jaw clenching as if he's seconds away from ripping your clothes off..." A pleased purr I hope to never hear again rumbles from the back of her throat.

"I think he'd rather rip my head from my body." I attempt to shut down her impish grin with facts. "You need to cut back on those Turkish soap operas, Dottie. You're seeing secret love and angsty pining in places they don't belong."

She gasps. "You leave my Turkish dramas out of this, young lady."

Uh oh. Pulling out the "young lady" means she's done with the ribbing for a bit and is settling in for a good, hard lecture.

"You and Jensen may have had a somewhat rough start, but we both know he's a good man. And handsome. When I was your age, I'd have jumped on that in a heartbeat. And I mean that literally." She gives me a lewd eyebrow waggle.

I'll admit that the month I moved here, I was in shambles. So, she's right about our rough start. When I'm stressed or nervous, my symptoms heighten. I'm clumsier, frazzled, distracted. Almost like my body and brain refuse to be on the same wavelength for even a moment. And often they aren't, but I'd made so much progress over the years with managing my condition that my struggles while settling in here were especially irksome. And humiliating.

"Well, unlike you, I'm not attracted to grumbly jerks."

Pfft. That's a complete lie.

"That's not what I heard," she says, unfazed by the attention we're drawing. The two Council members at the table in the back corner are leaning so far forward, there's a good chance they'll fall right out of their chairs, trying to eavesdrop. I'll leave that up to karma.

"Word was you tried to climb him like a tree your first day in Vaughn, but he was still sore about his ex leaving him, so he turned you down."

I shush her, pointedly darting my eyes to the women at the back table. Thankfully, that bullshit version of events wasn't one I ever saw in *The Vine*. But the last thing I need is more rumors flying around about Jensen and me. There's been more theories bouncing around about how Jensen *really* broke his ankle.

According to some of the more impressively creative lunatics in this town, I must be a trained assassin or a WWE wrestler.

Bringing up the night Jensen and I met would only add fuel to the already out-of-control fire. Because technically, I *did* end up in his lap.

"That is *so* not what happened," I assure Dottie. "It was an accident. And we barely spoke."

I tripped, and either clutched onto him to break my fall or he caught me from where he was sitting. I'm still not sure about that part, since falling comes a little too naturally. All I remember is looking up and *him* being there.

Hell, for all of about two seconds, I was on the same page as Dottie. Tingles of awareness flooded my body as my mind played out all the potential romantic scenarios of this chance meeting.

Out of sorts, I remember awkwardly laughing and then attempting to introduce myself. But Mr. Biceps with the entrancing molasses-colored eyes framed by lashes most women would drop a good chunk of their paychecks to obtain just glowered. He spouted off several cutting words and attempted to remove me from his lap. I slid straight off him and onto the floor. For a moment, I thought he felt bad about it—he even offered me a hand up—but then he opened his asshole mouth and made it worse. It's one of his most sharply honed skills.

His words aren't worth repeating, and neither is the embarrassment they caused. For weeks, I seethed every time I saw him.

Dottie raises her chin and moves to another table. "I like my version better. You straddling him, demanding he tell you everything about himself because you can't wait to get to know the last man you'll ever *fall* for again. But he was too heartbroken to see that the universe was doing him a solid."

If that were a show, I'd watch the hell out of it. Even with subtitles. Wait, was he really heartbroken or is that just Dottie's dramatic retelling? I'd heard he had a bad breakup that spring but got no details because it was before I lived here. But I'm having a hard time imagining a "heartbroken" Jensen. Maybe that version looks like the caustic, rude, overbearing asshole you met your first night here.

Roughly clearing my throat, I emphasize each word for her. "I. Tripped."

"And fell on his dick? Now *that* is a better story."

"A completely fictional one, you hussy!" I hiss at her, trying not to laugh. She's utterly shameless.

She clicks her tongue. "Unfortunately. You two had all that tension built up and all it led to was you pushing our town's hottest firefighter down a flight of stairs."

My mouth drops open in indignation as I stalk after her.

She sets the bin on the front counter and releases a noisy sigh. "You're right. My Turkish soaps have set me up for disappointment, at least with you two. I'm still holding out hope for the other Vaughn boys."

The kitchen door swings open and Dani glides out with two baking sheets in her hands.

"Hold up. *Declan* is Vaughn's hottest firefighter," she corrects, setting the sheets on the counter.

"You're biased since he's giving it to you on the regular," Dottie says, not bothering to lower her voice.

My mouth hooks up into a grin as Dani's face turns an adorable shade of pink.

"I'll admit your man's a close second. But there's something about a burly, wounded man that gets me going."

I smother my smile, refusing to give her the satisfaction of my amusement when she's being a cheeky little meddler.

"Well, there's a little more motivation for Jensen to get back on his feet as soon as possible," barks a grumbly voice.

Mr. Gillespie, the crusty but sweet town busybody, stands on the other side of the counter, hands perched on top of his walking cane as he stares me down.

"Raymond Gillespie!" Dottie says. "You take that attitude

somewhere else, or you'll find us all out of snickerdoodles the next time we host your bridge tournament."

"A minute ago, you were harping about her pushing him down the stairs," he argues.

"I was *teasing*." She rolls her eyes before raising her voice. "Anybody who believes Gracie tried to take out her least beloved Vaughn, who is my favorite, but don't tell Jaxon, he'd be crushed,"—she stops, standing up straighter while she scans the store—"is an idiot."

I grin, darting a glance at Mr. G for his reaction. God, I love this town, ridiculous gossip and all.

The bristly man opens his mouth to speak, but Dottie cuts him off again. "I mean, look at her! She's barely five feet tall. She might be strong, but there's no way she'd be able to budge any of the Vaughn brothers if they didn't choose to move."

Mr. G and several others, still rudely eavesdropping, shift their attention back to me in appraisal. I clutch my elbows, holding myself a little smaller to help sell it.

"*I'm* allowed to give her crap because she knows I don't mean it." Dottie turns to me, but keeps a hostile finger pointed at Mr. G. "Except the dirty stuff. And the part where I was disappointed that your life hasn't turned into a racy foreign drama."

Mr. G huffs. "Dottie, she might not have pushed him, but she was involved. And I think we all know it wasn't malicious, despite some of the more inflammatory stories circulating." He swivels, looking down his nose at the two Council members who we all suspect write some of the "anonymous" articles for *The Vine*. "But it still leaves us one first responder short when we're already overextended. Jensen planned to mitigate that issue with his Volunteer Training Program, but that is now on hold until he can return to active duty."

"He'll be back on his feet soon, won't he, Gracie?" Dani asks, her reassuring tone full of confidence.

I nod, despite not knowing enough about his current condition to make any guarantees.

"I hope so," he replies bleakly. "For a man like Jensen Vaughn, having to stay behind when those alarms sound in the station will be torturous."

That's been eating away at me. From what I've gathered, Jensen's career is *everything* to him.

After dropping that guilt-inducing nugget, Mr. G shuffles over to the far side of the bakery case to point out his usual assortment of muffins for Dottie to pack up.

Gripping my box of Jensen-approved baked goods, I summon a confident smile and tell the ladies I'm heading out, mouthing *wish me luck.*

I duck out of the bakery, heading to my bike, only to realize I'll have to cram the pastries in my backpack since they won't fit in my bike's side pouch.

I've nearly got the zipper to close without busting back open when I hear, "Ms. Parker?"

I turn as Mr. G comes to a stop a few feet from me.

"Yes, Mr. Gillespie?"

"You're a good girl."

I blink twice as I blush and mutter a confused, "Thank you."

"Normally, I find the trouble you get yourself into quite amusing. But I'll confess something I'll expect you never to repeat." He points an arthritic finger at me. "I've got a soft spot for our wounded firefighter."

I bite down on the sappy smile that's pulling at my cheeks. "I won't say a word." No one would believe me anyway.

"That young man once saved my late wife's life. Before he was even a firefighter. He's a stand-up man, just like his father was. And he's saved your ass more than a few times too."

Giving him a sheepish smile, I admit, "He has."

"Now it's your turn," he says, his gaze pressing on me. "People accustomed to always helping and saving others often have trouble accepting help themselves." Yep. Definitely noticed. The intensely serious senior in front of me taps the Baked Delights box that's peeking out of my bag. "That'll work in your favour when you offer to help him again." With a tight smile and a wave of his hand, he shuffles off.

Looks like my *please accept this olive branch* treats have turned into a *let me be your physical therapist* bribe. I'm not the type to give up, and the clock is ticking on Jensen's recovery time, so I'm going to need more than pastries and an apologetic smile.

I need a plan. And I only have the fifteen-minute bike ride to his house to figure something out.

The first step is getting past his front door. So, as I hop on my ride and pedal away, several ideas come and go. But one sticks out. It's stupid. Risky. And not entirely legal.

Which means it's probably my best bet.

CHAPTER
THIRTEEN

JENSEN

"**G**et the hell away from my ass!" I growl at my shower curtain, slapping it out of the way in frustration.

Something as simple as basic hygiene has become an entire production of plastic wrap, curtain placement, balancing, and risk assessment. Sadly, it might be the most exciting part of my whole damn day.

My casted leg is propped up on the outer edge of the tub, poorly covered with food wrap, while the clingy curtain I've placed around it slowly creeps up to attach itself to my ass.

As soon as this ankle heals, I'm ripping this shower out and installing a walk-in with doors. I don't even fit in the damn tub, so there's no point having it.

Roughly pushing the curtain away for the sixth time in as many minutes causes several bottles on the lip of the tub to fall on my foot.

"Motherfucker!"

If I put my other foot out of commission too, I'll be shit out of luck. Worse, I'll be forced to take my mom or brothers up on their offer to live with them as I recover. And I love my family, but no.

I hear a bang, and the cracked bathroom door flies open.

Sighing, I turn off the water, ready to lay into whichever brother was sent to check on me. "Knock next time, asshole!" With more force than necessary, I yank the curtain open, ripping it off several hooks. "I'm calling about therapy today, okay? So you can lay—"

I stop short when I notice the long, white-gold hair on the much shorter than expected visitor standing in the doorway.

Scanning the rest of her in shocked silence, I scrutinize the wrinkle of concern on her forehead, the teal donut-covered hospital scrubs, and the widening of those bright caramel eyes.

She's staring at my ass. My bare ass.

Well, the one ass cheek that is unavoidably on display.

Her unwavering gaze roams over every exposed inch of me. Feeling left out, my dick perks up. For the first time, I'm grateful for my injury. The awkward position of my propped-up leg may be exposing half my ass, but at least it's blocking my junk from her curious gaze.

Grabbing the mangled curtain, I throw it closed again.

"Grace!" I bellow, not even sure where to fucking start.

A few seconds of silence pass before she speaks.

"You're super naked."

Tightening my grip on the curtain, I attempt to gather some semblance of control. "For fuck's sake." My undisguised fury echoes through the small space. "I'm *showering*. That's usually done without clothes. Or spectators."

"Right..."

A couple more hooks tear loose from the thin sheet of plastic separating us, making me lose my balance for a moment. I slap a hand against the shower wall to keep myself upright. "You broke into my house." Her uninvited presence in my home makes that a statement, not a question.

"I heard you shouting and thought you needed help."

How long has she been in my house? How did she even get in?

"You heard me from clear across town?" I ask, my tone clipped. "Those are some good ears you have, Grandma."

More silence.

"Do you need a hand?" she offers.

Seriously?

"Grace. What are you doing in my house? And how the hell did you get in here?" I know my brother locked that door when he left last night. So she either broke in or one of my siblings is a traitor.

"Tomorrow, I'll bring you a shower stool and a cast cover," she offers, her tone too sweet. "That way, you won't have to yell obscenities at inanimate objects."

Inanimate? I suspect the souls of repressed Catholic school girls who think "butt stuff doesn't count" haunt this curtain.

"I don't need that shit," I growl. "And you aren't welcome back tomorrow."

"I wasn't welcome today either, but here I am." *Yeah, and I'll be finding out how she got in here.* "So let's skip all the back and forth and jump straight to letting me help you."

Not happening.

"Get out of my bathroom," I demand.

"I've got your towel."

The simmering anger I've barely kept at bay for the last few days roars to the surface. I snap the curtain back, gripping it as I lean forward to glare at her.

She extends the arm with the towel clutched in her little fist.

"Leave the towel." She looks between the towel and me with a furrowed brow. "I don't need your help," I bark at the woman standing—uninvited—in my bathroom.

"You going to make me leave? I'd like to see you try." She tosses the towel on to the counter. "Seriously." Eyeing my cast sticking out of the shower curtain, she jerks a thumb behind her. "I'm fascinated to see how you're making it down those stairs. If only you had someone who could help make your home more manageable, who could show you how to use your crutches properly, and help your body heal and strengthen faster. But sure, scoot down the stairs on your butt like a toddler. Or hop down them and reinjure yourself. Solid plan." She leans one small shoulder against the door frame, throwing out a sassy thumbs up before crossing her arms.

Something between a huff and a growl leaves me.

That's when I see it—the challenge in her eyes, and the twitch in her cheek. Pissing me off is amusing the hell out of her.

"And putting myself in your care would be better? Spending *one* morning with you resulted in surgery and a sling." Her expression immediately softens into one of grim remorse.

She's not actually to blame, and I should probably acknowledge that. I made my choice and taking that fall to prevent Grace from breaking her damn neck was one of them. But I'm sure as shit not interested in the pity I see building in her gaze. I've gotten enough of that from everyone else this year.

"You've been a problem since day one," I tell her.

"No, I haven't. You saw what you wanted to see." Her gaze flickers uneasily to the side.

Still holding the curtain, I raise each finger as I count. "The coffee shop incident." First finger. "Driving your car down a ravine." Second finger. "Getting trapped under a counter at Dani's bakery—"

With clenched fists, she cuts me off. "Those were accidents, and I offered to pay for your dry-cleaning bill after the coffee thing."

I continue, hoping she takes the hint and just leaves.

"Your first day in town, you fell and spilled beer all over the both of us."

"Maybe that was intentional," she says through her teeth.

"Next time you hit on a guy, try buying him a beer instead of making him wear it."

With an eye roll, she blows out a breath. "I wasn't hitting on you. Get over yourself."

"I could have, had you not been on top of me." I bite back a grin as her face reddens.

"My actions were unintentional. Yours weren't. I barely had a chance to apologize and introduce myself before you slid me straight off your lap and onto the floor."

Fuck. I forgot about that part. I may have also—

"You told me you might be interested in what I was 'offering,' but you weren't drunk enough yet." Her eyebrows shoot up as she stares at me, expecting some kind of explanation. "Then you offered to introduce me to your brother."

So here's the thing…

I *do* owe her an explanation. And an apology.

I was in a dark, fucked up place. Most people know the wedding didn't happen, that I lost my cool at the church, that my ex-fiancée left town afterward. But Grace didn't know any of that. She moved here weeks later when gossip had started to die down.

My threatening to leave town if people kept talking about it helped squash most of the chatter. But not all of it. So I have no idea what she knows. Few people know all the details—*why* Erika left me—and I plan to keep it that way.

I point at the towel. "Unless you're waiting for another opportunity to check out my ass, hand over the towel and get out."

With a glare, she picks up the towel from beside the sink. "For someone who looked scandalized when you saw me in here, you talk a big game." Her lips twist, eyebrows scrunching. "Did it live up to the hype? No. But I'm cutting you some slack because you're injured and temporarily letting yourself go is understandable."

Letting myself go?

She presses her lips together, but a laugh bursts free before it's cut off. "I didn't think your face could furrow more than it already was."

A warning rumble leaves my chest.

"I was kidding, hotshot. There was a lot to look at and I only got a few seconds before you yanked the curtain closed. I barely caught a glimpse of your ass." Those soft pink lips stretch wide, lighting up her face in a way I realize I haven't seen enough. And definitely never directed at me.

The harsh words I was about to throw her way stall in my throat.

"Now, get that well-sculpted ass out of there and I'll show you a few ways we can make getting around your house easier. Your mom is worried about those stairs, and also indicated that keeping your kitchen stocked requires a step stool and a shift schedule of some kind."

Towel in hand, she walks over and extends it toward me.

I take it and wrap the plush white cotton low on my hips.

Covered, I throw the curtain wide. She's standing in the same spot, eyes trailing across my chest, down to my abdominal muscles.

Inexplicably satisfied with her reaction, I ask, "So you *are* interested in another show, then?"

That seems to snap her out of it. She tears her gaze away and spins toward the door.

"No. Just surprised you didn't yell at me to get out... again."

"Don't worry, you'll hear it again after I get dressed." A pair of sweats is all I can comfortably manage right now, and even that takes more out of me than it should.

She hesitates. "I can help. If you need it."

I ignore her and she steps up to me as I take a seat on the edge of the tub and swing my good leg over.

Leaning down, she lifts my arm and drapes it around her shoulders, her soft hair tickling my cheek. She supports me, her warm hand splayed across my back. Once she's settled against me, she counts down from three and we move together when she gets to one.

I try not to put too much weight on her petite frame, but she lifts me seamlessly. And I have to admit that was a heck of a lot faster and easier with her help.

Her fingers trail across my spine as she slips out from under me, and I stifle the reaction her proximity always brings.

A crutch appears between us, and she smiles up at me. "Like this, okay?" She positions the pad a couple of inches below my armpit. "Typically, you'd use it on the injured side, but with your shoulder, that's not an option. So you'll have to adjust your center of gravity since all of your weight bearing is on your left side."

She watches a couple of my steps and tells me I'm moving the crutch too far ahead. Her adjustments are gentle, words kind and helpful.

This is why Grace can't be my physical therapist. It would mess with everything. Put her way too fucking close.

"You can wait in the living room," I bite out. "I'll be out in a few minutes."

Surprisingly, Grace listens and leaves with no sass coming out of those pink lips.

When she's halfway down the stairs, I grumble, "Thanks for the help."

She glances over her shoulder and flashes a small but dazzling smile before continuing down the staircase.

I take my time putting on my sweats and t-shirt, prolonging the inevitable, not sure what to do about the pint-sized blonde in my living room. With my career hanging in the balance, the potential repercussions of working with her are setting off some serious alarms.

We can't get along for five minutes, let alone for several long physical therapy sessions. Yet, despite our past, and my shitty attitude, she's been apologetic and determined to help me.

She watches me from the couch, and I keep my face neutral as I descend the stairs slowly, not wanting her to see how much it's kicking my ass. She gets up to help, but I shake my head.

"I got it."

"Sure you do, hotshot. How many teeth have you cracked, clenching your jaw in pain?"

"I'm fine," I insist.

"We should set you up down here. At least until you get your walking boot. I'm surprised they didn't give you one right away."

Landing at the bottom of the steps with a small grunt, I say, "They didn't think I'd take it easy and put the cast on so I wouldn't fuck it up worse."

She nods, with a slight tilt of her lips.

I sit next to her on the couch and she grabs the pillow between us and places it on the coffee table. "Elevate," she reminds me.

After placing my foot on the pillow, I recline into the cushions and shift my gaze toward her. "I don't want your help," I say bluntly, not sure how else to put it while ensuring she leaves.

Her mouth dips down. "Look, I know we have our issues. But it's not like I fantasize about your demise. Not seriously anyway. Stubbed toe? Yes. Getting crapped on by a flock of birds? Absolutely. But not *this*." She waves a finger between my injuries.

"Believe it or not, I don't mean to do any of what happens to and around me. It's just part of..." She pauses, taking a dejected breath. "It just does."

Her despondent tone pulls at me.

"I've heard a few people in town seem to think this may have been intentional." The corner of my mouth lifts a little. Saw that *Vine* post the day after I got out of the hospital, and it was the first time I smiled since realizing I'd be out of commission for months. "There are questions about whether this was an attempted homicide you perpetrated against your nemesis."

"Oh. *That*. That's just a few people drumming up drama.

You're their beloved town hero and have a face women without standards want to ride, but deep down, I'm sure everyone realizes you deserved it."

An unexpected choked cough sputters out of my mouth.

With a few awkward back pats, she continues on like she didn't just casually mention face riding. "We both want the same thing. You want to get back to work, and I want to help you do that. I'll even come to you since you can't get to the hospital on your own." She holds out her hand. "Deal?"

I stare at her hand. The pale, soft skin. The short, polish-free nails. She's a confusing mix of wildly exorbitant and naturally effortless.

Grace drops her hand, sighs, and ducks down to her backpack. She wrestles something out and rises to face me again.

"I came prepared with incentives," she announces with a grin, handing me a bulging, light blue box.

I can smell what's inside even before I see the *Baked Delights* stamp.

"Why?" I ask, shifting my gaze from the box to her.

Regret flashes across her face before her attention drops to her hands. She knows what I'm asking, and it has nothing to do with the sweets.

"I owe you."

"You hate me," I remind her.

Her shrug seems indifferent, but it's impossible to ignore the emotions simmering beneath the surface. I just don't know what they mean.

"Who else is going to save me from all the shit I get into? I kind of need you back on the job, Jerksen."

I snort before mumbling, "That's actually a hell of a lot more believable than you being concerned about my health and well-being."

A smirk pulls at her lips. "Plus, what better way to diffuse the crazy rumors circulating about us than the town discovering this accident brought us together as friends while I nursed you back to health?"

I raise an eyebrow at her. "What?" That's the absolute last thing I need. Because I know what they'll be thinking if Grace and I suddenly become chummy. And I have no desire to draw that kind of attention my way.

My only goal is to focus on recovering so I can go back to work. Plus, the town believing that the hostility between us caused my injuries was kind of benefiting me. Catching *The Vine's* attention can go either way sometimes. But after announcing the delayed start date of the training program, more people have been helping recruit and promote.

My face must give me away because she holds up a hand. "Fine. Maybe that's pushing it," she admits. "But if I'm going to be your physical therapist, we'll need to put aside our differences and be civil. Professional. Maybe even friendly." She tilts her head in question. "Just until you're back on your feet. Think you can do that?"

Can *she*?

"Afterward, we can slip back into our usual routine. I can continue being the menace to society you think I am, and you can return to saving lives and pissing me off."

Why am I even entertaining this idea?

I shake my head and open the box on my lap. "You don't owe me," I mutter.

"I do. You fell because of me. Let me fix it."

She's a distraction. A risk.

But she might be my best shot at recovering faster.

"Fine," I say. "But you bring food every session." I pull an apple fritter from the box and eat half in one bite. If I can't go out to get my favorite foods, she can bring them to me. "I'll get my usual places to create a tab."

"Deal!" The couch cushions bounce when she celebrates with a cute jump, causing the box to teeter off my lap. I lunge for it, catching the corner, but not before half the contents spill onto the hardwood floor. The sudden movement has me groaning in pain.

"Oh, shit. Sorry. Five second rule?" She aims a smile at me but one glance at my face has her slowly rising from her seat. "I'll get something to clean this up. Try not to move."

I protect my shoulder as she hurries off to the kitchen.

She sets the cloths and cleaner on the coffee table but knocks over my cup of water in the process. I bark out a few expletives and jerk my feet out of the way as she lunges across me to snag the cup before it crashes to the floor.

With jerky movements, she flutters around to set everything back where it belongs, mumbling an apology.

My laugh is dark and derisive as I drop my head to the back of the couch. Something deep inside me whispers *this woman is going to wreck you.*

If I come out of this unscathed, it'll be a miracle.

CHAPTER
FOURTEEN

GRACIE

What. An. Ass.

Between his extra churlish disregard and the glorious strain of muscles I witnessed in his bathroom, that's all I could think about after leaving his house the other day.

Though my thoughts *mostly* pertained to the rounded globes of his glutes. He's always a cantankerous ass, more so when he's injured. But it was hard to focus on that with mental images of his olive-toned ass dive-bombing my every conscious thought.

I nearly keeled over when he ripped the shower curtain back.

He's built, I knew that. I see the way he stretches out his VFD shirt. On many occasions, I have accidentally appreciated his physique before noticing his face.

But fresh from the shower, dripping wet, the sprinkling of dark hair over his hard pecs, the rigid planes of his thick muscles?

He had no right looking that good. It's fucking infuriating.

Appreciating the ripped body that hides the rude, bossy asshole underneath only further proves my toxic taste in men.

And somehow, I pushed all my conflicting feelings aside and

got the stubborn bastard to agree to let me help him. And it went pretty well, I think.

Right until the end.

But that was a one-off. It has to be. I refuse to let this become another way for him to give me shit about my inadequacies. Because I am freaking amazing at my job.

There's a lingering concern, though, that I won't be able to keep myself in check around him. We're explosive. When I'm around him, I'm always wound up and that spells disaster—both emotionally and physically. In order to keep it together, I'll have to act as if he's just a regular patient.

My phone buzzes as I'm scooping his bribe into a large food-storage container. He's paid for me to pick up food at several places in town, but I enjoy cooking. And after confirming with Jaxon that I'd be handling his brother's therapy, he sent me a list of Jensen's favorite foods. And his pet peeves, which I will store away for future use.

I put the lid on the container and pick up my phone, wondering if it's Jensen messaging to cancel at the last minute. However, he probably wouldn't text me. I doubt he even has my number. He just wouldn't bother to answer his door or he'd tell me he changed his mind and slam that door in my face again.

MOM:

> Miranda says we should stay at the Bradford Inn
> & Resort when we visit at the end of the month.
> Want me to book us pedicures? They have a
> full spa!

Somehow our town's mayor and my mom have become friends even though they've only met in person the handful of times my parents have come here for a visit. Since then, I've done my best to keep a tight lid on all my issues—romantic, professional, and personal. Otherwise, everyone would know.

> Sounds good.

Going off a hunch, I probe a little.

> Is Miranda joining us?

> Is that okay? Her girlfriend is away for a convention, and she'd love to have a girls' afternoon. And catch up with you too. She mentioned you've been busy and will be even busier over the next few months.

At least Miranda didn't totally rat me out.

> That's fine. She could definitely use a spa day. The town is gearing up for the Spring-a-ling Festival and there's been some drama with the performers. Two local bands are vying for the headliner spot, so they've been popping up all over town with unsanctioned concerts trying to garner support.

The fact that headlining for a small-town event kicks up this much of a ruckus is half the fun of living here. And it's not even the tourist season yet, which might be my favorite. Between our wine festivals, guided mountain tours, and the increasingly popular Valley Ventures setting up various recreational activities for water thrill-seekers, it's chaos central here from May until September.

All that commotion keeps the fire department, Town Council, and lookie-loos plenty busy. And I get to people-watch with an iced latte and whatever delicious new summer treats Dani has me taste test.

> Perfect. We are booked!

> So you've decided to ignore my subtle prying about what's keeping you so busy this spring?

I snort.

> Yep. That was the plan. But know that I still love you.

> Did you convince Dad to do something about his plantar warts other than slapping duct tape on them? Those are a pain in the ass to get rid of.

> You'd rather talk about nasty warts than tell me what you've got going on?

> Wrong move, sweet pea.

Oh, shit. She's going to dig deep now. We've gone from casual interest to unrelenting curiosity.

> Mom. Wait. Don't do anything crazy. I have somewhere I need to be soon. Can we chat about this later?

Or never. Preferably never.

Another message pops up.

DAD:

> You better tell your mother something, Gracie.

I scramble to think of something that will appease her, but not invoke a barrage of questions.

> She's reading something on The Vine and gasping. Good luck, honey.

She promised me she'd stop reading that! It triggers tons of questions and perplexed concern.

MOM:

> You nearly killed that firefighter?

Shit. Shit. Shit.

> Are you busy with community service? Is that
> what it is?
>
> Gracelyn Anne!

The phone rings, and I spend the next fifteen minutes giving Mom the Coles Notes version of the incident and assuring her I have it all under control. She lets me go when I tell her I need to head over to Jensen's house for our first session.

But the confidence I exuded while talking to my mom flees as I pack my bag with the homemade stew and warm loaf of bread.

Today I assess Jensen's injuries and come up with a treatment plan. And that includes helping make his house easier to live in. The man thinks he doesn't need help, so my goal for today is to not look overly smug while I prove him wrong.

"I GET around the house just fine," Jensen insists, moving in front of me and blocking my path to his stairs.

"Oh, yeah? Let's see you walk up that staircase."

"No," he says, avoiding my stare.

"Because you can't," I state. "At least, not well."

"No. Because I don't want to."

I smile at him. "Okay." I feign right, he shifts, then I rush left —to his injured side, which is the only way I'm getting around him.

"What are you doing?" he grumbles.

"I'm going to snoop in your room."

"Like hell you are."

"I'll have unearthed all your secrets by the time you get to me."

He growls at me as I reach the top landing.

I turn around and place both hands on the banister, looking down at him. "Or you can admit that moving to the main floor for a little while is a good idea because you hate having to do these stairs multiple times a day."

We glare at each other for a full minute before he answers.

"The couch is too small."

"You have a spare room," I remind him.

"It doesn't have a bed."

I wave him off. "I can bring your mattress down. Easy."

"Dammit, Grace." His eyes smolder with something I can't decipher. "You can't bring that mattress down by yourself. That kind of bullshit thinking is how we ended up here."

Problem is, he's not wrong.

The challenge to come up with a retort simmers in my veins, but I quash it.

"I already asked Jaxon to come over after our session and move whatever you need," I tell him, making my way back down the stairs. "I have no desire to rifle through your things."

A loud exhale rushes out of him, his tongue swiping along the front of his teeth in a display of agitation that's oddly enthralling.

"You're a bigger pain in the ass than I thought you'd be. And that's saying something."

"Thank you," I respond, demurely. "I always exceed expectations."

He scoffs, his long, thick lashes shielding his eyes as he diverts his gaze.

"Is that it for today?" he asks.

"We've barely started. There's still the initial assessment of your injuries and discussion of your therapy program."

"Didn't they do that at the hospital?" he asks, using his crutch to beeline to the front door.

"That was a post-op assessment. I need to gauge your range of motion, strength, pain, muscle function, and several other factors. You'll need to answer questions about your health history, daily routines, and physical demands for when you return to work." I put my hands on my hips. "It's an entire process, Jensen. Are you going to fight me the whole way?"

He tips his head back, murmuring something before coming back. I hold on to his good arm and help him sit in the chair I've set out.

After he's answered my questions, I test the muscle in his shoulder, watching his face for any sign of intense discomfort. He's exactly the patient who wouldn't tell me if he's in pain. His jaw is tight, eyes fixed on the wall behind me.

"Are you still taking your pain medication?"

His pain should be more manageable now that he's a week into recovery.

"No. I'm fine."

"The bead of sweat at your temple says otherwise."

"I'm sweating because of you. All your—"

"I make you hot?" I feign a gasp. "Flirting with your physical therapist is frowned upon, hotshot."

"Christ," he mutters. "You're exhausting."

"Just wait until we get into our treatment sessions. I'll have you sweating for real, and you'll be cursing me in whole new ways."

At that, he actually perks up. Whether it's because he's looking forward to the exercise or reaming me out, I can't be sure. But I suspect it's the former, because I've seen how hard he goes at the gym. I'm sure he's missing it.

"But if you're in a lot of pain, that's going to stall your progress. So make sure you're taking your pain pills, elevating your leg—toes above your nose—and icing if you notice any inflammation."

"Yes, ma'am," he chirps, disgruntled.

"Oh," I tease. "I like that."

His jaw tightens so hard I wonder if I'll hear his molars crack. I decide teasing him might be more fun than fighting with him.

After a few more tests, updating of his file notes, and showing him a few movements that will help with stiffness, I pack up my things.

"How's the full cast treating you?" I ask.

"Like shit. Doc said it'll be another couple of weeks, minimum, before it comes off."

I nod. "We'll be working on your shoulder first. I'll show you a few more stretches and small exercises you can start doing this week. Once the doctor puts you in a walking boot, we can do more with your leg and ankle."

His hand comes up to rub at the back of his neck.

"Is your neck sore too? Shoulder tightness and spasm can radiate into your neck."

He shakes his head. "No, a little stiffness from staying in certain positions at night, but that's it." He scrubs a hand across his face. "I was actually wondering when I could start working out again. I need to be doing something physical. It's driving me crazy to just sit or hobble around."

I've had a lot of patients who feel this same restless need to get moving again. Usually it's those with physically demanding jobs, athletes, or fitness enthusiasts.

"I'll come up with a few things you can do here that isolate motion in your injuries but can still give you a decent workout."

Jensen leans back in his chair, noticeably more relaxed. "Will I have to wait until our session next week?"

"No, I'll bring you an exercise plan tomorrow."

"You don't have to do that. Just send it to my work email or text it to me. That way, you don't have to make an extra trip out here." He grabs his phone. "I'll send you my email address."

I frown, tilting my head in question. "Um, Jensen, how often are you thinking our physical therapy sessions will occur?"

His head snaps up. "Once per week? Once every other week?"

I grimace and concern flashes in his eyes.

"For these kinds of injuries, it's typically two or three times per week. Especially once we get started on your ankle, since we'll work on both your shoulder and your ankle at the same time."

His hand swipes over his mouth again. "Fuck." Slowly, his eyes lift back up to mine. "You can't be coming out here that often."

Telling myself not to take it personally, I let it roll off me. "Too bad. If you want to do less, we can. But it'll mean you take longer to recover. You said you wanted to get back to work as soon as possible. This is how I help you do that."

Those smoky eyes flicker away. "I meant that's asking too much of you. Of your time. That's three nights a week you're heading out here." His face lifts into a soft smile. "What will the bowling league do without you?"

I snort. "Win more games. They know I'm mostly there for the beer, mile-high nachos, and colorful insanity that flies out of those ladies' mouths each week. I've been trying to get Dani to join, but she's in post-engagement bliss and prefers to cuddle at home with your chief. If it wasn't so damn cute, I'd be annoyed."

Jensen's lips quirk and I try to recall a time I've heard him laugh.

"Well, maybe we can schedule around your game nights."

"That would be…nice."

Confusion, disappointment, and relief war inside me. I lean into relief. Because this is good. Maybe if he's nice, I'll find him less attractive, and those horrendously intrusive feelings will dissipate. That would make things *so* much easier.

"Good." His tone hardens. "Now get out of here. For fuck's sake, try not to break anything on the way out." My jaw goes slack, and his gaze flicks to the kitchen. "I don't have a clue how that bread knife flew from your hand and landed in the soup pot earlier, but I'd like to eat in peace and you're a walking disaster," he grumbles at me while rising from his chair.

Fuck. I'm doomed.

CHAPTER
FIFTEEN

JENSEN

I miss the station. I miss the gym. I even miss popping in on Brody's paintball league.

But today...

Today, I miss tacos.

It's Mexican night at Rocky's and this will be the third time in a row I've missed it. The staff is probably worried sick.

Technically, I could go. I could get the guys to pick me up, use my crutch, and prop my foot up on a stool. But I have no interest in answering the metric shit ton of questions people would inevitably throw my way. And I have even less interest in attracting more pitiful, sympathetic glances.

Declan brought me some tacos last week, knowing I'd prefer to lie low. But the guy seems to think hot sauce is optional. Like a condiment or something. How are we friends and he doesn't know the freshly made guacamole at Rocky's is a religious experience? The bastard also snuck in a tofu taco like I wouldn't fucking notice.

Or maybe he did all that to piss me off and force me out of my house to get my own damn tacos. Or to distract me from bugging him about what's happening at the station.

Grumbling at the realization, I send him a text demanding he bring tacos when he comes over tomorrow night. Everything on them, no bullshit weird tacos.

I open the fridge and dig for a disappointing substitute. Two small pieces of chicken pot pie are better than nothing. Grace will bring me something today, but I won't make it through the next two hours without some food. Especially given the amount of workouts I've been doing.

I scarf down the pie cold, straight out of the container. After tossing the container and fork into the dishwasher, I make my way over to the main floor bathroom to shower before Grace gets here.

I smell like sweat and paint. She's much too observant not to notice and will give me shit for not "resting." I rest enough.

Once I turn on the shower, I take my time getting undressed and covering my cast. As I ease into the shower, my muscles relax. I raise the temperature of the water cascading down my chest and try to stretch my shoulder with a painful flinch. I'll admit I might have been pushing a little too hard the last few days.

I've built somewhat of a routine, but I'm still restless. Without the station, I'm not sure what the hell else I have, where my life is heading. My focus has been almost exclusively on work this year. And this house. Now the house projects are almost finished, and the training academy will start shortly after I return to regular duties.

This is a minor setback. Nothing has changed.

Except for one pint-sized intrusion in my life.

And I'm real fucking worried things won't ever return to normal after this.

She's been here three times over the last week. Coming up with new exercises, fine-tuning the ones I'm already doing, and checking my range of motion. Those bright eyes watching me.

Her soft hands touching me. The sweetness in her encouraging smiles is wickedly tempting.

Don't get me started on the leggings. Those fucking leggings pulling tight around her thighs and ass. And that thick, silken braid swishing around her shoulders, begging for my grip.

I've held her close a mere handful of times and it was too much and not enough all at once. It was perfunctory. Necessary. The softest parts of her pressing against me wasn't something I allowed my mind to linger on.

Until now.

She bends over so goddamn much to pick up the shit she drops. Does she know how maddening that is? Her ass is perfection. And I have no interest in getting near it.

Yet it's here three fucking times a week.

Don't pretend you've never noticed before now.

Maybe I noticed. Maybe even at that first moment I saw her.

I thought she was hitting on me, and it pissed me off. It had only been a month since Erika had left and there was no way I was allowing another hot, manipulative, forward woman to twist me around again.

Turns out she legitimately fell on me. And does so often. Also turns out she's tenacious, but in a way that's admittedly admirable.

As shown by her constant presence in my home.

I can smell her everywhere. In the living room. My kitchen. On my sling. Her soft summer scent has infiltrated my senses.

And with me feeling better, it's all too much, too good. Not just because she's excellent at her job—serious, patient, attentive. It's her presence. When she's here, it shouldn't feel so damn good.

I close my eyes to shut out the memories of her flitting about my house, moving around me, setting up whatever "enticement" she's brought that day. Some days, as I watch her in my kitchen, I barely notice the food.

The heat traveling up my thighs has nothing to do with the scalding water that's pummeling my shoulder. Not knowing whether to wrap my hand around my cock or stop the torture by flipping the water temperature to icy punishment, I press my head against the tile.

Grace will be here soon. And I have to find some relief or my dick will not cooperate.

I picture her bent over, showing me how to let my arm hang gently from my shoulder and rotate. While the scene plays in my mind, I don't have to divert my attention away from the soft swell of her cleavage. In this fantasy version of our sessions, I smooth my hands over her hips and pull her ass against me, my cock rubbing along the subtle seam of her pussy through her thin navy leggings. She grins at me over her shoulder, shaking her head. But the way she bites her bottom lip, as if she's trying to stop herself from begging for more, has me rock hard and determined to make her squirm and writhe. I'll rip those leggings from those sexy as fuck thighs and bring her to the brink over and over before letting her come. The first time I draw out her moans, make her shake, leave her soaked and sloppy, I want it to be with my tongue. I want to feed on her ferocity and make her melt.

I grip the tip of my dick, imagining it's notched against her entrance, waiting for her to come down from her first orgasm before plunging inside her. I want her desperate, still aching for me to fuck her thoroughly.

Not ready for this to be over so soon, I slow my fist, loosen my grip.

I shouldn't be imagining her. Fucking my hand with her in my head. Wishing for things that can't happen. Fantasizing that she wants me as much as I've begrudgingly wanted her. She might think the worst of me, but I wonder if her body has betrayed her in the same way mine has.

I get impossibly harder, closing my eyes and squeezing slowly from tip to base as if I'm sliding into the phantom heat of her pussy.

Fuck yes.

Grace would be tight and eager, bouncing against my dick, trying to control the pace. Maybe then I'd bend her over the kitchen island, slapping that tight ass bent before me as I drive my cock into her warmth. Grace would grumble and whimper, trying to get me to go faster, her hips undulating desperately. I'd push her back down to the counter and hold her there, telling her I'll give her what she needs. If she wants to come, she'll take my cock like a good girl.

My breath comes in hard pants, head rolling back on my neck as I think about what she likes, how I'd play with her pussy.

A guttural groan rips from my throat. "Fuck…"

She'd gasp, her slick heat clenching around my throbbing, desperate—

"Jensen? I'm coming…"

At the muffled sound of her sexy fucking voice, I send a loud moan to the ceiling, my cock jerking.

"Yes, Grace. Come with me, baby." Waves of pent-up release paint the wall in front of me. Shaking, my leg almost buckles. I drop my head to the tile, exhaling roughly.

"Jesus," I grumble.

Jacking off in the shower, while teetering on one leg…stupid.

Coming to thoughts of Grace—catastrophically absurd.

"Cut it out, asshole," a feminine voice says.

My body locks up tight as my neck whips toward the door. The voice that pushed me over the edge was *not* the product of my vivid imagination.

Grace is in my house.

At my bathroom door.

Listening to me grunt out her fucking name.

"I hope you had a good laugh," she shouts from the other side of the door. "You're going to need it for our session today. If you think pretending to be in there manhandling your ham candle is going to send me running for the hills, you're mistaken." *What?*

"I can fake moan too."

And then she does.

"Oh god, that's it," she coos, slapping against the door. "There, baby. Yes!" I turn off the shower, needing to hear every damn sound from her mouth. "Mmmm." Her voice is a deep, quivering spectacle she raises to a level anyone within a mile of the house could hear. "That mouth of yours," she pants. "Finally put to good use."

She thinks I was fucking with her.

"Stop imagining my mouth on you and go wait for me in the living room," I grit out through clenched teeth. "And next time, *knock.*"

"I did," she hollers at me. "But there was a creature in your bushes making a meal out of a bird. Feathers everywhere, violence abounding. Your walkway looks like a crime scene." She audibly shudders. "I refuse to step willingly into the brutalized, real-life version of *Jurassic Park* that was playing out on your property."

I carefully step out of the shower and wrap a towel around my waist, glaring down at the dick that's hard again. The effect her sass has on me is troubling.

"Good to know you have *some* self-preservations instincts."

"You're going to have to walk me out later. Preferably with a weapon. Your crutch doesn't count since you don't seem capable of properly using it."

As I rub the towel through the wet strands of my hair, a wide, bemused smirk stretches across my face.

"It's my neighbor's cat. She hunts birds and mice. Doubtful she'd attack you. Though you are very tiny. She might get confused."

"Shut up and get your pervy ass out here."

"That's not very professional, Ms. Parker."

A choking sound filters through the silence. "You were moaning, pounding walls, and calling out my name not two minutes ago, *Mr. Vaughn.*"

"And now you've learned to stop letting yourself into my house."

She mumbles something I can't quite hear.

I pull open the door and she's standing there, arms crossed, cheeks flushed as she glowers at me.

Her gaze dips for a moment, just like last time.

My grin is intentional, letting her know I caught her.

She might like what she sees, but she doesn't like *me*. And that kind of shit has fucked me over enough in the past.

With a sharp but cute huff, she spins on her heel and disappears down the hallway. That angry little pixie is going to make me pay for this during our session today.

"I brought over the gloopy broccoli cheddar soup you like from Kozy's. And if you're not out here in five minutes, I'm sacrificing it to the cat to get me out of here in one piece."

Oh, damn. That soup may be semi-congealed and smell like something in your fridge started growing its own ecosystem, but it's amazing. Disgustingly amazing.

"Reaper's not getting my soup, shortcake."

She spins to face me. "*Reaper*? Please tell me that's not her name. Is it safe for her to wander around? Is she feral?"

A laugh barrels up from my chest.

A quizzical expression lights her face as she plunks her hands on her hips. "You made that up."

"I did. Don't call my dick a ham candle ever again. It's disturbing."

She grins. "Oh, come on. You must have heard that one before."

"Definitely not."

"What about five knuckle shuffle?"

My brows dip low as I shake my head.

"Summoning the semen demon?"

"No."

"Hand to gland combat?"

"Stop."

She laughs, turning away from me. "You started this little game, Jensen. And I always step up." She nods toward the guest bedroom. "Get dressed. And put on a shirt today."

After she leaves, I throw on some sweats, but leave my shirt on the bed. I take a few moments to compose myself before I slip out of my temporary bedroom.

Her ass greets me the moment I enter the room. She's bent over my island, watching the hockey game I left playing on my tablet.

I'm well and thoroughly fucked now.

I've opened the door. The one that kept out all the forbidden thoughts and fucking filthy mental images.

"Oh, come on, Karlsson! Matthews was open in the slot!"

Ah, she really *is* a Sharks fan. How great would she look in nothing but a jersey? Those sweet legs on display, explaining player injuries, shouting obscenities at the TV.

So. Fucked.

HARPER:

What's my bestest, blonde-bombshell friend
doing later tonight?

The correct answer is "Not a thing, Harp. I'd love
to hang out with Ava while you drive to
Bakersfield to bail out your sweetly naive,
delinquent sister again."

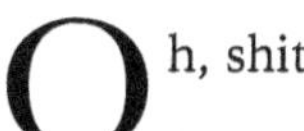

Oh, shit.

Yes, of course! I'm about to start my last PT
session, then have to stop by the hospital to deal
with that inappropriate patient I told you and
Dani about, but I can be there by seven o'clock
for sure.

Perfect. I love you. Thank you! I didn't want Ava
to see her auntie coming out of a seedy police
station until she was at least twelve. It'll be a little
easier to explain who Kitty, the half-dressed
woman with the pretty makeup, is at that age.

Snorting, I nearly choke on the chai tea Jensen poured me

when I got here. I'm not sure if I was more surprised that he had chai tea or that he made some specifically for me.

> You're a wonderful mom.

I try. So is that guy still being a creep? Is it common for patients to be inappropriate?

> Well, not usually, but I currently have two. One who wants to fuck me and the other who wants to strangle me. I'm going to get the sleazy patient moved to another—preferably male—therapist. Unfortunately, I'm stuck with the other patient.

Unless he fires me as his physical therapist. But so far, even though I've sassed him, pushed him hard, and broken several of his things, Jensen still arranges our next appointment time before I leave.

I mean, depending on what you're both into, the strangler could also want to fuck you. He's just kinkier than the sleazebag.

I glance over my shoulder to the hallway where Jensen disappeared to get changed. Illicit images flutter through my mind. That man would be dominant in bed. He'd make all the decisions, expect his every command adhered to, exert his physical strength over his woman. He'd spank, demand more of my orgasms—

What the actual fuck?

I'm blaming Harper for that depraved-thoughts cliff dive.

> Stop. The strangler patient is Jensen.

Oh. That might be hot. What do you think he'd do if you asked him to choke you? Use your raspy, flirty tone when you ask.

I'm ignoring that. I'll see you at seven.

"Let's get this over with," a deep voice barks directly behind me.

I squeal, flinging tea all over the counters, stools, the floor —everywhere.

"Christ," he mutters.

"Dammit, Jensen! You scared the shit out of me." I snatch the roll of paper towels near the sink while I shoot daggers at him. Thankfully, we've fallen into a routine now. I clean up whatever mess I've made, and he focuses on his exercises.

Once I've cleaned the counter and floor, I move to where he's attempting to release his arm from the sling. He glances up at me from his spot at the table before letting me ease it off him. Even with him seated, I'm only slightly taller.

The heat of his gaze caresses the side of my face, and I wonder if he can see the retaliatory gleam in my eyes. During these sessions, I have to remind myself to stay detached and remain professional. I'm his physical therapist. I've worked with much more challenging patients.

"You're wet."

"Mm. Yep." My shirt is soaked in tea, creating a cold and uncomfortable cling against my skin. "That happens when you fling liquids in every direction." The droll tone has a grin pulling at his mouth.

"I've got a shirt you can change into," he offers.

"I'm good. It'll eventually dry."

"Just take the shirt, Grace."

I shoot him a glare, but glance down to inspect my top. Sighing, I lift the soaked fabric from where it's sticking to my stomach.

"I have an extra in my bag." For situations like this one. "Do you mind if I change in your guest room?"

His dark gaze shoots down the hall where the guest room is

located, then back to me. He consents, tipping his head in that direction.

"Do your shoulder rotations. I'll be right back."

Backpack in hand, I hustle to the room.

Realizing too late that the guest room is now *his* room.

I set my bag down on his hastily made bed. As I dig through my backpack, my gaze wanders around the room. A hamper with a few articles of clothing is in one corner, a lamp and laptop sit atop the nightstand, and on the opposite side of the room is a short dresser with a few photo frames on display. Otherwise, the room is bare.

Curiosity gets the best of me, and I find myself in front of his dresser, staring at a picture of him and his siblings, quite a few years younger. The boys have lined up—laughter creasing Jaxon's face, a surprisingly warm smile on Jensen's, and a stoic, almost cocky slant to Brody's mouth. Liv is horizontal in front of them, posing as Superwoman while her brothers hold her up.

Next to that, there's a photo of a handsome man with familiar chestnut brown hair, standing next to Lilah Vaughn. He has Jensen's eyes and jawline and is wearing a police uniform with pride. In his hands, he balances a few awards. I lean in and see a Mayor's Award, an Exemplary Service medal, and another I can't quite make out, but it looks nearly identical to the first. The Mayor's Award plaque reads *Ethan Vaughn*. Jensen's dad, the man who lost his life in the line of duty.

I study him for another minute before moving onto the last frame, which is a collage of images depicting parties, camping, his brothers, and friends. In the bottom corner is a picture of a pretty strawberry blonde woman with a wide, Julia Roberts-like smile. She has her arms hooked around the necks of the twins, with Jaxon smiling sweetly at someone out of the shot and Jensen...

My breath leaves me in a rush. This mystery woman and her flawless beauty might be what first drew my attention, but it's Jensen's adoring gaze that catches me most off guard.

He's looking at her like every woman dreams about. And she's missing it. Instead, she's looking at the camera with a wild exuberance that's almost contagious. An uncomfortable heat rises in my chest. He loved this woman.

I jerk upright, feeling as though I've crossed a line, grossly invaded his privacy by looking at the photographic memories he keeps close.

I slink back over to my bag and burrow my hand to the bottom. It closes around wet, goopy fabric. What the hell? The container I brought Jensen's food in must have leaked.

When I pull the shirt out, I spot the deep red stains. I groan in frustration and shove the shirt back into the bag, making it tumble off the bed with a thud.

"Fuck a duck."

The thunk of Jensen's crutch hitting the hardwood gets louder and then stops. "Grace?" he asks from right outside the door.

"Yeah, come in."

The partially closed door eases open.

"I, um…I might take you up on your offer of a shirt. The pasta I brought leaked throughout my bag."

"Pasta?" He cranes his neck, looking for my bag.

"Yes. It's in the fridge. For *later*."

He grumbles, shooting a glance down the hallway to the kitchen.

"Shirt, PT, then your hollow leg," I demand.

He throws me a dark glower. Practically the opposite of the look he was giving the mystery woman.

"Stop pouting and get me a shirt, please."

He mumbles something about how he "doesn't fucking pout" and moves past me to the dresser. As if he knows I was looking at the photos, he glances back. I keep my expression blank, but my traitorous eyes dart to that last frame for a fraction of a second, and he notices.

He turns back to the dresser, yanks open a drawer, and pulls out a black t-shirt.

"Here. It'll be enormous on you, but it's dry And clean." He tosses it to me, but I'm too deep in my thoughts and my reaction is slow.

It hits me in the face and slides down to my chest before I snag it.

He sighs like I've disappointed him yet again.

"Thanks," I mutter.

He's staring, fists clenched, as his eyes travel down my front.

I twirl my finger in a circle, motioning for him to turn around. One brow dips as he follows my directions with a hint of confusion on his face.

The question of whether he should leave so I can change lingers between us.

Yes. Yes, he should. So what the hell am I doing?

I turn around as well, as if that'll make it okay.

With my arms crossed in front of me, I drag the bottom of my shirt up my chest like I'm performing a chai-scented striptease. When was the last time I felt compelled to undress for someone?

Never.

Straightening my arms above my head isn't as smooth as it should be, so my movement stalls at an awkward angle. My arms are trapped. I yank harder, releasing a huff. The back of my shirt won't go up any farther. It's tugging at my compression sports bra, the tight kind that keeps everything on lockdown. The kind that requires advanced yoga skills and a background in acrobatics to remove.

A trickle of panic seeps in as my shirt tightens around my arms like a boa constrictor locked on its prey. I twist and heave, trying to pry it loose. All this does is pull at my bra so the bottom half of my boobs are now reveling in freedom while the rest of me tries to buck this form-fitting, polyester cage.

But I can't see, my balance is shit, and I know by now Jensen must have turned around to assess the situation. So naturally, that's when I trip on the backpack at my feet, going down like a felled tree.

I bounce off the bed and land with a grimace-inducing thud on the carpeted floor. The air in my lungs expels with a deep, "Oof!"

"Grace."

"Don't look!" I shout.

"Way too late for that, shortcake," he drawls.

"Oh god," I groan.

"Why am I not surprised that this is how I hear you moan for the first time?"

What?

Is he mocking me?

Flirting?

No.

Yes?

Shit, my tits!

I tuck and roll onto my stomach. It's difficult but I inch up to my knees. I look up through my top to catch movement beside me.

"Need a hand?" The way he says it sounds like he's offering to fingerfuck me.

My core flutters with anticipation.

No more assholes, Gracie! No matter how thick and strong his fingers look while he's undoing the straps of his sling. Or the intense way he'd stare into your eyes while watching you come, darkly satisfied that he can toy with you any way he chooses.

"No," I grind out.

After a few more pulls, I'm ready to find some scissors.

"Need a hand?" he offers again, failing to keep the wry amusement from his voice.

"Don't laugh at me."

"I'm not," he says, and this time he sounds earnest.

His hand brushes the bare skin at my waist, drawing a shiver from me as it skims past my navel. He stops at my hip, his large hand wrapping around it. I let him pull me up but make sure not to lean too far into him. And not just because he's only got one functional arm and leg to hold us both up.

When I regain my balance, my back brushing against his front, I'm glad for the shirt that's blocking my face. His warmth disappears and fingers find the edges of my bra.

The rumbling hmm that comes from him is erotic and wholly unsettling.

"How the hell…" His breath hits my bare skin as he ducks down to assess the problem. "You rolled your top up in your bra."

I nod, unable to find my voice.

Sure, hot fingers sweep up my spine and across the tight band.

"Be still," he demands. I freeze, holding my breath in hopes I'll make it through this with at least a few scraps of my dignity intact. "Mmm…good girl. Almost there."

My eyes roll up as a full-body shiver blazes through me.

Oh fuck. Oh fuckity fuck.

Jensen stills, and I have to bite down on my lip to keep the needy sounds from bubbling to the surface.

Jensen Vaughn can*not* know about my praise kink. I would die. The ways he would use that against me would be innumerable.

Apparently, it doesn't even have to be on purpose. Because a hot, wounded firefighter asshole who grumbles sexy praise?

Fuck. Me. Sideways.

Please.

No.

Harper's kink talk earlier has my mind going to naughty places. That's all this is.

"You want me to take it all the way off of you?" he whispers against my hair.

Yes, yes, *yes*!

A flush of desire races down my spine. Unable to cut off the trembling squeak of desperation that falls from my mouth, I turn it into a cough.

"Definitely not," I lie. "Just get me free and then turn back around."

"You've been free for a bit now."

Then why are his hands still on me?

I rip the shirt off and shoot daggers over my shoulder at the man apprising me with a shuttered expression. Lightning fast, I snatch his shirt off the bed and whip it over my head. A quick glance over my shoulder reveals his unwavering gaze.

He didn't turn around.

And I don't tell him to.

As I throw my arms into the gargantuan armholes, his gaze burns down my body as he says, "I want that shirt back. In one piece. I've had a few of those go missing over the years. Unlike some guys at the station, I don't let women keep them as souvenirs."

A disgusted scoff bursts from my mouth. "Souvenirs? Seriously?"

Those roped shoulders lift in an indifferent shrug.

Do they really do that? Anders, maybe. Bradford, definitely. Jaxon? I don't know. For as much as he flirts, I've yet to see him leave the bar with anyone.

"Gross. I feel tainted wearing this."

His eyes wander down to where the shirt ends a few inches above my knees.

"You can always give it back. I've already seen what's under it."

His dry tone, with a hint of mockery, makes my eye twitch.

"You're impossible, you know that?"

"Back at you," he grumbles.

We move for the door at the same time, nearly crashing into each other. He holds out a hand, gesturing for me to go first. I sidestep him, narrowly avoiding shoulder-checking the wall, and clamber down the hallway at a pace I know he can't match.

After a few moments, he still doesn't follow, so I shout, "We've got forty-five minutes left of your session, hotshot. Get out here."

"I want the full sixty, shortcake," he shouts back, appearing in the hallway.

Months, I remind myself. I still have months of being mixed up with Jensen's mercurial ass. His rock-hard, biteable, grumpy ass.

Nice guys only, Gracie! Jensen is not a nice guy.

And I'm determined to give dating the sweet, adorable dreamboats with smiles for days a real try. A guy who will text me good morning, open my door, ask how my day is, surprise me with gifts...

That's what I should want.

But maybe he could be a little prickly. Gruff, but with a heart of gold.

A sweet, molten center he'd only allow *me* to see.

He'd be a rough, dominant, pussy-pounding, kitty-devouring god in the sack. Taking me from behind, handling me with confidence and ease. Enjoying every damn bit of me. Whispering what he likes and how he likes it. How good I please him.

Mmm...yes, please.

My core throbs in quick successive beats, making me clutch the dining table in front of me.

Jensen's arm brushes mine as he moves to grip the back of the chair next to me. His head turns and those keen eyes assess me. Concern flickers across his face, the heat of his stare intensifying. All the questions left unasked, explanations left untold, grudges fortified, form a shield between us.

"That wet shirt, evil sports bra incident stays between us, got it?" I warn him half seriously. "I hope you now feel less inclined to use something like that against me. Like say in a *Vine* article, or to shit-talk me to your crew." Hurt filters through my tone unintentionally.

"You're never going to let that go, are you?" He lets out a resigned sigh.

I suck in a breath before I admit, "I might have a few trust issues after being publicly ridiculed."

His gaze roams my face for several seconds before saying, "*The Vine* shouldn't have put up that article about your car accident."

I chuff out a breath. "Agreed. Having your nipples featured in a small town news report your first month in a new town isn't ideal."

He swipes a hand over his jaw, a guttural sound coming from his throat.

"That may have been the one aspect of the article worth remembering, but I was actually referring to what I said in the article." With a shake of his head, he adds, "I was taking some shit out on you that you didn't deserve." His confession confuses the hell out of me. "You're not a menace to society. I know you didn't crash your vehicle on purpose." He blows out a breath, bending forward to lean his arm across the back of the chair. "I didn't mean any of it."

I place a hand on the table to keep myself steady as I turn toward him. His dark gaze lifts to mine, the intense sincerity in his gaze pins me in place, silencing the flippant response on the tip of my tongue.

"I'm sorry if what I said hurt you. I was an asshole."

"*Was* an asshole?" I tease, wrestling back a smirk.

He stands and presses a finger to my lips to quiet me.

"Mmpf dis…" My words come out muffled as I talk around the finger. I wrap a hand around his wrist and tug.

"But I stand by my comment that this pretty face lets you get away with just about anything. It's a problem." A playful smirk tugs at his mouth, and it's utterly disarming.

I forgot he'd called me pretty, but the fact he said it in the middle of a brutal character assassination overshadowed the compliment.

"You don't let me get away with *anything*," I whisper, the hushed tone all I seem capable of right now.

"I've let you into my house. Let you help me, despite serious reservations. I pretend like I don't see you trip on every rug I own. I've let you into my life, Grace, and I haven't let a woman get this close in a long time." His hand works the back of his neck while his gaze flickers to me, those long lashes shielding the emotions stirring in his eyes.

"Why?" I can't decide if I'm asking why he hasn't let a woman get close to him or why he's letting me.

With a swipe of his tongue, he wets his bottom lip and every part of me fixates on that movement, on the anticipation of his answer.

"You're not the only one with trust issues. Or who's had their worst moments broadcast to the entire town. *The Vine* might do more good than harm, but no one's safe from the gossip." His gaze flits away, the muscle in his jaw flexing. "They feature my family in there a lot, and it's not all glowing commentary."

I snort in disbelief. *The Vine* loves the Vaughn brothers— they're practically town royalty.

"You don't believe me." He turns toward me, his expression candid. "On the day of my wedding, someone took photos of me destroying decorations and shouting at everyone to leave. Those images were shared all over town and in *The Vine*."

"You're *married*?" I yell, my voice cracking.

In the recesses of my mind, I know he's not married. But that's buried under shock and an endless stream of questions.

"No." His stare is unrelenting and just as uninformative.

That's all he's going to say? Just *no*?

I jut my chin out. "Anything to add to that 'no'?"

A smirk pulls at his cheek, distracting me. "What I'm getting at is that people talk, and sometimes they get it all wrong."

Is he saying *The Vine* was wrong to post that article about me?

Or is he saying that *he* was wrong about *me*?

Our mutual disdain for one another has been my safety net, and he keeps snipping away the strings.

Avoiding that train of thought like a log truck ahead of me on the highway, I veer into another lane. "Mhm, so true," I say, briskly. "But let's rewind to the bit about your wedding. I have questions."

"No."

Yep, should have seen that answer coming.

"Come on. You can't just drop that you had a wedding and then clam up."

His warm eyes apprise me, and I hold my breath. Maybe he'll tell me if I stop asking questions. He'll fill the silence.

"My fiancée left me on our wedding day. She wanted a different kind of guy, someone I couldn't be. I didn't take it well. And news about how I handled it traveled quickly."

I take at least five seconds to close my gaping mouth and say something. "Fuck."

I'm fully aware that's not a sufficient response, so I scramble to come up with something more appropriate to say to a jilted groom who now lives alone, in the woods, with a near-permanent scowl and a penchant for scathing lectures.

But nothing feels right. Because there's a hell of a lot about Jensen Vaughn I was oblivious about.

His attention stays focused on the wide, rectangular window that takes up nearly the entire length of the dining room.

My mind goes in a dozen directions. Sure, he's a pain in my ass and hates me, but I wouldn't kick him out of bed if he looked at me the way I saw him looking at his ex-fiancée.

"Well, she's a cunt," I announce. "Good riddance."

He chokes, coughing into his fist.

"What? You disagree?" The realization he might not be over her hits me. "Oh god. You're not still in love with her, are you?"

If so, I just moved up several spots on his shit list.

He scrubs a hand over his jaw, shaking his head. "Nope." His eyes sparkle at me with a look of unconcealed amusement.

"Good. So did you—"

"That's enough questions for today, shortcake." He nods to his workout area. "Let's get this over with. I'm starving, and I doubt even that newfound pity shining in your eyes will result in me getting fed before we're done."

I scoff. "It's not pity. It's shock. I mean, you *apologized* to me. Honestly, that might be the bigger of the two surprises you unleashed on me today."

He gives me a dismissive grunt, but his expression looks less guarded and his hunched shoulders have relaxed.

"And Jensen?" He shoots me a curious look. "I'm sorry that I threatened to report you for the shit you said about me. I didn't. I wouldn't have." Dropping my gaze to the yoga mat, I admit, "You saved my ass. The things you said just poked a few sore spots." Particularly when he said I was too much fucking trouble and hoped I wasn't staying in town, so he didn't have to deal with me. "You've seen me. I accumulate a lot of bruises." When you're told you're "too much" often enough, it leaves some marks.

The corner of his mouth lifts in a half-smile. "You do." He presses his lips together before asking, "Did I add to them?"

The bleak concern etched into his face has my heart clambering to my throat.

Unable to answer, I shake my head.

What would it look like if Jensen and I put the past behind us and became friends?

Well, friends-ish.

But becoming even friend-ish with Jensen Vaughn feels big. Risky.

Because despite his brute-like personality, when he's not being a complete dick, I could like him.

Not just the way he looks. Those shoulders, the massive chest with the perfect amount of dark chest hair, his devastatingly handsome face.

Despite his growly introverted tendencies, I think I could like the total package.

Because *damn*, it's an attractive package.

"If you ogle my chest one more time, I'm raiding whatever food you brought, and you'll have to wait to finish our session."

I feel like someone just slapped a cupcake out of my hand right as I was about to take a bite. Stupid nice-guys-only diet is messing with my head.

I amend my previous statement.

I *might* want to be not-enemies with Assistant Fire Chief Jensen Vaughn. If he ever learns how to keep his rude mouth shut.

SEVENTEEN

JENSEN

I'm officially losing my damn mind.

I'm a homebody. I like the quiet of my house, my projects. I head to the station a couple of times a week and have Jax pick me up to meet the guys for food and beer on their days off.

But I feel off. Restless. Like I'm missing something vital.

Everything feels different, and it's making me uneasy.

Maybe it's being off work and having my schedule completely off-kilter. Or that the Vaughn Volunteer Firefighter Training Program was supposed to start next week.

Grace hasn't been by in a few days either. Not since I shocked the shit out of both of us by apologizing for the way shit went down after her car accident. Not since I saw her underboob, and she called Erika a cunt.

Our session afterward was fine—normal—other than the dread that sunk deeper in my stomach with every soft, sympathetic gaze she shot my way.

I probably should have kept my mouth shut, accepted her hostility, and left it alone. But I owed her an apology for the shit I said the day I helped rescue her from the ravine. I had just found out Erika had dropped by the station to return my engagement ring. She left it with the first crew member she saw and left town again. And I took it out on the wrong woman, the one who was drawing my attention and distracting me in ways I resented.

Having Grace hate me was easy. Smart. It kept the lines clear.

Now there's no line. No way to push everything down like I'd been doing for months.

My teeth grind together as I attempt to ward off the numerous images that plague my head daily. After watching her get bested by a shirt, I discovered Grace might hate me, but her body definitely doesn't care. Now every fucking time I'm in bed, alone and frustrated, I think about her. And the way she looked in my shirt.

I wonder if she's been wearing it to bed. I told her I wanted it back, but I'd rather know if she's bare beneath it as she slides between the sheets at night.

Then maybe I'd demand it back. Watch her peel it off, ready to catch her if she falls.

I'd get her on her knees before taking me in her hand. Instead of putting me in her mouth like I told her to, she'd tease me with little licks of her tongue. But when she wraps her lips around my dick, when I hit the back of her throat, I'd tell her how fucking amazing her mouth feels. How she sucks like a goddamn dream.

The fourteen knocks on the door set to a rhythm I can't quite put my finger on, drags me from my fantasies. With an irritated growl, I throw the door open and glare down at the persistent pixie who has shown me more patience than I deserve.

"Do you have to do that every time?"

"Does it bother you?" she asks.

"Yes."

"Then, yep!" A delighted smile dances across her face as she slips by me, not bothering to wait for an invitation.

She lays down a thick yoga mat and sets up some resistance bands before turning back to me.

"So good news is your sling comes off today. Bad news is your sling comes off today."

That sounds like I'm about to have a rough day.

I move over to the mat, rubbing at my shoulder as I try to relax my tight muscles.

"You've been overdoing it, haven't you?"

She already knows the answer, so I don't bother responding. Between the range of motion exercises, stretching, and whole-body strengthening workout, I've been doing at least triple what she recommended.

"If you can promise to take it easy and limit any anterior motion and lifting with your arm, you can keep the sling off. But the moment you think you know more than I do about your shoulder mechanics and healing, I'll wrangle it right back on you. Got it?"

"Like to see you try," I murmur.

Given the slight narrowing of her eyes, she heard me.

She unzips her jacket and turns to the chair she normally hangs it on. With a grin, I undo the sling.

"Couldn't wait, could you?" I glance up and do a double take. She's wearing the hip-hugging leggings I love and a long-sleeve crop top that leaves an intriguing amount of skin on display. The loose braid hanging from her high ponytail swings along her nape as she saunters over to me, reaching for the sling.

I hand it over wordlessly and she sets it aside. When she turns back to face me, I follow her hands as they smooth down the tight, black fabric covering her thighs.

Today's session will undoubtedly test the limits of my concentration and willpower.

"I thought we'd start with some manual release to ease some of the tightness in your shoulder."

"Huh?" I ask, distracted.

But the words slowly trickle in.

Manual release? That can't *actually* be what it's called.

"To help with joint mobilization and stiffness. I'll use a hands-on approach for trigger point release and soft tissue manipulation."

Heat burns low in my stomach. It's a really fucking bad idea for her to give me a massage. I've barely touched *myself* since she caught me. Plus, who wants to have to explain to their medical team—let alone family and friends—that they dislocated their shoulder again by masturbating too vigorously?

"Is that okay?" she asks tentatively.

Shit. "I can always book a massage. You don't have to do that."

The corner of her mouth tips up, the professional mask she's been putting in place each session slipping for a second. "It's part of your therapy now that we're getting your shoulder moving more. But we can stop if it gets too painful."

"That's not what I'm worried about," I mumble.

"Have you never had a massage?"

I've had therapeutic massages and sexy massages, and my body is primed for this to become some kind of fucked up combination of the two.

If Grace's gaze dips below my shoulder, the growing boner in my sweatpants won't go unnoticed.

"Fine," I answer, rotating to lie down on my stomach.

"Nope, on your back."

I'm fucked.

I throw her a glare, wondering if she's doing this on purpose.

She snorts. "You're impossible, you know that? I do this every day. Now take off your shirt so I can get you back to pushing yourself too hard during workouts."

I put this shirt on specifically because she was coming over and she tells me to take it off. Like it's no big deal to undress and let her put her hands all over me.

She kneels beside me, eyes connecting with mine. "I'll help until we can get this arm moving better." Her fingers find the hem of my loose t-shirt and inch it up. As she skims the skin along my waist, up my ribs, my abs tighten and I hold my breath.

My cock is going to be laying like a steel pipe in my sweatpants for the next hour. The chances of her not seeing it are slim.

I pull my arm out of the sleeve and wait for her to shove the shirt over my head. After it's lifted off me, my eyes immediately find hers again. Her usually pale skin is rosy at the cheeks, lower lip tucked beneath a row of sleek white teeth. If she weren't keeping her gaze fixed on my shoulder instead of reprimanding me for roughly yanking the shirt off my injured arm, I *might* have believed she didn't look down.

Fuck.

"Lie back," she orders, but her voice has a slight tremble.

I don't dare look at her as I get in position, because I don't want to see the feelings that are always displayed on that pretty face.

Soft, cool fingers meet the top of my shoulder and trail down my bicep. I keep my face set, eyes on the ceiling as she moves my arm into a few positions, testing for movement and tenderness. Soon, she adds some oil to her palm and her fingers glide over my skin. There's some soreness, especially when she moves my arm into various positions, but...it feels really fucking good.

The scent of her shampoo wafts toward me. Apricot and sunshine. It's taking everything in me not to grab that braid swinging enticingly above me and bring her to my mouth. Tip that head back and dive into her neck, memorize her smell, taste her skin, shove my hands under the hem of her deliciously short—

Fucking fuck.

My dick is throbbing, and if there isn't a wet spot on the front of these dark gray sweats, it'll be a fucking miracle.

I've never let her get to me like this before.

It's because she's around all the time. Looking good, smelling incredible, sassing me with that smartass mouth. Probably just need to get laid. I've been more cooped up than usual and it's been months—a lot of months—since I've fucked anyone.

Her arm grazes my nipple and I groan.

"Sorry, I know this can be really sore. Just a few more minutes."

I won't need a few minutes. If she so much as breathes on me, I'm done.

She lays my arm into her lap to prop it up at the angle she needs and leans back over me. If I stretch my fingers, the tips will brush her pussy. They twitch, liking that idea.

Stop getting ideas. This woman would turn your whole life upside down.

Grace sits back on her legs and rests my arm by my side. I'm not sure how long I've been staring at her, but when she inhales slow and long, causing her chest to push against her snug top I have to clench my fist to keep my hands in check.

Then it happens.

Her gaze darts over.

Lying down, it's slightly less noticeable, but the moment her attention moves to my cock, it jerks. Fucking backstabbing bastard.

She's hot. I'm allowed to think Grace is hot.

But I shouldn't be planning more jerk off sessions to thoughts of her. Or letting myself want things I can't have.

With that sinfully sweet face, sassy mouth, and legs that would look fucking incredible draped over my shoulders, her appeal is unquestionable. Doesn't mean I should act on it.

"Alright..." She huffs out a breath and quickly stands. "Take your time getting up. I'll go grab you some water and we'll get started on your homework exercises."

I don't bother telling her that my water bottle is two feet away and full. I'm going to need a goddamn minute and we both know it.

Footsteps filter in from outside just before my deadbolt flips.

"Oh!" my mom gasps as if she didn't see Grace's car parked in my driveway.

"Mom. Thought you were coming by this afternoon." I get up and move toward the menace in my kitchen.

Come to think of it, she hasn't broken or dropped anything yet today. Not even tripped on the living room rug like she usually does.

"I forgot there's a Town Meeting this afternoon." She gives us both a warm smile. "Can't miss that, so I thought I'd stop in a little early. Am I interrupting?"

My gaze flicks to Grace, which she skillfully avoids.

"Nope," I say, sitting on a stool at the island, hoping it'll hide the boner my physical therapist gave me. "Thanks, Mom."

"Hi, Mrs. Vaughn." Grace waves from in front of the sink, a glass of water grasped tightly in her hand. Her eyes finally dart over to me, briefly dipping to my dick as if to check its progress.

Still fucking hard for you, Grace. That's how he's doing.

"Please, call me Lilah. And do you prefer Grace or Gracie?"

"I prefer Gracie. Jensen calls me Grace to poke fun at my general gracelessness."

My teeth grind at the poorly disguised hurt in her tone. Another wave of shame punches me in the gut. That's not why I call her Grace, but there's no way I'm explaining the real reason.

Mom's gaze wavers between the two of us. "I'll call you Gracie, then. And I'm sure my son will too now that he knows it's your preference."

"Like hell," I murmur low enough she can't hear it.

Mom sets down the bag she brought in and starts taking out food and groceries. Ah, shit, she got the peanut butter pretzels I love. And is that a roast?

"You making me a pot roast?" I ask, suddenly starving.

"Yes. It's going in the slow cooker, so don't touch it until at least 6:00 p.m."

"Deal. I'll have whatever Grace brought me to tide me over.

And Brody promised to bring over pizza and beer for when we watch the game later tonight."

Mom whirls around as Grace turns on the oven. "Oh! That reminds me. I ran into Brody. He had a change of plans and asked that I tell you he's babysitting, so you'll have to reschedule. I think he said there was another game in a few days. Sorry, sweetie."

I respond first, completely baffled. "Babysitting?"

Grace is not as perplexed by Brody being around a child as I am, and calls out, "Next game is Tuesday at 7:00 p.m."

Is she going out to watch the Sharks game?

"Right! That's when he said he'd come instead," my mom tells Grace.

"Brody is babysitting. How is no one as concerned as I am?" I ask.

"Harper was in a jam. Something about her sister and with Brody living right next door..." She shrugs it off while she pours and sprinkles things into a crock pot she keeps here, but that I have never actually cooked with.

Grace appears beside me and thrusts a glass of water into my hands. "Drink. Then we have to get back to it."

I finish the glass in three gulps and hand it back. Her eyes widen, but she remains silent as she turns to take the glass to the sink.

She strides back just as I'm putting my shirt back on, and that's when she trips on the kitchen mat.

There she is.

I catch her with my good arm wrapped around her, tucked just under her cropped top, my palm meeting the soft skin at the side of her waist.

"Shit," she mutters, righting herself.

"Almost made it through incident-free this time. There's only twenty minutes left. I think that's a record," I say, the soft teasing lilt to my tone surprising us both.

Stop grinning like an idiot or she'll know you thought it was cute.

She's enough of a danger to herself and others without encouragement.

Grace shows me a few new exercises, ensuring I understand the potential repercussions if I push too hard or go too fast.

Mom finished putting the roast on a while ago but stuck around to watch the session. She remains quiet, but her expressions are exceedingly loud.

By the time we're done, I'm a little sweaty, but I'm not sure I'll make it through a shower without a snack. My stomach lets out a demanding growl.

"Hungry?" Grace asks with a chuckle.

"Always," my mom answers for me.

"Well, I'm glad your mom set you up with a roast."

Wait. Did Grace not bring me food? It's my reward. She's only had to take it away once because I was in pain and acted like an asshole. No caramel nut bars for me that day.

"I got home too late last night to make anything. But I snagged the leftover hot wings from my date."

"Date?" my mom and I say together.

"Yep. Super nice guy." She gives us a casual smile, and continues packing up her things, coming to kneel beside me as she rolls up her mat.

I cut my gaze away, hoping my brain didn't get enough of a visual of her on her knees to taunt me with later.

She's dating someone. Tanner? Someone new? She was alone on Valentine's Day and at the hockey game.

Whoever this guy is, she can't seriously be trying to offload his leftovers onto me.

"Giving me scraps of your boyfriend's meal isn't holding up your end of our agreement, Grace." My voice bounces around the room, dark and ominous. And slightly petulant. I hate it. Because it almost sounds like jealousy, and I don't do jealousy. Not anymore. That would involve feeling as though someone has something I don't and caring about it.

You do though, don't you?

Grace stands, glaring daggers at me.

"Jensen James Vaughn." My mom's face is stony, tone appalled as she perches one hand on a jean-clad hip. "You're expecting this sweet young lady to neglect her personal life while she works at the hospital, comes here three times a week, volunteers at the elementary school helping kids with disabilities, and then makes time to cook for you too? I can't imagine how you plan to explain that level of ignorant entitlement."

"She offered," I mumble, tucking my hands into my pockets. Apparently, you can be a grown-ass man and still feel like a child when your mom scolds you.

Grace leans over and whispers, "As much as I'd love to be here while your mom hands you your ass, I've got to go." She turns to my mom. "Give him hell, Lilah. He's been a pain in the ass. I'm off to meet Dani at Rocky's. We're watching the game. She doesn't care about sports but loves the food and cheering."

"Well, that *is* the best part," my mom agrees.

With a chuckle and a little wave, Grace slips out the door.

I round on my mom, preparing for the lecture, but she's already standing right in front of me.

"Christ, you're fast for a sixty-year-old."

There's this thing my mom does where she can look through you and find the shit you don't want anyone to know. She can unearth feelings you keep buried and yank them out of their murky depths.

It's mystifying. And frightening.

"You like her." Whatever minute reaction she discerns from my blank expression makes her pause. "You ready to do something about that or—"

"Nope. Not interested. I like my life as it is and without whatever crazy she'd bring. If I were ready to date anyone, it would be someone serious. Someone quiet. Someone like me."

"Pfft. That's the last thing you need."

"Not for you to decide, Mom."

"Well, I like her."

"Better get in there and ask her out before she gets serious about this new guy."

"Hush, you," she says, smacking me on the arm. "Do me a favor though? Keep an eye on her. Those dating apps can be ripe with predators."

Brody needs to stop talking shop at family dinners.

My gaze shoots to the door, wondering if Grace is still here. She better not be meeting up with random men on those apps. The number of fucked up calls first responders get from dates gone wrong grows every year.

Mom changes the subject to detailed updates regarding Liv and Sawyer's engagement party while she makes tea. My attention drifts. All the shitty scenarios Grace could get herself into race through my mind.

I've seen her handle skeevy asshats who approach her at The Hole, only interested in getting laid. But what about the ones who don't quite appreciate her sassy mouth as much as I do? Or the ones who don't take no for an answer? The pricks who could easily take advantage of her small size and overzealous nature.

She gets into enough shit all on her own. Adding online predators to the mix is going to make my life fucking hell. I can't protect her if I'm stuck here, in a cast, unable to move my arm properly, let alone beat some asshole who touched my girl.

"Oh, fuck." I drop my head, letting out a deranged, scornful laugh.

My girl.

"Jensen? What's wrong?" my mom asks, bringing over two mugs of tea.

"Nothing," I say, scraping a hand across my jaw.

Moving past my mom, I snag a tea towel from the counter and rip open the oven door. The wings smell amazing.

"Oh. Those will probably need a few more minutes, honey."

I remove the tray and toss it on the stovetop. No way in hell I'm eating another man's leftovers.

"What's going on?" she asks. Her eyes bulge as I take out the garbage bin from under the sink and toss the wings in. "Are you feeling a little jeal—"

"Mom. I love you, but no."

"You don't even know what I was going to ask."

"I don't have any answers." Not for her or me.

She's quiet for a few moments before ambling over and handing me the mug of tea. "Want to prank call your brother at the police station? He's handling the complaint line this afternoon." She blows on her tea.

That drags a half-smile from me. Mom always seems to know exactly what to say.

While she makes the first call, I text my brother.

> Change of plans. Let's head out to Rocky's for the game.

JAX:

> You're shitting me?

> Are you in or not?

> Man, normally, I'd be all for it.

> But Reg's girl works there, and she hit on me last week. On purpose, in front of Reg to piss him off. So I'm gonna need to give that some space. The guy is huge.

Fuck.

> What's up? You never want to watch the game anywhere but at one of our places anymore. Unless Mexi Night and a game fall on the same night.

> It's nothing. Stupid idea. Bring pizza.

> It's Brody's turn.

> He's babysitting tonight.

> WHAT?!

See? *That's* the appropriate response.

> Yeah. Harper's kid.

> Shit. I'd pay money to watch Brody try to entertain a five-year-old.

> Maybe you can stop by before you come over.

> Don't forget the pizza.

> And no barbecue sauce on it.

That shit was disgusting. And I'll eat almost anything.

> Extra barbecue sauce on at least one pizza. Got it.

> Jax. Don't fuck with my pizza.

> If I don't put shit you hate on it, I won't get any.

That's his problem.

But something tells me he'll get more than his fair share tonight.

Because my mind's not on pizza. Or the hockey game.

CHAPTER
EIGHTEEN

GRACIE

He's a lefty and I should *not* know that. But his sweatpants have made that impossible to ignore. It's been on replay in my mind for days.

I don't think I'll ever be able to look him in the eye again. His erection was enormous. The effort to not gawk at it had me sweating. Thank god his mom showed up because I wasn't sure I had another half hour of pretending I didn't see it in me. I mean, I didn't have it in me to pretend anymore, not that I was pretending it was *in* me.

Goddammit.

Fine. I've had two sex dreams about his cock, and it's making me feel insane. I'm not sure I've ever woken up after a dream and had to peel off my soaked panties in the middle of the night. And getting myself off to the mental image of straddling him naked and rubbing myself over his hard length was certainly a new low.

That *does not* mean I'm interested in him. He's more tolerable than he's ever been, and seeing him with his family has been sweet. But nothing else has changed. He's apologized and been notably less of a dick. I've been professional, supportive, and called his ex-fiancée a cunt.

I think that means we're *friends-ish*…maybe.

But there's a niggle of doubt worming its way in my brain, causing me to question if maybe there's more to him. That I've misjudged him.

And that's dangerous thinking.

Before I can even raise my hand to knock on his door, it swings open.

"You're late."

I check my phone. "No, I'm not. I'm on time."

"I've been waiting to let you in."

Awesome. He's in a mood. These were more noticeable during our first few sessions, but I guess they've returned. Goodie!

I follow him into the living room, preparing for an extra surly Jensen kind of day.

"Did you hurt yourself? Feeling sore?"

"No." His voice is strangely sharp.

"Okay…"

He rounds on me, making me stop short. "Are you really dating random idiots online?"

I halt in my tracks and glance around, searching for a fucking clue. "What?"

"You fill in your information online, blindly trusting he's being honest with his. Then he'll tell you the kinds of sweet shit that'll make you all hot and heart eyed. You believe him and welcome him into your life, your house, your bed. But he's a total fucking stranger and you're being moronically reckless," he growls.

I press my fingertips together, going over his words again in case there's something in there with some merit. Something that might make me withdraw the junk punch he just ordered.

Nope. Sure as fuck isn't.

"That's a lot of assumptions you just strung together there, big guy. You get help with that, or did you shovel all that bullshit in one place by yourself?" I ask, outrage searing every nerve ending, pulling at every muscle to prepare to leap down Jensen's stupid throat.

"You're predator bait. You're chaotic, challenging, spunky, and sweet as hell—like a damn treat. I'm not there to keep an eye on you, Grace. I'm stuck here until this fucking thing comes off." He lifts the foot with his cast. "So, can you at least fucking date responsibly?"

Like a treat?

Keep an eye on me?

"I've been on like four dates in the last year, asshole. *Four!*" I snap, storming past him to the kitchen.

"Call me an asshole. Hate me. Think I'm bossy. I don't care." The gravelly rumble of his voice is unlike the usual timber he uses around me. Even when he lectures me. Even when I'm knee-deep in trouble and we both know it. "But no more meeting these random fuckers. You're smarter than that."

I remind myself to maintain a professional attitude. Shut down this personal affront and find out what's really bothering him. He must have fucked up his ankle or shoulder today. Or maybe something went wrong at the station?

"We're starting our session in three minutes. Go get set up." Those few minutes won't come close to giving me enough time to calm down. "I won't be answering any more personal questions. And if you keep it up, I'll leave."

"Tell me you understand me, Grace." He crowds me, moving so close I can smell his clean, woodsy scent, see the copper specks highlighting his deep brown eyes. "Who was the guy you saw the other night? Are you seeing him again?"

I squeeze my eyes shut and mentally count to five before I bite out, "Are you serious?"

"Of course I'm fucking serious. I'll get Brody to look him up. If he clears him, then—"

"I can't even go out with a boring as fuck college instructor without a lecture?" I shriek, throwing my hands in the air. "Goddammit! See? This"— I wave my finger to encompass his dick-mode stance—"is why I'm sticking to *nice* guys from now on. No more dicks for me."

Oh god, that's truer than I intended.

So I scream again. Because I'm angry, confused, and so goddamn sick of feeling more for this asshole in front of me than any of the guys I've tried to convince myself are perfect for me.

The other guys might not make my heart flutter in unexpected ways, or challenge me, or make me feel oddly safe, but they also don't fill me with unfettered rage.

"I'm leaving. And I'm taking my bacon double cheeseburger sliders with me."

His mouth tightens, but he doesn't say a word. He also doesn't move out of my way. I'm trapped in the kitchen with an unreasonable, overprotective lunatic.

Fine.

I slip off my backpack and take out the dish of sliders. His gaze narrows.

After carefully removing one, I hold it up, grease slipping through my fingers. He watches, his gaze sharpening in a way that says *Don't you fucking dare.*

I slap the sloppy, cheesy mess onto the bare counter. As I gleefully recall the list of pet peeves Jax was kind enough to share, I yank open the cutlery drawer and grab a knife. His jaw tightens when I cut the burger in half. Cutting a burger *and* not using a cutting board is two peeves in one.

"That's not bothering me." *Pfft!* Liar. "What else you got, shortcake?"

I raise the knife to my mouth and lick it clean.

The muscle in his temple jumps. Excellent, hit a nerve.

I take a bite of the slider, moaning obscenely and chewing with gusto. Jensen's practically vibrating, and he crosses his arms to contain himself.

Ready to eat every bite in front of him, I bring the burger to my mouth again. The bun shifts and the beef slips out, landing with a *squelch* on the hardwood floor.

Frozen in place, I stare down at the burger patty. When I look up at Jensen, I press my lips together to hide my amusement at the shock and devastation on his face.

His throat works as he swallows roughly.

With an eat-shit grin, I drop the rest.

A feral growl comes from him as he rushes at me.

I yelp and dart away, but he snags me around the waist almost immediately.

He lifts me onto the counter.

"Jensen! Your shoulder!" I shout.

He ignores that reminder, bracing his hands on the granite counter on either side of my hips. Almost as if he's searching for something, he tips his upper body forward, getting in my face.

"Let me down. I'm leaving. And I'm going to take the rest of your food to Jaxon." I could never eat it all and can't bring myself to throw it away. Someone should get to eat those amazing sliders. Plus, giving the food meant for Jensen to his brother is likely just as traumatic for him.

"Don't use my brother against me," he says, voice rough. "You won't like the consequences."

"Then don't attack my personal life."

"Only if you start being more responsible with your personal life."

He's so close I can see the specks of copper in his irises.

Leveling him with a look as intense as the one he's throwing at me, I ask, "How much do you know about the women you date before you fuck them? How often are *you* on dating sites and apps? Ever gone home with someone you just met?" I hurl the questions at him, not bothering to pause between. "Do you tell *them* to be more responsible?"

His shoulders heave with an aggravated breath. The rich

warmth of his heated gaze flickers away before returning to me. "No," he admits.

I tilt my head. "That's some hypocritical bullshit."

"I don't care about them," he answers between clenched teeth. "I care about *you*."

He's mere inches from my face, his eyes searching mine. A shocked puff of air leaves my lips, drawing his gaze down to my mouth.

More layers of my safety net fall away.

"You don't even like me," I murmur through numb lips.

He grunts out a wry laugh. "That would have made this so much fucking easier," he grumbles.

Stepping even further into my space, he nudges my legs apart. I fall back in surprise, knocking my head on the cabinets behind me.

He tangles one hand in my hair. Tingles rush from my scalp to my neck, all the way down my spine.

The breath seizes in my lungs as I press a hand to my jittery stomach. With a rough swallow, my gaze falls to the teeth he's sinking into his full bottom lip.

Oh god.

I think he's going to—

"Fuck it."

He swoops down, crushing his mouth to mine. His tongue slides along my lips, demanding entrance. And I open to him.

My hands desperately grasp at the counter, trying to find purchase on something, anything, for stability as my brain melts and my body soars.

His kisses are rough, needy. Mentally catching up, I tilt my head and grip the sleeves of his t-shirt. Clinging when I should push him away. I suck the plump bottom lip that I missed out on at the hockey game with that chaste brush of his lips against mine.

I moan against his lips, loving the taste of him. Like dark mint chocolate. Like indulging in decadence after months of dieting.

And as his tongue tangles with mine, I forget I *am* supposed to be on a diet. I'm not supposed to be kissing assholes.

But then an arm swoops under my ass and pulls me to the edge of the counter. Eagerly, my legs lock around him. He bends further and our centers line up. His hardness grinds into my seam. Pressure builds, burns through my veins, ripples through my quivering muscles.

I drop my head back. God, I want this. If he stops touching me, if he's doing this to prove a point, I might actually push him down a few stairs. On purpose this time.

His lips skim and suck along my exposed neck. He lays open-mouthed kisses against the sensitive flesh before he takes my chin and turns it to the side. I'm panting, confused, and needy.

Jensen nips at the skin below my jaw, and I whimper, my eyes rolling up.

"I love your noises. Let me hear you, beautiful."

My pussy clenches. I'm about to fuck Jensen Vaughn, and I really, *really* shouldn't.

How did we go from yelling at each other to fucking on his kitchen counter?

But then his lips find my collarbone and that question becomes less important. And it's forgotten completely once his hands skim under my top, caressing the sides of my breasts through my thin bralette.

I release my grip on his shirt and shove my hands through the soft, subtle waves of his mahogany hair. How is his hair so amazing? I bet he doesn't even use conditioner. Tugging at it, I move him back up to my mouth. The scruff he's grown scrapes against my mouth and chin. I relish every abrasion and beg for more.

Barely able to keep one thought going at a time, my hands flutter over him, wanting everything. All of him, all at once. I let my hands smooth down over his wide shoulders and curve over his pecs, earning me a throaty moan. Lower and lower my hands travel, dipping over the bumps of his abs until they get to the top of his sweatpants.

Slipping beneath the band, I find warm, bare skin. No underwear. My breath pulls from his while his mouth consumes mine. I'm drenched and swollen, already imagining him slipping inside me.

I wrap a hand around his shaft and groan. Oh god, maybe not. He's silky smooth but so fucking thick. I stroke him a couple of times, feeling him harden to steel beneath my grip. He'd fill me right up. Completely. *Perfectly.*

My legs clamp around his waist, needing him inside me. I pick up the pace, stroking more wildly, but a wave of nerves has me loosening my grip, my movements faltering.

I chase the mouth that lifts off mine to find him staring down at me, the searing heat of his hand wrapping around my wrist.

"Touch me. Feel what you do to me." His voice is a husky rasp, somewhere between a whisper and a groan.

His other hand comes up to grip the front of my throat. The pressure is assertive, commanding, but not suffocating. Gentle and rough. Fierce and sweet.

My pulse thrums against his palm in a frantic beat.

Lips meet mine once more. After a few more curious strokes, I remove my hand and push at his sweatpants. A rumble vibrates through his chest as he pulls me down from the counter.

With his mouth still attached to mine, his hands search for the top of my leggings, ripping them down seconds before his fingers find my soaking wet slit. His hand comes back up to my throat, holding me steady while fingering me.

He hooks my knee over his arm, opening me up. Back arching, hips pumping in a frenzied rhythm, I cry out for more. His fingers enter me, hooking to rub with deep strokes along the sensitive spot most men can't seem to figure out.

Yes, yes, yes!

I break away with a moan, panting and looking down at where his hand is playing with me. I trail my fingers down his arms, watching.

"Pretty fucking pussy," he grunts out. "So wet for me."

A shockwave of hot, crippling pleasure blasts through me. I pulse around him, muttering incoherent stuff about his magic fingers and addictive lips. Bone-melting hormones have flooded my system, and spasms wrack my body as I cling to him, riding out my release.

His fingers slip from me, and I whine.

I climb him.

I literally climb him like a tree.

Forgetting about his leg, his shoulder.

He groans, hooking an arm under my ass and pivoting. He hops—fucking hops—a few feet over. Before I can come to my senses or utter a single warning about his injuries, he plasters me against the fridge.

"Hold on tight, shortcake," he demands.

He lowers me down so his dick is sliding against my entrance.

"Shut up and get inside me, hotshot."

With a devastating grin that nearly makes me come again, he eases the tip of his cock into my wet heat. I wiggle and grind, pushing down, getting him to fit. But he's holding me still, waiting.

He blows out a breath against my neck. "Fuck," he mutters. "Hold still. Your pussy is trying to kill me."

A laugh bursts from my lips right before I grab the back of his head and kiss the hell out of him. I lick, plunge, suck. Needing him to jump off the ledge with me. Because if I stop to think, if I pause and let myself feel anything but this, everything changes.

His hips shoot forward, filling me. He groans, and I gasp. His cock drags back out achingly slow. He's stretching me and it's so much, too much. Then he pistons back inside, and I see stars. I shift into a grind, asking for more while taking it slow.

With a shaky exhale, his head drops back, hips pumping. To keep some of my weight off of him, I move my hands up to grip the top of the fridge, legs still locked around his hips.

A low moan leaves him, but his jaw locks as he brings his gaze to mine. "I'm too close. Play with your clit, Grace," he demands roughly, slowing his pace. "I need to feel you come."

Clenching around him, flutters of my release swooping down on me, I let one hand drop between us. He tracks the movement, and excitement ignites in my belly.

I circle my clit with soft strokes, speeding up at the sounds of grunts and pants coming from the burly, domineering man wanting to feel my core milking him. He's holding off on his release so he can feel me drench him, wring every drop of pleasure out of him.

"That's it," he whispers. "Good girl. So fucking good."

Heat flushes through my chest at his praise, and I detonate with a keening moan. "Jensen..."

He stiffens and his voice joins mine as he releases inside me. The warmth of his breath against my neck makes me shiver. His muscles twitch involuntarily as he relaxes into me. Within moments, his grip loosens and he slips out of me, gently sliding me down the fridge.

I unwind my legs from around him and place my feet on the cool tile beneath us. His breath is still coming in hard pants and my heart is still racing.

I get an eyeful of his dick before he pulls up the sweats he didn't fully remove. It's still glistening from our combined releases. Legs wobbling, I slap my hands against the fridge in an attempt to steady myself.

The silence surrounds us like a physical presence, thick and stifling.

One of us needs to say something.

And I'm afraid if it's me, I'll fuck it up. Because that was the best sex of my life, and he was working without full use of all his limbs. Against a fridge. Still mostly dressed.

"Stop thinking so damn hard, Grace."

I gape at him. *That's* the first thing he says?

"You fucked all rational thought from my brain. Give me a damn minute, Vaughn."

"Back to 'Vaughn' even after I shot you full of my cum, huh? Guess it's better than 'Jerksen.'"

We didn't use a condom.

"Shit," I whisper.

I've never had sex without a condom. No matter what excuses guys have thrown out or assurances they've given.

What the hell is wrong with me?

Stupid. So fucking stupid, Gracie.

Not only am I horny for assholes who are only good for making me crazy, but apparently, I now let them come inside me.

Awesome. I've officially leveled up.

I scramble for my pants while he leans against the island in front of me.

Fuck.

"We should talk about this," he says, sounding calmer than he should.

"Not today, we shouldn't," I tell him, my voice hoarse.

"Then when?"

I scoop my backpack off the floor and leave the food on the counter. I can't even look at it right now.

"I don't know," I admit. "That wasn't some innocent flirtation, a taunting touch, or a brief, spontaneous kiss. That," —I point behind me— "was so much more." It was wrong, but felt *so* right.

Swallowing down the panic, I snatch my pants off the ground. "Oh god, I've lost my mind."

A noisy exhale huffs out of his flared nostrils. "You're freaking out."

Of course I am! I'm spiraling into a pit of self-loathing and regret.

"There are so many reasons this shouldn't have happened, Jensen." I groan, covering my face. "I'm your physical therapist."

The many expressions that were flitting over his face suddenly shut down. "What do you want to do?"

At his terse tone, my chest pinches with something much deeper than regret. I eye the door, needing to escape. Needing to think.

"You want to pretend this didn't happen," he guesses. "Again."

I don't respond. There's no need.

I pick up his crutch from the floor and extend it toward him. "I should go." My voice is barely above a whisper. "You good with rescheduling your session to Thursday? Same time."

He takes the crutch, his face still blank. After a few long moments, he answers, "Yeah. Thursday works."

I slip out of his house, shutting him out as I close the door behind me.

"You did what?" Dani shrieks after a coughing fit.

I could have waited to tell her until she put down her hot chocolate, but I couldn't keep it in any longer.

The Kozy Kitchen diner provides the comfort foods I was craving and slightly more privacy than we'd get at her bakery or Rocky's midday, but Dani's screeching is like a flashing, neon "juicy gossip" sign.

After a quick check to make sure the other tables aren't eavesdropping, I whisper the confession again, "I fucked Jensen."

Her eyes widen and a surprised laugh shoots from her mouth before she's able to cover it.

"And it was *good*, Dani."

A flush heats my chest and cheeks, even though I've locked those memories down and refuse to think about how his dick felt oh-so-much better than I imagined. Or that the way he touched me was unexpected and addictive. That I felt cheated by how quick it was, and his lack of nudity.

"No way." Her eyes dart around and then come back to me, widening enthusiastically. "When? Wait…how good?"

"A few days ago." I close my eyes and groan. "And really, *really* good."

I'm not sure why that's so upsetting. I got two orgasms out of it and satisfied the niggling curiosity I've smothered for years.

"So, like hate sex?"

I'm sure that's how Jensen would explain it, but I've never had hate sex. Never understood it.

"Maybe?"

"You don't know what kind of sex it was?"

"It's not that simple. What kind of sex did you and Declan have your first time in the supply closet?" I ask, my tone haughty.

Not liking that question when it's pointed her way, she scrunches her nose at me. He's fourteen years her senior and the fire department couldn't afford anymore scandals after people exposed our former chief's pretty shitty behavior. So, those two danced around each other for a while, with Dec keeping Dani at arm's length until last winter when he found out about her sexy holiday wish list.

"You two never hated each other. Jensen and I on the other hand..."

She stirs her hot chocolate and takes a sip. "Hate sex can still mean there's something about the other person you find enticing. Even if it's just on a physical level."

I consider that while pushing the barely touched fries around on my plate. "True. Physical attraction isn't solely determined by your feelings about them as a person."

Yes. Hate sex.

One-and-done hate sex.

Relief washes over me and the plate of food I was too distressed to enjoy earlier suddenly holds a lot more appeal again. I pick up a fry, douse it in ketchup and shove it in my mouth.

"Right." Her voice exudes confidence, then softens as she asks, "So, if you found someone attractive and then got to know them and hated them, would you still be attracted to him? You'd still want to get naked with him?"

"Nope," I quickly answer before shoving in another fry. "If I hated someone, they would be vile to me."

My eyes fly up to meet Dani's.

Oh fuck.

She grins, and both her hands come up to slap over her mouth. She gives a little head shake, assuring me she won't say it out loud.

I glare, holding up a finger. "*No. I—*"

"Who's vile?" Harper asks, dropping into the booth with us. "Also, I'm offended you two didn't want to come to the bar. Do I not pour you enough free booze?"

"Sadly, we both have to go back to work," Dani tells her. "And because you're fifteen minutes late, you missed the start. And it's *big*. Or I think it was. Gracie? Was it *big*?"

I snort at Dani's obvious taunt, sliding over so Harper can get settled into the booth.

"I've only got thirty minutes left on my break before I have to head back," she says, checking her phone. "Come on, you both know I need this. Tell me everything."

"I thought you hated gossip," I remind her.

"Yes, I do. But this isn't gossip. It's personal life updates. And I can almost guarantee yours is more interesting than mine."

"Right, because finding out your sister is stripping to pay off the thugs who beat the shit out of her boyfriend is boring?" I ask, hoping to distract for a while longer.

"The mess Nova's made for herself—and subsequently me— might be interesting, but not in a good way. Give me something else to think about."

I debate for a moment. Jensen's sister, Olivia, is one of her best friends. And while she's the most trustworthy person I know, I don't want to put her in an uncomfortable position.

"You can't tell anyone. Even Liv. Or um, *especially* Liv. You okay with that?"

Her brows jump, and then her mouth forms a neat circle. She nods solemnly.

When I tell her, she turns into some kind of "woo girl" and gets us shushed by no less than three tables. Apparently, she'd called this months ago.

Nothing slips by Harper. It's eerily impressive how she can read body language and pick up on things others overlook.

I prop my elbows on the table and cup my face in my palms. "Tell me not to do it again," I practically beg. "I'm on a jerk-free diet. Cinnamon-roll type guys only. Because I'm the girl who always thinks there's a gooey sweet center to these gruff men and then finds only stale raisins and trickery."

Is it asking too much to find a good, kind man who's got a rough exterior? One who works with his hands, insists you walk on the inside of the sidewalk, doesn't let anyone talk shit to or about you, and picks you up when you stumble?

A dreamy sigh leaves my lips as the girls stare at me. "I mean, there're all kinds of men out there who aren't assholes. I don't have to find the perfect one in the wild or anything. I'm willing to teach him."

Dani reaches across the table, placing her hand over mine. "Jensen's a good guy, Gracie. Maybe there's something there worth exploring." She grins. "Plus, Declan and Jensen would *hate* double dating. So that might be kind of fun."

I laugh. "There's no dating, double or otherwise. There's no *anything*."

"Wait, can you even date a patient?" Harper asks.

At my grimace, she slumps against the back of the booth seat.

"Shit," she says. "Do you need a bright side?" The woman searches for the bright side of most everything, and more often than not, it's what I need. When I was younger, the negative self-talk would take over. The positive mindset shift pushes me to challenge myself and lets nothing stop me from doing the things I want. Not even me. But sometimes my brand of optimism is the kind that pushes me harder, not necessarily one that is emotionally comforting.

With a deep inhale, I say, "Give it to me, Harp."

She tilts her head. "Well, it sounds like you got dicked real good. And there are some people in this diner—in this world—who haven't had sex in years." Dani and I lock eyes, silently agreeing to move forward with our plans to set Harper up because damn, her sunshine seems to have a nun-like dark cloud hovering in front of it.

"Plus, this might actually improve your relationship with the surly Vaughn twin," she adds.

Pfft. Doubtful. It'll just be a thousand times more awkward now.

I give her a stiff smile.

"Sorry. Between Nova's poor taste in men, Ava's troubles at school, and our rental house turning out to be a lemon, finding the positives has been a little harder." She lets out a long breath. "Want me to give that another crack?"

I hold up a hand. "All good. Still valid points." Hooking an arm around her shoulder, I draw her into me. She's almost as short as I am, so it's not much of a reach. "You know, I might have thought of a bright side all on my own."

With a wink, I snatch her phone and download a dating app. "I get to focus on finding you a man and ignore my mess of a sex life."

Her nose wrinkles, and she shakes her head at me. But a moment later, she tilts her head, eyebrows raised. "Actually, if you could make him a handyman…"

Dani's eyes widen before she softly squeals. "I know you two are dealing with a lot right now, but I feel good about this new direction."

"This new direction being getting laid?" I ask.

"Exactly."

CHAPTER
TWENTY

Quiet surrounds me. The kind of serenity I seek after long days, disturbing rescue scenes, or socializing far past my limit. Especially this year. All I've wanted is to disconnect and focus on the shit that matters to me.

But today, the quiet isn't giving me what I need.

I'm on my second cup of coffee, and I've already checked in with Declan. Soon, I'll be heading into the station to work light-duty shifts, so we've been chatting in the mornings and he updates me on station and town happenings.

Today's brief was run-of-the-mill. Apparently, someone needed rescuing from the Lark Pass lookout point after treeing themselves. Not as uncommon as some may think.

People reported seeing a pack of coyotes or wolves on Main Street. Turns out it was two dogs who were off leash, enthusiastically enjoying their freedom. They eventually found them playing in the Town Center fountain.

And Mr. Abernathy, a retired teacher—my former math teacher—was taken in again because he smoked too much pot and thought he had an alien growing inside of him. Surprise! It was gas.

Feeling more grounded in knowing nothing has changed, I spent the last couple of hours working on anything and everything Declan allows me to do from my dining room table.

Consequently, the crew's schedule is complete until the end of summer. I've set up a trip to the elementary school, organized some media coverage—including *The Vine*—for our yearly open house, talked to the Fire Commissioner, and ripped out the flooring in my main bathroom.

That last one wasn't work-related, but it needed to be done, and I had put it off for long enough.

That reminds me, I need to replace some planks on Mom's deck.

The sound of a motorcycle coming up my drive has me reaching for my coffee mug. I pour a second cup and lean against the island, waiting for yet another visitor to barge into my house. And I'm not as irritated by it. Maybe because I know I've been insufferable for far too long—since before my fall. Hell, probably since before Erika left me. Trying to be everything for someone who doesn't want you is fucking exhausting. And depressing as shit.

And Grace doesn't want you either—she wants a nice guy.

Fuck. Those were the kinds of thoughts I was supposed to avoid today.

Jaxon checks the knob to see if it's locked before using his key.

He throws the door open and walks inside with a wave. Holding his helmet against his side, he eyes me. "You look like crap. What's up?"

I take another gulp of my coffee and extend his mug out to him. "I'm good. Keeping busy."

Since I'm not interested in dwelling on shit I have no control over, I put my coffee down and gather the old flooring pieces. With my crutch tucked under one arm, I walk past him to the front deck.

"New project, huh?" he asks, trailing behind me.

"Old project. Just finally getting to it."

"Ah." He toes the scrap pile, grimacing as it topples over.

I shake my head at him. "You gonna pry now or later?"

"I said nothing, bro." He holds up his hand.

Yeah, sure.

He heads back into the house, shouting, "Coffee's not going to do it. I'm grabbing a beer. You want one?"

"It's not even noon," I tell him with a half smirk.

"It's my day off. And Friday."

Fair enough. I grab the boxes of vinyl plank and carry it into the house on my good shoulder.

Muffled moans reach my unsuspecting ears. Jax eats like he's auditioning for porn.

"Who made this?" he mutters around a mouthful of food.

He better fucking not be eating the layered dip Grace brought over the other day for our session. It was our only session since I fucked her against my fridge, and it was torturous. Long pauses, minimal touching, and enough space between us to park a truck. She made it clear she didn't want to talk, that she wanted to forget what happened. That I snapped and took what I'd been wanting since the moment I met her.

I wanted to go back to that moment and take back everything I said, get to know her instead of intentionally pissing her off and pushing her away. I wanted to fix it. It's what I do everyday on the job. I'm sent to a problem or crisis, and I fix it.

But I can't fix this. Because Grace doesn't want me to. She's my physical therapist. And I'm not the kind of man she wants to be with.

So yeah, that seven-layer dip is the only good thing I've got right now.

And I absolutely will *not* share.

I clomp over to the kitchen and catch my brother shoveling

another heaping chip into his greedy gob. "Put that the fuck back!" Before he can take more, I pick up an empty water bottle and launch it at him, nailing him between the shoulder blades.

"Ouch. Shit. Put a label on it if it's not meant for sharing."

His sneaky-ass grin tells me he knows what he's doing.

"It's *my* fridge. Assume everything has my name on it."

His head dips back into my fridge to return the leftovers I plan to devour for a pre-physical therapy snack today.

"You touch the chocolate pudding mom made and I'll end you," I threaten as he scours the refrigerator for food.

The asshole laughs as he backs away with a beer, letting the door swing closed.

I sidle up to the large, handcrafted wooden table and set myself down with a groan. From here, I have the perfect view of the place I lost my goddamn mind and fucked Gracie. There's always been something about her that gets under my skin, and that something has since grown into a needy fire I can't extinguish.

She wants to pretend like it never happened. As if I could forget the feel of her pussy clamped around my dick. Forget the throaty sound of her coming or the memory of her juicy fucking ass in my arms. As if her smell, the feel of her hands on me, doesn't make my cock twitch.

The only regret I have about the whole damn thing is agreeing to pretend nothing happened.

"Got two new recruits signed up today," Jax says before cracking open his beer. "And people have been asking what the new start-up date is."

Fuck. I return to work in less than a week, and in the process of keeping myself focused on work—not *her*—I forgot about the project that represents three years of certification, planning, and county-wide recognition. That's how fucking distracted I am.

And Jaxon knows how I operate better than anyone, which is

why he's checking where I'm at mentally and pushing. Because I don't deal well with failure, and I've done a fuckton of failing lately. He knows how much this means to me. To him, not picking a date means I might have given up on the program...or myself.

"Working on it. Should have a new date and details out this week."

"Good," he says, sitting down next to me and handing me a beer. "Chief will be glad to hear it. And I'll also win the pool, so thanks for that, buddy."

"Pool?" I ask, knowing I shouldn't.

"Guys made a betting pool on how long before you knocked off the secluded-recovery bullshit and came back to the station with all your militant, rule-following swagger. It's weird without you there."

"I don't know if they would have wanted me there the first few weeks. Not sure if you noticed, but I was a whiny, angry bastard."

He claps me on my left shoulder. "Nah. Didn't notice much of a difference." We grin at each other, and my brother takes another swig of his beer.

"Heard the C shift crew is heading to The Hole this weekend for drinks. You going to meet up with them?"

Hadn't given it much thought. Declan has been over a few times in the last couple of weeks to check on me and to hand over my work laptop so I can at least keep up with the admin duties.

"Nah. I still can't drive and it's Olympian Night at The Hole." I shake my head and my brother laughs.

Lately I've been feeling guilty about my lack of effort in hanging out with him, into going out at all. Last year, I poured all of my energy into work and home renovations—shit that's easy, that I'm good at.

Of the people I let see how fucked up I was over Erika, I took it out the worst on Jaxon. Not with words, and not on purpose, but our relationship still suffered despite insisting I'd never let her come between us.

Truth is, Jaxon is everything I'll never be—fun, charming, social—and I let that comparison eat at me. I didn't let Erika come between us, but in some ways, I let what she said the night of our rehearsal dinner taint our relationship. And I need to fix that.

"I was hoping you wouldn't remember that. You know, if you participated you might have more fun." He eyes my leg. "Though I don't think Gracie would approve of you fucking up your recovery over a game of beer pong or dizzy bat."

With a snort, I slump back into my chair. She'd storm in there and throw a fit, maybe even drag me out—or try to. Then convince the guys to do her dirty work. My brother would take me on if Grace was the one asking. Not that I'd fight to stay. Hanging with the guys is a good time, but I don't need to be there to the bitter end. I prefer to slide in, grab some grub, a beer, shoot the shit a bit and then Irish goodbye the hell out of there.

Eyes on my beer, I keep my voice level as I put forward a suggestion I've been mulling over for the past two weeks.

"Maybe we could see if the guys want to come here for some drinks on a weekend we're all off? We could have a fire in the pit, maybe even allow you to bring your guitar out. If you promise not to sing." His eyes light up as he shouts so loud birds scatter from the trees near the porch. "I'll take that as a yes."

"Oh, Jenny, that's a hell yes. I've been waiting for the day you pulled your head out of your ass and started living again." He points at me. "And putting me in charge of this party—"

"It's not a party and you're not in charge."

He continues like I didn't speak. "...is smart since you will not want to plan it. You'll be busy with returning to work and your physical therapy, which is helping get you back to your usual hulking, bossy self. You look much less intimidating with crutches."

This one's on me. I decided to reconnect, attempt a wholesome, brotherly moment. I should have expected this.

But I owe him for putting up with me and being one of the few who knew I needed time to process alone. And even though he never left me truly alone, he let me deal with shit at my pace.

He mutters something as he types away on his phone.

"Not too many people, Jax."

He waves me off. "Anders is inviting some of the ER staff. Let me know if you want to invite anyone other than the crew."

I shake my head.

"Alright. I'll keep it under fifty people." *Fifty?* "Ha! Your eye twitched. It'll be fine. I'll take it easy on you, given this is your first large gathering since…" He cringes and I know he was going to say *your wedding*. Instead, he asks, "You sure you don't want to invite anyone else?"

"Like who? I'm sure you're already inviting everyone I know."

"What about Gracie?"

"She wouldn't come," I tell him, hoping my tone carries the finality I'm intending.

"I suspect she *would* come." His grin mocks me, and my gaze narrows. "If I see her before the party, I'll convince her to come out."

"Have you seen her?" I blurt out.

"What's that information worth to you?" he asks, leaning back in his chair.

"Look, she left here angry the other day. Things have been tense. I want to make sure she's good."

"Three dip scoops," he demands.

Cocky little shit knows he's got enough leverage to go after my food.

"Two."

"Deal." He rubs his hands together and struts over to the fridge.

"Answer my question first."

"I'll answer with a mouthful of your food, and you won't say a damn thing about it."

The calming breath I take as he brings the food to the table does fuck all. My eye twitches as I watch him eat the food Grace made for *me*.

"I've seen her out a bit. Twice with Dani and Dec, then at Rocky's, sitting at the bar and talking to Harper. Her parents were in town last weekend. Dad's a big dude, the mom's tiny like Gracie. Her bowling league lost another game, so all the ladies got drunk. When they were kicked out of the bowling alley, they moved to lawn bowling on Brody's lawn."

He chuffs with a wry grin, stuffing more chips into his face. "He wasn't home, but Harper let everyone into her place next door when Brody showed up. Gracie accidentally fell into our brother and thought he was going to arrest her for assaulting a police officer. Then Ava woke up, came outside, and told Brody off, saying he can't arrest her friends. It was a whole thing." He inhales another ridiculously huge bite, ignoring my death glare. "I wasn't called out, but it was in *The Vine*. Oh, and she had a date last week." Before I notice and swipe it back, he pilfers my beer and guzzles half of it. "That's what you're really asking me about, right?"

I give him nothing. Not even a blink.

When he doesn't get the reaction he wants, the one he knows I'm burying, he continues.

"Didn't go well, from what I could tell." He was there? Why didn't he tell me?

Why would he? She's not yours.

"Guy was the buttoned-up kind, looked like a snooze-fest. But Grace looked hot as fuck." I pounce, punching him straight in the chest. Chips go flying, the rest of my beer spills across the table, and Jaxon...laughs.

"You don't get to talk about her like that. And you sure as shit don't get to call her Grace." He grins at me, holding up his hands. "She's off-limits, got it?"

The teasing smirk falls.

"I'm just fucking around," he says, his tone instantly sobering. My jaw tightens, fists clenching as I push away, falling back into my chair. "Jen, you know I'd never—"

"I know," I tell him, dropping my gaze to my fists and willing them to relax.

He gets up to put the food away, and my attention strays.

The station, my family, the community, the legacy my dad left. Grace, Grace on a date, Grace's ass. My ankle, my shoulder, training, therapy. Grace sitting on my face.

Fuck.

"Oh, hey," he calls, leaning against the fridge. "One other Gracie update you should know." I lift my chin, waiting for him to spit it out. "There's a barely visible, irrefutably awesome ass print on your fridge,"—he points to the stainless steel—"and I'm pretty sure it belongs to your pint-sized PT girl." He snaps his fingers and points at me. "Probably already knew that one though?"

My head swivels to the fridge, but I can't see shit from this angle.

"Mom's coming later today, so you might want to, you know...remove the flashing 'we fucked here' sign you two left."

"Jax." That's all I say because he'll know if I lie to him, and I can't risk saying anything else.

"I'm taking the cookies as a thank you for keeping that shit a secret. Love you, bro. Don't do anything stupid. And maybe try to get out of the house a little before the party. The thrilling baseboard replacement project you've got on the docket for this month can wait until you're all healed up." With a wink, he adds, "And I hope Gracie comes again for you."

It takes three quick strides to get within swinging distance of him. He holds a hand up in defense, but his stance tells me he's ready in case I decide to give him the ass kicking he deserves.

He backs up, ducking behind the door. "Whoa, whoa! I meant I hope she keeps coming over here for your sessions."

"No, you didn't."

Dropping the act, he bellows a laugh. "No, I really didn't."

One lunging step in his direction is enough for the idiot to take the hint and fuck off. With a slam of the door, he's gone. I lock it behind him with a resounding clunk of the deadbolt. Won't actually keep anyone out, but it makes me feel like I've tried.

I swipe my laptop from the dining table and take it to the couch to get comfortable, leg propped up on the coffee table.

Working will get me out of this funk, put my focus back where it belongs. It will fix this feeling inside me—the quiet discontent. Once I get back to work, get back to what I do best, things will turn around.

So I'll choose a date.

A date when I'll be back and able to run training. That's all I need.

Two months from today. There. Done.

I send an email with updates and details.

Two months of physical therapy and light duty.

Two months of seeing Grace and not fucking her.

Two months until I can go back to my regular routine. Back to my life before Grace barged into it. Hell, even before Erika mistakenly set her sights on me.

I wait for the restlessness to ease, for the sense of accomplishment and fulfillment to seep in.

When that doesn't work, I haul my ass over for another workout. Sweating and getting stronger at least gets me a little closer to the life I was supposed to have.

Because having Grace here, in my house is more torturous than I expected. Part of me wants her to stay, wants her here all the time. But I'm not what she wants. And believing it could be different this time, that I won't repeat the mistakes of my past, undoubtedly makes me an idiot.

TWENTY-ONE

GRACIE

Last night—at 11:52 p.m.—I finally gathered the courage to send a long overdue text message. I'd been holding off, at first forgetting, then stalling. Because Jensen and I were supposed to pretend we didn't have sex. Which makes the "were we both safe?" talk infinitely more awkward.

Especially if you've made a complete ass of yourself by text-bombing him repeatedly and incoherently, to where you will cringe if you hear the words "proof" or stupid" again, for the rest of your life.

Hi.

I know we decided to act as if certain "events" never happened, but we still need to be responsible.

I'm on birth control. Clean. All that stuff. In case you were wondering after the other day.

I can get you proof.

That sounded weird. I've never had to have this talk. Unprotected sex is NOT something I do. Ever.

> Being around you has made me stupider.

> That's an actual word. I looked it up, so don't give me any shit about it.

And he left me on "read."

I need to stop torturing myself by re-reading those messages, so I close out of the app and place my phone face down on the table.

I take a sip of my London fog and try to get back to my book. Having a weekday off every other week used to be a little boring, since no one else has a random Tuesday off. But I've settled into appreciating my "me time."

Not today, though, because in a few hours, I've got a session with Jensen. After mind-blowing, whimper-inducing, maybe-hate sex and a string of remarkably awkward text messages. I try telling myself that it was going to be awkward either way, and that having the are-we-both-safe-and-clean chat would not go any better in person.

He has a doctor's appointment this afternoon and will probably have his cast replaced with a walking boot. It should be an exciting time. My more eager patients often can't wait to get into more rigorous training exercises, move around easier, feel closer to freedom. But my stomach is a mess, nerves jittering uncontrollably.

Jensen's been compliant about pretending we didn't have sex, and that might be throwing me off even more. Maybe he regrets it. Or didn't enjoy it as much as I did. I know he came because his release became a continual presence between my thighs for a full day afterward—even after showering. Twice.

And it was hot. I should have freaked out, my stomach churning with regret. Instead, it turned me on in unexpected ways. After each time I had to clean myself up, I'd see the lusty flush on my skin in the mirror, point an accusatory finger at my reflection and mouth, "You're disgusting. Stop."

My phone vibrates against the patio table where I'm trying to soak in a little sun. I flip it over and drop the phone when I see who it is.

I'm not supposed to go over there for hours yet.

What if he needs help? Had an emergency? Is canceling?

What if he just wants to talk to you?

I pick up my phone and quickly scan his messages.

JERKSEN:

I'm clean.

You off today?

Need a favor.

That's it?

I roll my eyes before responding.

Well, hello stranger.

Why yes, I am off today. Thank you for asking if I'm enjoying my day off.

I'm taking in this beautiful spring weather with a cup of tea and a book over at Lit Latte's rooftop patio.

Is this how you prefer texting?

Every thought in a separate line?

If this is another one of those "Let's see if this annoys Jensen" things—the answer is yes.

Good to know. I wasn't doing it on purpose before, but now…

Jeannette helped me choose a new urban fantasy featuring a powerful gender shift where women rule over men.

> Picked up a few interesting conditioning ideas for our session later today.

> I think we'll focus on mobility and MANNERS.

> I'm not interested in your dominatrix books. You can fantasize about torturing men on your own time.

> It IS my own time, asswipe.

See, we can be normal. We can go back to snipping at each other and act like he didn't make me come so hard I thought my lady bits blew up.

> You going to help me or not?

He's fucking with my good day and making me think about things I promised myself I wouldn't. I should have known his response to my texts would only lead to frustration.

I *needed* the rest of "me time" to get my head on straight.

It's weird he's asking for my help though.

> Depends on what you need, hotshot.

> My doctor's appointment is in thirty minutes. My sister was supposed to come with me, but she had to bail. One of her patients went into labor.

> So, you want me to come with you? I don't do patient handholding.

But apparently fucking them is fine?

I groan, anticipating his scathing response.

> I don't need you to hold anything, shortcake.
> Just drive me there.

Oh, hell. Nope.

After a few minutes of hoping he finds someone else while waiting for me to respond, the three dots pop back up.

You're ghosting me? Really?

My cast is on the right leg, Grace. If I could drive myself, I would.

Brody and Jaxon are on shift. Can't get a hold of Dec. And my mom is in Landry for some kind of raunchy book club you'd apparently be really into.

Come on. You've got other friends, right? What about exes? Maybe there's one or two you're still on speaking terms with? Oh! Heather, over at The Hole, would kick her current boytoy out of bed in a heartbeat and chase after you if you gave her the nod. And she drives an old Buick. Tons of room for you in that thing.

I don't want Heather anywhere near Jensen, but I also don't want to admit that I haven't driven since the accident.

Grace.

It doesn't take much to imagine the deep, disapproving rumble with which he usually says my name.

This shouldn't be a big deal. It's a quick drive from his house to the outpatient clinic. I ride my bike there and back multiple times a week, and it would be much easier in a vehicle that's not as susceptible to gravel or potholes.

Okay. But you owe me lunch afterward.

What are you doing? Stop spending time with him. You cannot pretend like his dick didn't hit that spot that makes your legs spasm if you're around said dick all the time.

Oh god. What if I accidentally fuck him again?

Accidentally? You didn't exactly fall on his dick the first time.

To be fair, if anyone were to fall on and/or impale herself on a dick accidentally, it would be me.

Dottie would be so proud.

> Fine. Be here in fifteen minutes.

> And I get to choose what we eat.

> Are you on your way yet?

I sigh and tuck my phone away. I'm ordering dessert too, and I'm getting it to go so he can't swipe any. I've seen him eat off his brother's plates. I bet he eats his date's too.

I bet he eats his dates really good.

It's not a good idea to go to Jensen's house in this state of mind.

I shake those thoughts loose, and remind myself of the asshole who never fails to enrage me, who is an overbearing, contemptuous ass.

"How the fuck did she end up down there? She's lucky to be alive. Christ, that woman is way too fucking much trouble, I can feel it. She's going to be nothing but problems."

That moment after my car accident acts as one of several reminders I recall anytime I let myself think he cares. That a good guy lurks beneath the surface.

But in hindsight, I realize that fixating on his rude comments and attitude was my way of coping. Because that wasn't the worst part.

It was the memories of how the accident felt. The tipping over of the vehicle, being suspended for what felt like hours, the fear, the waiting, the blur of panic and intense anxiety. That's what left me shattered on the inside.

And Jensen wasn't an ass the whole time. That's the

confusing part. He was careful with me. Calm and confident. Gentle. But the moment I was out and on level ground again, he stormed off.

Fire fills my veins as I remind myself why I keep my back up around Jensen.

I no longer waste my time or my heart convincing people to respect and accept me just the way I am. No matter how big their dicks are or how sweet they might be beneath their prickly outer layers.

NERVOUSNESS HAS my body in a state of constant fidgeting. I was practically vibrating while I rode my bike here. I glance over my shoulder to where I leaned my bike on the far side of the garage, almost looking forward to the shit he's going to give me about riding my bike here again.

I knock on the door, wishing for the crunch of gravel that would mean someone else has arrived to take Jensen to his appointment.

No such luck. Instead, the door swings open, and a freshly showered Jensen steps out.

He eyes me warily but says nothing.

We make it down the couple of steps from his veranda and move toward the garage.

"Where's your car?" he asks.

With a smirk, I lead him over to my bike and pat the handlebars. "Hop on!"

There's no way those handlebars will hold the beefy man beside me, and the bell would probably have to be extracted from his ass after, but I *really* want to see him try.

His jaw clenches. "You didn't bring your car?"

I plant my fists on my hips, and answer, "Don't have one."

"What?" he barks, spinning toward me.

I shrug and hope this means he has to call someone else.

Someone further down the call list than you? Unlikely.

"How have you been getting here?" He peers around, head craning until his gaze lands on my bike. "Tell me you don't usually bike here."

He's going to make a thing of this, and I don't have the mental capacity to deal with it today. There are only a couple more months before he's completed physical therapy and returns to work. After that, I'm sure not a single thought of me will cross his mind until I get myself into a mess that requires his services.

"Jaxon was supposed to tell you to stop."

I snort. Oh, he did. Apparently, Jensen thinks I can't be trusted to ride a bike and doesn't want any kind of incident reports or insurance claims to occur on his property.

"Hm. Weird. If only I was the type of woman that listens to over-bearing men who think they can tell me what to do." I tsk. "Shame."

"There's wildlife that roams the mountainside and creeks near my property. Wild boars. Snakes. Badgers. What would you do if you came across one of those?"

I put my hands on my hips. "Pedal my ass off. Sacrifice whatever food I brought for you. Climb a tree." It's not like I haven't thought about it, but it's a fifteen-minute bike ride and all I've seen so far are squirrels, rabbits, and a deer.

He keeps his mouth firmly closed as he growls at me, rubbing at his jaw.

"Catch a ride from now on. I can arrange something with my brothers. Liv might be able to bring you after work sometimes since you're both at the hospital."

I open my mouth to argue, but he holds up a hand, a scowl stressing the sharp edges of his face. "We'll figure something out later. Let's go get this damn cast off."

He puts in the code at his garage panel, and it swiftly opens, revealing his large gray truck. I knew I'd have to drive it, but knowing and coming face-to-grill with the beast are two different things.

Frozen in place, I stare at the monstrosity. It might not seem bigger than any other 4x4 trucks, but I've driven nothing other than a sedan or hatchback. And the one time I did, I wound up upside down on the side of a ravine.

"I don't think I can—"

"It's easy to drive." He pauses and I look over at him. Those dusky eyes assess me with doubt. "Just don't crash it and we'll be good."

My breath hitches.

He throws his crutch in the truck's bed and gets into the passenger seat.

And I can't move.

"Get in, Grace," he calls.

My feet advance, but my mind is stuck in the past. I take a deep breath and pull open the door. As I climb into the truck, I make a vow to myself that fear won't keep me from doing something difficult and intimidating.

Without looking at Jensen, I hold out my hand for the truck keys. If he senses my fear, who knows what he might do with it, so I keep my gaze on the windshield.

He drops the keys into my hand, and I start the truck.

Backing out of the garage is fine. Cruising down the long driveway is also fine.

See? Everything is fine.

But my body is not getting the message. My shoulders have hitched up by my ears, and my back snaps ramrod straight.

"Grace?"

I ignore him, keeping my focus on the upcoming turn. Panic creates a problematic mix of hyperawareness and numbness. A red car comes around the bend, and I feel myself slipping. I pant through the fear, hands shaking and sweat trickling.

"Grace," the deep voice on the outer edge of my awareness is firm. "Grace, pull over."

Hard heat meets my side, but I can't look. I have to keep my eyes on the road.

A massive hand envelopes mine on the steering wheel and I gasp. My eyes dart from the hand, up an arm, and lock onto a handsome face.

Jensen.

Fuck.

I force my gaze back to the pavement, letting out a strangled breath as he shifts the truck into neutral and guides us to the side of the gravel road.

"Foot off the gas, shortcake." I lift my foot, fingers still white-knuckle gripping the steering wheel. "Good girl," he murmurs and a tingling warmth ignites in my chest. "Now, apply the brake nice and easy for me. If you can't, that's okay. We're already slowing down."

His voice is gentle, reassuring, like he knows exactly what to say. The tension in my body dissipates, leaving me feeling drained but safe.

I tap the brake a little too hard, but then gently ease us to a stop.

The man crushed to my side immediately shifts the truck into park and releases a gusty breath. "You did good, Grace." Nearly in tears, I nod, keeping my eyes focused straight ahead, letting his voice soothe me. "You're okay. You're safe."

Fingertips caress the side of my face before moving to my chin. Jensen tips my face up to him, coaxing my eyes up to his. The concern in his eyes, something vibrant and real lingering in those dark irises. This is the way I've always wanted a man to look at me.

Checking to see if what I'm seeing is more than worry, I drop my gaze to his mouth. A hum vibrates through his chest into my arm. Pressing even closer, his fingers slip into my hair, cradling the back of my head. I crane my neck, lifting my face closer, searching, needing something from him I don't dare ask for. But I don't need to ask, he already knows.

His mouth brushes mine with a few soft strokes of his lips as he murmurs, "You're okay. You're safe, Grace."

And that's when I fall off the ledge I've been keeping myself on. Tilting my head, I capture his mouth and move my hands to cup his jaw, holding him to me.

Our kiss is soft, tender—unlike any I've ever had. It's so damn good but also unquestionably intimidating.

Jensen pulls back a few inches and looks down into my kiss-drunk, bewildered face. He places one more light peck against my mouth and one on the tip of my nose.

Silence passes as my heart rate slowly returns to normal.

After clearing my throat, I still only manage a rough whisper. "Sorry. I didn't think I'd...I haven't..."

Jensen shifts beside me, but I don't dare look. I'll end up kissing him again.

What was numb a moment ago now burns with pins and needles in the aftermath of my adrenaline dump. All I can do is close my eyes and hope the tremors don't start.

"You haven't driven since the accident?" he asks.

I nod. "Sorry."

"Don't apologize. I didn't consider that was why you biked or walked so much. I should have pieced that together."

I shake my head. "I didn't need a car to get around, Vaughn. Walking and biking keeps me in shape, and it forces me to keep working on my motor skills."

"What?" he asks.

"Nothing," I blurt, horrified at the near slip. "Biking is good for me." Even if it's annoyingly difficult sometimes.

"You should have told me. I wouldn't have pressured you into driving."

I wrap my arms around myself like I usually do when my body is feeling out of sorts.

"Fuck." His hand wraps around my thigh, right above my knee, giving me a comforting squeeze. "I'm sorry, Grace." With a few swipes of his thumb against my inner thigh, even through leggings, I'm about to melt.

I shake my head, trying to clear it. Shit, I'm a mess.

"It's fine. Give me a minute and I can absolutely do this. I'm not a quitter. This will pass and I'll be fine." I'm not sure how much of that was me convincing him and how much was to convince *me*.

He says nothing, but his other hand goes to the back of my neck, fingers caressing from the top of my shoulder to the bare skin at my neck. It feels so good, I almost tap out.

Beneath his asshole exterior, Jensen Vaughn has the gooey, sweet center I convinced myself was merely a myth.

"No, you're definitely not a quitter, Grace Parker. But everyone needs help sometimes. Even me."

Startled by his confession, my head whips to look at him. He's pulling out his phone, tapping at the screen before holding it to his ear.

"Hey. You guys busy? I need you to come out to Valley Pine Road, about a mile from my place. There's a problem with my truck." He pauses and I can hear someone on the other end. "Yeah, Grace is with me." Another pause. "See you in five."

He hangs up and tucks his phone away, a deep glower tightening his features. I avert my gaze, preparing for the impending lecture I usually get from him, but after a few moments, the cab is still silent. When I peek at him, he's slumped against the backrest of the middle seat he's much too big to occupy. His pensive gaze wanders the ditch next to us while his fingers move back to my neck.

I stare at his chest as he takes a deep inhale. There's something calming about watching him breathe, falling into a natural silence as he broods. Or whatever the hell he's doing right now. My body automatically attempts to match his slower breaths with a steady, deep inhale. Awareness trickles in as his scent invades my senses. That warm, tantalizing musk of whatever soap or grumpy recluse brand of cologne he uses provides a slight distraction from the embarrassment of my unhinged episode.

His thumb pulls at the lip I didn't realize I was chewing on, smoothing over it with two gentle strokes before retreating. "What's going on in that head of yours?" he asks.

My eyes lift and there's an amused expression on his face. Yep. He caught me staring at his chest.

"Do you use body wash?" I ask, diverting for as long as I can.

"Is that your way of asking if I showered today?"

That gets a tiny smile out of me. "No. Believe it or not, that was leading up to a, uh, positive observation about your scent. A compliment-adjacent comment."

The left side of his mouth perks up. "An *almost* compliment? From you, that's high praise."

I blush, hating the effect his pleased smile has on me. The "good girl" he dropped on me earlier was bad enough.

"I smell nice, Grace? And I assume you're surprised by that?"

Keeping my eyes wide in astonishment, I reply, "Ogres live in swamps, yet you smell oddly un-swamp-like."

His tongue pokes at the inside of his cheek, a playful glint in his eyes. He dips his head toward my shoulder, and I can feel his warm breath on my skin as he makes obnoxious sniffing noises.

I roll my eyes, suppressing the shudder that erupts when I feel his nose lightly grazing the spot just above my collarbone.

"Hmm," he says, the deep vibrations causing goosebumps to scatter along my exposed flesh. "You smell pretty damn good yourself." My head snaps over to him. Shit, he can't say nice things to me. "Like...trouble." His rumbled words are so inconceivably different from the other times he's called me trouble. "Tempting, delicious trouble."

A tingle hits my core, causing my thighs to tighten. Warring emotions battle inside me. It's not like he said my scent is one he'll remember every time he slides that monster cock through his fist.

I immediately know I've done a terrible job of keeping the confusion off my face when his eyes come up to meet mine.

I'm about to ask him what that smirk means when a horn blasts.

The Vaughn Fire Department command vehicle pulls in front of us, revealing Declan and Dani.

I need to get out of this truck and come up with a game plan for how I can exist around Jensen Vaughn. I've clearly done a shit job of pretending our mind-destroying sex didn't happen.

Jensen eases out of the truck as Declan strides up. His door is still open as he fills his friend in, and I wait to see if he looks back at me. And if he does, what will I see on his face?

A knock on the window startles me. "Gracie?"

I give Dani a reassuring smile and open the door. Neither of us says a word. I'm usually the talker. It's how I've always distracted or redirected on the days I felt my mask slipping.

She leans in and whispers, "It wasn't truck problems, was it?"

My smile falls as I shake my head.

"Did he make you drive him?" Her face screws up with a short huff. "Never mind. I doubt even Jensen could convince you to do something you didn't want to. Or maybe *especially* Jensen."

I spent years building a backbone strong enough to withstand the jackasses I grew up with. Jensen's been the recipient of the full extent of my unrelenting resolve on many occasions.

"He asked and I agreed. It's fine. I had a tiny freak out, that's all."

Her eyes jump to Jensen.

She's about to mama bear all over the only man I can think of who might be stronger than her boyfriend. Not that Jensen would do anything other than try not to let Dani hurt herself while thumping him.

"Don't," I warn. "He was nice about it."

Her eyes widen, the mama bear glare softening.

Though, I wouldn't mind seeing those two guys take off their shirts and get a little—

Focus, Gracie.

"I thought I was over it," I admit.

"Have you driven since the accident?" she asks.

"Um, no."

She scoffs, dropping her chin to stare at me over the top of her sunglasses. "Were you avoiding it on purpose?"

So many questions.

"Maybe."

She sighs, throwing her arms around me and hauling me in for a hug. For a few calming seconds, I ignore the fact that Dani's boobs are cushioning my face.

"God, those are nice," I tease, pulling back and wagging my eyebrows at her.

She laughs. "Stop. I'm trying to be serious here. Comforting."

"Oh, I was comfortable alright." I turn to Declan and Jensen, who are now watching us with rapt interest. "You sleep on these bad boys, Dec?"

"Amongst other things," he replies, voice low and full of innuendo.

Feeling lighter, I chuckle and give Dani one last quick squeeze. "Thought so." Jensen has checked out of the conversation, his face stoic and indifferent once more. "Well, we should get Vaughn to the hospital. He's eager to get that cast off."

"He'll probably insist on driving the command vehicle back after. It's a good thing his truck is out of commission," Declan says. "He'd probably start showing up at calls."

Confused, I look at Jensen. His eyes flicker to me, giving me a subtle shake of his head.

He didn't tell Declan what really happened.

I suck in an uneven breath and plaster on a smile. "Looks like I'll have to make sure the doctor is specific about your medical clearances, then."

With a near-grin at my sweet but vaguely threatening tone, he says, "Wouldn't expect anything less, shortcake."

Dani mouths *what was that?* to me as we all pile in the SUV.

I don't have an answer because I have absolutely no idea anymore.

CHAPTER
TWENTY-TWO

JENSEN

I've seen it all.

Rage, tears, blackouts, incoherent stuttering, fainting.

But never have I felt as helpless as when I watched Grace melt down behind the wheel of my truck. And I caused it by coercing her into driving me to my appointment.

The shittiest part: I didn't bother asking anyone else to take me. I immediately thought of *her*. I wanted to see her. Even though she ran after we had sex. And ran again after I berated her about dating idiots online because *I* wanted to be the guy she dates. But I'm not, and I've still let her get under my skin. As if I don't know how that ends.

Now that I'm free from my cast, I should celebrate this small taste of freedom, rather than lamenting on not being what a woman wants long term. Reminding myself this is the reason I'm focusing on work has become tedious. Especially around Grace.

"Why do you look madder than before your cast came off?" Grace asks from beside me at the raised eating bar of the Sandwich Ship. "I didn't eat your pickle when you went to the bathroom like I wanted. I've seen your proprietary food complex in action and—" Her eyes flash to me, like she just realized the last time she messed with my food we ended up fucking against the fridge. "I just meant I've seen you gut punch your brothers for nabbing fries from your plate. I haven't got the abs for that, so I've kept my hands to myself."

She's full of shit. The brat likes to steal my food. She does it casually, like it's just part of our conversation. But she's right, my brothers don't get away with it.

She takes a big bite of her corned beef sandwich, immediately followed by a chomp of her pickle. She moans, chewing with her eyes closed.

I clear my throat, averting my gaze as I adjust myself on the barstool.

"God, their corned beef is incredible. And this bread. Did you know they make all their bread in-house? I want to live here, surrounded by the smell of sourdough, spiced meats, and baked cheese."

She devours the rest of her meal and practically whimpers at her empty plate. Sliding her the last quarter of my spicy chicken sub and the tomato bisque soup I haven't touched earns me an adorable, baffled expression.

"Come on." I jerk my head toward the food. "Eat so we can go. You said it was your day off, so maybe we can knock out the therapy fast and then you can go do whatever it is you normally do on your day off."

Her sugar-sweet eyes dart from me to the food.

"It's not a trick. Just eat." Pushing the plate closer, I add, "Coffee isn't food. From now on, whatever food you bring to our sessions, you stay and eat with me. Got it?"

She doesn't answer, but I also don't wait to hear what she has to say. Because most likely she'll fight me on it. The woman fights me on damn near everything.

As she polishes off the sub, I drop some bills on the counter. Warmth hits my abdomen as I watch her chewing while she sways side to side on her stool. Cutting that emotional shit off, I slide off my seat and grab my crutch. I hate the damn thing, but it makes hobbling around easier.

Grace suggested I use a cane for better mobility when I go back to work next week. When I expressed my opinions on senior citizen canes, the doc had someone bring one over to me. Grace kept quiet until they left and then offered to hook me up with what she called a "hot silver fox" cane.

Whatever the fuck that is.

She spins on her stool and hops off, rubbing her tummy. "Oh man. I'm probably going to need a nap on your couch before we get started." She bends to pick up the black backpack she carries everywhere, and I avert my gaze from her killer ass. But a beat too late. She glances up and catches me staring. That will not help our situation.

"Maybe we could stop and grab a coffee—" She yelps, slamming into a guy carrying a white takeout bag.

"Shit!" he mutters as the bag of food crashes to the ground. "Oh, hey, Gracie." He ogles her, not irritated in the slightest.

"Oh no. Your food. Sorry, Kaiser." *Kaiser?* Like the bun? "Here, let me clean it up."

He wraps his hand around her arm—touching her—and I automatically step closer. "Nah, don't worry about it," the scruffy guy with shitty bleached-blond hair tells her.

While I size him up, I try to place him. He's familiar. I've seen him around town wearing an orange, reflective safety vest...

Shit. *Kai.* We were never in school together since he's quite a bit younger than me, but his parents own Irvine Construction. They were good friends with my parents, probably still friends with my mom.

Kai gives me a cursory glance. "Hey, Vaughn."

Ah. He doesn't know which twin I am. Pretty sure he's about to find out the hard way. Regardless of whether this gets back to my mom, he's got two seconds to wipe that predatory look off his face before I do it for him.

His focus shifts back to Grace. "Actually, I'm glad we bumped into each other. Bound to happen with you, right?" He chuckles at his own stupidity. *Asshole darted in front of her, maybe even tripped her. I was too busy trying not to look at her ass again to notice.* "I'm considering the trashed meal a happy accident. Because now I can convince you to make it up to me by taking me to lunch tomorrow. Or you can bring it over to my place." Grace rears back, that little vein in her forehead—the one I always seem to coax out of her—making an appearance.

And now I'm feeling possessive of her you're pissing me off *vein? Fucking ridiculous.*

"Uh, Kai..." she falters, confusing me. *She never has a problem telling* me *off.*

"You owe me a date, Grace," he states, his voice dropping a few octaves.

"She doesn't owe you shit," I tell him, keeping my tone more composed than I feel.

His head jerks up, but he doesn't remove his hand from her arm. Unclenching my fists takes conscious effort. The discomfort in my leg becomes an afterthought as I decide how to shut this situation down.

"This is between Gracie and me." The smarmy bastard grins down at her, but she's eyeing the exit. "She helped me after I fell off a ladder a couple of months ago." The man who looks like he slept in the clothes he's wearing and forgot how to groom himself points at me with a smile, as if we're buddies. "Actually, I think you were one of the emergency crew guys who brought me in from the worksite." *I don't give one single fuck.* "I made her promise to let me take her out once I was no longer her patient. But this one has been hard to pin down."

And you won't be pinning her down. Ever.

"Technically, you have a few more sessions scheduled," Grace tells him.

"Mm, well, I guess I'll see you soon then," he teases, lifting his hand to tug on her braid.

This fucker.

I shift over, tucking Grace off to the side with one wide palm splayed over her belly. When her hand moves to rest on my back, the muscles in my shoulders ease.

"I've actually got a session with Jensen this afternoon. He just got his cast removed." Grace tries to redirect the conversation, but I doubt this guy will let her off that easily.

Not missing the placement of my hand, Kai shoots me a hardened glare. That's right asshole, she'll never be yours.

Eyebrows raised, his expression turns cocky. "Guess that means we're free to break your rules and have lunch together too."

"Well...we..." she stammers. "They aren't *my* rules. It's part of our code of ethics." Her gaze darts over to me, weighted and filled with guilt. "Jensen offered to buy me lunch since it's my day off and he needed a ride to his appointment. It's his right foot." She points at my new walking boot. "So driving"—she blows an awkward raspberry—"not happening."

Her gaze flickers between the two of us. "Yeah. So, did you guys hear about the bird's nest in the park bathrooms by Moraine hiking trail? Those buggers were dive-bombing innocent hikers as they dropped their pants." She barks out the craziest laugh I've ever heard.

I have no idea if this rambling approach to turning down persistent jackasses works, but it's definitely hard to witness.

"Soooo," she continues, a fake smile on her sweet face, "we should be going. Dani is waiting for us over at the bakery. Byyyye," she draws out in an odd sing-song voice.

Reaching back, she grabs a fistful of my dark denim jacket and steps around Kai.

He forcefully grabs her arm and pulls her back, causing her to loosen her grip on me. We both reach for her, but she lands against Kai, his arms wrapping around her.

"Hold up, pretty lady. Let's set up a—"

I knock his hands off her. "Don't touch her." I'm in front of him and I don't remember moving.

Grace sidesteps away from him and places herself behind me.

Good girl.

Kai squares his shoulder and lifts his chin. "Listen, J-man…" Did this fucker just throw out a nickname like we're friends? I've got several inches on him and the tenuous hold I have on the willpower keeping me from shoving this asshat to the ground is slipping. "It's cool. I was just helping her find her footing."

There's a shift in his stance the moment he meets my gaze. He's finally realized he's way the fuck out of his league.

"You're the reason she tripped." The violent rumble of my tone lashes out at him. I step closer, wanting so badly to fuck this guy up and get Grace out of here.

"Jensen." A hand on my arm pulls my attention off the idiot who is reminding me why I keep my circle of friends tight. "It's fine. I—"

"No," I tell her. "He purposely walked into your path so he could weasel his way into your pants." I point to him. "He's *not* one of your 'nice guys.' Tell him to fuck off and be done with it."

"You for real?" asshole-guy says. "Didn't she push you off a balcony or something?"

I don't respond. The sharp glare I fix on him is a warning, one I almost hope he doesn't heed.

His mouth twists with a crude grin as he tucks his hands into his pockets, eyeballing us. "Oh, I see what's going on here. She must have made it up to you, huh?" With a mean gleam in his eyes, he leers at Grace. "I've heard sweet, clumsy Gracie falls to her knees pretty often."

Big. Fucking. Mistake.

A wrathful blaze ignites in my chest, spreading like wildfire, making every muscle in my body twitch with the desire to fuck this guy up.

"Wow, Kai. You're pretty damn full of yourself for a tiny-dicked piece of sh—"

My gaze locks on Kai as I cut Grace off, putting a hand on her hip and easing her further behind me. With one barely restrained shove, he shuffles backward to stay on his feet, anger lighting his eyes. When he charges forward, I've got less than a second to make a choice.

I grasp him by the shoulders and push down with more force than is necessary. The charging momentum he put into his attack works against him as I drive his face directly into my raised knee.

Ignoring the gasp at my back, I release the sputtering moron, and he collapses to the floor.

My mouth hooks into a smirk as I watch him wipe away the blood dripping from his nose and mouth. Shifting to stand over him, I feign concern. "Oh, look...now who's the clumsy one?" I drone in a harsh whisper. "Now, I don't listen to all the town chatter, but I heard shitheads who run their mouths about Grace are having lots of 'accidents' lately." He flinches as I extend my good arm to make it look like I'm helping him up. "Got me?"

"Jesus," he mutters, smacking my hand away. "Yeah, got it."

"Good. Pick up your shit and leave."

He mumbles curses while still wiping at his nose, but he snatches his bag up and storms out of the door.

"That was..." Grace stalls, at a loss for words. A rare occurrence.

Probably because I lost it. Looking around, I only see the staff and one other customer. Both pretending nothing happened. Fuck. I'll be getting a call from Brody any minute.

And Grace. She's going to read into—

"What the hell was that?"

Dumbstruck, my head jerks back.

"You acted like we are *together*," she whispers.

"We are. At least in the sense that we had lunch together." Her forehead scrunches in a way that usually means she's about to yell at me. "I'm not going to let some guy touch you, and try to talk his way into seeing you naked with me right fucking here. He was a pushy, slimy—"

"Not your problem. If he was trying to hurt me, a different story. Step right in because I have the combat skills of a baby koala."

"He was—"

"Flirting," she says, cutting me off again. "Then when he didn't get what he wanted, he got mean. It's what a lot of guys do. And I'm an easy target for ridicule." She waves a hand toward me, the pink in her cheeks deepening. "Hell, even you make fun of my clumsiness. Regularly."

She thinks I treat her like that fucker did?

"I've said nothing remotely like that." My attempt at whispering comes out as a growl. "I give you shit when you're careless or putting yourself in danger. You still think I'm an asshole? Fine. But every fucking time something happens to you, I think to myself, 'This could've been it. She could have really gotten hurt this time.' And it makes me crazy."

Her mouth is slightly agape, her eyes opened wide and blinking at me. We stand motionless for what has to be a full minute, just staring at each other.

"Nothing to say for once?" I goad, hoping to break the tension I can't seem to shake around her.

"*You're* careless!" she barks at me, her lips pressing into an adorable pout.

"That all you got, shortcake?" I ask with a bemused smirk.

Her sunshine eyes narrow to slits, and an irritated grumble vibrates her minuscule frame a moment before she storms away.

I follow her path and dodge the heavy glass door swinging closed behind her. "What? No piggyback?" I hobble outside.

"Don't baby koalas cling to their mom's backs, Grace? I'd let you hop on, but you'd have to call me Daddy."

She lurches to a stop and spins. Shit. Never seen that look on her face. I might be seeing what I want to, but there's a heat in her glare that's not all fury.

With clenched teeth, she says, "I think you'd like that a little too much, hotshot."

Damn straight, I would.

She turns away, hotfooting her cute little ass down the sidewalk again. I pick up my pace to keep up with her. Thankfully, her short legs make that easy, even with crutches.

I nudge her over to the inside part of the sidewalk, and she shoots me a confusing half-frown.

"So the 'nice guy' search seems to be going well?" I ask, knowing this is a risky way to get her to talk to me. But getting a reaction out of her is all I've got right now.

She comes to an abrupt stop. "I like assholes!" she bellows.

I knew she'd yell at me, but those were not the words I was expecting to come out of that sweet mouth.

TWENTY-THREE

GRACIE

That sounded better in my head than it did out loud.

But I'm done with this day, done with overwhelming feelings lingering between us. Just *done.*

Jensen blinks at me, his eyebrows drawing up on his forehead.

I point back at the sandwich shop. "Not that kind of asshole. Kai's a creep. But the broody, prickly, quiet kind? I'm inexplicably attracted to those guys."

The side of his mouth curves up. "Like *me?*" he asks, pointing to himself.

"Unfortunately. I've found you annoyingly attractive since the first time I saw that upside down grin, the one that's more scowl than smiling. But then I met you and you were awful. Even so, it only *mildly* deterred me," I admit with an irritated huff. "Until the car accident and your big, stupid mouth."

Casually leaning on his crutch, looking much too pleased, he says, "I can do a lot of things with my mouth, shortcake. I promise if you give it another chance, you won't have any complaints."

The right side of my face twitches as I grapple with the warring emotions from those two tempting sentences. "I confess that I found you attractive even though you were a jackass from the moment we met, and now you're flirting with me?"

One muscular shoulder rises in a shrug. I force my eyes from his thick deltoid muscles, wishing only his body attracted me. Because that would be manageable and none of this feels manageable. There's a reason he completely unsettles me, and only a small part of that involves his shoulders.

"I'm supposed to be dating nice, normal, sweet guys," I whisper. It's a plea, an excuse. "Cardigan-wearing guys. Elementary teachers, yoga instructors, interior designers. *Not* rude, overbearing firefighters."

He cocks his head at me. "If this is your way of asking me to wear a cardigan in the bedroom, I'm game."

No. No, no, no. Do not laugh, do not envision him in a tight navy cardigan. All buttoned up. With elbow patches. And nothing underneath.

I give him a stern, "Jensen," but it comes out as more of a resigned sigh.

"You realize those professions are mainly female-dominated fields, right? Were you trying to make it harder on yourself on purpose?"

We quietly assess each other, the smoldering taunt in his gaze meeting my mirthful one.

"I like a challenge," I answer, holding my head high.

His gaze drops to my mouth as he asks, "So that's how you'd describe your usual type? Assholes?"

I lock eyes with him. "Growly, intense, brown-eyed, cocky assholes who have a gooey center and heart of gold. I'm chasing unicorn men. While alluring, they've proven to be mythical. And their lookalikes—regular assholes—are consistently bad for me. So this"—I point between us—"is probably another mistake." I blow out a breath, feeling a teensy bit lighter. "There, glad that's out in the open."

"Wait. So, your type is brown-eyed, cocky assholes?" I lift one shoulder, offering him a crooked smile. "I might be an asshole, but I'm not cocky. Wrong twin," he grumbles, his mood shifting once again.

Pressing my lips together in contemplation, I consider this. "You're not *traditionally* cocky. But you have the intensity and the confidence. That air of fearlessness mixed with the arrogance of someone who thinks he knows best."

The way he can give off eye roll vibes without actually rolling his eyes is fascinating. He communicates more with his face and body than his mouth.

I fling a hand in his direction. "Your turn. Share your truths. It's cathartic."

"You're saying I'm not good for you and then want to skip to my turn?"

"I'm not saying you wouldn't be good for me. But you, Jensen Vaughn, scare the shit out of me."

His eyes search mine. "Ditto."

"I'm not scary," I assure him.

The sharp features of his face soften. "You've scared me since the moment you landed in my lap."

I snort in disbelief. "Say something nice to me," I demand. His brow furrows, so I explain. "I need to check something. Be sweet and thoughtful for one minute. I can give you some time to prepare if you need it. You could Google 'things nice guys say to women' if you're unfamiliar."

If this attraction is simply my ridiculous need to win over jerks, to prove him wrong about me, then once he's nice to me, my interest should take a nosedive. And when that happens, I won't have to think about the ramifications of being unable to control myself around him. Or worry if he's another man I'll put everything into, only to realize he's nothing more than the tantalizing rough exterior that lured me in. Most importantly, whether he'll show me everything I've ever wanted and then break my heart into tiny pieces won't matter.

"You're the most adorable, confusing woman I've ever met," he says.

"That wasn't overly nice. Dig deeper."

"Grace—"

"Also, how am I the confusing one?" I ask. "You save me, then ridicule me. Protect then lecture. Tease then taunt." I crane my neck, glancing around us before whispering, "Fuck me, then fight with me. Fight *for* me."

"I wanted to fuck then *talk*, Grace. You didn't."

"I needed time to process. And you wanted to what? Chalk our indiscretion up to hate sex, draw lines, lecture me on being reckless again? No thanks."

"I made it pretty damn clear how I felt." My eyebrows hike up to my hairline. He smooths a finger down my forehead. "Stop making that face at me. I told you I care about you."

Did he though? Pretty sure he just yelled at me about being predator bait.

As if in slow-motion, he moves closer, towering above me. I'm breathless, my heart hammering at his closeness, not knowing what he's going to do next. And hoping he does something he shouldn't.

Waves of hair, which he's let grow out, fall over his forehead as he dips down, placing his lips at my temple. "It wasn't hate sex," he states, emphasizing each word as his lips brush my skin.

I twist my neck to peer up at him, our mouths only inches apart. "What was it then? Because you hated me from the moment we met, went out of your way to piss me off. The only reason you agreed to let me help you was so you could get back to work sooner. And the free snacks, of course."

He shakes his head, full lips pulling to the side. "I never hated you, Grace."

A doubtful huff leaves my lips.

"You being pissed at me worked in my favor. I wanted you as

far away from me as possible." His voice is little more than a rough whisper.

"Why?" I ask, hoping for the kind of answer that will change everything. Even if nothing can change. Not yet.

"Because I *liked* rescuing you—way too fucking much. But the fact that you were constantly putting yourself in danger drove me to the brink of insanity," he grinds out, his focus dropping to my mouth. "You walked straight into walls, tripped your way through every room, flirted with my twin brother. You were a ridiculous, gorgeous, distracting, unavoidable pain in my ass, Gracelyn Parker."

I suck in a breath and hold it.

Yeah. An answer like that.

"You were a temptation during a time I refused to be tempted." He shifts closer, softly gripping my chin like I'm delicate, cherished. "Erika had just left, I was still paying for a wedding that would never happen, lost a future I thought we'd both wanted. Until recently, the only things I gave a shit about after that was my job and my family."

The breath I was holding releases in a rush. I not only made his job harder, but was the reason he couldn't work for weeks and had to delay the start of the volunteer training program.

His thumb flits over my lip causing a shiver to zip down my spine.

"I didn't know any of that, Jensen." I wrap my hand around his wrist and squeeze reassuringly. "And I never flirted with your brother." Not once I realized he wasn't just an overly moody bastard, but an identical twin. And of course, I had to have the hots for the broody one like the asshole-loving fool that I am.

"You gave him your smiles, all your playful sweetness," he explains, a possessive edge to the way he's holding me. "It pissed me off."

"Because... you *didn't* hate me?"

"Not even a little," he asserts.

I blow out a breath, my eyes darting between his. "So where does that leave us?"

"One way to find out..." he murmurs, sweeping a thumb over my chin once more before stepping back. "Let me walk you to Dani's. I'm going to head to my mom's tonight."

He's ten feet away before what he said sinks in. "What about physical therapy?"

"Going to need to cancel that today," he shouts over his shoulder.

I hurry to catch up, moving to his uninjured side to keep out of his way, but he stops and jerks his head to his right.

"What?"

He frowns and moves to the outer part of the sidewalk again. "Not taking any chances, Damsel."

My scoff hides my smile as I lengthen my stride to stay a step ahead of him. I can't risk seeing that upside down grin, or the hypnotic sparkle in his umber gaze. He's able to rattle me one frustrating poke at a time. And I let him. I engage because I like it just as much as he does. I more than like it.

And with every interaction, every argument, every confession, I know that soon, I'm going to have a much bigger problem than tripping around Jensen Vaughn.

I might end up falling all the way in love with the jerk.

DANI DROPPED me off at home earlier and stayed while I word vomited every detail of my driving fail and the sandwich smackdown.

And then I whispered the confession I couldn't say aloud after the 'hate-sex,' "I think I like the jerk."

My best friend, who should have reminded me that Jensen

isn't the type of guy I'm supposed to get caught up in, said, "Good! You don't even like the boring 'nice' guys you think would be perfect for you."

"What if he just wants a physical relationship until he tires of me?" I asked her, the insecurities I typically keep on lockdown, bursting out of the cracks Jensen put in my walls. "Of the way I am…"

"He knows the way you are. And he clearly wants you."

"Other guys have said the same."

"Those guys aren't Jensen," she argued. "Do you know any man as protective or intentional as Jensen? That man is loyal, dependable, and doesn't do anything without being fully committed."

"I'm his physical therapist though. His top priority is recovering so he can get back to work. That was the initial reason he was so pissed at me. I unintentionally messed with his career, and I need to make that up to him."

"How much longer will he require PT?" she asked.

"At least a month." Dani sucked in an uneasy breath. "But as long as he doesn't touch, text, or talk all gruff and dirty to me, I'll be fine."

My best friend, my kindred spirit, and platonic love of my life…laughed.

Who am I kidding? If I don't get my shit together, I'm going to be ass up on his couch with him driving deep into me, over and over, while he commands me to touch myself again.

Dani made a few reasonable suggestions, like deciding what I want and going after it. The problem is, I already know what I want. Trusting myself to open up and accept it is another matter.

After she left, I went to bed, but ended up tossing and turning in my much too empty, king-sized bed. After the highs and lows of today, my mind can't shut off.

There's no point in dwelling on things I can't fix right now, so I scroll through social media instead. Probably a bad idea when trying to sleep, but I'm hoping I'll catch some celebrity news that's bound to put my troubles to shame.

Instant regret hits partway through a deep dive into a country music duo's recent breakup. Dozens of articles and videos reveal the heartbreak of two beautiful singers going through a nasty divorce despite clearly loving each other. All this distraction manages to do is make me ugly cry for twenty minutes while I sing along to their breakup songs.

I'm about to enter a third rendition of his musical proclamation of betrayal when a text pops up.

JERKSEN:

Tomorrow, 6pm.

Wear the black crop top.

For motivational purposes.

Something flutters wildly in my chest as I trap my lip between my teeth, reining in an eager grin.

He's still sending single sentence texts, and I'm determined not to be amused by that.

I plan on wearing a turtleneck.

Supposed to be a storm rolling through tomorrow.

You know I take weather precautions and safety VERY seriously.

But thanks for the outfit suggestion, buddy.

I stare at my phone with a smile on my face, waiting for a response, imagining his rumbly growl of disapproval.

I'm bumping the thermostat to 90 degrees, so you'll want to bring a change of clothes.

Brody says he can drop you off.

I can take the heat, hotshot.

I bet you can.

And Grace?

We are not buddies. Not even fucking close.

THE VINE COMMUNITY UPDATE

Jensen Vaughn returns to the fire station on light duty starting next week. We haven't seen much of the handsome firefighter while he works through physical therapy and rearranges the start up for the Vaughn Volunteer Firefighter Training Program (beginning June 1st). But that doesn't mean he's been taking it easy. He was present for an unfortunate accident involving Gracie Parker and Kaiser Irvine yesterday afternoon.

Blood was spilled, roast beef sandwiches destroyed.

We are not laying any blame on our lovely, spunky physical therapist. Though she appears to be a magnet for these types of incidents. And while Jensen and Gracie have a rocky history that has led to growing hostility, he stepped in when needed.

Yet some unanswered questions remain...

We all know these two have never gotten along, insults have been hurled, scathing glares observed, taunts dispatched. But is this all in the past?

Have Jensen and Gracie buried the hatchet now that she's helping with his recovery? Is this merely a temporary truce?

The appointment took longer than expected. Heading out to Santa Rosa only takes an extra fifteen minutes—twenty with my mom driving. But I've been anxious to get back home, and my patience is shot.

"Come for dinner? It's Pie Night," Mom offers as we drive through town.

Ah, shit. Pie night? Three different pies all served in one incredible meal. Usually it's a mix of either pot pie, shepherd's pie, dessert pies, quiche, or hand pies.

"That sounds great, Mom. But I have plans tonight." I lean over and kiss the top of her head. "I'll stop by tomorrow after work to finish your deck and the leftovers."

"I figured. Between your jittery leg shaking the whole car on the drive home and checking the time every thirty seconds..."

"Grace is coming over."

"Ah. Good. I was wondering why you were seeing a new physical therapist in the city. I figured you either had a falling out after the fight at The Sandwich Ship—and yes, Sylvia Irvine informed me it wasn't an accident—or something was happening between you two."

"It's the latter," I confirm.

With an excited glimmer in her eyes she's trying to tamp down, she offers, "Why don't you invite Gracie to Pie Night?"

I think of Grace eating dinner with us. Convincing my mom to join bowling, teaming up with Jaxon to goad Brody into the nonsensical conversation he hates. Chiming in on the new statue in the Juniper Street meridian that looks like a giant bluebird with freakishly large balls.

Do birds even have balls? Dicks? I bet Grace would know.

"Gonna have to get back to you on that." I have to see if she even wants to give this thing between us a real try. "We've got to work out a few things."

Mom pulls into my driveway, putting the vehicle in park.

"Have you worked out your own things first?"

I open the car door and hop out. "I've been ready to move on for a while. I wanted to be sure. I wasn't her favorite person for a while."

"Oh, honey. You weren't anyone's favorite person last year. It was like communicating with a bear. You did a lot of growling and let us feed you, but god forbid anyone try to approach." One side of my mouth drops into a frown. "Still loved you to bits, and no one complained about your task-focused intensity during that time. Though I could have done without the 6 a.m. yard work."

I lean over the car door. "Your pep talks could use some work."

She waves me off with a half-snort, half-laugh.

Mom circles around my driveway and drives out. My neighbor's cat sits on the walkway a few feet from me. Since I don't know her actual name, I've started calling her Reaper, and she likes it.

Once I look her way, she moves, winding herself around my legs. I scoop her up and let her climb up to my shoulder. She nuzzles my cheek, making me grin.

"You hungry?" I ask, already knowing the answer. The only time she cuddles this much is when she's looking for food.

I open the garage door and grab cat food and treats. Reaper follows me to the bowl that I keep on my porch for her.

As I'm closing the garage door, Grace arrives—on her fucking bike.

"Shortcake. We talked about that bike."

She hops off, unclipping her helmet and tossing it to me. "We did. But your brother's dealing with something at the hardware store. There was a slap fight in the nuts-and-bolts aisle."

I squint at her, determining if she's messing with me, but all I can see is the dark green turtleneck she's wearing.

"How's your leg feel?" she asks.

"Weird," I answer, watching her closely as she fidgets with the straps of her backpack.

"That's normal," she says, giving me the flash of a sweet smile before shutting it down and looking away. "Ready? We're moving on to stage four of your rehab today."

I tip my head and hold a hand out toward the house. She moves past me, peeking at me out of the corner of her eye as her shoulder brushes against my chest.

She greets Reaper with a head scratch and some cooed words, no longer scared of her after I introduced them a couple of weeks ago.

There's an eagerness to each step as I follow her into the house. All because Grace shouted about assholes in the street.

I'm exactly her type—in ways she might not be ready to admit, but I'm willing to prove. Until yesterday, I didn't think she'd let me be anything but the man who keeps saving her, fighting with her, and watching her only when she's not looking.

Grace Parker's perfect man is *me* and we both know it. And I plan to get her to admit it. No more excuses, no more boundaries and lines we can't cross.

"I'll get your binder updated and everything set up while you go change," she tells me, placing her backpack on a chair.

She tugs at her turtleneck before she scans the room, looking for my thermostat. Her gaze lands on me, and my grin widens. She gives me a scowl in return.

I practically vault the stairs to get changed. With my heart pounding, I toss on the clothes laid out on the bed as quickly as possible.

I make sure not to put all my weight on my walking boot as I descend the stairs. The minute I hit the bottom, she turns around.

"Wha—" Grace covers her mouth and stands still, as she takes in my outfit. "Jensen. Seriously?" she mumbles through her fingers, eyes locked on my chest. "No. This—"

"Eyes up here, gorgeous." I need her focused, so she knows how serious I am.

"That's the exact color cardigan I imagined you in," she mumbles.

"I'm not changing, Grace. Tried that once, and it blew up in my face," I tell her, prowling closer, stopping a few feet away. "But I'm more than willing to put on a stupid sweater if you're looking to keep lying to yourself about what kind of man you want." I give her a wicked grin.

"That sweater isn't doing what you think it is, hotshot," she announces, her tone distracted, subdued.

I stalk closer again, leveling her with a look that tells her exactly what I want, not holding back anymore. "You don't want a cardigan-wearing, agreeable, nice guy. You want a man you can battle. You want to be challenged, cherished no matter what you throw his way."

I watch the rapt attention on her face, the sharp intake of breath. Questions lurk in her gaze, but her lips press closed as if opening her mouth will cause all her truths to spill out. She's still holding back.

Probably because she still thinks we can't be together, that there's a line between us she can't cross.

"I'm not sweet or friendly. I don't sugarcoat shit. I'm impatient, and stubborn, and rough around the edges. And when it comes to you, you bet I'll be overbearing and possessive."

"Shit," she whimpers, retreating, keeping a few feet of distance between us.

Her ass meets the back of the couch and I settle in front of her, tipping her chin up toward me. "I'd take you to my bed and fuck you hard and rough, the way I know you like it." Her cheeks flush, eyelashes fluttering. "You can tease and taunt, knowing I'll spank your bratty ass and make you beg like a good girl. And then we'll both know the truth."

"Jensen…you're making it really hard to be good."

"You want to be good for me, sweet girl?"

Grace bites her lip, a restrained groan escaping.

"You fucking *like* me, Grace. And I'm prepared to prove your asshole theory wrong. Because"—I lean into her, arms wrapping around her sweet body, her chest pressing into mine—"I'm your unicorn man."

A rough swallow moves down her throat, as one of her hands slides up to my shoulder. Uncertainty edges its way in as I search her face in the tense silence that hangs between us.

This could backfire hard and then I'm fucked. Because I'll never not want Grace. But if she doesn't want me, all of me, the torture of being around her before I acknowledged how I felt will be like comparing a paper cut to a gaping chest wound.

"One month," she rasps, placing her other hand on my chest. She toys with the hair on my chest, and I push my hips into her, needing more of her touch, more of *her*.

Wait…one month?

My mouth dips into an amused frown. "No."

"Six weeks tops. When you're done PT. We pretend like—"

"No," I repeat. "No more pretending." Pulling her in tighter, I study the emotions that light her eyes—want, need, turmoil. "You're fired."

"*What?*" Her jaw drops, her lashes fluttering as she blinks up at me.

Ah, shit.

"I'm working with another physical therapist in the city," I explain.

Her hands push against my chest, so I give her a few inches of space.

"There's no one who will work harder to get you back to 100 percent than me, Jensen!" she hisses, tears clinging to her lashes.

"I have no doubt about that." I bring my hand around to her nape and assure her, "And you can still whip me into shape at home. I'll do whatever you fucking want. But you can't be my PT anymore."

Doubt and accusation smolder in her heated glare.

"Are you more mad I'll be working with someone else, or that there's no more obstacles in our way?" I cup her face, my thumb drifting to caress the mouth I want to taste again.

I don't give a shit about who my therapist is as long as it means I get to kiss Grace, have her in my bed, catch her every time she falls.

"Tell me you want me," I demand, dipping my head down to place a kiss on her pliant mouth and steal another taste of those lips. "Admit you like I'm a bossy, overprotective asshole. Tell me you love our bickering as much as I do."

I wrap my hand around to the front of her throat. My thumb strokes gently along her neck, giving her ample time to move away or tell me to stop.

She sucks in a ragged breath, her pulse thumping against my palm. Her irises darken to a golden caramel, still bright and captivating as they mingle with mine.

And then her fist tightens in the fabric of my ridiculous cardigan. She surges up on her toes and tugs. I willingly follow, eager for her mouth to meet mine, curious what she'll do with me now that she has me.

Her kiss is fierce, drawing a grin from me before I welcome her wicked tongue. She whimpers, her arms lifting to wind around my neck.

With one hand still circling her throat, I move the other down to her ass, squeezing the plump cheek. I pull at her hips as I rock my erection into her.

Fuck, she feels incredible.

I hold her tighter, change the kiss, let her know I'm taking over. She fights me on it for a few moments, trying to regain control, desperately pulling at my mouth with hers.

Easing back, I say, "Tell me, Grace."

She frowns and tries to get to my mouth again. I give her throat a firm but gentle squeeze. A delicious moan vibrates against my palm.

On a gasp, she says, "Goddammit. Of course I want you, Jensen. You know I do."

"What else?" I ask, my dick angry I'm doing shit that's delaying getting inside her.

"Fine! I love fighting with you, okay? It annoys me how I'm attracted to every damn part of you—you sex-withholding asshat! Now take me to the bedroom you said I'd never get to see."

That's when it hits me.

In this moment, with her sweetheart face tipped up, heated eyes burning into mine, I realize the resentment and bitterness it took me nearly a year to get over was worth it.

Because it ended with *her*.

"I want to haul you over my shoulder and fireman carry you into my bedroom, but my new physical therapist wouldn't approve."

"Hey! I'm still your physical therapist—in private—and I also wouldn't approve. But I want a rain check on that fireman carry. It might be a fantasy of mine."

I lift the hem of the shirt covering way too fucking much of her. She shivers and glances down as I pull it up past her breasts.

They aren't compressed into a sports bra like usual. Today, it's semi-sheer black cups with a lacy trim. The stark contrast of her pale skin against the dark lace draws my touch. I trace the edge of her bra, from the strap down to the space between.

"Only girlfriends get to go into my bedroom though."

"Girlfriend*s*? Plural?" Her voice rumbles in warning. "Yeah, I don't fucking think so."

She shudders when I swipe a thumb over the nipple poking through the thin fabric.

"I like your possessive side, shortcake." I pull her shirt the rest of the way off and stare at the skin I've uncovered. Skin I didn't get the chance to see last time. "I'm yours Grace. Only yours."

Her hands come up to run through my hair. "Damn straight," she says with a satisfied smirk.

On her toes again, she kisses me, this time softer, sweeter.

As she slips away, she snags my hand and threads her fingers through mine. She spins to walk backward, her other hand undoing the buttons of my cardigan, but struggling.

"Next time we're keeping it on," she says.

"You think it's hot?"

"It makes me smile." We get to the stairs, and she stops to run a finger down my chest before slowly undoing another button. "You're like the Big Bad Wolf dressed up as grandma, attempting to trick Red Riding Hood into entering his bedroom so he can rail her."

Moving her fingers aside, I take over and rip the sweater off.

"You're twisted." She shrugs, looping a finger into my jeans, dragging me up the first step. "And I really fucking like it, shortcake."

We're role-playing that scenario soon. My cock strains against my zipper just thinking about it. I'm ordering her a red cape and a basket full of sex toys and we're going to make a weekend of it.

When we reach the top of the stairs, I hook my fingers into her pants and shove them down while backing her into my room and toward the bed.

Her legs hit the frame, and she falls with a giggle, holding her feet up to me to remove the rest of her leggings. As I rip them off, I catch a glimpse of her pussy, covered by a skimpy black thong. The round, tight curves of her ass beg for my hands.

She shifts up on the bed to make room for me.

I get on the bed, take both knees in my hands, and spread her open.

She reaches for my zipper, but I stop her, holding those wandering hands against her stomach. "Not yet. I'm hungry and you look fucking delicious, baby."

Her feet fall to the mattress, knees still open. I trail my fingertips up the back of one calf until I reach her knee and smooth a rough palm against the velvet skin of her inner thigh. Brushing my thumb over the sheer black material elicits a desperate whimper.

I push the thong aside and graze my thumb over her clit all the way down to her entrance.

"Yes," she whispers.

"Up," I demand as I grip the wet part of her panties.

She lifts her ass, and I remove the delicate material.

"What are you—oh fuck..." She gasps, watching as I bring them to my face and inhale her intoxicating scent.

Blood pounds through my body, and I'm confident most of it is heading straight for my dick. A tingle zips its way up my spine. I'm torn between the need to eat her and fuck her.

"I'm keeping these," I tell her, stashing them in my pocket before lowering my jeans with one hand. There's no chance I'm stopping to remove my walking boot.

I dive between her legs, trailing a teasing lick up to her clit. Unable to restrain myself for another damn second, I lap at her, swiping up and down, flicking her clit. She moans my name, gripping the hand holding hers in place. And I'm fucking gone— drunk on her taste and sounds.

I flatten her thigh to the bed, opening her up for me. "I love the sounds you make for me, pretty girl," I tell her before moving my hand to stroke myself. I could come just like this, but I don't want the first time to be with my mouth on her pussy, so I release my cock.

My tongue finds her clit as I slide two fingers into her. Still gripping her hands, I press them into her lower stomach, creating more pressure for her as I find the spot that will make her blow.

"Oh god. Jensen, that's—" Her eyes lock with mine, dark amber boring into me with wonder-filled elation.

"There, babe?" I press a kiss to her swollen bead before sucking it back into my mouth.

"Yes! Faster."

I drag my mouth from her pussy, and she gives me a frustrated growl. Smirking, I place a kiss on her clit.

"Say please, Grace."

I get another growl, so I place another soft kiss on her throbbing pussy.

"Please, faster. More."

I do as requested, and she clenches tight as those thick thighs clamp around my head. A low, whispered moan leaks from her lips, followed by my name.

Fuck, yes.

Her pussy spasms hard, pulsing against my face and gripping my fingers. I keep swirling my tongue, drawing out her orgasm.

Once she's settled, I lick my lips clean and move up the curves of her perfect body.

"You taste fucking incredible, shortcake." Even better than she smells. Better than peaches or apricots. Better than anything I've ever had my mouth on.

With a panting breath, she says, "Coming from a man who will eat anything…"

"That sounds like a challenge. You want me to prove it to you, Peaches?"

Reaching behind her, I unclasp her bra and slide it down her arms, revealing dusky pink nipples. They tighten as the air hits them, and I brush my lips over one before sucking it into my mouth.

Her legs skim the outside of mine, wrapping around my waist.

"Say something nice, hotshot," she murmurs.

Finding out what makes Grace hot, what she likes in bed, is officially my new life goal.

"You're perfect, baby. I want to discover every fucking thing about you." I drop to my elbows, holding myself above her. "I've been dying to get between these thighs again. You coming with my name on your lips beat every fantasy I've ever had." I kiss her, my dick slipping through her wet heat, and I groan into her mouth.

"Fuck me, Jensen." Her demand is full of sass and desperation.

"Beg me, Grace."

She lifts to her elbows, extending her slender neck to tip her face up to me, her tight nipples pushing into my chest. My throat rumbles with another groan, loving the feel of her soft skin. I want her rubbing herself all the fuck over me.

Her plump, delectable lips graze mine as she repeats, "Fuck. Me," in a haughty, seductive tone, without a hint of begging. "*Now.*"

Heels dig into my ass as she raises her ass off the bed to line herself up. The tip of my cock slides against her entrance, the head slipping right in.

The beautiful, confounding pixie plaguing my every damn thought grins up at me with a saucy triumph in her golden gaze.

I drop us down to the mattress and seat myself fully inside her with a barely restrained thrust. She gasps, her head dropping back.

"So fucking hot."

She hums incoherently, thighs tightening.

I slide out of her just enough to dip my head down to kiss along the side of her breast before twirling my tongue around her nipple.

She keens into the muted silence of my bedroom, hands raking into my hair.

"Look at me, baby." I move back to hover above her, and this time she keeps her eyes on me. "Good girl," I praise her.

Her lashes flutter and her back arches.

I hiss out a strained breath as I try not to come just from the view of her sweet tits and the feel of her legs wound around me.

Pumping harder, I pin one of her legs back, pressing her knee into the side of her chest.

"I'm going to come inside you."

Close. I'm too close, my balls drawing up.

"Yes. Please. Jensen…I need it."

"Such pretty begging," I grunt out. "I'm going to fill you up, give you what you need."

Waves of heat drag up my thighs, my ass flexing as I push deeper, grinding into her, eyes locked on her beautiful, glowing face.

"Fuck you feel too good, Grace."

Her hips rock with mine. I jerk inside her and she cries out, her walls spasming, gushing, milking me. I hold still inside her, unable to move or breathe as I come so hard I'm barely able to hold myself up.

Eventually, things come back into focus and I feel her hands skimming over my abs.

"You've made a mess of me," she says, her pussy squeezing my sated dick once, twice.

Sexy little tease.

I kiss her on the nose and tell her, "I'm nowhere near done with you, shortcake." Her eyes stay on me, still playful. "One more."

I lick my thumb and bring it to her pussy.

She rises on her elbows, looking down at where we're still connected. With my dick half-hard again, my hands circle her waist and smooth over her hips, tucking under her to grip her ass. It's going to get a good spanking tonight. She can't even help herself—she's a feisty brat and I can't fucking wait.

"You don't have to. I've already come twice." She wiggles, backing off my dick, but I grip her hips, not ready to pull out.

"Now it's two more."

Her eyes widen and I can't contain the crooked, self-assured tilt of my mouth.

Oh yeah, I'm going to make sure she never thinks about "nice" guys for the rest of her life.

CHAPTER
TWENTY-FIVE

GRACIE

A distant, persistent melody pulls me from a magical dream —literally. I snuggle deeper into the warmth surrounding me as the details of my dream mingle with my semi-conscious mind.

I had been attending an academy meant for witches and wizards. And as the only half-breed witch selected for the international wizarding tournament, the pressure was on, stakes high. In the last round, we had to face off against our greatest enemy, the person who could cost you *everything*. Naturally, the person waiting for me in the arena, my opponent, was Jensen Vaughn.

I approached him with caution, wand raised. His dark eyes burned into me and traced my every movement. He corrected my stance, said something borderline flirtatious, and grinned at every sharp comment I threw his way.

We got closer and closer, neither of us hurling our magic at the other. Instead, we stripped down and fucked. Yep. Magic exploded from us the moment we touched, vanquishing everyone else. Jensen held me close and told me he'd destroy anyone who came near me. He'd do whatever it took to help me.

Afterward, he kissed me and whispered, "I love you, Gracie."

And that's when I sighed, disappointed at the realization it was fantasy, not reality. You'd think it would have been the magic that tipped me off. Nope, it was Jensen calling me *Gracie*.

"Your alarm, babe," a deep voice rumbles, sliding a hand along my bare back down to my ass.

My eyes flutter open, and all I see is chest hair and golden skin.

For the third night in a row, I'm snuggled up into the warm chest of a man I've always thought hated me. Now I'm dreaming about magic and *I love you*'s while breathing in his addictive scent and warming my cold feet between his hot calves.

I never imagined myself being one of those women who has amazing sex and then gets all giddy and dreaming of forever.

The sex has been *amazing* though. Five orgasms? I've never had that in one night—let alone one *hour*. And he's so attentive, dominant but tender. He takes charge, guiding me exactly how he wants, completely in control of every bit of pleasure he wrings from me. A big part of me loves how he dominates me, because then I can't screw it up. But the other part of me wants a turn taking the reins too.

And after last night, I'm more sore than I've ever been, yet...

I move my hands down his chest, to his abs, my eyes following the trail. Goddamn, he's pretty. The roped muscles, the smattering of hair, the narrow hips, and the ass that looks like someone chiseled it from marble.

He's facing me, eyes closed, an arm looped around me, a single pillow fluffed under his head. He hums, a deep sound that vibrates from his chest to my hands. The arm at my back pulls me tighter against him.

I cut off a laugh and kiss him. As if he was waiting for me to make a move, he rolls over on top of me, mouth still on mine.

Somewhere nearby, my alarm is still blaring music, but my priority is the man hovering over me with warm, sleepy eyes.

My heart squeezes, giving a few distracted thumps before hammering away. That look—the one that's equal parts devious intent and possessive pride. I would wake up to this look every day thinking, *Damn, life is good.*

"Morning, shortcake."

"Morning, hotshot." And because I don't have the sly sexy morning smolder he does, I add, "Thanks for the orgasms and living up to all your big dick energy."

I expect him to shake his head or grumble something that's half curses.

But there's a smile lighting his eyes as he dips down and captures my lips in a slow kiss. Before I know it, my body wraps around his. We're both still naked, and his hard length jolts against my belly.

"You promised I could play with you after all the orgasms you claimed last night," I remind him. He made it very clear my orgasms were *his*. And that's something the independent woman in me threw some side-eye at…until he told me how good I came for him.

There's no doubt in my mind he knows what those words do to me. But he hasn't said anything. Yet.

"You passed out before I could clean you up."

I vaguely remember him using a warm, wet cloth between my thighs as I star-fished on his bed, utterly spent.

"Oops," I say with an apologetic smile. "You off today, or will I have to wait until the weekend?"

His thumb caresses the side of my boob, sending tingles of pleasure through my chest. My nips are standing at attention, waiting for him to turn his focus on them.

"I've got a shift today, but then I'll be off for two days."

My voice cracks as I try to respond, but I'm distracted, so distracted. His cock twitches against my belly button while his thumb taunts my nipples.

Clearing my throat, I mutter, "Bowling."

"Bowling?"

"I have bowling this weekend," I manage to explain.

Just ask him, Gracie.

"Want to come?"

The confusion flickering in his gaze has me squirming.

He hesitates, then says, "That's…public."

I frown, trying to figure out what that means. Is he wanting to keep our relationship quiet? There's no reason to anymore. Isn't that why he switched to a new physical therapist? At least on paper, I still plan to work with him, regardless.

"Were we not still talking about when I'd let you play with me?" he asks. "Because I don't normally take my cock out in public. It's frowned upon." He winks at me. Between that and his hot, heavy cock pressing into my stomach, I'm nearly panting. "It would be all over *The Vine*. Probably cost me my job. Which you threatened once, but of all the ways to get fired, an under-the-table handy at Gutter Ball might not be so bad."

He's teasing me, I know this, but I can't ignore the obvious provocation in his tone.

"First, reporting you to Declan was an empty threat." *Mostly.*

His disbelieving hum vibrates through his chest, the roughness of his sexy morning voice making it a growl.

I give his hair a playful tug. "I was distraught, okay? I had a concussion, seatbelt injuries, a sprained wrist. And on top of all that, you were being a prick." I slide my hands down his back. "Second, you're a *Vaughn*. I'm sure you can get away with anything in this town."

"Being a 'Vaughn' guarantees nothing. Sometimes it works against us. There are high expectations and family legacies to preserve." His droll tone pulls at my cheeks as I attempt a somber expression.

I think back to the photo of his dad holding up his awards, and my expression softens. "And now?"

His dark gaze sweeps down my chest to my aching flesh. "My

focus is on you." He shifts his hips, the thick head of his cock so close to where I need him. "Sore?" he asks.

I shake my head. It's not exactly a lie. I'm sore, but not so sore I don't want to have sex with him.

He squeezes my breast, his thumb moving over my nipple in a firm stroke.

"I have less than an hour to get to work," I murmur as his lips find that spot under my jaw that makes me shiver.

I watch the muscles at the top of his shoulders flex. And then that mouth of his is devouring me, his scruff scraping against my neck, collarbone, the tops of my breasts.

One hand dives beneath me, lifting my ass. He sinks in, and I arch into him, eyes glued to his abs as they clench with each swing of his hips. I'll never tire of the sexy visual of my pale thighs contrasted against his bronzed skin.

Getting brave, I whisper, "On your back."

Eyes locked on mine, he hums as if considering my request. He slows his rhythm, shifting slightly, moving deeper. I moan, heat flooding my lower abdomen.

I know what I have to do to get what I want, and I can be his good girl for a few minutes...until I get on top.

"Please? Let me ride you, Jensen."

It's something I haven't tried in a long while, but I've been fantasizing about having him under me, watching his face as I draw out his pleasure.

His hand skims up my stomach, between my breasts, to cup my cheek. When his thumb moves over my lips, I open. The digit slips inside and I close my lips around it.

He releases a groan, and rasps, "Suck."

I swirl my tongue around him before sucking hard.

"I need that mouth on me. Soon," he grunts out. "Sucking me so fucking good."

He removes his thumb, wet from my mouth, and uses it to circle my clit. Lightning zips up my thighs. I will not last like this, and I'm now determined to climb on top of this man and make him moan.

"Jen…"

Dark, heated eyes drag up to my face from where he's playing with my pussy.

In a series of swift movements I could never accomplish, he flips me on top of him, still buried deep inside me—deeper now.

Groaning, I plant a hand on his chest. The wide grin pulling at his mouth distracts me as his hands grip my hips, wrapping around to my ass.

God, he has huge hands. Everything about him, everything I feel for him, is huge.

I grind, slow and easy at first, because this is going to take all of my concentration. While I love the idea of being on top—teasing, testing, driving him crazy—my lack of coordination is making it more difficult than I remembered.

I remind myself to stop overthinking, to focus on him, how he fills me, the way he's biting down on his lower lip.

"You look so fucking good riding my dick, babe." He swats my ass and my walls flutter around him. It's been less than a week and he's already got me figured out.

When I lean forward to kiss him, I lose my balance, knocking over the lamp on his nightstand. His grip on me is the only reason I didn't face-plant on the floor. I right myself, holding onto the headboard with determination.

He guides my hips, and that ridiculous insecurity creeps in, causing me to wonder if it's because I'm not doing it right.

There have been incidents in the past—bleeding lips, kneed balls, a concussion, unintentional teeth scraping, and one fractured penis. So, I might have a few bedroom hang-ups.

Make it good for him. He doesn't want to fuck the Energizer Bunny. Just move, do whatever feels good and he'll like it.

Something shifts in him as he reads my expression. I'm

undone by the tenderness in his gaze when his hands move to my face.

"Easy, baby. I got you." Holding his stare, I move again, but with hesitation. "You sure you're not sore?"

I shake my head, keeping my eyes on his darkened gaze. An insatiable hunger lingers, obliterating my pesky anxieties about taking charge.

"I want it to be good for you," I admit.

"Grace. You're on top of me, naked, your pussy squeezing my dick, your tits bouncing like a goddamn dream. The only thing that isn't good is knowing I'll have to wait two days to have you like this again."

And that's when it hits me. Jensen is long-term. He wants *me* —all of me. I don't *need* to tell him about my condition. I *want* to tell him. Because I know he won't look at me any differently. How he feels about me, the way he views me, won't change because there's an official name for my clumsiness.

Rough hands trail down my back to my ass. My clit rubs against his pubic bone, breasts swinging against his chest. His fingers clench, pulling my cheeks apart as he pumps into me with swift thrusts.

He licks his thumb, and I move faster, knowing what's coming.

"No. You first," I tell him.

With one hand, I reach behind me to cup his balls, grazing my nails over them and grinning at his hiss of pleasure. Using two fingers, I massage the spot right underneath.

"*Fuck.*" He groans.

I may not be as nimble or smooth during sex, but I know a few fun tricks.

"Give it to me, hotshot," I taunt, my hips swaying in wild circles, but he doesn't seem to mind.

"Not the way this works, baby," he growls, thickening inside me. His dick rubs along the deep spot I can never stimulate on my own, even with toys.

Moaning, I keep my hips moving as my fingers massage him with firmer, deeper strokes. With a few rumbles of pleasure, he pants my name, his body locking up as he releases inside me.

Oh yeah, I like being in control of this big man.

"Grace, baby. Fucking incredible," he says, heaving out a breath.

His eyes shift from enthusiastic appreciation to wicked retribution. And then he comes after my clit like it stole something precious from him, and I explode on a scream.

I FLY past the kitchen to snag my bag off the chair in the dining room. Jensen has a more flexible schedule since he's on light duty, but I have less than thirty minutes before my shift.

"Coffee."

Turning, I spot my hot-as-all-hell man in the kitchen holding out a travel mug.

"Declan will be here in fifteen minutes to give us a ride into town."

Flicking my still-wet braid over my shoulder, I stride up to him and accept the coffee. "Thank you."

He grunts a response and leans against the counter.

"Where's your crutch?" I ask.

"I'm at my desk a lot," is his non-answer.

I roll my eyes. "I'll bring you a cane tomorrow night. And make sure your new PT goes over how to properly walk in that boot." I bend to check it. "Did you make sure it's on right? It goes tight, tighter, tightest—bottom to top."

"Baby, I got it." He dips down and kisses me—chaste and sweet.

"Good." I smile up at him. "So… Couldn't find my panties. Again."

There's a devious glint in his eyes as he leans against the island.

"I'm going commando to work, Jensen." That full, bossy mouth of his twists into a grin. "Is this how we're playing things? I have to carry extra panties in my bag?"

Warm eyes sparkle at me as he takes a healthy swig of his coffee.

"You're a dirty, dirty man, Jensen Vaughn."

A wolfish smile spreads across his stunning face. I haven't had a chance to ride it yet, and I'm going to need to fix that soon.

"Keep the panties." I step into him and steal a kiss, allowing my lips to linger for a moment.

"Already planned to," he says against my mouth.

I place my coffee on the counter beside him and loop my arms over his shoulders. "Fingering my panties and having a raging hard-on while surrounded by a bunch of dudes all day won't be weird at all."

He smacks my ass and lunges forward to crush his lips to mine. I'm defenseless to his soul-melting powers.

When he pulls back, he asks, "What time is bowling?"

"Hm?" I tear my gaze from his mouth. "Oh. I need to be there by 7:30 p.m."

"I'll be there." His voice is low, assertive.

"At bowling?"

"Yes."

"Just to watch me?"

"Yes," he repeats.

"It'll be boring." I consider what a usual game is like, and change my statement. "Actually, no. It'll be loud and flat-out nutty. You'll hate it."

His hand moves from my ass as he puts his coffee down next

to mine and reaches for my face, tilting it up to him. "You trying to convince me not to come?"

I shake my head. "Just making sure you set your expectations accordingly."

"I'm aware what a night with you might entail, shortcake." With a peck on my lips, he hands me back my coffee. Naturally, I fumble with it, sloshing coffee all over my pants and the floor.

He helps me clean it up with a wry smile.

"I can be a bit of a bowling disaster. Haven't quite got the hang of it yet. Some days are better than others…" My lips twist and I toy with the hem of my shirt, thinking of the best way to tell him.

"There's nothing disastrous about you, Grace. Not a damn thing." He draws me back into him, my hands splaying against his chest. "It doesn't matter what you do—it's all sexy to me. Hell, even at the Fire & Ice game, you impressed me. Between your skills and hockey knowledge, the chirpy commentating, and that one brief taste of your lips, I was hard for half the game."

The raw honesty in his eyes leaves me stunned.

"I'm not pushing you away anymore, Grace. The stupid shit I used to say instead of dealing with how you made me feel, that's in the past." He draws me into him again. "So even if you're not the best bowler, I won't notice, babe. Though I'm sure you're being modest—you have an innate ability to knock shit over, so those pins don't stand a chance." He grins down at me and my face aches from the size of my sappy smile.

"Jensen…"

"I'll mostly be watching your ass, anyway," he adds.

I drop my forehead to his chest, chuckling. "Jensen," I try again, lifting my head to give him a soft smile. "There's a reason for my knocking-shit-over skills."

"I make you so hot, you lose bodily function?" He's joking, but there's a frown marring his forehead.

"Well, you often do make me nervous and keyed up, which

can make things worse." His hands roam over me in comforting strokes. "I have a neurological condition called Developmental Coordination Disorder or Dyspraxia. I prefer Dyspraxia because it sounds like a superhero name or like I'm some kind of human-alien hybrid with special powers. Or that's what I thought when the doctor diagnosed me at seven-years-old."

His eyes search mine like he's trying to figure out if I'm fucking with him.

"There's a broad range of symptoms and severities. The type I have is called ideomotor dyspraxia, which affects organizing single-step tasks, movement sequences, and both gross and fine motor skills. My handwriting is atrocious, which is fine since almost everything is digital now."

He shifts, leaning heavily on the counter behind him, his hands slipping from me to grip the edge of the granite.

I pause, unsure if I should continue.

"What else?" he asks, his lashes lift, dark irises flicking up to me briefly. An array of emotions clouds his eyes—confusion, surprise, anger. And then something else, something that steals my breath. Anguish.

"What else, Grace?" he repeats.

I pick at my fingernails, not wanting to see any other reactions. "I'm fortunate not to have any speech or significant learning disabilities. But I can be scatter-brained and impulsive. Heightened emotions and stress exacerbate all of my symptoms."

"Jesus Christ," he mumbles, scrubbing his hands down his face.

Well shit, it's not like I'm dying or something. I thought this would be a lightbulb moment, an explanation. He'd ask some questions, and that's it.

"It's honestly not that bad. I've spent years learning how to train my brain and body to function the way I need it to. I don't let it stop me from doing anything, so I don't talk about it much. People know I'm clumsy. They can accept it or not." I shrug.

As an adult, it's straightforward, but as a kid, it took years to cultivate that acceptance and confidence.

Jensen is quiet, his gaze shifting around as if lost in his thoughts.

So I continue. "Muscle memory is a huge blessing since those tasks are the easiest for me. I learned early that the more I practiced something, the sooner it became an automatic action instead of one that requires more mental processing. New physical tasks can be brutal. Hell, I still have trouble biking some days if I don't make sure I'm doing it regularly."

His face is full of torment when he pushes off the counter, wrapping an arm around my waist again. "You should have told me," he grinds out.

Not something he gets to decide.

Resting one hand on his arm, I bring the other up to tap a finger to my chin. "Huh. I must have missed your slumber party invitation where we were going to stay up all night and reveal all of our deepest, darkest secrets," I tease. "I thought you hated me, remember? That doesn't exactly inspire the desire to share personal, private life details. At that point, I figured you'd either use the information against me or worse— feel sorry for me and treat me differently." He grimaces, his chin dropping with a defeated sigh. "I wanted to tell you now, so I did."

"And I appreciate that."

"You don't seem appreciative. You look pissed."

"I am. I gave you so much shit, Grace. Every fucking time I saw you." His hands come up to cup the sides of my face. "Fuck, Grace. I practically bullied you."

The rawness of his voice hurts my heart. I want our past to be in the past.

"You didn't bully me. You yelled at me for being reckless, and for—"

"And you couldn't help it." He thrusts a hand in the air. "It's like yelling at a visually impaired person to watch where they're going."

I mean…not quite.

It might have riled me up whenever he came at me with his lectures, or hurled prickly comments my way, but his reactions make more sense now.

"I still expect you to give me shit when my impulsiveness gets the best of me. I love pushing myself and can't turn down a challenge. But sometimes I need to pause for a beat and inject a little rationale into the thinking process."

His chest moves with a deep inhale. After a few moments, he mutters, "I called you careless, a menace. Several times."

I shrug. "I've been called worse."

"By whom?" His tongue slicks over his teeth like he's trying to keep his overprotective instincts at bay.

"Long time ago. Really, babe, I'm good."

He dips, gripping the backs of my thighs, and with a quick spin, deposits me on the counter. "Don't sugarcoat it, shortcake. I fucked up, and you might not want to admit it because you're strong as hell, but some of the shit I said must have hurt you. More than I knew at the time." I tilt my head, giving him a small smile. He's taking this harder than I expected. "And I'll be replacing every negative word, every moment I've given you crap about things you had no control over, with good memories—with orgasms and smiles, with praise and affection."

"Not going to say no to that." I waggle my brows and lean forward for a kiss.

Right as his tongue delves into my mouth, there's a knock at the door, and I pull back.

Jensen frowns. "Shit," he says, helping me off the counter. "Declan's here."

I'm a little disappointed at the interruption, but I also know Jensen will need some time to process.

"Jensen!" Declan's voice booms from outside. "Your murder

cat is lurking in the shrubs by the garage. Get your asses out here before it pounces."

"She's not my cat," Jensen shouts back.

I snort, having seen the food he's set out for Reaper on several occasions.

With a laugh, I grab my coffee and backpack.

"Shotgun!" I shout before racing to the door.

CHAPTER
TWENTY-SIX

JENSEN

"Two gutter balls and then a strike!" Grace shouts from the lane. "That's how it's done." High-fives and boob bumps break out around me.

My tongue slicks along my teeth to keep from laughing. These ladies are batshit crazy. Grace is one of the few women here on the "safe side" of menopause, and yes, that's been a topic of conversation tonight. I knew better than to ask *any* questions about the subject.

I've heard things I can't unhear and learned more about unwanted nipple hair than any man needs to know. I've also resorted to issuing a wide variety of non-answers to evade the sneaky questions Grace's teammates asked while she bowled her frames.

Lonnie, the sixty-year-old "team manager," is three beers in and has spent most of the game peppering me with questions. She can't bowl because of ongoing arthritis issues, but she started the team years ago and recruited Grace within weeks of her moving to town. Her best friend Nina also attends every game but doesn't bowl. The best way to characterize Nina's role is "team fluffer." She doles out compliments, neck rubs, and boisterous shouts of encouragement to each bowler—even on other teams.

Their husbands are here as well, but they play for another team. When the ladies introduced us, Lonnie's husband clapped me on the back, wished me luck and then both men fucked off to their own team.

That left me with one other husband, several menopausal women, and a few younger ladies here to drink, bowl, and over-share in ways that had Grace watching my every reaction with open amusement.

"That's a special girl you've got there," Lonnie says to me after the boob thrusting ends.

"Yes, ma'am," I agree.

It's only been a few days since Gracie told me about her developmental coordination disorder. And I've spent countless hours researching everything I can about it. There are a wide variety of symptoms and severities, but my research made one thing very clear—I'm a giant asshole.

Grace wants to put my ignorant remarks behind us, but I keep circling back to one especially stupid remark I made...*Are you capable of acting normal?*

"Normal" for her is a sore spot, one I didn't know I had poked. Her delays brought her years of turmoil, but it also made her into the woman who works endlessly to accomplish exactly what she sets out to. Her fierce tenacity and drive drew me to her from the start.

But the idea I added to her struggles, hurt her in hidden ways, still doesn't sit right. I've been making it up to her every day, with my actions, my words, and my mouth. I've been having the most fun with the latter.

"Beautiful, inside and out," Lonnie adds, interrupting the appealing turn my thoughts took.

I tip my head with a grin. "She is."

"Terrible bowler," she adds with a cheeky smile.

Astonishingly unpredictable is the only way to describe Grace's bowling style. But every so often, she pulls back and releases an incredible throw. Her advice for her teammates and knowledge of the game is spot-on though.

"You're lucky to have her on your team."

She pats my hand. "Not a bad answer."

Grace plops down next to me at the *Bowling Babes'* reserved table. "They might have won the first game, but we've got the next one." She rubs her hands to warm them and gets up to kneel in front of Kerrie, the unfiltered redhead. "I'm going to work on Kerrie's calf cramp while one of you gets us nachos to power up for the next game."

Every woman looks at me.

Kerrie's husband avoids eye contact as he flips through a fishing magazine, muttering, "Not it."

Right. I'm on nacho duty. Just as I'm sliding out of my chair, someone moans.

"Thanks, Gracie," Kerri shouts over the racket of the bowling alley. "Devin and I tried a new position called Leap Frog, and it was quite the leg workout. Should have stretched."

Being the nacho bitch is looking pretty damn good right now.

I head to the concession area and put in our order, including drink refills, a pizza, and a lime slushie for Grace.

When I get back to the table, trays of food in tow, Grace is talking animatedly with her hands, not noticing my arrival. I move my chair to the empty spot next to Grace and hand her the slushie.

"Oh! How did you know lime is my favorite?" she asks a second before the straw is in her mouth and she does an excited little wiggle.

Christ, she's cute.

"So, this will be our only break tonight," she tells me. She nods to her teammate, who's singing a lullaby into her phone.

"Mandy's babysitter can only stay until ten tonight, so we'll have to finish up our last two games back-to-back."

"Maybe Brody could stop by..." I offer.

She laughs, her eyes sparkling from the multicolored LED lights illuminating the lanes. "Actually, he's fantastic with Ava. She digs his serious demeanor and the way he pretends not to know anything about kids. She thinks he's performing a bit."

Definitely not a "bit."

She shoves a nacho in her mouth, closing her eyes in ecstasy. "So good. Hot sauce?" Her eyes scan the table until she spots the side of hot sauce. She leans over to grab it, placing a noisy kiss on my cheek as she does.

"So..." Kerrie points between us. "Tell us the story. How did you two get together?"

The other ladies clamor in agreement, wanting the details.

"She pushed him down the stairs," Devin answers, emerging from his magazine to snatch up the largest pizza slice.

Focus, man. There's more pizza, and these people are important to Grace.

His wife elbows him and looks over at Grace. "He's kidding."

"Um..." Grace widens her eyes at me, waiting for me to chime in. "I brought him food, and he started being less of a dick?" she tells them, the hesitant inflection on the end making it sound like a question.

My lips press together, the corners dipping down as I nod in silent affirmation.

"So you never hated him?" Kerrie asks.

Interested in her answer, I raise my brows at Grace.

"Hate is a strong word. But were there days I would have liked to see him tied up and left in the shallow waters of Cragg Creek for the leeches to snack on? Yes."

That was a little too specific.

"You imagine these kinds of scenarios often, shortcake?"

She smacks a kiss on my lips and answers, "Not today."

"Well, look at that. Beauty tamed the beast," a familiar voice booms from behind us.

Grace straightens and moves to look around me. She smiles and waves at my brother.

Jaxon moves closer and greets everyone, causing even Devin to perk up and start a conversation. I add two slices of pizza to my plate and stretch my arm behind Grace's chair, toying with her hair while I eat.

She listens to everyone and takes part in the various topics around the table, her hand slipping to rest on my thigh. I have to contain a possessive groan, liking her hand there a little too much.

She's laughing at something a teammate says when her other hand reaches across to my plate. The sexy temptress picks up my pizza and wraps those succulent lips around the slice she's folded lengthwise to take a bite—*folded*.

And I don't care.

My fingers go to the back of her neck, skimming the soft skin of her nape. She puts the pizza back on my plate and relaxes, leaning into my touch.

But then a hand drops onto my shoulder. "So I guess Brody and I don't have to keep a close eye on Grace anymore?" Jaxon asks. "Looks like you got her covered."

"Keep a close eye on me?" Grace repeats, her gaze narrowing on me.

Fucking Jaxon.

"I was worried about what you'd get up to without me around to rescue you."

"Bullshit," Jaxon responds. "He wanted us to keep other assholes away from you."

I never said that. But it was definitely my intention, whether or not I wanted to admit it.

"Interesting…" Grace says, her eyes flicking back to me. "How long ago was this?"

I glare at my brother, and he grins but clams up.

Deflecting, I slide her green drink over. "Drink your slushie."

Grace flashes me a wicked smile before placing the straw between her lips and returning her attention to Lonnie, Kerrie, and her other team members.

"You sticking around for a bit?" I ask my brother, hoping he'll join me for beers while the ladies bowl.

"Nah. Just got a text that you two were getting cozy bowling and had to see for myself." He points toward the parking lot. "I'm meeting Anders at the gym. I'll swing back and pick you two up when I'm done."

"Thanks, man. Boot comes off next week, then I can return the favor."

"You're going to regret that, Jenny. Your ass is easy to cart around town since all you do is go to work and run a few errands. Me, on the other hand..." He drags a hand down his chest suggestively, like the endearing shithead he is. "I'll be out late, heading into the city on weekends, hanging out in the loud, obnoxious places you hate."

My cheek twitches at the front he puts on.

"Or we could skip some of that shit and I'll let you, Anders, and Sawyer take the quads out with my new paintball guns. We could make it a weekend, either at my place or head out to Cooper's Pass, do some camping. I can bring all the shit we'd need."

It's something we all used to do a lot more, but between my failed wedding that spurred a singular focus on work and Brody's recent appointment as Chief of Police, we haven't had many opportunities.

"Hell yes. Sawyer will want to bring our sister, which means Anders will ask about bringing his new lady friend, who, by the way, is the worst."

I shrug. "Grace might want to come too."

My brother's perma-smirk eases off his face and turns into an approving appraisal. When his gaze shifts to Grace, the side of his mouth tips up, and he nods at me. I always knew he liked Grace, not in the same way I did, but he definitely liked the way she got under my skin.

"Is this before or after your house party?"

Grace's braid whips me in the face as she turns to look at us. "You're having a party?" she asks, her eyes wide in confusion.

Shit. I forgot about that.

"Apparently," I tell her with a small smile.

"Still in the works, but it will probably be the weekend after next," Jax informs us.

"Am I invited?" she asks with a sassy head tilt.

I press my lips to her ear and say, "You're required. Wouldn't be bearable otherwise."

"Ah, shit," my brother grumbles, squatting down beside my chair. The faint chemical smell of spray paint wafts off of him, mingling with scents of cheese and salsa around us. I have my suspicions about why he smells like that, but it's best for both of us if I don't ask. "That's 'Meghan-with-an-h.'" Jax lowers his tone. "I may or may not have told her I was helping you with a bathroom reno tonight. If she comes over here later and asks, I'm at your house tiling shit."

"You don't have the skill or patience to tile a damn thing. Let alone my bathroom. You hate renovations."

"She thinks 'North' is whatever direction she's facing. You've got a distinct intellectual advantage here, bro," he informs me, his tone hushed. "Just use big tiling words like leveling fin, garnet gauge, and grout. She'll get confused and walk away."

"Only one of those was real," I point out.

"You and I know that. *She* will not."

Nachos spew from Grace's mouth before she covers her choking laugh.

"She's heading to the concession. I'm sneaking out. Text me when you're ready to go. I'll park at the staff exit out back by the dumpster." My brother straightens and double-times it straight out the doors.

"Gracie!" someone yells. "We're starting, doll."

My girl hops up and one hideous shoe slips on the floor. With a shriek, her arms flail. I lunge forward in my seat and catch her, toppling her back into me.

She lands on my lap with a little *whoop*.

"Sorry, bowling shoes are bad for me," she says, gripping my arms.

"Not the first time I've had you fall in my lap, and it better not be the last."

Her eyes narrow as she adjusts her position. "Last time, you didn't seem happy about it. I believe I still wound up on the floor. No thanks to you." One brow arches in challenge.

"Wasn't really in the right headspace to be around people, shortcake. You got a little too close, and believe it or not, I liked it a little too much."

"Yeah, I liked it too," she whispers. She runs a finger along my lips. "Until you opened your mouth."

I grin at her sass. "You still liked me."

"Your surly ass got my shameless bits tingling, sure. Doesn't mean I liked it."

I ease a few strands of hair behind her ear and slide my fingers to wrap around the side of her neck. Her pulse pounds and her cheeks heat. "How about now?"

"In this moment?" She gives a noncommittal shrug. "You're alright."

A flash of light makes us both flinch. With my retinas burning, I try to locate the person who took the picture, but there are too many people around.

News of the two of us will be everywhere by tomorrow. Grace's body is wound tight as she also peers around. I hold her hips still, shifting slightly so she can feel what she does to me every time she's near.

Her eyes widen, chest flaring on a sharp inhale.

I place my lips on her ear. "I was hard for you that first time too, Grace."

"Gracie! You're up, doll," Lonnie hollers. "You can fondle your big firefighter later. We need to win this game, or we're sunk."

"Go knock some pins down, babe." I smack her ass.

"Yes, sir."

I grip the back of her neck, pulling her close and growling, "Good girl," against her ear.

Her cheeks flood with heat and a soft, pitchy moan escapes.

"Fucking knew it," I mutter. My girl has a praise kink. I've been wondering for weeks, toying with it, but now… "That's going to be a lot of fun, shortcake."

"No." She glares at me. "You are not using that against me, Jensen."

"Oh, it's not 'against' you, baby. It's foreplay." I nip her earlobe. "And I'm going to work you up every fucking chance I get."

She jumps up, jogs over to the ball return and grabs her ball. Her braid flies as she twists to wink at me over her shoulder. When she lines up, she gives me an intentional booty shake before squaring her shoulders and taking a quick five-step approach to the lane.

Then my girl bowls a strike.

And again on her next frame.

The Bowling Babes win their first league game of the year.

While celebrating, Lottie informs me I'm required to attend every game—as if I'd be anywhere else.

TWENTY-SEVEN

GRACIE

THE VINE COMMUNITY UPDATE

Spring has sprung, and love is in the air. Between this year's Spring-a-Ling Festival, a fully booked wedding season, and tourists trickling in, two of our residents must have thought they could fly under the radar.

Gracie Parker and Jensen Vaughn are official. We spotted the duo cuddling at Gutter Ball. The way they stared deeply into each other's eyes, hands casually draped over one another, confirmed our suspicions.

From their first meeting, these two have been dancing around each other like MMA fighters, looking for their opponent's weakness.

When word of Jensen heading into the city to see a new physical therapist reached us, we worried our burly firefighter was being especially obstinate. Apparently, he was simply paving the way for Gracie and him to be out in the open.

Want to find your perfectly imperfect love match yourself? The Rec Center is having their monthly singles meetup next weekend starting at 7:00 p.m. Register on the Events Page of The Vine Community Bulletin site and don't forget to bring your balloon (this is not a euphemism —balloons are part of the ice breaker game. Please do not bring condoms to this event.)

I forward the post to Dani and Harper, chuckling at the safe-sex messages *The Vine* will probably receive today. How many men will think this is an invitation to a bareback orgy? God, I have so many questions.

Now that I can sit down for a break, I put my phone on the cafeteria table and snap off a piece of the Kit Kat I spent too long deciding on at the vending machine. I collapse against the chair back, shove the entire piece into my mouth, and close my eyes to rest for a few minutes.

Jensen and I have spent most nights together this week. We didn't bother with any pretenses or false intentions to go out or engage in any social activities.

I had wondered if we would end up staying naked and in bed, if Jensen was looking for just a physical relationship. But the man is so damn good to me. It's almost intimidating.

He cooks, listens, anticipates my needs. It's almost annoying how incredible he is at being a boyfriend when he was the sharpest thorn in my side for so long. It's official. Jensen has accomplished his goal of proving that kind-hearted assholes really do exist.

My stomach flutters with excitement the moment my eyes land on any part of him. He makes me weak in all the best ways. I've lowered my walls, let myself fall all the way into him, knowing he'll catch me. Jensen Vaughn will always catch me.

He was doing it even when I thought he hated me.

An unruly smile stretches across my face as I chomp into another Kit Kat piece. I feel like the nerdy schoolgirl waiting for her date with the captain of the football team, who turns out to be much more than a jock with an attitude problem.

"Heard you met with HR today."

The sudden presence beside me causes me to jostle in my chair. The wall behind me is the only reason I don't topple backward.

Oblivious, Tanner takes the seat beside me, arranging his sandwich and chips in front of him before looking over at me with expectation.

Gossip travels around the hospital almost as fast as it does in town. Except the outpatient clinic is usually a bit of an island in some ways. We stick to our area since we don't use any of the hospital facilities and our staffing is separate.

"Yep," I say, taking a small bite of my chocolate instead of inhaling it like I did the first few pieces.

"About your new boyfriend?"

I'd rather not have this conversation with a guy who tried to stick his tongue down my throat only a few months ago.

"They wanted to confirm dates and get a statement about when our relationship began, since there was a lot of speculation around town."

Kai also made some comments when he came in to rebook with a different therapist. HR made notes of the details and took a statement from me regarding my relationship with Jensen. They also reminded me I could not continue treating him, which was a moot point, since they already knew he was no longer a patient.

"We should have placed a bet," Tanner says, unwrapping his sandwich.

"A bet?"

"At the hockey game. You refused to believe Jensen had a thing for you."

I tsk at him. "He *hated* he had a thing for me. Not sure that counts."

"It definitely counts," he mumbles around a bite of his turkey sandwich.

My phone vibrates against the table, so I flip it over.

JENSEN:

Grace.

There's a hole in my door.

Did you install a cat door while I was at work? Because I just reamed out Jaxon, and after he finished laughing, he insisted it wasn't him.

He sounds a lot less impressed than I imagined. I'd venture to say he's leaning toward pissed.

New phone, who dis?

Nope. That was the wrong thing to say. Immediate regret.

Grace. Explain.

I should have asked him first. But he does so much for his mom and others, I thought this would be a cute gesture. Plus, I was restless, being in his house without him while he was at work, and his tools from flooring the bathroom were *right there.*

Technically, it's a dog door. I messed up the measurements for the cat door and had to upsize to the dog door. It was that or buy you a new door.

I don't have a cat. Or a dog.

Reaper is practically yours. Now she can come in to eat and snuggle.

As can squirrels. And raccoons.

I did not think of that. But what are the chances random animals will use that tiny door?

Unlikely.

He sends me a picture of an adorable squirrel—on his kitchen counter.

Oh shit.

Do you have secret Photoshop skills?

He reads it, starts typing, stops, starts again, stops.

Babe?

Our only hope is to lure Reaper in here to scare this fucker off.

The "our" makes me all kinds of giddy.

Blowjobs!

What are you doing, Gracie? Are you really this thirsty for his dick?
I haven't given a blowjob in years. Past experiences have put me off, but I can't stop thinking about getting on my knees for this man.

Babe...

I can hear his voice as I read the word, and it's filled with exasperation and confusion.

I fucked up. I know you like that damn cat, and I was trying to be helpful.

I'll consider that after I get this menace out of my house. I've already got my hands full with one menace, and this squirrel isn't as hot or fun as her.

I can't decide whether his statement should offend me or delight me.

Since I'm the reason he has a wild animal loose in his home, I'm choosing delighted.

I owe you a new door.

Don't worry about it.

It was sweet.

By "sweet" do you mean impulsive and short-sighted?

Yes.

I snort. I'm surprised he's not giving me more shit about this. I'll probably get a full lecture in person.

Pfft. You knew what you were getting into by dating me.

Mayhem, sexual torment, bodily harm, and now squirrel invasions.

Oh, please. You love me.

I frantically press the delete button, but the message is already sent. We have *not* mentioned love yet. I've been too timid. I mean, he was in love with someone else, ready to marry them, less than a year ago. And I'm joking about how he *loves* me?

You think so, huh?

There's no chance at a favorable damage control outcome. Anything I say now is guaranteed to make it worse, so I send a smiling angel emoji.

He takes ten agonizing seconds to respond.

> Come over after work. I have a surprise for you. Wear something comfortable.

I'm half disappointed, half relieved he's choosing to ignore my comment. But mostly, I'm grateful. Now I have a surprise to think about instead of imagining the horrified look on his face to what he likely views as an attempt to Jedi mind-trick him into loving me.

I SHOW up at Jensen's house on my bike again. The main reason is because asking for rides has become tedious—for our friends. It's too much of a burden to ask someone to drive me or him four or more times a week. This will piss him off, but goading him into an argument about my bike is preferable to discussing the dog door and the "you love me" awkwardness.

As I prop my bike against his garage, the front door opens and shuts. I spin around and see him striding toward me. Without his walking boot.

His eyes narrow on my bike for a moment, but he doesn't pursue it. Huh. Weird.

"Your boot came off today? I thought that wasn't for a few more days."

He kicks his right leg out. "They had a cancellation and had me come in this morning."

I saunter closer and place my hands on him, moving them up his biceps, over his shoulders, and down to his chest. It's my favorite spot on him. There are many parts of him packed with muscle. His formidable strength strains under my fingertips in a way that makes me weak-kneed. But there's something about his chest, his steady heartbeat, the vibrations of his gravelly voice that's comforting.

"Feel good?"

"Yeah. Feels fantastic."

"Is this my surprise?" Or maybe the surprise is what he can do now that he's not restricted by his boot?

His mouth tips up on one side. "No."

"Oh." I glance around, trying to spot what else it could be.

Jensen cups my jaw in his hand and kisses me on the nose before moving around me. He enters the code for the garage, motioning for me to join him.

What kind of surprise would he hide in the garage?

And then he points to his truck.

Oh. He can drive now.

I smirk and hook my arm through his. "You taking me on a date now that you can drive?"

"Just want to go for a drive with you." He captures a wayward hair that's fallen into my face and tucks it behind my ear. Unlike me, he seems to relish my rebellious strands. "Then stop somewhere for a picnic. Maybe even make good on that blowjob offer."

My heart skitters in an uneven beat.

"But first, we need to talk."

Here comes my lecture. At least I know how to handle this.

"About the dog door?" I ask with a hesitant smile. "I can get you a new door. And I'm sure I can find another YouTube video to show me how to install it."

"Not what I wanted to talk to you about."

"The squirrel? Did you get him out? Did he damage anything?"

"The squirrel is gone. Had to throw out everything that was left out on the counters though. He gorged himself, which made it less difficult to capture him."

"Sorry." It comes out as a whisper to hide the laughter in my tone.

"We need to talk about what happened in my truck last time."

I really hope he's talking about the kiss.

"You're fishing for compliments?" I tease. "Fine. It was by far the best truck kiss of my life."

His eyes soften as a tentative smile graces his face. "Babe, you're terrified of driving. And I made you do it. I caused your panic attack." He ruffles a hand through his hair. "Let me help you."

"Jensen, I'm fine. I don't need to drive, and I wouldn't call that a panic attack."

That's a lie. I completely lost it, and I haven't thought about it since because I am worried it'll happen again from just the memory.

"You can practice with my truck, with me beside you, until you get comfortable again." He points at my bike. "And then you can stop riding that fucking bicycle everywhere."

"I've been riding that bicycle for six months and it hasn't been an issue. I get where I need to go. It's therapeutic and helps shape the ass you lo—like."

His eyes dip down, upper body shifting to get a better look at the ass I mentioned.

Once his gaze comes back to mine, he says, "You have not been riding that bike for six months. That's your second bike. The first one got fucked up when you were a 'bystander' in a collision with some parked cars."

"That wasn't my fault."

"Never said it was. But it still happened." The intensity of his concern makes me pause.

"I enjoy biking. So...no." I pat his chest and add, "Thank you."

"You helped me, even when I refused it. Now it's my turn."

Twisting my lips, I question whether I'm being stubborn like he was or if I don't want to showcase my weaknesses to the man I'm falling for.

"I bet I can get you back to driving with ease before I can return to full-time duties at the station."

I huff at the obvious goading. "That's different. Your injuries are physical and require time to heal. My issue with driving is… well, complicated, but it'll take a lot less time than recovering from an ankle fracture." Though, he did just get his boot off, so he'll be back to full duties within a month, two tops.

His grin widens. "So we agree it'll be quick and painless."

"I'll think about it," I grumble.

And I will. I've pushed this aside for too long and now it's become a giant obstacle. I'm not one to give up on anything, but I also felt like I *shouldn't* be driving, despite having a clean record for a decade prior.

"Great. You can think on the way to our picnic spot. And then drive us back."

"Today? You want to start *today*?" I shout.

"Exposure therapy," he explains.

I glare at him, but I want to do this. It's been on my mind for months—especially after my failed attempt—but something has held me back.

I was *so* alone last time. The stubborn independent part of me made excuses, rationalizations. What I needed was someone to push me into getting behind the wheel again. Because that accident made me question myself.

He reaches for me, cocooning me in his embrace. "I can't stop thinking about it, Grace. The sheer panic in your eyes, the way your hands shook. Let me help you."

His thumbs caress my cheeks in slow, careful strokes. The way his brows draw down, the skin around his eyes tightening as if he's in pain, has my breath catching.

"Okay," I whisper. "But if I break your truck, that's on you, mister."

The kiss he lays on my mouth has my toes curling and my worries about driving his monster truck around town vanishing.

"I care about *you*, Grace. I will not let anything bad happen to you." His gaze flicks to the garage. "Or my truck." He winks and jerks his head to the side. "Now get your sweet ass in there. We are conquering your fears today."

Getting back behind the wheel with a capable fire/rescue specialist who cares about me—even when he's giving me shit—might be exactly what I need.

I slip out of his arms and move to the truck.

He fishes the keys out of his pocket. "We'll take some of the back roads that don't get much traffic." He places a hand on the hood, his mouth twisting into a grin full of provocation. "With you being hesitant to drive—which is more than understandable —I can take us out there. You're stubborn, so it'll probably take some time for you to come around to the idea of driving again. It's better if I drive us anyway, even though I just got out of a leg cast and survived an attempted homicide."

I shake my head at him, knowing what he's doing.

"It's gonna be like that, is it?" I ask.

"You tell me," he answers.

Not too long ago, letting Jensen see me in a fragile state would have had me reinforcing all my walls with stone and brick. I'd have lashed out, brushed it off, turned it around on him, anything to take the attention off myself.

Today is a different day. I climb into the passenger side and slide across to the driver's seat.

I honk the horn and yell, "Get in, hotshot."

"THAT'S MY GIRL." Jensen's hand massages the back of my neck as I pick up speed to merge onto the highway.

It's been two hours of driving the back roads. I may not be

ready for any solo driving adventures yet, but driving around in the country has been less torturous than I expected.

For the first hour, the muscles in my neck and shoulders felt as though someone coiled them into a tight ball. But Jensen's been the patient, calm presence I needed. He's kept his body pressed against mine, a hand on me, bringing me comfort. When he felt my anxiety creeping up, he'd redirect my focus by distracting me. I only had to pull over once, but after some deep breathing and his murmurs of "You're safe, baby," I was back on the road within five minutes, more determined than before.

"Ready to head into town?" he asks, pointing to the left instead of saying it, since following verbal directions is difficult for me.

With a different idea in mind, I scan the surrounding landscape. To my right, I spot a side road, splicing through a thicket of trees, and turn onto it. I can feel Jensen's gaze on my face, but he doesn't ask where I'm taking us.

"I think we need a little break," I tell him.

"Thank fuck, I'm starving," he says.

I pull off to the side, park the truck, and twist to face him.

A slow, devious smile stretches across his face as he reaches for me. His fingers hook into my leggings.

"Thought you said you were starving."

"Oh, I am. But not for what's in the picnic basket."

"No?"

"I think my girl deserves a reward."

"I pulled in here to give *you* a reward," I rasp as his hand dips into my underwear.

"Baby, my reward is eating your pussy."

He kisses me, and my hands dive under the bottom edge of his shirt. I want to feel every bulging part of the hard body that makes me tremble. His fingers slide through my slit, gently parting me.

I press forward, deepening the kiss as I remove his distracting hand from my pants. "After," I say. "First, I want to try something."

The corner of his mouth lifts. "We can try anything you want, Grace."

"I don't do oral very often. The rhythm, the overthinking..." I pause. "With the uh, *feedback* I've gotten in the past, I've mostly avoided it."

"This part of your issue with assholes?"

I nod and flick his hands away so I can work on unfastening his pants. Damn buttons are always a problem. I wonder how pissed he would be if I changed his jeans to Velcro or snap closures...

When I lower his zipper, his hard dick commands my attention.

"I might be bad at this," I confess.

He captures my mouth in a fierce kiss. "Impossible," he murmurs against my lips.

"You want references?"

"Fuck no," he growls.

"Keep your expectations low or be prepared to help me out. Because I've been told I'm only good for face-fucking."

Those relationships lasted longer than they should have, but I was young then and my self-confidence is no longer affected by rude-ass fuckboys.

"*Jesus fuck.*" His gruff voice rumbles through the truck. "Those selfish bastards missed out." He takes my hand, opening my palm and skimming his thumb over it. "Unless you're using sand for the hand job, I'm going to want you touching me as much as you want, Grace." There's fire in his eyes, part anger but mostly molten desire. "You want me to show you how I like to be touched, shortcake?"

At my nod, he presses my palm to his boxer briefs. "Tease me like this." He guides my hand up and down his shaft. "Makes me think of you pressed against me, pussy begging for my cock, needing me to make her come."

I lick my lips, wanting to skip a few steps and get him in my mouth, make him beg and moan.

"Do you feel how hard you're making me, baby?"

Instead of answering, I tug at the waistband of his underwear. He leans back and lifts his hips so I can slide the material down to his thighs.

The thick head of his cock bobs in anticipation. I wrap my hand around him with a firm grip. He hums in approval and the resonating rumble has wetness pooling in my panties.

To avoid the awkward angle I'm at on his left side, I swing a leg over him and sit astride his thighs. He grins at me as I readjust my grip. I move up and swipe a thumb over the head of his cock.

"Yeah. Just like that," he rasps, watching me touch him. "You can play with rhythm and pace. But start slow, like when I play with your pussy."

"Do you like dry handjobs or do you prefer lube?"

His eyes lift. "I just like it when you're touching me, babe." I focus on the head of his length and pick up the pace. "Fuck…"

"If you had to choose?"

His jaw tightens as he tracks my motions once more. "Feels too damn good right now to decide, babe." The rise and fall of his chest stalls like he's struggling. "We'll try lube next time," he mutters.

Those full lips of his part in ecstasy as I make faster strokes. I want to nibble on those lips, but I can't keep this going and think about kissing him.

"Two hands," he pants, guiding my other hand. "Use your other hand. Play with my balls."

He moans when I roll his balls in my hand. I slow my strokes, a frown on my face as I battle to keep the rhythm he needs. All I want to do is watch the tight rippling of his abs. Watch the pleasure light his eyes aflame.

His huge hand wraps around mine, tan against pale, leading me. Hot. As. Hell.

I lean forward and kiss him with all I have. "I want to taste you," I whisper against his lips. "I want your hands clenching my hair and your cum coating my tongue."

"Jesus Christ, shortcake. You take care of me so fucking good."

Before moving off his lap, I crush my lips to his one more time.

He slides back to the passenger seat and uses the controls to ease it back before reclining slightly.

I crawl over and drop to the floor in front of the passenger seat, kneeling between his legs.

"Get those lips good and wet for me, Grace." He strokes himself as he stares at my mouth.

While wetting my lips, I smack his hand out of the way and take over, licking him from base to tip, swirling my tongue around the head.

"Fuck, Grace," he murmurs, his fingers threading through my hair. "Wrap a hand around the base. You can either stroke in time with your mouth or hold it still."

His dick is thicker than any I've seen in person and while it makes my thighs quiver thinking about how good it feels inside me, I'm hoping my mouth can keep up.

The silky head of his cock slips past my lips, and I slide up and down a few times before easing him deeper.

"Your mouth feels like heaven."

He groans when he hits the back of my throat, and I gag before easing off a little.

"Suck hard, baby. I want to see those pretty cheeks go hollow." Heat zips through me, my thighs pressing together to relieve the ache he's causing. "Look up at me while my cock is in your mouth." He moves the hair away from my face and cradles my cheek. "You look so damn beautiful sucking me, baby."

I moan, so hot for him I can barely stand it.

After a few more bobs, I lift off him and ask, "Show me the pace you like."

He guides my head, and I follow his lead. My jaw hurts, but I don't care. I'm enjoying myself too much. I suck with enthusiasm, watching his face, feeling his muscles jump beneath my touch.

When I swallow around him, he hisses, his hips flexing.

His hand is still in my hair as I release him with a soft pop and move lower, running my tongue over his balls.

"Oh, fuck yeah," he utters, his voice husky and rough.

He's wrapped his hand around mine again, helping me jerk him off as I tease, lick, and suck.

Less than a minute later, a growl reverberates deep in his chest. "I need your mouth back on me, babe."

I grin up at him, guiding his throbbing cock back into my mouth, taking him deep—too deep.

"The sound of you choking on my dick is fucking perfect, babe."

Both of his hands are in my hair now, but they're not moving. He's just holding me, letting me finish him off.

I'm not sure if he's too far gone to keep showing me what he likes or if he knows I don't need it anymore.

He murmurs for me to go faster, and then he groans long and loud, his fingers curling into my hair as his dick jerks in my mouth. His hot release coats my tongue and I swallow it all.

When his body calms, he draws me up to his chest. "That was sexy as hell. Anytime you want to practice, you tell me. But just so you know, you're fucking incredible at everything you do, Grace."

With a lazy grin, he kisses my lips and shifts me so I'm sitting beside him. He tucks himself away before reaching into the back and producing a flannel blanket.

He opens the truck door and holds out a hand for me. I take it and hop out, giving him a curious look. He leads me to the back of the truck, lowers the gate, and spreads out the blanket.

"What are we doing?" I ask.

"It's time for my snack, babe." He lifts me and places me on the blanket in the truck's bed.

"Jensen…" I look around to make sure no one is out here. There're only trees and blue sky. But with the sexy gleam in his eye, like he's desperate to have me, I wouldn't care if there was an army of people nearby.

He rips my leggings off, and before I know it, he's tongue fucking me. Occasionally, he stops to remind me I'm going to come at least three times like a good girl. He tells me how much he loves my pussy, my taste, my sounds.

I melt into his truck with his tongue flicking against me. The pressure builds and I thrash, my orgasm barrelling through me like a freight train. I gush against his mouth, and he laps at it, grinning proudly.

Unicorn man, indeed.

TWENTY-EIGHT

JENSEN

Leaning against the porch rail, I survey the chaotic scene before me. I gave up on asking for a guest list for this gathering my brother arranged. From the sea of bodies milling about my yard, I'd hazard a guess he sent out a bunch of texts that simply said, "Jensen's place. Friday. Bring a camping chair, bad beer, and every fucking person you know."

Jaxon doesn't even know some of these people.

"Lana said she can't come until after the Parent Council meeting at school," Sterling, one of our volunteer firefighters, tells Jaxon. "But she's picking up a case of craft beer from Loco Brew on her way here."

I hoped by telling Jaxon to keep it small, that meant it would be under twenty people. There's over thirty people on my property right now, and more coming.

But hey, Lana's bringing more beer.

There's commotion inside and high-pitched voices mixed with laughter filter through the double patio doors behind me. Jax jogs up the steps, slapping me on the shoulder and claiming he should go greet *his* guests.

A few minutes later, he barges back through the doors

carrying bakery boxes. "Your girl's here with Dani, and they brought treats." He's already digging through the top box as he strides over to the fire pit.

Thank fucking god.

I push off from the railing and head straight inside.

When I spot the mass of blonde waves put into one of her usual complicated half-braid styles, I shoulder my way through a few of my crew to get to her.

I press my chest against her back and slip my arms around her waist, splaying my hands across her stomach. Her warm amber eyes peer up at me while an easy smile curves her lips. She's in a soft, aqua-colored dress with thin shoulder straps. The bottom half flares out, ending at her knees, but the top is snug, dipping down to show the curves of the breasts that perfectly fill my palms. I grin, knowing if I graze the side of one, those sweet nipples will appear.

I tear my gaze from her to greet Dani and Declan, letting them know Brody's manning the barbecue if they want some food.

"Jax stole the dessert we brought. Sorry, babe," she says.

I lower my mouth to her ear. "We both know that's not the sweet treat I was most looking forward to tonight, shortcake."

"Stop making Gracie blush, and leave us to get to know your girlfriend," my mom says, shooing me away.

I frown as Grace slips from my arms.

"You're adorable when you pout," she whispers.

"I want her back in ten minutes," I demand.

"Twenty," my mom barters, whisking my woman away.

I sigh and run a hand through my hair as I glance outside. This crowded party is not my thing, but I figured it would be bearable because I'd get to spend time with my family and have Grace with me.

Since Mom stole Grace from me, I'm going to steal the treats she brought from my brother.

When I get to the fire pit, about a dozen people surround the flames, talking and roasting hotdogs. I snatch the bakery box from Jax's lap, barely getting it out of reach before he lunges at me.

Laughing, I drop into one of the camping chairs.

Declan joins us and hands me a beer. I clink my bottle with his and take a drink. Unlike my brother, Dec is content with the quiet.

"Dani with the ladies?" Jax asks.

"Yeah," Declan says. "They opened a bottle of Kahlua and were whipping up some chocolate drinks. Looked like sludge with whipped cream on top." He takes an indifferent gulp of his beer, used to Dani and Grace's shenanigans. A spark of jealousy flares to life inside me, hating the idea that Declan got closer to Grace while dating Dani and I kept myself away.

"Come get your burgers, lazy bastards," Brody shouts from the back deck.

I sink further into the chair, deciding to eat when Grace comes out.

Well, I'll have one pastry. Two tops.

Brody's booming voice floats over to us as he talks to some of the fire crew and EMTs. Eventually, he makes it over to us and takes a seat.

Ross, Sterling, and Bradford all bring heaping plates of food over to the fire. A few more of our crew are having drinks on the patio. Some are inside with their wives, others are playing lawn games on the side of the property by the garage. Everyone else is wandering around, likely just wanting to see my place or looking for a fun night out. No one's getting rowdy, but I'm certain that will change in a couple of hours.

Brody finishes his sausage and throws the paper plate into the flames.

"Mom's pretty damn excited, man," he says, his eyes still on the fire.

"About what?" Jax asks.

"Gracie Parker. And the 'upside down grin' on Jensen's notably less hostile face."

"Upside-what?" Dec asks.

"That's how Gracie described Jensen's face when Mom said she enjoyed seeing her baby boy's smiles coming back."

Oh, fuck me. They're talking about me in there. Knew I should have kept her with me, on my lap, in my arms all night.

Jax laughs, looks at my face, and then laughs again. "She's not wrong. I see it now. He disguises his smiles with a frown. Like he can't remember how to smile."

Brody snorts, lifting his glass of whiskey and taking a healthy swig. He's not going to say a damn thing because his face displays a perpetual scowl most days.

"If my face was hostile, it was because I was planning on marrying a woman who secretly wanted my twin brother," I grumble.

Shit.

I've kept this hidden for almost a year and now I'm spewing it around a bunch of gossipy idiots. I consider my crew family, but I'd think twice about telling them the location of my candy stash, let alone one of my deepest secrets. Realistically, I know they'd keep serious shit to themselves if I asked. But there's a certain amount of shame in what the woman who was supposed to love me and share a life with me said to me the day of our wedding.

"Ah, hell," Dec mumbles from beside me, shifting to the edge of his seat, preparing in case there's a fight.

There won't be. I don't blame Jaxon, but it took some time not to resent him for having everything Erika considered lacking in me. Jaxon is all the things I'm not. And that never bothered me until I saw how much I disappointed her. Erika needed the outings, the parties. Like Jax, she made friends everywhere we went, never enjoyed spending an evening at home. She flirted, joked, drank, was willing to try everything at least once. She was a whirlwind I was in awe of for a long while. Too long. My thoughts were so preoccupied with our future, I didn't stop to think if it was right for us. If we should even have one.

"Guess I didn't really have much to smile about until recently," I confess.

I've moved on with a woman who has my whole fucking heart.

"You saying all that overtime at the station, then coming home to messy DIY projects didn't make you giggle with glee?" Jaxon's trying to goad me into a silly argument like he usually does when something serious comes up. "The guys are going to take that personally, man. They thought bitching about the schedule, purposely fucking up training drills to mess with you, and their mere existence fulfilled you."

I snort. I thought it would too, actually. "I couldn't afford to slack off. You fuckers need constant supervision." I'm fucking good at my job. And making Dad proud is the intent with which I begin each day.

"Yeah, we do," Anders shouts from a few spots down.

"But I found someone better, smarter, and way more attractive," I tell them with a smug grin.

"Gracie's definitely something special," Declan says, covering his smirk with his beer bottle. "Don't tell her I said that though. It'll go to her head, and she'll give me more shit."

"I already like Gracie a hell of a lot more than Erika," Brody adds. "Then again, I never liked her."

"Didn't think you liked anyone, bro," Anders says, sitting beside Jax and joining the conversation.

A soft, peach-scented body drops into my lap. I set my drink down and wrap my arms around her.

"Who don't you like?" Grace asks my brother.

Everyone's quiet for a few beats before Brody answers, "Erika."

"Oh. The cunt," she replies, winking at me.

Beer sprays out of Jax's mouth and nose.

"Nice," Anders comments with an amused laugh, slapping my brother on the back as he chokes.

"Well, I like her even more now." Brody lifts his glass, and Grace lifts her own, whipped cream dripping from it.

"What is that?" I nod toward her drink.

"No idea. Tastes like one of those boozy chocolates."

"You hate those," I say, remembering her not-so-discreetly spitting one into a napkin during the Santa's List party at The Hole in December.

"Yep, but your mom made it for me."

I kiss her, tasting the drink on her lips. "They added cinnamon schnapps?"

She nods with a grimace. "There were a lot of things added to this concoction that had no business being in a cocktail." Her eyes lock onto mine and I know.

This woman belongs here, on my lap, in my house, with my family. The woman I tried to keep out by acting like an arrogant jerk slipped right past my defenses and went straight to my heart.

Shouting and cheering comes from the other side of the garage. I like most of the people here, but my capacity for parties sure as shit isn't getting better with age. I did a lot more of this when I was with Erika because she expected it. Changing who you are for someone else—someone who supposedly loves you—means they don't love you. Learned that the hard way.

Yet Grace wants me despite seeing me at my worst. She put up with the aftermath of how I handled my broken engagement, how I fought my unwanted feelings for her, and forgave me for the venom I spewed from the moment I met her.

I'm one hell of a lucky asshole.

My girl wiggles on my lap, and the need to show her what she's done to me, every part of me, is overwhelming. I plan on showing her how I feel every day, but with her in my lap, I can't help but tease her a little.

"That perfect pussy is taunting me, baby," I whisper in her ear. "You make me so damn hard."

She blushes as a shiver wracks her lithe body.

"When we're alone tonight, you're going to ride my face. I want your pussy smothering me while I swallow every drop of you."

"Jen," she practically moans.

"If you're a good girl and stay right here"—I gather her closer—"the rest of the night, I'll put the cardigan on later."

She giggles, causing her ass to shake against me again. "Something tells me you'd wear the cardigan any time I ask, hotshot." Her fingers skim along my jaw. "These are your favorite people." A vehicle honks and there's more yelling. "Well, most of them."

"I always have time for my family, my crew, for this town, but I can only withstand these kinds of things in limited spurts."

But lately, I've found myself less drained and disinterested in outings. In fact, Thursday we're headed to The Hole with my brothers, sister, and Sawyer to watch the NBA Finals, then next weekend it's Liv's engagement party at Rocky's.

Grace places a kiss on my lips, her hand still at my jaw. "Do I have a limit?"

I slide a hand under her skirt and ease it high on her thigh. "Grace, you don't have a limit. You make everything better. Every damn thing. Got me?"

With a teasing frown, she nods, but her eyes taper as she asks, "Are you ever going to stop calling me Grace?"

"No."

"Why not? That nickname was an immature, dickish—"

"You told me your name was Grace," I interrupt, voice low. "Well, technically, you went through all the versions of your name, but I was distracted and not fully sober." My eyes roam her face, gauging her reaction. "You fell into my lap and spilled my beer. And your name was Grace. It stuck."

"You said the nickname gave me something to strive toward."

The corner of my mouth pinches as guilt and regret take hold. I *did* say that. "I know. I'm sorry." I was sorry within moments of that comment spewing from my mouth. But she'd always been Grace. And after a few times of accidentally calling her Grace, I stuck with it.

"So…" Her brows raise in question.

I kiss the tip of her nose and her forehead scrunches again. "I'm the only one who gets to call you Grace. And I like that. A lot," I admit. "I was never teasing you. It was my way of claiming a part of you no one else could. I got your fire when I couldn't have anything else."

Her eyes search mine. "Fine," she huffs, her mouth twitching to conceal her smile. "But only because I always secretly liked how you growled *Grace*,"—she drops her voice to mimic me— "all sexy-like when I annoyed you."

Dani comes over and hands Declan another beer and a plate of food.

"Lawn darts, babe," she tells Gracie, gesturing to the side of the house.

I growl as Grace shifts to stand. Who the fuck brought lawn darts?

"Hell, no," I say.

"No to me taking her from you, or no to the lawn darts?" Dani asks.

"Both," I reply. "We're getting food. Dec, can you deal with the lawn darts?" I'd rather nobody left here bleeding or with any extra holes in their body.

Someone cuts off Declan's response by hollering, "Fuck! Carson, what the fuck, man? You got me."

Jax jumps up. "On it," he says, jogging toward the screaming, with Declan following close behind.

Grace practically falls off me, twisting around to see the commotion behind us in the diminishing light of the sunset.

Lawn darts at dusk. This is the stupidity most of us deal with all week, so it really shouldn't surprise me.

"Should we go help?" Grace asks.

"They've got it."

"So…food?" Dani offers.

"Jensen!" my mom shouts from the patio doors. "Sawyer and Liv just got here. And bring your girlfriend inside. Jane wants to meet her."

I crane my neck and spot her on the porch with her best friend. Sawyer's mom waves from beside mine.

I raise a hand to wave back before asking Grace, "Ready to meet more of my family and friends?"

"Definitely. Let's grab you a burger on our way in. Then, while you're chewing, I can answer all their questions."

She's so fucking perfect.

"We need to save your mouth strength for later."

She hops off my lap, and I follow, standing to tower over her as she gives me a cheeky grin.

"Damn straight," I tell her.

"So this is how it feels when you overhear Dec and me talking dirty to each other?" Dani asks, reminding us of her presence.

"Yep," Grace confirms. "But Dec's dirty mouth has no filter. He gives no shits that I'm there. Jensen usually has the decency to whisper, so maybe pass that along."

Dani's cheeks darken. "Declan probably thinks at some point it'll scare you off."

"I'm harder to scare off than he thinks."

She certainly is.

After a thirty-minute interrogation disguised as a "getting to know you" conversation, and Mom nearly fainting at my willingness to share food with my woman, we head back out to the fire where most people have now gathered.

This is the part I love. The quiet conversations, the reminiscing and shit-talking. The comfortable ease of sitting around a crackling fire.

I keep Grace in my lap, even though there's other available seating. She's small and soft and mine. So I keep her exactly where I want her.

My hand finds its place under her dress, stroking the bare skin of her hip. Grace turns in my lap, moving her hands up my chest to grab the panels of my flannel shirt. She tugs and her mouth is on mine, the taste of chocolate and cinnamon infiltrating my tongue.

Heady from the feel of her against me and everything I could want within my grasp, I deepen the kiss. And hope this time, I'll be enough.

"You coming in?" Grace calls from somewhere inside her house.

We're supposed to head straight to Rocky's. I wasn't supposed to come in when I picked her up because we always end up getting distracted. But I follow her voice through the living room, taking in the blankets draped on the couch and her usual pile of books on the side table next to the over-cushioned chair. In the opposite corner of the room, the yoga mat and exercise equipment I've used for physical therapy are scattered on the floor.

"I just needed a little caffeine boost before our night out," Grace says, leaning against the counter in her cute, but comically small, galley-style kitchen.

Behind her is the fancy coffee-producing monstrosity that takes up most of her counter space, which I've yet to learn to use. Knowing all the incredible food she's brought over came from this tiny kitchen, only proves how impressive and relentless Grace is in everything she does.

If she wants to stay here, I'm ripping out this kitchen and building her something that's a hell of a lot more functional.

"I know you don't drink coffee after four o'clock because you're old, but today was my early shift, so…espresso." She holds up the miniature coffee cup.

I'm barely five years older than her, but she's not wrong about the caffeine issue. I sleep like a rock—unless I have caffeine after dinner or eat spicy wings late at night.

I make it over to her in two steps.

Her head tilts as she assesses me. "My kitchen feels like Polly Pocket with you in it."

"It's fun-size. Like you," I tell her, capturing her jaw and laying an appreciative kiss on her mouth.

Her hand moves to my chest, like she's grounding herself. Without looking, she sets her mug down, nearly missing the counter. Then she spins out of my reach.

"Don't tempt me. We have to be at the party in ten minutes. Liv and your mom are both sticklers for time, and we all know the girlfriend gets blamed in these situations."

I snort. "They know better. With the activities they have planned for tonight, they'll expect me to drag my feet to this thing." I trap her against the counter, one hand planting on either side of her.

"Did you know there's a camera crew coming? It's part of the whole Love Vine small-town bachelor show they did."

Fucking great.

Having the production crew at our family dinner last year, basically inviting the whole town into my mom's home and Liv's life, was bad enough. Making a spectacle of the engagement party festivities with five times the number of people taking part sounds like a nightmare.

I've been dreading this event all damn day. It makes me wonder if not telling me was intentional. My family had to know this was going to be hard enough for me as it is.

After my own disastrous attempt to get married last year and the photographic proof of my reaction that circulated, the thought of being filmed tonight is a big *fuck no.*

"I missed most of that because of my accident. But Liv filled me in, and she's only slightly less keen on the idea than you. But it'll be fine. We got this." She tries to chest bump me but rebounds off my chest and into the counter behind her. "Oof."

"*Grace.*"

"Why do I find it so hot when you get all riled up? It's not you who gets hurt in these situations." Precisely the problem. She's covered in little bruises I hadn't even noticed until the last couple of months. "But if you said it like that and then spanked me? Not too hard though. My dress is thin and I'm wearing a thong."

"You keep talking like that and we're staying home."

"Nope. It's your sister's engagement party. We're going." She snags the mini coffee cup once more and tips it back to finish it. "Ready!" she announces with caffeine-fueled zeal.

I let her lead the way, following behind as she collects her bag, a jacket, slips a puffy hair elastic onto her wrist, and walks out the door. I take her keys and lock up before leading her to the passenger side of my truck.

She's gotten a lot more comfortable driving, but I figured she could let loose tonight, and I'd drive us both back to my place afterward.

Once we pull out of her neighborhood, her phone buzzes in her bag.

She pulls it out and says, "Harper is already there. She says they're pulling everyone aside for a quick interview about the couple."

Fucking great. Probably should run my answers by Liv or Grace since my first instinct will be to tell them no, it didn't thrill me that my brother's best friend was fucking my sister while he supposedly simultaneously dated other women for the reality dating show they set up.

What we didn't know until afterward, and what they've kept from the town, is that Liv and Sawyer set the whole thing up to get him through the matchmaking charity event without having to choose a girlfriend he had never wanted in the first place. Liv offered to fake fall in love with him. But they ended up *real* falling in love with each other.

"Oh!" she yelps, scrolling on her phone. "Ha! You won't believe this."

I jerk my chin at her, waiting for her to tell me what else to expect tonight.

"*The Vine* has an article about the engagement party and it's filming tonight, but also a headline about us again. Like an official relationship announcement showing our relationship status has gone from cute-dating-flirtation to serious-and-long-term."

I'm not surprised. After the Spring Festival, *The Vine* does a "Love is in the Air" monthly feature. They highlight all kinds of love-inspired content, including couples in town, romantic date night ideas, and wedding announcements.

She scans her phone while I pull into a parking spot at Rocky's.

"What the…" She covers a chortle. "Um, there's a picture from the other night when we were watching the game at The Hole."

She hands me her phone, and I see the headline "Possible Vaughn Double Wedding?" above a picture with the caption *Jensen Vaughn and Gracie Parker finally embrace their chemistry while enjoying a night out with friends.*

And that picture?

It's of Grace and *Jaxon.*

She's smiling up at him, a hand on his shoulder, eyes crinkled on the sides, affection radiating from her sweetheart face.

"How are they not able to tell you two apart by now? You may be identical, but you're *so* different." The faint ringing in my ears can't distract from the sharp jabs her pointed words inflict.

"What?" she asks. "I'm sure this has happened to you before."

She has no idea.

Because you never told her all of it. You hate admitting you weren't good enough for the last woman you cared about.

"It definitely looks like you're with him," I mumble, "so maybe that's why they cropped me out."

"Oh, come on, it's funny." She points at the photo with a bemused raise of her brows. "Look, there's your arm! God, your arms are hot. Wish I was conscious when you carried me to the ambulance after I got knocked off my bike." She still refuses to admit she was involved in that accident, and it *almost* has me smiling. "Oh, could you carry me into the party bridal style? Really have Mrs. Vanderham and the rest of *The Vine* ladies swooning."

As my mind reels, my breaths come out in short, agitated huffs.

"Also, it's probably not the right time to remind you about this, but you still owe me a sexy fireman carry into the bedroom."

The firefighter angle. The assumption we're all hot, brawny, heroic, fearless thrill seekers. The reason my ex initially chose me over my twin.

"Maybe we'll save that for the wedding night." *What?* Why would she say—"Because according to this article, there may be a double wedding in our future." Her laugh is light but somewhat tense. She's trying to play this off, lighten the mood, but it's not working. "A double wedding would be the worst, by the way. Too many cooks in the kitchen, too many people to trip over on my way down the aisle. I'd want two bridesmaids, a short ceremony, and preferably a destination wedding so everyone can get a vacation out of it too."

She's thought a lot about this, and all my hopes of avoiding thoughts of my past and wedding talk evaporate.

Grace then tries to convince me that tonight will be fun or some other upbeat take on the night, yet I'm more skeptical than ever.

"There's Sawyer's parents." She waves before turning back to me and freezing. "Jen? What's up?" Concern darkens her eyes. "You don't really have to carry me inside. In fact, you should give your ankle another week of strength training with the boot off before you carry anyone."

That propels me out of the truck, determined to show her I'm more than capable. And part of that is thanks to her.

Yeah, I'm fine. The night will be over in a few hours. I'll head home and banish all the shitty thoughts that article dredged up from the pile of repressed feelings I've worked hard at pushing down for almost a year.

I make my way around the truck, taking in the excitement in Grace's eyes as I scoop her up. She giggles as I carry her to the front door of Rocky's where they have a staff member checking the guest list.

The bouncer nods us in and Grace shouts "Thank you" over my shoulder before winding her fingers into my hair.

The bleakness lurking inside me—the part that took over after Erika left—is warring with all the good feelings Grace brings. I don't love Erika. I don't miss her or wish she'd stayed. But I *am* still angry I put every fucking thing into that relationship and she still found me lacking.

After our interviews, we sit at our booth and listen to speeches. Miranda and Stella—who runs the naughty book club my mom has told me about, despite my asking her not to—are hosting the filmed portion of tonight's celebration. The speeches start with Liv's matron of honor, Elle, and then move to Sawyer's best man, Jaxon.

Before I know it, I've had a few drinks more than intended. Grace left my side a bit ago to play a few games with her friends. I've hugged my sister, congratulated Sawyer, had a drink with my brothers, and now I'm ready to leave.

I head to the bar and order my last drink before arranging rides home. I set up a later ride for Grace and their earliest one for myself. I need to get my head on straight and watching my girl with my family, having a blast while I'm all fucked up inside, is only complicating things. But she's having a good time, and I will not cut her fun short because I'm having a shit night.

Someone claps my back, and I crane my head to see my cousin. Honestly, he's exactly the distraction I need right now.

"The hell?" I say, bringing him in for a hug. I spot my aunt and uncle nearby with my mom. "Didn't know you guys were coming down for this." As an elementary teacher, we don't see Griffin outside of the summer holidays.

"Yeah, school's already out this year, so timing worked out great."

Fin orders us shots of rum while we catch up. He secured another one-year contract teaching in his hometown, and has plans to travel around Ireland for half the summer before school starts back.

"Auntie Lilah says you started up a firefighter training academy and you're getting an award for it?"

I try to muster up the energy to think about anything other than how much fun Grace has been having since the moment she left our table. She tried to convince me to play some games and join her in the team karaoke they're about to start up, but I turned her down.

"They don't decide until next month."

"I'm sure you've got it in the bag." He holds up another shot I wasn't aware he ordered us. "Your dad would be proud."

I lower my gaze to my drink. The volunteer training program starts next week, and it's all set, but it's become an afterthought. I've been so caught up in Grace, in practically existing *for* her, I haven't given it much thought.

I've neglected my responsibilities. The goals I had this year are still in motion, but the effort is minimal, the drive considerably less.

Because I want to be everything for Grace. Can I still do that and be me? Does that mean sacrificing my career goals?

We down the shots just as we hear, "Testing, testing."

Turning, we face the stage as the karaoke starts. Singing pop songs and show tunes in front of dozens of people while tipsy is something my sister occasionally enjoys, but my brother—he lives for karaoke night. I bet he's even brought his guitar.

Fin nods toward the stage the production crew set up. "That your girl up there?"

Scanning the stage, I spot Grace setting up in front of a microphone.

"Yeah," I answer in a low voice.

She tries to detach the microphone from the stand but tips it over instead. Jaxon appears, catching it before it hits the ground. He hands her the microphone, while holding one of his own, and everything other than their duet performance becomes a blur.

I'm up and weaving through the crowd, my feet moving me closer. Grace laughs at Jax, singing with a smile, happy and fucking perfect.

She shoves him at the end of the song, making a grab for his mic. I can just barely hear her tell him he's an attention whore who doesn't know how to be a team player.

She's still laughing as they make their way down from the stage. "You were supposed to be the pretty face up there, Jax, not the talent." He offers her his hand to help her down the steps, and she takes it. "You can't be good at *all* the things. It's show-boat-y and not fair to the rest of us."

"She's got your brother pegged," Griffin comments from beside me. I didn't even realize he'd followed me.

Jaxon releases her hand. "Life's not fair, Smalls. Thankfully, there's plenty of beer here to cry into."

"We're supposed to be on the same team," she chides.

That's when Jaxon sees Griffin. The two wander over to us, Jax practically lifting our cousin up in an excited hug. Grace ends up introducing herself, making me feel like the asshole I am.

"You good, man?" Brody's at my side, arms crossed, eyes surveying the room.

"No," I mumble.

He leans in closer, dropping his voice low enough so only I can hear. "You going to be an idiot about this? Decide something's going on there when there's not?"

I rub my partially numb mouth. "Probably. It'll end the same either way, won't it?"

Rationally, I know nothing's going on with my brother and Grace. But is my twin brother the kind of guy she can have fun with? Is he all the things I'm not? Is he the perfect combination of nice guy with an edge of cockiness she was looking for? Yeah.

Losing Grace because I'm not what she needs would gut me. I'll put everything I have into us, into *her*. Only to find out she wants more, different, better.

Because the reality is I may not be able to give her what she wants. What she *needs*. Not long term. She'll realize that soon, and then what?

"You're drunk," he comments.

"Maybe a little," I admit. "Shots with Griffin pushed me over."

"I promised Sawyer I'd rescue him from Miranda and Stella after karaoke with your girl, so I better go." Jaxon points at Fin. "You coming or were you planning on getting up there?"

Our cousin makes his escape with my brothers, leaving Grace and me alone. My eyes wander to the stage, still mentally seeing them up there together.

She bites her lip guiltily as she says, "I didn't think you'd want to go up first, but I added us to the sign-up list. There are five songs until we go up. I figured I'd need at least that long to convince you. How about it? Want to serenade me? Woo me with that raspy singing voice of yours?"

I want to give her everything. Any damn thing she wants. A few minor concessions for a woman I love seems innocuous. And maybe it *is*. But right now, in this moment? I'm not sure.

Changing in order to gain the love and acceptance of others is how I got my mind all fucked up in the first place.

"Nahhh," I drawl. "I don't think I'll be staying much longer." I hate the look of confused disappointment she hits me with. "You'll still have my brother to have fun with though." I pat her awkwardly on the shoulder, watching my hand do shit I can't control.

Fuck. How many shots did I have with Fin?

"What? Babe, this is your family's party. I'm here for *you* and you're planning on leaving *without* me?"

My jaw locks tight to prevent any of the storm that's raging inside me from spilling out.

"You need food. I'll go scrounge something up." She darts away and I scrub a hand down my face.

Not a minute later, Grace pops up, thrusting a plate of fries at me. "Eat," she says. "Then we sing, hotshot."

"No, Grace."

"You don't even want to try to have fun?"

I'm not the fun twin, I want to tell her. *I'm the boring one. You chose wrong too, baby.*

"I'm not the fun boyfriend, Grace. I don't do karaoke, or play games, or stay late. I don't do a fucking thing I don't want to," I say, my voice raised and slightly slurred. "Okay?" I ask, softening a little.

"No, not okay. What's your problem?"

"You," I say. "All of this. Us." I don't mean it. I could never mean it. But right now, it's the simplest answer.

And judging by the look on her face, the wetness gathering along her lashes, I'm not going to be able to take it back.

I shouldn't have shown Jensen that stupid article.

He's been off all night. When I got out of the truck, I realized it likely had to do with the fact he almost got married a year ago and now has to attend his sister's engagement party. The article implied he and I would head down that road too, maybe even for a double wedding. Given how his last relationship went, it probably brought up bad memories.

So, I gave him space, something I've found he needs when he's processing. But he also told me everything was better with me, so I encouraged him to participate. He turned me down a few times, but I kept at it, kept checking in and asking him to join.

I pushed. And now he's telling me we are a problem.

My mouth hangs open as moisture gathers in my eyes.

"What?" I ask, my voice breaking partway through.

He grabs the back of his neck. "I don't know. You're pushing me and I..." He pauses while I'm hanging on every word. "Last time we were all together like this, it was for my wedding. And it all went to hell. Not sure I want to do that again. "

I search his face, but his eyes stay glued to the stage. "That was different. We're not engaged. I'm not Erika. No one's leaving anyone."

He blows out a breath. "It's feeling really familiar, Grace."

He was fine last night, his usual sexy, confident self all week. Now he's wigging.

"Let's go sit and talk," I suggest.

He shakes his head. "I can't."

"Jen—"

"You go have fun. I need some time."

"Time for what?" I ask, not sure I want to hear the answer.

"To think."

"About what?"

He grumbles and finally looks at me, a sweeping glance that ends in a sad frown. "About if you were right about being with a nice guy. If I'm the right guy for you. About focusing on my work. I've been ignoring my responsibilities by chasing things I can't keep."

I take several moments to break all of that down. And then it hits me.

"You're ending this?" I need clarification.

"You'll be happier with someone else. You should consider that."

A non-answer.

I cross my arms, my fists clenched in indignation. "You think I want some normal nice guy? I enjoy spending time with lots of different people, Jensen, but I love going home to *you*."

"For now," he mumbles. "People make mistakes, they fall out of love, they give their love to the wrong people. But apparently, even when you think you've found the *right* person and love them, it doesn't mean they'll believe it." He laughs, but the sound is dark and broken. "And it sure as hell doesn't mean they'll love you back."

"Then they weren't the right person," I respond, hurt sharpening my tone. "But you have to be willing to *let* someone love you, Jensen. And I—"

"Don't. You don't love me, Grace. You like fucking me, fighting with me. You'll get over it," he says, his tone unsteady but devoid of emotion. "Probably with some nice guy you'll love for many years. Really love him. Not just get a thrill from winning the attention of a man you think isn't capable of love."

I blink at him, my composure breaking. "You think you were just a thrilling challenge for me? That I'll 'get over it'?"

"I don't know what to think right now." He releases a short, derisive laugh. "But I know I will not change. Just like I don't expect you to change who you are." His mouth dips into a deep frown as he whispers, "It's too much and not enough at the same time."

And what I hear is *I'm* too much. *I'm* not enough.

Because I've heard those words from other men in various situations. But I never thought I'd hear them from Jensen.

He's mumbling as he works a hand over his jaw. All I catch over the shrill voice of whoever's singing karaoke is, "...can't be what you need."

Heat rises in my cheeks, and I blink away every emotion, every angry tear. I bottle the devastation and heartbreak.

He's choosing to believe I don't want him because some bitch made him think he wasn't good enough. And for a bit, when I feared what we could have, I might have made him doubt he was my dream man.

He's upset, drunk, and completely full of shit. There's a part of me screaming *he doesn't mean it; he's just freaking out.*

But it doesn't matter. Because it still means there's a part of him that doesn't want me as much as I want him.

The first tear falls before I can turn away. He reaches for me, but I jerk away, slamming into a cocktail table. Jensen's hands wrap around my arms, but I bat them away. He moves in closer, crowding me against the table. I can't even look at him.

My palms push against his chest, needing space. What I don't need is to feel him, breathe in his clean, earthy scent. But he doesn't back away. I slap at his chest harder, but he's not letting me go.

When I drop my head to his pec, it no longer feels as safe, as sturdy.

"You're an asshole," I cry.

He clears his throat. "I know. And you deserve better than assholes, baby."

I lift my head and take a breath. "Let go of me," I demand.

"I never wanted to hurt you, Grace. I just need a minute—"

I cut him off. "Now, Vaughn."

His arms tighten momentarily before easing away.

I slip out from between him and the table and walk straight out the door of Rocky's. Not stopping for my jacket. Not saying goodbye to anyone. And definitely not looking back at the man who stole my heart and returned it damaged—too far gone to beat for anyone else but him.

CHAPTER
THIRTY-ONE

JENSEN

"**G**o home," Declan orders, throwing my jacket at me.

I've spent enough time at home. It's too fucking quiet there. Even with Reaper coming and going as she pleases. Work is a better distraction.

Even if it's not as effective of a distraction as it once was.

I keep my eyes on the laptop I brought into the kitchen area, ignoring the Chief.

"You're pissing everyone off and you're near the end of your shift anyway."

Tough shit.

I fucked up the one truly good thing in my life, so now I'm here, putting everything I have into the station once again.

"I'm back to regular duty now and volunteer training starts tomorrow, so I want to make sure the crew is good, and I'm caught up on my admin shit."

"You're months ahead on most of the admin shit. So whatever you're pretending needs doing"—he gestures to my desk—"is busy-work, and two of the guys have threatened to walk out if you go back out there to terrorize them again today."

"Who the fuck threatened to walk?" I bark.

Emerson chooses that moment to walk through the swinging door. The moment he spots me and Dec, he spins on his heel and marches straight back out.

"Something's up with you. I can probably guess, but you didn't push when I needed time to get my head on straight, so this is me returning the favor."

I nod. "Appreciate it."

"For one week."

Pointing out how badly I fucked up will not do anything but piss me off right now. I've been keeping busy so I don't spend every minute rehashing last weekend.

What happened last weekend was the culmination of too many repressed issues hitting at once. It was a slow burning build up and a knee-jerk reaction rolled into one dark spiral.

Because reality caught up to me, but I wasn't ready to face it yet. And the whole night, all I could see around me were those realities...

Grace's attraction to assholes was likely temporary.

My aversion to weddings and marriage hadn't changed— might *never* change.

My twin brother *is* more likeable than I am. And for the first time, I felt jealous of him. Hell, I wanted to punch his permanent grin right off his face and tell him to stop reminding my girl of what I'd never be.

That's when I realized I needed to step back. And she needed to think about what she wants too. I needed to give her an out. And I needed to face the shit I let fester all year, that I pushed down so I could focus on work and the shit I was good at.

Because a part of me wondered if I can make Grace happy, if I'm enough for her.

Would Grace eventually resent me too? Because I don't go out enough, I'm too bossy, too protective, too serious, rude, boring, quiet.

All of those thoughts burned through me, the fire spreading, raging, burning away all rational thoughts until I imploded—half-drunk and reeling over shit I believed I'd gotten over.

Tones go off for EMS. I stand and move to the door since I'm on ambulance with Jax today.

"Jensen," Declan says.

"I'll go home after this call," I assure him.

I'll go home and think about all the shit I said, the look on Grace's face.

Deep down, I know I made a mistake.

One I can't take back.

One I'm not sure I deserve the chance to take back, even if I could.

"How long have you suspected you're bleeding from your rectum?" I ask the man who we haven't been able to convince off the toilet.

"All day," he answers, white with panic.

I wrap the blood pressure cuff around his arm. "Can we look?"

"At my ass?" the patient asks.

"Inside the toilet," Jax clarifies.

"I don't think I should get up. What if that makes me hemorrhage?"

I don't have the patience for this shit today. Literally. Thankfully, I'm better able to keep myself together when I'm on shift helping people with *their* problems.

"Is it bright red, red-brown, dark red? How much blood?"

"Dark reddish. But my urine's pink."

"You didn't mention your urine before. When did you notice it turning pink?" My brother keeps asking the man questions as I record his vitals and move out of the bathroom.

If this guy needs to be taken in and refuses to get up from the toilet, we are going to need the stretcher and a game plan.

As I pass the kitchen, a dozen bottles propped on top of the raised eating bar catch my attention.

Beetroot juice.

I sigh, snag an empty bottle, and stalk straight back to the bathroom.

Leaning against the doorjamb, I clear my throat.

Jax glances at me as the patient continues talking about the number of times he's defecated today—*a lot*.

I hold up the empty bottle of juice with a tight smile.

Jax's mouth opens in question and he looks closer. Then it clicks. He adjusts his glasses and schools his face before turning back to the man on the toilet.

"You doing a juice cleanse, Phil?" he asks.

"Yeah. Supposed to help cleanse my liver, so it works better, and I can drink more on weekends without feeling so rough."

I scrape my tongue along my teeth and shake my head when Jax's eyes dart to me. He's on his own with this one.

"Not how that works, man. But it *can* discolor your stool and urine. It's a fairly harmless condition called beeturia."

Phil scrunches his face and glances over at me as if needing confirmation. I raise my brows and nod.

"It can also increase the likelihood of kidney stones, so if you have a history of kidney stones, that abdominal pain you're experiencing could be the start of a stone moving," Jax continues. "Or it could simply be a symptom of all the beetroot juice."

"Oh," Phil says.

"They can do a quick urine test at the hospital to check for blood, if you want us to take you in."

Phil pulls his shorts up a little higher, the wild panic dissipating. "I'll just, uh, finish up in here and then decide."

We step out of the bathroom, and Jax heads to the truck to put his kit away. He comes back in with a sheen in his eyes. No doubt he laughed his ass off in the truck.

Phil decides to skip the hospital visit and stop the beetroot juice. I'm disappointed because a trip to the ER meant I'd be working longer, but we wrap up with Phil and get into the ambulance.

Jax pulls away from the curb and mutters, "Fucking beet juice."

With a laugh, I reply, "Not the 'bleeding orifice' call I thought we'd be walking into."

"Right?" he says. "I was sure we'd be transporting someone to the hospital for the removal of a rectal foreign body. We have a little competition going. Whoever's chosen object gets the most action"—he winks at me—"wins the pool at the end of the year."

"What object did you choose?"

"Cucumber."

This is why I prefer fire shifts.

"Weirdest object you ever had to bring someone in to have removed?" I ask.

Without missing a beat, he says, "Kitchen timer shaped like an owl. We could still hear the whirring sound as the time counted down, and when it dinged, it took me a full minute before I could look the patient in the eye." He snorts out a laugh. "The nurses barely blinked. One said, 'sounds like he's ready to come out,' and snapped on a pair of gloves."

I shift my focus to the window with a smile on my face as Jax pulls us into the ambulance bay at the station.

Before he even puts it in park, he asks, "You ready to talk about whatever the hell happened with Gracie?"

"No."

"Heard she left the engagement party crying," Jax points out like I didn't already know. I fucking hate I made her cry. "Then when I saw her at Kozy's, she fled the moment I made eye contact."

I frown and open my door, eager to head home.

"Does it have anything to do with that picture of her and me in *The Vine*?" he asks, as I'm hopping out.

I slam the door, my boots hitting the concrete at a fast clip as I move around the truck.

"Jen," Jax shouts from behind me. "You're reading into shit and letting it mess with your head."

I spin and face him. "Or maybe I'm getting myself into the same fucked up situation as before. Dating women who would be better off with *you.*"

Jax throws his hands up. "You're full of shit. You got scared because you love her and you're too much of a pansy to find out if she feels the same. Instead, you pull away, shutting yourself into your secluded home to hang out with your murder cat."

"Better off that way."

"So you and her are done?"

Never.

"I said some stupid shit. Probably wasn't ready for a serious relationship yet. And with Grace, it was always going to be serious."

"So you're just going to avoid her until you get your shit straight? Or are you hoping for a casual physical relationship? If so, can I be there when you offer that idea? Haven't seen anyone get junk-punched in a while."

And I'd deserve it if I ever suggested anything like that.

"No. I just need some time to sort shit out. And give her a chance to think about what she wants too."

He sighs, crossing his arms. "Gracie isn't Erika."

Patience waning, my voice rises. "Yeah, no shit. I kept trying to make it work with Erika, but I wasn't what she wanted, wasn't enough. Look where that got me."

Jax stares at me and I take advantage of the silence to walk away.

"You're an idiot," he shouts. "Let's be honest, your pride took the biggest hit when Erika left. Because you might have loved her in a way, but it's not the same as what you feel for Grace, right?"

I stop and glance back at him. After Erika left, I was angry, defeated, lost. But how much of that was heartbreak?

Not much.

Because part of me already knew what the rest of me refused to acknowledge.

In a shitty way, Erika did me a favor.

"Maybe you're right though, man," he says with a shrug. "Grace deserves to find someone willing to love her without doubts. Better to watch from afar as someone else gives her the future you could have had with her."

My jaw clenches. Accept a future where she's building a life with someone else? Where I'm not the one loving her?

"That's not fucking happening."

His easy gait eats up the space I put between us. "Yeah? Better do something about it then." He shoulders past me, making me take a step back.

He disappears into the kitchen, leaving me standing outside the door with my thoughts reeling.

Jax's head pops out of the door. "Want to go for drinks?" he asks.

"It's nine in the morning."

He smirks. "That's a yes, right?"

"No one is serving liquor yet."

"Oh, have a little faith. I have friends in low places."

Knowing Jax, I'm going to end up in some shady prick's basement drinking gin from a vase.

Before I can speak, he reads the answer on my face, and his grin widens.

He shoves my jacket at me and heads for the exit, spinning around and walking backward, adding, "Come on, Jenny. You're buying. Least you can do, considering I'm helping you with your lady."

Drinking won't bring Grace back to me, but it might help burn away the residual damage of my past and give me the courage to face the one woman who holds the power to either revive or destroy me.

"Wait. What do you mean you're helping me with Grace?" He busts through the front doors, turning to shoot a grin back at me. "Jax?"

I catch his booming laugh as I follow him out the doors.

THIRTY-TWO

GRACIE

I'm dabbing coffee from my nose and chin as Dani pulls into the parking space in front of Grind. I swallowed wrong—not choked, just somehow fucked up a swallow—and coffee shot out of my nose like I was a human espresso machine.

Dani rounds her vehicle and wraps her arms around me. "Your eyes and nose are all red. Were you crying again?"

I shake my head. "Coffee shot out of my nose."

She tucks her lips between her teeth and slowly blinks at me. "That's a plausible cover story." Her eyes narrow as she assesses my general well-being with her sharp gaze.

"For real." I show her the napkin. That's not to say I didn't have a loathsome ten-minute sob-fest in the shower this morning.

We make our way inside and choose a table that's away from most of the other diners.

"I'm going to put our order in with Dell or we'll never get the right food." She dashes away, sidling up to Dell, who wraps her arm around Dani's shoulders in greeting.

I take out my phone and send a message to my mom. They're coming down again in a few weeks, which was unfortunately spurred by the article in *The Vine*. Shortly after Jensen came to my first bowling game, I told them about us. It thrilled my dad to find out I'd started driving again, and he spoke to Jensen on the phone about it. They were looking for a new car for me and I'd have been offended they weren't including me, but I couldn't know less about vehicles. The guys were giddy when I told them they could choose.

My phone lights up and I see an incoming call from my mom.

I answer, infusing enthusiasm into my voice. "Hi, Mom."

"Hi, honey. Glad I caught you," she shouts over the racket in the background.

"Where are you?"

"Home, but Dad's got some friends over for their weekly card game."

Dani waves at me from the front counter and mimes holding something to her lips. I frown at her and mouth, *What?*

"Poker?" I ask my mom.

Dani shakes her whole body and mimes sucking through the fingers of her lips. We're playing diner-food charades.

A milkshake? I mouth.

She gives me a thumbs up and I give her one in return.

"No, a work friend of your dad's introduced him to Dungeons and Dragons. It's a lot more intense than I realized."

"Dad is playing D & D? Does he dress up?"

"Do you honestly think I stick around for all that? I go to the den and read smut."

That checks out. I'm proud to have inherited my reading preferences from my mother. I meant to drop that little tidbit on Jensen since I caught him glancing at a few of my fantasy romance novels with undisguised intrigue.

"Anyway, I wanted to let you know we are taking you up on your offer to have us all stay together at Jensen's beautiful cottage." *Shit.* "We'll cook breakfast each morning and bring the liquor. Mimosas and margaritas sound good?"

I figured they'd want to stay at my place and have it all to themselves.

"Um, well…"

"It'll be like a mini family vacation in the woods."

I have half a mind to just let them show up and have Jensen choose whether he wants to explain or just awkwardly host them until I come to save him.

That would amuse me, but it wouldn't be fair to my parents.

"I think we should stay at my place where we can easily walk to Town Center and enjoy some of the weekend festivities," I tell her. "Plus, my place will allow us more flexibility since I believe Jensen's weekend plans have changed." I cringe before the last word leaves my lips. Not because that excuse is shaky, but because my voice broke when I mentioned Jensen.

"Honey…what happened?"

"Not sure yet," I answer in a soft whisper.

"I saw something on *The Vine's* Facebook group about how the two of you were getting serious. There was a super sweet picture of you two…"

The reason I hadn't told her yet is because I don't know what to tell her. It's confusing and it hurts.

"You're not supposed to be in that group anymore, Mom," I remind her.

"I got invited into the group again and then tagged in that article."

How thoughtful.

Dani lands in the seat across the table, plunking a tall strawberry milkshake in front of me.

"Hey, Mom, I'm at dinner with Dani. Can we chat later? I have a few ideas about your visit."

"Sure, honey. But I refuse to do that bicycle beer tour thing. Makes me motion sick."

"Deal."

Once my mom hangs up, I take a long draw of my shake.

Dani's is chocolate and we always switch halfway, so we can get both of our favorites.

"Your mom saw the article?" she asks.

I nod. "And she said they decided to take Jensen up on his offer to let them stay with *us* at his place when they visit." I prop my elbow onto the table and drop my head into my hand.

"So are you going to tell them you broke up or will you tell Jensen he'll have to pretend for a weekend unless you get some answers?" Her eyebrows jump as she plucks the cherry off the fluffy whipped cream atop her drink. "Oh, I like that idea."

"Dani…" I lean in and whisper, "I don't even know if we're broken up."

"Wait, he didn't break up with you? I thought you said he did. Or he implied you and he weren't serious, just fucking?"

I throw my hands up. "I don't know! But he made it clear we don't feel the same way about each other. So maybe that means he didn't want to say it and just hoped I'd have enough self-respect to tell him it's over?"

"He's not exactly the passive-aggressive type. If he wanted you two to be over, he'd have said that," Dani says, pointing at me with her striped straw.

"He says he needs time and that I should consider if I'd be happier with someone else."

"Well, that's bullshit. If he didn't make you happy, you wouldn't be with him. Since I've known you, there hasn't been one guy who interested you enough to make it to the end of the date."

"Well, after my 'nice guy' relationship quest, I think he's got it in his head I deserve or want that."

"Tell that to Tanner. Poor guy's been after you for months. He's good-looking, sweet, and saves sick children *daily*." Her gaze narrows on me with a glint of humor. "But men like that aren't what you crave. You need the foreplay fights, a grappling for dominance, a good spanking when you've acted out."

My mouth drops open. "Dec has been a bad influence on you, Dani. And I like it."

"So, are you going to storm over there and set him straight?" she asks, a cocky tilt to her mouth.

"Part of me wants to confront him, tell him he's being an idiot, prove to him I don't just like fucking him—I love him, all of him. Even when he's grumbling and rude and bossy."

Even if he's too scared to love me back.

I give her a weak smile and she tsks.

"*He's* the one who needs to do the proving. If he wasn't ready for a serious relationship or to admit you're the best thing to happen to him, he had no business messing around with you."

"I think that's why he walked away. It was too much and not enough," I say, repeating his words from the other night. "Me, the relationship—either way."

Her gaze narrows, her mouth twisting to the side. "Honestly, babe, I don't think so. But I *do* think he's freaking out."

"At the very least, he's put us on hold while deciding if he can put up with me long-term. And I'm not waiting on a man to determine if I'm worth his time. Fuck that."

"Definitely fuck that." She taps her chilled glass against mine. "Is that what it feels like he's doing?"

"No idea."

I reach over and swap our milkshakes, sucking down the cold, creamy chocolate while I attempt to separate facts from feelings.

She gives me a sympathetic smile. "I ordered us loaded fries and chicken and waffles to share." My favorites…because best friends just know when you need cheesy fries. "Then I was thinking we could go to Rocky's. Harper's off tonight and will meet us if she can find a sitter."

With a sad smile, I remind her, "I have bowling tonight." And Jensen will be notably absent. He's only missed one game, and that was because he was on shift. I still have his shift schedule on my phone, so I could technically find out if he's working tonight, giving me a legitimate reason for his absence. But checking his schedule now feels like an invasion of privacy.

"Okay, no problem. I'll let Harper know I'll meet her at Rocky's." She grabs her phone from her bag. "I'll pick her up at the end of her shift and head straight to the bowling alley."

My eyes water. "You're going to come bowling?"

"Of course." She holds up a hand. "I mean, not to bowl. I'm there for the company and crazy shenanigans. I missed the lawn bowling last time."

Our food arrives, and I inhale it until I'm uncomfortably full. Loaded fries and a milkshake can temporarily fix almost all my problems.

Dani offers to drive me home so I can pick up my bowling stuff, but I need to walk off the deep-fried food and clear my head, so we decide to meet there in an hour.

As I start toward my house, I check my phone and stare at the notification of a missed text message from Jensen. I take a breath and try not to guess what he's texting about before I open it. That way leads down only two paths: undue hope and misery.

JERKSEN:

I'm an asshat. I'm sorry. Can we talk? Preferably in person.

My heart pounds as I take in those words. I've only gotten one other text from him this week, and it was a couple of brief sentences checking on my ride-to-work situation. I told him I took care of myself just fine before we started spending nights together, and I'll continue to do so with him gone.

Hello, asshat. And no.

If he thinks he can just say, *Oops, my bad*, and things will go back to the way they were, he's wrong.

> You can say what you need through text and
> then I'll decide if we need to meet up.

Fair enough. Guess I'll have to convince you with
my oral charms.

I glare at my phone. He better not mean sexting, because I am *so* not in the mood. A dick pic and hot fantasy talk won't repair the damage of what he did.

> Heard you were hibernating in your cave. You
> can duck back in there unless you're ready to
> shed some light on what the hell happened this
> weekend.

Chicken-shit, I want to add.

Hibernating?

> That's what your mom said when I ran into her. I
> think she was trying to rationalize your
> disappearing act.

Yeah, I do that sometimes. Drives my family
crazy.

I can relate.

He deals with things by shutting himself off until he can work through the emotions.

I tackle most things head-on, sometimes before I'm ready.

> Hopefully, you give your family an explanation
> first.

It's usually a shitty explanation, followed by a lot
of grumbling, overanalyzing, and tackling of
unnecessary home projects.

Sounds like a blast. You better be fitting in your physical therapy around all that fun.

Worried about me?

The town still needs you in top shape.

Just the town?

Look, you said you needed time. You said a lot of things. Yes, I pushed your boundaries at the party, which I feel badly about...

But you're a grown-ass man. If you don't want to do something, just say "Nah. But thanks, babe. You go do body shots off the nice stripper. I'm good here." And then give me a kiss or an ass pat and return to skulking around or watching me from a dark corner, if that's more your thing.

Including you isn't holding you to unrealistic expectations. It's being goddamn polite.

You're right.

I'm an idiot. A sulky emotionally challenged prick who flipped out.

Are you ready to tell me what happened? Was it the article? The idea of getting married? Regrets or residual feelings about your ex?

Erika?

Yes, Erika. The sexy brunette with the motorboat-able tits. The woman you were in love with and set to marry last year.

Her tits weren't that great. And to be honest, the idea I was head-over-heels in love with her is a stretch.

She was on the wrong side of the hot-crazy
scale, even for me.

I stop on the sidewalk, a half-groan, half-laugh rushing out of me.

That son of a bitch.

Amusement pulls at my mouth moments before disappointment hits me in the gut.

With a sigh, I type a response.

> Jax, you fucker.

> Stop meddling.

A GIF of James Franco winking pops up.

> He was worried you wouldn't want to hear from him, so I swiped his phone to test the waters. Ease the way. Grease the shoot. Preheat the oven.

> Wait. Not those last two.

> Fuck. Jen's going to kick my ass when he sees this.

> I'm not interested in your shoot or your oven. Can we agree to delete these last few texts?

> Gracie?

> Smalls?

I don't respond. He got my hopes up and can suffer the consequences of his actions with no reassurances from me.

Jaxon *and* the Jerk can both fuck right off.

It's late by the time Declan drops me off at home. I'm high off another league win and a short, nostalgic foray into our younger years. The latter happened by taking some booze out to the high school football field and having a dance party.

A patrol car did a slow drive-by with flashlights, so Harper and I distracted them by racing across the street and into the woods while Dani and Kerrie helped the arthritic matriarchs of our group make their escape. I believe Dani's exact words were, "My boobs will be our downfall. They're meant for comfort, not running." Kerrie said her own boobs would be fine, but the rest of her wouldn't be.

Declan picked up the other ladies first, then came to get Harper and me. We were proud of ourselves for not getting injured or lost, but Declan wasn't as impressed. He didn't say a single word on the drive to my house, and we goaded him. *A lot.*

I wave at the ladies as I reach my front door. "Thanks, Dec!" I shout. "You're going to make an excellent husband!"

"Get your ass inside your house, Gracie, or I'm calling Jensen. It's his turn to deal with you three."

"Don't you dare," Dani barks. "He has to earn back the privilege of being around us again. Right, Gracie?"

"What she said!" I shout back. "Night!"

I let myself into the too-quiet space and take off my cross-body bag. After I dig out my phone, I head upstairs to shower.

I'll only sniff Jensen's body wash once. Then I'm throwing it out because it's taunting me.

I drop my phone on the nightstand before I take a quick shower and dispose of the yummy shower gel. Once I dry off and dress for bed, I plug in my dead phone and chug water as I wait for it to turn on.

Four notifications await.

> Hey, it's Jensen. Sorry about my brother. He
> can't seem to help himself.

But he was right. About all of it.

Just needed you to know that.

Night, Grace.

321

I scroll up to reread everything Jaxon sent me earlier. Unable to process what any of it means, I mumble, "Night, Jensen," right before my head hits the pillow.

THIRTY-THREE

JENSEN

THE VINE COMMUNITY UPDATE

Vaughn police investigated a suspected underage party at the high school football field late last night. Empty bottles of wine, bags of corn chips and popcorn, several brassieres, and an open box of effervescent electrolyte tablets were found on the premises.

Two petite female suspects were seen fleeing into the nearby woodland with officers Zach O'Riley and Bree Morales giving chase. With no apprehensions or suspects, police are chalking it up to a group of teenagers having a wild night out.

Neighborhood Watch and the school have been notified.

My knee bounces as I sit at the bar, waiting for my food. Spending most of the afternoon in the gym did nothing to ease this nervous energy.

Grace hasn't responded to my messages. And I haven't seen

her in over a week. Without her, it feels as if part of me is missing.

I need to come up with what I'm going to say to her. I'm going to explain what happened. And fucking *beg* her to hear me out, let me back in, give me her future—or at least a chance at it.

For now, I'm picking up tacos to take home to a brother who's likely spread out on my living room sofa again, watching my television and eating all my snacks. I'm terrible company, but I'm trying.

I haven't taken away Jaxon's key. I let him fill the silence with his ridiculous chatter. I even pretended to believe his hot water tank was being replaced, and he needed to stay with me for a few days. Because while I like my space, especially while I'm struggling with something, I'll admit that being alone doesn't make the time go by faster. It doesn't make the problem easier.

And as a sign of my appreciation for keeping me from throwing myself back into the dark hole I lived in last year, I'm going to feed him and not say a damn thing about him taking over my house.

The door to the kitchen swings open and Harper strides out. She stops in front of me, holds out my bag of food, and lets it drop on the bar top with a crunchy thud.

"Thanks," I say, picking up the bag of freshly crushed tacos.

"Mm-hmm." Her usual smile is notably absent.

She glides past me, and that's when I hear *her.*

I swivel on my stool and find Grace hugging her pissed off bartender friend.

When Harper pulls away, she whispers something that has Grace stiffening. Her eyes dart to me at the bar. I give her a slight nod, which she ignores, and move to stand.

The two women give me a wide berth as they walk around me. Grace hops onto a stool at the opposite end of the bar.

An internal debate roars in my head. Talk to her now or wait until I come up with a better plan than whatever the fuck comes out of my mouth once I catch her peach scent.

With a wince, she pulls at the sleeves of her denim jacket, slipping it off her arms.

What was that?

Concern has me stepping closer, allowing me a better look at her arm. A massive bruise covers the upper half.

"Jesus fuck." I place a hand on her thigh and spin her toward me. She clutches the bar, mouth open in surprise. "Grace, what the hell is that?" I pinch the edge of her t-shirt and gently lift it. The bruise goes to the top of her shoulder.

"Back to this, hm?" She tugs at the edge of her shirt to cover the garish purple welt. "I'm fine, so can we skip the lecture?"

"I'm not trying to—" I take a breath and try again. "Did someone do this to you? Did something happen?" I bite out.

She jabs one dainty finger into my chest, holding my gaze with a steely one of her own. "Not." Poke. "Your." Poke. "Business." Poke. "Anymore."

My jaw tightens as I lean closer. "The fuck it's not."

She continues glaring, but there's a lingering sadness that breaks me.

In a pleading, raspy whisper, I say, "Baby, tell me what happened."

She glances away and sighs. "First, I'm not your babe. Second"—she points to her arm—"this was just me being me."

"Tell me, shortcake."

Delicately examining the discolored contusions, I trail a finger over her arm and watch as goosebumps break out over her skin.

"I ran into a door," she admits. "It was one of those heavy bastards that attack the moment you let go."

"Shit," I grumble. "A door did all this?"

"I thought I'd pulled it open enough, but something distracted me. When I charged forward, *bam!*"

"How many times did you run into it, babe? There are multiple bruises here."

"It was one of those decorative, vertical door handles. Thick metal, protruding parts." My frown deepens. "It slammed into my forearm first, and then my momentum drove the rest of me into the edge of the door. So I guess I hit it twice."

I nod, switching my focus back to her face. "What distracted you?"

"Hmm?" She hums, her cheeks coloring. "You know, life, people...stuff."

"Try again, shortcake," I murmur.

"No. It was stupid."

I scrape my teeth over my lower lip as I strive for patience. Her eyes drop to my mouth and linger.

By the time her eyes lift back to mine, there's a knowing curl to my lips.

Her eyes taper and her nose wrinkles. "I thought I saw you."

The corner of my mouth twitches. "And that caused you to walk into a door?"

She shrugs, but there's a stiffness to it. "It happens."

"But it wasn't me?" I ask.

"No. It was Jaxon."

"And he was with Ainslee," Harper chimes in.

Our heads turn, finding Harper with both elbows propped on the bar, face in her hands as she openly eavesdrops on our conversation. "That's what distracted her." Harper looks at Grace and then stammers, "Because she's, uh...she's never met Ainslee."

It only takes me a few seconds to figure out what they're not saying.

"You saw Jaxon and Ainslee together and thought it was me with another woman? That's what you thought you saw?"

She doesn't answer.

I lean a hand on the bar and dip my head, dropping my forehead to hers. "Baby, I don't see anyone but you." I take her hand and press her palm against my chest. "I have no room left in here for anyone but you."

"You said I was 'too much' and that you needed time."

I lift my head and stare down at her. Is that what she thought? "*You* are *not* too much. You're exactly fucking perfect." I bring my hand up to grip her chin. "What I felt for you was too much. It had me wondering if maybe *I* wasn't enough for *you*."

"Jensen..."

"So you need to think about this, shortcake. Because even if you tell me I'm not what you need, I'm going to be in your life and I'm going to make sure you're being taken care of. That you're being treated right. That you're living your best life. And I'll spend every day hoping like hell that life will someday be with me."

A soft exhale flutters from her parted lips, and I want more than anything to kiss the breath out of her mouth.

"You're probably still in the running...if that eases your mind at all."

The beginnings of a smile tug at my mouth. "Good to know." I retrieve the bag I tossed on the bar as I was looking at her arm. With one final swipe of my thumb against her smooth skin, I release her. "Gotta get these to Jax before he eats everything in my house."

I don't want to stop talking to her, or looking at her, but I prefer to end our conversation on a good note. Which means I need to go before I fuck it up.

Moving backward a few steps, I keep my gaze locked on her, knocking into a couple of guys. She presses her lips together to keep from laughing.

When I reach the door, she calls out, "Jensen?" I stop and wait. "You still have a lot of explaining to do."

"I know," I say with a smirk on my face, eager to tell her and then put it behind us. Burn my past to ashes. "And I will."

As I walk to my truck, I think about how it upset her to think I was with another woman. And I hate that I wasn't there with her, so she had no doubts. I hate that I put those doubts there. Most of all, I hate I let my past fuck up my whole damn future.

If revealing the details of my past will let me have the future I want with her, I'll tell every-fucking-body.

Maybe that's exactly what I need to do.

CHAPTER
THIRTY-FOUR

GRACIE

JERKSEN:

Can I buy you lunch? Or a coffee? Dinner?

The Sandwich Ship now has delivery. I'll take an Italian sub on cheese bread with extra banana peppers.

May I join you or should we see how you feel after the sub?

How do I know this is really you?

When you're on your knees for me, all I have to do is tell you how amazing your mouth feels, how fucking pretty you look with my cock between your lips, to get you wet and squirming at my feet.

Jesus.

Wherever I go now, I look for tripping hazards. I reach for you at night. In my truck, I stare at the empty seat beside me. I hate myself a little more each day, not wanting to admit that the reason I told you I needed time was because you truly scare the shit out of me, Grace.

That text was uncharacteristically long for Jensen.

Trying to pour my heart out here, shortcake.

You can't pour your heart out in a text, Jerksen.

But I'll admit that was the most impressive, poetic, and lengthy way I've ever heard someone say, "I miss you."

And I'm willing to do whatever it takes for however long it takes to earn your love again.

Never said I loved you, hotshot.

I never said it either. Doesn't mean I don't love you.

Is that your ass-backward way of telling me you love me?

OVER TEXT?!

"No" feels like the safe answer here...

Meet me somewhere tonight?

...Where?

Anywhere.

Food Truck Friday at Horton Beach. You can buy us some churros and tamales.

A half hour later, an Italian sub showed up at my work, along with my favorite Italian soda and enough cookies to share with everyone on shift. And in a separate bag was a container of Arnica cream for my bruised arm.

The weak part of me, the slice of my heart that wants to lap up everything Jensen has to offer, is overjoyed. The rest of me is determined to be cautious.

Because he has a lot of explaining to do and I need to be prepared in case what he tells me changes things between us.

I give my patients all of my attention for the rest of my shift, not interested in overthinking or letting myself get nervous hours before necessary. That time will come.

By the time I leave work, I have less than an hour to bike home, change, and walk to Horton Beach. I'd have more time if I biked there, but I plan on wearing a floral maxi dress—pretty, casual, comfortable, but unsuitable for biking.

After showering, I check my phone and see a handful of text messages. I get another two while I'm responding to Dani's text of "Have you seen it yet?"

All my messages are about an article in *The Vine*. And Jensen.

Moisture gathers at the back of my neck. What now? The timing could not be worse.

My stomach churns and I brace for the worst.

I call Dani, too scared to look online. I'd rather she just tell me, break it to me gently.

She answers on the first ring.

"Did you read it?" Dani asks.

"No, I haven't seen anything," I tell her, frantic. "What happened?"

"There's a post about the two of you. It's...you need to read it."

Maybe it's speculation about our relationship since I walked out of Liv and Sawyer's engagement party? They love posting those things because the whole town chimes in with their theories.

"You're freaking me out. How bad is it?"

She squeals.

"Dani! I swear to—you know what? Fine, I'll go read it but if it's bad, you're on a best friend timeout for a week," I threaten. "No hand massages, no specialty coffees, no one to binge holiday rom-coms with you."

"I don't start my Christmas movies until the end of June, so I'd be out of my timeout by then."

"You'd miss the hand massages," I press.

"Read it. I'll take an apology hand massage next time I see you." She sends a kiss through the phone and ends the call.

A text comes through while I'm opening up one of my social media apps to find the post.

Dani sent me the link.

FROM A FAILED WEDDING TO FALLING DOWN THE STAIRS TO FALLING IN LOVE, FIREFIGHTER JENSEN VAUGHN TELLS ALL

No. Fucking. Way.

I collapse onto my bed, eyes skimming the article, needing to know if this is in fact an interview with Jensen or something they pieced together with random quotes and conjecture. I can't imagine a scenario where Jensen would willingly tell *The Vine* about us, his past, or his injury—any of it—unless it applied to his work. He keeps his personal life practically silent.

Local hero, Jensen Vaughn, assistant chief at the Vaughn Fire Department, and director of the new Volunteer Firefighter Training Program, opened up to The Vine *contributors this week.*

This came as a surprise since Mr. Vaughn has previ-

ously expressed his preference for privacy. In fact, last year, after the event we refer to as Jensen's Dark Day [the day of his called-off wedding], he requested that all wedding talk cease or like his ex-fiancée, he would move and start over somewhere else.

Jensen has asked that after today, we stick to his present and future, because those are what matter most.

"That part of my past is only acting as an obstacle to the future I want," he told us.

When asked why he suddenly wanted to divulge the details of his failed wedding and his current relationship with the lovely Gracie Parker, Jensen indicated that this was a way for him to replace the bad memories with good ones.

He's still trying to make up for that article about my accident, trying to build me up after feeling like he let me down.

I scan the interview questions, noticing Mrs. Langerham started by prodding for details about his ex-fiancée. Jensen mentions he's willing to give some brief insight on what happened, but he'd prefer to focus the rest of the interview on his present, his future... *me.*

My heart clenches as I read through his responses about his past relationship. The details he's given are ones he'd already shared with me.

With one notable exception...

VINE: Did you and Erika speak after the wedding day to clear the air, get some closure?

VAUGHN: Not until the day she left town.

VINE: Well? Don't leave us in suspense.

VAUGHN: She'd realized she had feelings for someone

else. Someone who was the complete opposite of me. She'd hoped I could change, be a little more like him eventually, but I wasn't. And when she left Vaughn, I felt like I'd failed. Despite my best efforts, I'd failed at becoming the man she needed me to be.

I shout at my phone, "Well that's some bullshit."

VINE: So you took on all the responsibility for your failed relationship?

*VAUGHN: I did at first. But now, all I feel is glad. It was the right thing to do, even if it she went about it in the sh*ttiest way possible.*

VINE: You weren't glad right away, though, correct? Because as respected as you are in this community, your mood was just short of feral for quite some time.

[Vaughn smirks]

*VAUGHN: No, you're right. It's been pointed out I was a miserable a**hole. I hoped that moving on with my life, excelling at work, starting the training program, doing more for the community would turn things around for me, but...*

VINE: It didn't?

VAUGHN: It helped. But I needed more than that, more than time and professional accomplishments. I needed someone to make me feel.

VINE: Feel what?

VAUGHN: Anything. Everything.

VINE: And you found that person, right?

[Vaughn grins, nodding]

VINE: [whispers] This is the part where you tell us how you fell in love.

VAUGHN: From the first moment I saw Grace, she captured my interest. Which pissed me off. I didn't want to be tempted by another woman who would have unrealistic expectations of me, who would suck out my energy, take me for granted, and lead me around by the...uh, hand.

VINE: You weren't interested in getting into another relationship so soon.

*VAUGHN: I wasn't interested in a **serious** relationship or falling in love at all. And the more I got to know Grace, saw her smile, witnessed her strength and sass, I knew she'd be trouble for me.*

VINE: So you two didn't butt heads from the start then?

VAUGHN: Oh no, we did. I made sure of it.

VINE: Oh?

*VAUGHN: I was rude, short with her, gave her sh*t all the time. When she had her car accident, I was a complete jacka**.*

VINE: Your portrayal of the accident was noticeably harsher than expected.

VAUGHN: I was worried, angry that she got hurt, and intent on keeping her pissed off at me.

VINE: Instead of facing your feelings and opening yourself up?

VAUGHN: Uh, yes. That.

VINE: When did things change?

VAUGHN: When she pushed me down a flight of stairs.

VINE: Oh! I thought—

[He holds his hands up]

VAUGHN: I'm kidding.

VINE: Just to confirm, she didn't push you?

VAUGHN: Correct. I fell. And then she kept offering to help me with my recovery. I turned her down the first few times because I was mad about being on leave from work, but mostly because I knew what would happen if I let her into my life.

VINE: You knew you'd fall in love with her?

VAUGHN: I think I'd already been at least a little in love with her before then.

VINE: But you agreed to let her become your physical therapist anyway?

VAUGHN: Yes. Logically, it made sense...she offered to come to my place, and she brought me food each session.

*VINE: And with each session, she helped you heal— your leg, your shoulder, and your heart. That is **very** romantic.*

VAUGHN: She had every reason to hate me, to never give me a chance. Instead, she gave me all of herself. Her stubbornness and playfulness. Her kindness. And for a moment, I doubted if I was good enough to be the man who could make her happy, to give her everything she wanted.

VINE: And now?

VAUGHN: I'd love nothing more than to wake up with her every damn day. And I'd do it without a single doubt that I could be the man she needs. That she would be the best part of any future I could imagine.

VINE: Jensen Vaughn, you are quite the surprise today.

[He shrugs, bashfully]

*VAUGHN: My brothers are going to give me a lot of sh*t about this.*

VINE: But it'll be a wonderful surprise for the person you're hoping reads this.

VAUGHN: Yes.

VINE: Because something happened? There have been rumors that you and Gracie have spent some time apart recently. Since your sister's [Liv Vaughn] engagement party.

VAUGHN: Yes.

VINE: And you're hoping this will get you back in her good graces?

*VAUGHN: I really f*cking hope so. Because if she'll let me, I'll forever be her unicorn man.*

The screen blurs and my heart clenches. Blinking away the tears in my eyes, I devour the rest of the article. Jensen neglects to disclose any details about the conflict between us that sparked this interview. He tells the interviewer he doesn't think it would be wise to remind his lady why she should be irritated with him.

That has me snorting. Smart man.

Jensen then discusses his desire to have the same kind of family he had growing up. He talks about his dad as a role model and how Ethan Vaughn used to make big, showy apologies whenever he messed up with Lilah, which is how he got the idea for this article.

The Vine wraps up the interview with a few apology ideas and date night plans to help treat your significant other right. One of them is cooking them a homemade meal. The ladies then ask Jensen what his favorite meal of mine is, and his response:

"Nothing you can make in the kitchen."

I fall onto my back, laughing through the hands covering my face.

Oh god. My mom is going to read that Jensen's favorite meal is served naked and between my thighs.

ON MY WALK to Horton Beach, I get a few looks from locals who are coming and going. Food Truck Fridays are a popular weekly event that begins in May and ends in October. It's safe to say that I'm here every week, rain or shine. Last year, I didn't even let Jensen's presence deter me from enjoying my post-work indulgence. Did I choose times when I was fairly certain he wouldn't be here? Yes. Didn't always work out though, because it appeared he was doing the same thing. And then we'd eat in silence while ignoring each other despite there being only ten feet of space between us.

Today, though, his gaze finds mine the minute my feet hit the gravel lot of the food truck area. He's grinning at me, his eyes sweeping down my dress before lifting back up to my eyes.

He chose the table closest to the treed area that stretches to the north end of the lake. Despite the boats, the paddle boarders, and the kids shrieking as they enjoy the playground, it's as private as you can get in the open picnic area.

"Hi," I say. Ten minutes ago, I had a dozen questions to ask, but all I can think about when I see those warm eyes and his quiet intensity is *mine.*

My man. My heart. My future.

He's wearing his white VFD shirt that makes his complexion look warmer, his chest appear bigger. He looks like a rugged angel who's lost his wings and willing to fall into the wickedness of humanity.

"Hi, beautiful."

I take a seat opposite him and find the table filled with all kinds of food—not just tamales and churros. There are fish tacos, deep-fried pickles, funnel cake, grilled cheese, margaritas, and fresh lemonade.

"Figured more food couldn't hurt."

"So…" I lift a lime margarita from the assortment in front of me and take a long pull. "You told the whole town my pussy is your favorite meal."

"It is, but that's not what I said."

"Close enough."

His mouth twists into that upside down grin I love so much. "That all you going to say about the interview?"

"No," I assure him. "But that was one part that needed addressing."

"I prefer that part to be undressed."

I stifle a grin, but my lips still twist in amusement. "You're an idiot."

His head dips. "I am."

"That article was…unexpected. And enlightening. And heart-warming. It was a lot to digest."

He reaches to the far end of the table and grabs the plate of tamales. His eyes bore into mine as he sets them in front of me. "I wanted to replace another one of your bad memories with—hopefully—a good one."

I pick up a tamale. "You did. It was really sweet." I take a healthy bite and offer him the rest.

He shakes his head, and I frown at him in confusion. "Not hungry. I'd like a chance to explain everything if you'll let me. I'm sure you have questions."

"You explained enough in the article. But I have a few questions." He nods, resting his forearms on the table. "The night of Liv and Sawyer's engagement party, you looked so broken, like you'd given up. At first I believed you were giving up on *me*, but now I think you gave up on *yourself*. You thought I'd eventually feel differently about you, like your ex did? That I'd be happier with someone who was the opposite of you because Erika wanted that?"

He looks away for a moment, and I follow his gaze to the surrounding activity. But his attention is glazed over, unfocused. He's thinking, not avoiding.

"I didn't want to hold you back or break my own fucking heart by holding onto a woman I had no right keeping."

With a sad sigh, I say, "I'm sorry Erika made you think you came up short somehow, that you weren't worthy of love unless you changed to suit her. The idea of her molding you into being like some inferior asshat that caught her eye proves she was too stupid to—"

"It was Jaxon."

I'm sorry…what?

"What was Jaxon?"

"The man Erika had been in love with. He was who she wanted me to be more like, the guy I could never live up to."

I drop the tamale. "What? I—that…" I lay my hands flat on the table and lean forward. *"What?"*

"Jax and I have a lot in common with some of our mannerisms, the way we problem solve, even a bit with the way we think. But in terms of personality? Socially? We are two different people."

"Mm-hmm," I agree. "When did you find out she had a thing for your brother?"

"The night of our rehearsal dinner," he answers.

That's only slightly better than her confessing on the day of their wedding. Then again, she'd have had to show up to do it then.

"She'd been extra moody that day, lots of highs and lows. Found out she'd been drinking all afternoon. Not unusual for her during events and parties, but she'd had too much. We needed to be up early for the wedding, so I suggested we leave and get some sleep. She got worked up, let me know how much of a disappointment I was, and some other fucked up stuff."

I reach across the table, knocking aside the taco stand, and wrapping my hand over his. "You know she was full of shit, right? She sounds like a woman who was unhappy with *herself* and thought everyone else should fix that for her."

A soft smile spreads across his face. "Yeah."

"What else did she say to you?"

He grimaces and clears his throat.

"You don't have to tell me. I just want to understand."

"I know." He turns his hand, so our palms meet. "In front of most of my family, Erika told me she wished I were more like Jaxon. That she couldn't believe she ended up with the boring, anti-social twin. Asked him if he wanted to swap places with me the next day."

"*What?*"

If anyone deserved to be kicked out of her own wedding, it was this bitch. She disrespected and shamed Jensen by not showing up, knowing he would think it was *his* fault she decided not to go through with it. She left him there to deal with the fallout.

"And she wasn't wrong. Compared to Jax, I'm—"

"The fuck she wasn't wrong! Are you kidding me?"

Jensen's eyebrows shoot up to his hairline. He opens his mouth to respond, but I'm not done yet.

"You are *not* the 'boring' twin." I point at him. "You're serious and contemplative, cautious and deliberate. You like personal conversations and deep connections. You might not like parties, or karaoke"—I send him a playful glare—"or hordes of people acting like idiots, but that doesn't make you boring. Fuck her. You are my favorite person to spend time with. And not just naked time either."

He takes my hand and kisses the inside of my wrist. An irritated huff of breath rushes out of me, knowing what he's trying to do. I don't want to be calmed. His lips brush against my knuckles before he turns my wrist and places a kiss at the center of my palm.

"Grace..."

"Nope, you better not be defending her or tell me you believe any of that crap. Your brother's a riot, but not the kind of—wait. That's why you were upset at the engagement party? Because you thought I might prefer him over you?" The tightness around his mouth as he releases a long exhale tells me I'm right. "You actually thought…Jax? *Really?* Oh my god." I giggle, then cover it, trying to remain serious. "No. Never. So much no."

"It was his face you gazed adoringly at in that stupid photo. It planted the seed. Then you two were singing together at the party, getting along, doing all the shit he loves. Stuff I do my best to avoid."

"So you thought, 'Grace must be in love with Jax.'"

The aggravated grunt that comes from him has more laughter spilling from my lips.

"You think having to restrain myself from beating my brother to a pulp is funny?"

My shoulders shake in an effort to tamp down the laughter. A snort escapes, and then I'm choking on my laughter so hard I fall backward off the wooden bench.

Jensen's at my side almost immediately, staring down at me with an odd look in his eyes. I cover my mouth as I continue laughing. The fall onto the gravel might leave me with a couple of bruises, but I'm not feeling it at all right now.

"You okay, babe?"

I nod, biting my lip.

The handsome firefighter looming over me kneels at my side, running his hands up my arms, my neck, until they land on either side of my face. "You know, it wasn't long ago you were determined to find yourself a nice guy. It wasn't that crazy of a thought."

I dig my fingers into the front of his shirt and pull him closer. "I've never once met a nice guy and wondered what he'll do to me…if he'll argue with me, growl into my ear. If he'll be furious with me one second and promise to make my legs shake the next. Because I doubt those nice guys would make me feel as safe, as seen or understood, be as charmingly gruff or protectively bossy. And there's no chance they'd make me come with a string of dirty words, a hand wrapped around my neck, and a thick, unforgiving thigh pushed between my legs." I snort. "Nice guys don't do it for me, hotshot. *You* do."

He moves my leg and plucks me up off the ground, positioning me so I'm straddling his lap. People around us are looking over, the chatter picking up again.

Gripping my chin, his eyes search mine, a wide grin stretching across his gorgeous face. "I fucking love you, Grace. So damn much."

The breath stalls in my throat, the sound of my pounding heart echoing around us. I stare at him, at his heated, hypnotic gaze. "Ditto," I rasp.

"Give me the words, sweet girl."

I shift closer, needing to feel him everywhere. "Jensen Vaughn...you are the asshole of my dreams."

He swats my ass and I grin.

"I love you, hotshot."

"There's my good girl."

Warmth spreads through me as I squirm on his lap.

"Cocky jerk," I murmur against his mouth. His lips capture mine and his tongue slides into my mouth in a kiss that has me forgetting to taunt him the way I love to.

He pulls back just enough to warn, "Your sass is going to cost you orgasms, baby."

At most, he's going to delay those orgasms, which means a long night of him wringing pleasure out of me until my body stops working.

But he likes that control and I like giving it to him. Well, after testing his patience, making him growl in frustration and pleasure, and then watching that victorious smirk sweep across his face when I eventually succumb to his every touch.

I chase that delicious mouth again before jumping back up to my feet. His hands stay on my arms, keeping me steady. I lead us over to one of the trucks and ask for some to-go containers and a bag so we can pack up our food.

"We're not staying to eat?" he asks, wrapping one arm around my waist.

"Was there more you needed to tell me?"

"No, Grace. I told you everything—good and bad, past and present. Now I just want to take you home."

With another grin filled with wicked intention, I say, "Good. Want to wear the cardigan tonight?"

"Will you be able to restrain yourself from another 'nice guy' giggle fest, or will I need to keep your mouth busy?"

"So if I giggle, you'll make me choke on your cock? Not the threat you think it is."

His eyes darken, his lips curling into a wolfish smile. "Fuck, I love your mouth."

"Then take me home, hotshot. I want to use it."

THIRTY-FIVE

JENSEN

I open the cupboard beside the fridge, looking for the box of protein bars I keep in here.

"Grace?"

She sidles up next to me and slips a hand under my shirt, pressing her warm palm against my bare abdomen. "Oh. I already made coffee, babe. Mugs are now above the espresso machine."

Moving Grace into my house wasn't something we discussed or decided on. It wasn't a big proclamation or event. After the article, it was a natural progression that came about out of necessity.

Mainly because every time I went to her place, I started bringing bags and boxes full of her things back to my house. Soon, most of the things she needed were here.

At first, she thought I was trying to make my home more comfortable for her, which was part of my intention. But the moment I loaded up her fleet of coffee gadgets, she clued in.

I thought she'd fight it a little, argue that we should've discussed it or waited a few more months, demand that I persuade her in interesting new ways. But she loves it here and I love her being here. So no persuading was needed, but there was enthusiastic entryway sex after I carried her over the threshold to welcome her to her new home.

"Your mom warned me about the coffee, but I still feel unprepared for the quantity and varieties of coffee you have."

"*We* have. Right, babe?" Her sweet, heart-shaped face tilts up to me as she flutters those soft lashes.

When her parents visited a few weeks ago, Erin, her mom, fell in love with my kitchen and immediately started opening drawers and cupboards. She made some comments about how Grace's coffee supply must be running low because it only took up one cabinet.

I thought she was kidding or being sarcastic. Nope. Grace *was* running low—for her. She likes trying new roasts, different brands, and whole beans that she grinds with a special machine.

"Did you go to the farmer's market and score some new beans?"

Her hands move down my front, her fingers dipping below the band of my briefs. "The girls and I went yesterday. I got you a bag of the medium roast they were sold out of last time. You said it was the right amount of sweetness with that nutty flavor you like."

I have no recollection of that coffee. But if Grace hands me something to try, and looks up at me with those sparkling amber eyes, I'm going to tell her whatever it takes to keep that adorable excitement on her face.

Because I like coffee, but not nearly as much as Grace. Though my morning coffee has tasted significantly better since she's been buying and making it.

"Sounds amazing." I kiss her forehead and point to where my protein bars usually live. "Thoughts on where my protein bars might be?"

She grimaces, opening the drawer beneath the counter. "Sorry, I moved them here."

I snag one and shove it in my pocket. I have no idea how long the Mayor's Award ceremony is, but the speeches for these town events tend to be long-winded.

"Sure you still want me here?"

"What have I told you about doubting how I feel about you?"

"Maybe I'm looking to be punished…"

There's an unmistakable heat in her eyes as her mouth parts and her tongue sweeps across her plump lower lip. My girl is definitely looking to play.

"We have to be at Town Hall in less than an hour." My hands go to her hips as I move her backward out of the kitchen.

"Guess you'll have to make me come fast then."

I grin, looking forward to playing with her today. Grace loves being praised, and she loves dirty talk, but she often likes to play a little first. And today, she clearly wants to be spanked, possibly tied up, and then praised.

I bend and wrap my arm around the backs of her thighs, hauling her over my shoulder.

"You only get to come on my dick if you're a good girl, shortcake."

"Your fingers will do just fine then, hotshot," she calls from my back, her hands wandering over my ass.

As I charge up the stairs to our bedroom, her dress rides up her thighs. My hand moves up her smooth leg, landing on her cheek with a sharp *smack*. She yelps and giggles, shaking her ass at me as best she can from her position.

I release her, dropping her onto the bed.

"You want me to only use my fingers, baby? Fine. But you're going to watch and when I'm done, you're going to beg for my cock."

Her skin flushes and her breathing changes. She's feisty today, but I can already tell she wants to be good so I can reward her. When she goads me like this, it only makes me harder.

I grab her ankles and pull toward the end of the bed. The hem of her dress rests halfway up her thighs. I flick it up, exposing her pale pink panties. My hand smooths down the inside of her thigh to her center, toying with the edge of her panties. I graze my thumb over her sex in slow strokes that have her arching toward me.

I remove her panties in one hard tug of fabric, her feet lifting to help. My shirt comes off next, then my pants. She eyes me with a thirsty grin and reaches behind her to unzip the dress she put on for the ceremony this morning.

"Don't," I tell her. "I want you just like that."

I step around the bed and pick up the freestanding floor-length mirror I moved in here from Grace's old place. Grace stares curiously at me with one brow raised as I place the mirror at the end of the bed, near the corner.

I join her on the bed and position myself behind her, angling her toward the mirror. Her eyes widen as I push her legs apart while keeping a hand on her stomach as she leans into my chest.

I kiss her neck. "Watch, baby."

Our eyes meet in the mirror as my fingers trail down her thigh to the top of her pussy. I spread her open and whisper my fingers over her. "I'm going to show you how much I want you here, how much I need you. I never want you to doubt how much I love you."

I slip one finger through her folds, and she gasps. "Look how wet you are for me." Her hips grind into my hand as I stroke her. I avoid touching her clit while I toy with her opening, barely sliding in before moving my fingers over her again.

"You're fucking beautiful, Grace." I turn her face to the mirror again. "Every inch of your soft skin." I trace a finger down her neck to the cleavage peeking out of the top of her dress. Her nipples are popping through the fabric and I rub my thumb over one, teasing until her breath falters. She reaches up, covering her hand over mine and squeezing. I give her the pressure she's craving with a chuckle. "You're fierce and full of sass." My thumb rubs over her breast again before I move down to her lower abdomen. She lifts her hips for me, but I stay still. "Endearingly kind, and awe-inspiring."

"Jenson…" Her voice is breathy as she turns her head to kiss me.

For a few moments, I take her mouth hungrily before releasing her lips. I widen her knees to give me more room. "These thick thighs I can't get enough of. I want them wrapped around me all the fucking time." Her sweet ass presses against the base of my cock and she squirms. It's almost too much combined with the image of her laid out for me in the mirror.

"Eyes on the mirror, baby."

She does as I ask, and the moment her gaze drops to where my hand is, I sink a finger into her. I pull out of her and sink two fingers in next. She moans, her back bowing.

"Is this what you wanted? My fingers deep in your pussy, fucking you slow?"

She cries out as I hook my fingers, fucking her deeper.

I look at her in the mirror, writhing, eyes locked on the reflection of what I'm doing to her. My thick fingers disappear into her hot, tight channel, sliding in and out. "Or is that better?"

Her walls flutter and she gives me a desperate nod.

I pull out of her and suck her off my fingers. "Fucking delicious, baby. You'll always be my favorite treat." I move back to her slick heat, splaying my fingers on either side of her clit, massaging around it but never quite touching. "You're throbbing for me, baby." I need to feel her come on my fingers, my cock, all over my face.

Her hips writhe, encouraging me to give her more, move faster, press harder. But all it's doing is working my dick against her backside and tempting me to flip us over and pound into her from behind.

Her pussy is dripping wet as I slide my fingers over her in quick strokes. The shake in her legs and the erratic pulses of her swollen flesh mean she's close.

"You're mine, Grace. Tell me you're mine."

"I'm yours," she pants.

"What else is mine?" I pump my fingers inside her again, slowly, not letting her come just yet.

"M-my pussy is all yours," she says on a gasp as I pump deeper, angling to hit my favorite spot—the one that sometimes makes her squirt.

"Tell me how good you come for me, Grace."

"So good."

"Tell me how perfect you are for me."

"I'm the best thing that's ever happened to you. Now, make me come, Jensen." She moves my other hand from her stomach down to the top of her mound. A needy sound vibrates through her as my fingers circle her clit again.

I thrum three fingers over her swollen bud, then circle the way she likes, adding more pressure until she...

"Oh my fucking god, Jensen!" she cries out, her eyes slamming shut as she collapses against my chest. "Yes, yes, yes," she murmurs.

"Keep watching, baby, or you don't get another one," I warn.

She lifts back up and fixes her gaze back on the mirror, mouth open in a silent gasp, her whole body locking up. Wetness drenches my fingers as she comes. I gently tease her clit until she stops shaking and her pussy stops its rhythmic waves.

She moans, coming down from her release, and I kiss along her shoulder and neck, whispering, "That's my girl. Give me those sounds I love so much."

Turning her head toward me, she stretches up to take my mouth in a kiss. "I want to hear your sounds now," she tells me.

I move out from behind her and flip her over. She must have been partially sitting on her dress because it's a mess. I lift the back of her dress, staring at her plump as fuck ass. I smack it once before grabbing her by the hips and bringing her off the bed to stand in front of me.

I rip down my briefs, giving my raging hard dick a few strokes as she watches me.

I tap her right thigh. "One knee up on the bed."

She lifts her leg and rests it atop the mattress. I run my fingers through her pussy again, and she moans.

Gently, I wrap my hand around her throat and hold her against me. She cranes her neck, offering me her mouth, but she's too short like this, so I dip down and capture those sweet lips.

I keep my lips on her as I shift to line myself up. With one push of my hips, I slide inside her and she gasps against my mouth, arching her back. I grin and hold her closer, one hand at her neck and the other on her hip.

She's so fucking wet. I push all the way in and Grace's ass presses against me, cushioning each slam of my hips against her.

I pull my mouth away and whisper, "I'm going to come inside you."

"Yes, do it. Please."

"God, I love when you say please."

"Don't get used to it," she sasses.

I turn her head to look at us in the mirror while I grind into her, then pull out to the tip and thrust back in. A white-hot surge zips up my thighs, heat tingling at the base of my spine, as I pump into her, keeping her against me. She feels too damn good. And watching while I fuck her—watching as I make a goddamn mess of my woman—has me nearly there.

My hand moves from her hip to her clit, and I stroke smooth and fast until I feel her clench hard. Once, twice. I watch us in the mirror as I pummel in and out of her, finger caught in that perfect pussy. Pleasure rushes through me, peaking as Grace grinds her hips. I push into her, deep and hard. My release hits hard, tearing through me as I fill her full of my come. She cries out, moaning long and loud, her head dropping to my shoulder, legs weakening.

We collapse onto the bed, and I wrap my arms around her. She falls asleep on me, but I can only let her rest for a few minutes before I take her to the shower to clean her up.

I wasn't expecting this thoroughly enjoyable diversion from our plans this morning, and I have a surprise for her I don't want to put off any longer. Well, technically two surprises for her, but one of them will have to wait a little while longer...

"IT EVEN HAS one of those backup cameras!" she shouts from inside the vehicle, excitement rippling off her little body.

We spent longer than intended in the shower, which left little time for me to give her the gift I've been working on for weeks. So it wasn't until we returned from the award ceremony that she had a chance to fully check it out.

Her dad and I had talked about finding her something when she started driving again. It took us weeks to find the right vehicle—the safest vehicle. And it wasn't until a few days ago that my mechanic buddy, Sean, and I finished making sure it was in pristine condition.

Once Grace got over her shock of the new vehicle I'd hidden away in the garage, she jumped on me and peppered me with kisses. Then she told me to get my ass in her pretty new car because we had an important event to get to.

She had me grinning the entire ride with her *oohs* and *ahhs* over the interior and how "cute" it is. I told her the little Honda Civic is a hell of a lot cuter with her in it.

Grace continues tinkering inside the vehicle as I move to where her dad's looking under the hood.

"Looks good. You said it was in better shape than you expected?"

"Yeah. It was pretty easy to fix."

He nods. "She loves it."

I grin. "I noticed."

He props one sledge-hammer-sized fist against the car. "I can see how much you care about our Gracie. She's independent, capable, and stubborn as hell. She doesn't need anyone, but she deserves to be loved and doted on—when she'll let you."

I take a calming breath, and say, "She does. And I hope she keeps letting me be the man who gets to love and support her. Forever."

"Forever, huh?" He crosses his arms over his chest.

Tucking my hands into my pockets, I tell him, "I'm going to marry your daughter one day—if she lets me."

Cam tilts his head at me, his expression unreadable. "Is this you asking for permission?"

"Knowing Grace, I'm not sure asking your permission would go over well, since it's her decision to make. But I would appreciate having your blessing."

He stares at me, his assessing gaze boring into me.

There's a slight quirk of his lips as he steps closer. I stand my ground, waiting.

Shit, is he insulted that I didn't ask for his permission?

A laugh booms from him as he claps me on the shoulder. "Yeah, I think you'll do, Jensen." Then he stabs a finger in my direction. "Just don't fuck it up," he says menacingly. "Was that what you were looking for?"

I snort. "Yeah, something like that."

He finishes looking over the Honda and gives his daughter a hug when she gets out of the car. Cam nods my way and then heads inside to join our families.

Grace skips to me and wraps her arms around my waist. "I can't believe you got me a car. Is this because you don't want to share your truck anymore? I've only spilled coffee in it two times. Which, all things considered, is commendable."

My truck *still* smells like coffee, but I don't care. It reminds me of how fucking lucky I am to have her in my truck and in my life. Even if she's spilling coffee every step of the way.

"I know my truck feels too big for you, so I wanted you to have something comfortable to drive in and out of town."

She clutches the keys to her chest. "It's too much. I mean, this must have cost a lot. Like down- payment-on-a-house kind of a lot."

Grace and I briefly talked about finances when she moved in, and our incomes are similar. But even if they weren't, even though she'll likely bring in a bigger paycheck a few years from now, if Grace wants or needs anything, I'm going to be the man who will either support her in obtaining it herself or I'll step in to provide it.

"Got it for a steal. There were a few repairs needed, but I had a mechanic friend in Landry help me with some of it."

She narrows her gaze on me. "Today was supposed to be about you. You're the one who should get gifts."

The ceremony was short and free of pageantry. Winning the Mayor's Award was at the top of my list of goals for years. What started as a fun bet with my dad morphed into a career goal, something I could focus on to not only make him proud but to feel like less of a failure as my personal life went up in flames. I needed a win.

Turns out that wasn't what I really needed. My win came in a much cuter, feisty package.

"I already got my gift, baby."

She snags the Mayor's Award plaque from her bag. "You sure did. Where are we going to put it? Next to the picture of your dad with his?"

I take it, threading my other hand through her hair to pull her in for a kiss. She hums happily against my lips.

"Yeah, that's the perfect place," I murmur. "But this isn't the gift I meant."

Her face morphs from confusion to panicked concern.

"You've seen your gift? It wasn't supposed to arrive until tomorrow! I wanted to make sure it didn't get delivered while our family was here." I'm about to tell her I haven't seen anything, but she keeps going. "I hope you hid it because everyone is in the house right now." She leans sideways to get a better view of our front window that really only shows the entryway.

Shit. What the hell did she buy?

"I didn't hide it, I—"

Her eyes bug out. "Go hide it now! Please? I'll go in with you and keep everyone distracted while you sneak away. Don't be obvious or your brothers will notice."

"Babe, I didn't—"

"Shoo! Go." She drops her voice. "Unless you want everyone seeing our sex swing?"

Oh fuck me.

"Babe. You bought a sex swing?"

Her mouth drops open. "Shit. You didn't know?" I shake my head, unable to keep the sheer delight off my face. "What gift were you talking about, then?"

With a kiss to her lips, I answer, "You, babe. Just you."

Her face softens, a sweet smile lighting up her eyes. "I ruined my own surprise."

"It's impossible to ruin a damn thing about buying us a sex swing, Grace."

We head back into the house to visit with our family, but before she steps away, I whisper, "Once everyone leaves, we're setting up my gift."

Her brows rise, a sexy smirk on her lips. "Looking forward to it, hotshot."

I watch her walk away and wrap an arm around my mom in a side hug. They chat and I stare.

Brody cuts into my line of sight and hands me a beer. "When are you doing it?" he asks.

"In a couple of weeks," I reply.

He glances over to where Jax is talking to Grace's dad, gesturing wildly as Cam lets out a hardy laugh.

Brody turns his head toward me, lowering his voice as he says, "You should move it up. Jax is shit at keeping secrets, and he's seconds from adopting your future father-in-law as his own."

He's not wrong.

"I've got a plan," I assure him.

The kind of plan that includes a lifetime of cardigans and sex swings, and catching the woman I love every time she stumbles.

EPILOGUE

BRODY

I'm going to be late. And I fucking hate being late.

"Chief Broody, put the lights on!" Ava begs from the back seat of my police car.

She can't even see the lights from the inside. What she wants is the siren, and I'm tempted to use it so we can make it to Rocky's in time.

I glance at her in my rearview mirror.

Her cherub face tilts up to me, her tiny hands pressed together and tucked under her chin. *"Pleeeease?"*

Goddammit.

My gaze slides to her mom, who's sitting beside her. She's on the phone with the garage, arguing about the issues she's had with her car since they serviced it.

But since she has some kind of superhuman multi-tasking abilities, she reaches over and lowers her daughter's hands, mouthing, *No, Ava.*

Ava frowns and settles back into her booster seat.

When we come to an empty intersection, I flick another glance to the rearview mirror as I hit the lights and sirens.

She lights up, cheering and dancing in her seat. "Again! Again!"

Harper cuts me a glare.

"Oops. Wrong button," I say.

"Are you excited about the surprise party, Chief?" Ava asks.

"Not overly," I confess.

"Why not?"

"Not a fan of proposals," I answer.

"What's a proposal?"

"An unfair bargain that usually leads to years of regret," I tell her.

Her cute little face scrunches up in confusion.

"Chief!" Harper hisses.

She knows I'm right. For most people anyway. Thankfully, my brother and Gracie are pretty fucking great together. They're going to make it, and I'm happy for them. Truly.

"Why are we having a party for *that*?" Ava asks.

"You should probably ask your mom that, Fruit Loop." I nearly grin at the fire shooting out of Harper's eyes. She's not usually this easy to rile up. She has the patience and positivity of a saint. But between her car problems, her sister, and having to ask me for help, she's clearly reached her limit.

Covering the phone, she turns to her daughter and says, "We're celebrating our friends starting a life together full of love and new adventures." She shoots me a forced smile. "We're very excited for them. Right, Chief?"

I go with the safest answer. "Right."

By the time I find a parking spot across the street from Rocky's, Harper's off the phone and Ava's squirming in her seat, eager to get to the party. I park and turn to Ava.

"Wait for your mom to come around and let you out," I tell her.

Harper gives me a grateful nod and exits the back seat.

"Chief Broody?" Ava asks.

"Yeah, Fruit Loop?"

"I spilled my juice box in your car."

I shrug. "I've had way worse shit spilled back there, kid."

Her mouth forms a little circle. "Bad word!"

Fuck.

She tallies all the bad words I say and when I reach ten, I owe her ice cream.

I never agreed to those terms, but that didn't seem to matter to her.

Harper opens the door, and Ava yells, "Chief said a bad word!"

"Shit," I mumble.

"*That* word," she shouts to her mom.

I exit the vehicle but duck back inside. "We're running late, ladies. Hop to it."

I close the door and wait as Harper helps Ava out of the car.

When we make it inside, I spot Jensen and Gracie at a corner table. I point them out, and Ava races across the restaurant.

"Gracie!" she screams.

My brother's soon-to-be fiancée slips out of her chair and crouches down just in time to catch Ava.

"We got to ride in the police car," she tells Gracie.

Harper brushes past me, tucking a piece of her silky black hair behind her ear. My gaze drags down her body, from the pinched-in waist of her dress, over the pronounced flare of provocative hips.

Jensen waves at me to get my attention. I head over to him, intent on getting an update about his proposal plan—not on getting closer to the temptress who approached me with an entirely different kind of proposal just last week.

"You all came together?" Jensen asks.

"Have you turned from part-time babysitter to full-time nanny? I hope you get good benefits." Jaxon winks at me.

"Shut it," I tell Jax. "They needed a ride." I tip my head toward the girls. "Her vehicle broke down. Again. The shop is charging her for fixing it again, even though they didn't do it right the first time."

We only have a few vehicle repair shops in town, and one in particular is known for their shitty business practices, especially with female customers. Hopefully, a visit from me tomorrow morning will provoke a more agreeable response.

As a single mom working full-time, and raising an endlessly energetic kid, Harper doesn't have time, money, or energy to spare fighting with those bastards.

But I do.

I'll just have to deal with the consequences if she finds out I interfered.

"She can have it brought to my place," Jensen offers. "Sean and I fixed up Grace's new car in less than a week. I'm sure we can figure it out."

I hesitate, swiping a hand over my mouth as my gaze shifts to Harper.

Eventually, I nod. "That'd be great, but you might want to offer yourself. She's touchy about letting me help her."

"Who's touchy? Mom says we have to keep our hands to ourselves," Ava says, popping up at my side, her tiny hands clutching my pant leg.

"You eavesdropping again, Fruit Loop?" I ask.

"No."

I drop to her level, giving her my best interrogation frown. "Do you even know what eavesdropping means?"

"Nope!" Ava answers with a wide smile.

This kid kills me.

"Is it time for the poh-posal yet? Is there cake? There's always cake at surprise parties."

Fuck.

Gracie takes a step closer. "What?"

No one answers. No one moves.

She goes to take another step, but stumbles. Jensen's there, steadying her, looking down at her with a wobbly grin.

So much for his grand plan. He's going to do it right here, right now.

My work cell rings as Jensen gets down on one knee.

Of fucking course.

I'm on call, but everyone knows not to disturb me—unless absolutely necessary—for the next hour.

I slip away, hoping no one notices.

As soon as I push through the back exit door, I answer, barking, "This better be important."

"Chief, I know you're busy with a family event, but we have an issue here. One we think you may want to deal with personally."

"Tell me what's happening, O'Riley."

"We have a Nova West in custody."

Fuck. Harper's going to shit a brick.

"I'll be there soon."

I make my way to the front of the building, planning to pop inside to give my apologies to Jensen and Gracie, and make sure Harper and Ava know I'll be gone for a while.

But as I round the corner, I nearly ram into the newly engaged couple as they steal a moment alone.

"Greedy girl," my brother murmurs.

"I'll be your good girl later. Sing for me, hotshot."

I bleach that shit from my mind, and walk right on past with a simple, "Congrats, you two." Then, over my shoulder, I add, "Let Harper and Ava know I'll be back in about an hour to drive them home."

As I continue to my car, Jensen shouts, "Brody! Where the hell are you going?"

Sighing, I answer, "To fuck over my chances of getting laid."

———

Brody & Harper's book is next!
Grumpy/Sunshine | Age Gap | Single Parent |
Neighbors to Lovers | Law Enforcement | Small
Town Rom Com

> > > NEED JENSEN & GRACIE'S PROPOSAL SCENE? CURIOUS ABOUT THAT SEX SWING? *READ THE BONUS SCENE!*

SIGN UP FOR THE BONUS SCENE:
https://rebrand.ly/Bonus-FFTG

ALSO BY AMY ALVES

The Landry Love Series

(complete series)

The Experiment (Emma & Jess)

The Denial Game (Lauren & Taylor)

The Forever Plan (Willa & Evan)

The Love Words (Chloe & Hayden)

The Surprise Seduction (Aria & Garrett)

The Road Home (Sadie & Sean)

Vaughn Brothers Series

Falling for the Bachelor (Sawyer & Olivia)

Falling for the Grinch (Declan & Dani)

(A holiday novella)

Falling for the Jerk (Jensen & Gracie)

Falling for the Grump (Brody & Harper)

ACKNOWLEDGMENTS

These two characters had been in my mind for nearly a year. And when it was time to start Jensen and Gracie's book, life had other plans. So after many setbacks, I typed their final words with a wide smile on my face. I would absolutely not have been able to do it without my wonderful team.

First, a big thank you to my readers for all the love and excitement you've extended in anticipation of this book.

Next, my alpha and beta readers, Sara, Renee, Sherry, and Jeanine: I cannot believe how lucky I am to have you all supporting me, answering my endless questions, putting up with my rambling, finding my little Canadianisms (one *always* sneaks past me and my editors). I kept dangling this book, pushing back and when I needed you, each of you took time out of your day to help me. Thank you *so* much. *Special shout out to Renee's hubby, LW, who answered A LOT of firefighter questions for us.

Katie, my girl, my PA. You keep me on track and help prevent me from falling down the rabbit hole on a daily basis.

Julia and Molly, I am so glad to have found you. Publishing is *hard*, and having people you can trust, laugh with, cheer for, share anything with, and feel completely at ease around is a rare thing. Love you ladies.

To my review and promo teams, you are so very appreciated. I am in awe daily of your love and support.

Paula, my editor—you are a rock star. Your comments throughout crack me up, and I live to make you blush and write crazy things only editors do like "should she gag on his cock a little?" Makes my whole damn day.

ABOUT THE AUTHOR

Amy Alves lives in Alberta, Canada with her husband and two crazy cute kids. She is a romance-obsessed reader, a lover of wine and fuzzy socks, and a loather of laundry. For over a decade, she was a high school science teacher, but now substitute teaches in between writing novels and being a mom.

**Find Amy In All The Places
She Gets Distracted:**

Goodreads (goodreads.com/amyalvesauthor)
Instagram (instagram.com/amyalves.author)
TikTok (tiktok.com/@amyalves.author)
Facebook Page (facebook.com/amyalvesauthor)
Facebook Reader Group (facebook.com/groups/amyalvesreaders)
Bookbub (bookbub.com/profile/amy-alves)
Amazon Page (http://author.to/amyalves)
Website (www.amyalvesbooks.com)

www.ingramcontent.com/pod-product-compliance
Lightning Source LLC
Chambersburg PA
CBHW020904060726
47591CB00004B/1078